Hillsden Riots
and
Getting it Wrong

Hillsden Riots
and
Getting it Wrong

Rhodri Jones

André Deutsch Children's Books

Hillsden Riots
First published in 1985 by
André Deutsch Limited
105–106 Great Russell Street, London WC1B 3LJ

Copyright © 1985 by Rhodri Jones

ISBN 0 233 97827 5

Getting it Wrong
First published in 1986 by
André Deutsch Limited
105–106 Great Russell Street, London WC1B 3LJ

Copyright © 1986 by Rhodri Jones

ISBN 0 233 97910 7

This edition published in 1991 by
André Deutsch Children's Books
An imprint of Scholastic Publications Limited
7–9 Pratt Street, London NW1 0AE

Copyright © 1991 by Rhodri Jones

ISBN 0 233 98708 8 paperback
ISBN 0 233 98753 3 hardback

Typeset by
AKM Associates (UK) Ltd, Southall, London
Printed in Great Britain by
WBC Bridgend

Hillsden Riots

Rhodri Jones

Chapter 1

Wayne rushed to tell his friend Desmond. It was all over the school.

'Did you 'ear? They arrested Kingsley.'

Desmond's mouth dropped open with shock. 'Naw! What 'e done?'

Wayne was scornful. 'Don' be crazy, man. 'E don' 'ave to 'ave done not'in'.'

'That true,' Desmond admitted. 'Say, it 'appenin' all the time now. There was Simon an' Calvin last week, an' Willard a couple o' days ago.'

'Yeah,' agreed Wayne. 'It's gettin' so no black boy can walk down the street.'

'I 'ears they bring the Special Patrol in,' said Desmond. 'They got some kind o' drive on.'

'Yeah,' said Wayne. 'I 'ears that too. They calls it Operation Purge. They gonna clear the streets o' crime so they says. But it ain't gonna work. All they does is pick on black people. It just gonna stir up trouble. I'm tellin' you, black people just ain't gonna stand for it.'

'Yeah,' agreed Desmond. 'We got rights too.'

Another boy butted in. ' 'Ave you 'eard 'bout Kenny? 'E been drill up by the police.'

'Naw,' cried Desmond.

'That dread,' said Wayne. 'When did it 'appen?'

The rumours and stories buzzed and raged round the school all day.

It was Friday afternoon. It was the Friday afternoon before the summer half-term holiday. More than that, for Wayne and Desmond it was their last day at school before their exams — their last day as schoolboys. Unless they went into the sixth form.

Wayne didn't fancy that at all. He had heard that teachers treated you differently there. But you were still a schoolboy, weren't you? He didn't want to be like his brother Colin still at school at the age of eighteen. His mother had other ideas. That battle remained to be fought, and Wayne put it out of his mind. For the moment, it was enough to enjoy the exhilarating delight of coming to the end of what seemed like a term in prison.

When the bell rang at four o' clock, he raced out of the building.

'Hey, man, I'm free,' he yelled.

He hurled his schoolbag high into the air and let it land with a thud in the dust of the playground.

'It's all over,' he cried joyfully.

'Man, you crazy,' said Desmond gloomily. 'You forget 'bout the exams. It just begin.'

Wayne gave his friend a sour look. 'What you on 'bout?'

'Well, it's important, innit?'

Wayne blew out his lips. That was the trouble with Desmond. He was a worrier and a born pessimist.

'Ain't not'in' to worry 'bout,' Wayne said confidently.

'You doin' any work?' Desmond asked.

'Naw,' Wayne replied witheringly. This wasn't quite true. He had been doing some revision, but he wasn't going to let on about it. 'I'll get t'rough all right. I'm a natural genius.' He laughed smugly.

'That what you says,' sneered Desmond.

'I don' know what you on 'bout anyways,' Wayne continued airily. 'Don' you know there ain't no jobs for black guys like you even though you gets good results?'

It was intended as a joke — part of the fencing with words that went on constantly between them. But Desmond took it seriously. His mouth drooped with depression.

'Yeah, I knows,' he agreed.

Wayne clicked his teeth. That was just like Desmond, that was. So things were bad. So there was no guarantee of jobs for any of them — especially if you were black. But was that any reason to ruin this day of all days?

'Aw, come on, guy,' he burst out. 'You spoilin' my fun. I didn' mean it. Today we is free. Ain't no point troublin' ourself wit' t'ings that might never come 'bout.'

Desmond made an effort and brightened up. 'All right, man. Let's go see what 'appenin'.'

By the time they reached Hillsden High Street, they were sweating. Summer had finally arrived. The sun was beating down fiercely, and there was a clammy heat in the air. It was like walking through soup.

'Whew! It 'ot,' said Wayne, wiping his face with his hand.

'Yeah,' Desmond agreed with a smile. 'It 'ot 'nough to get a sun tan.'

Wayne grinned back. 'Well, you better watch it. You better keep in the shade. You quite dark 'nough as it is.'

Desmond aimed a playful kick at his friend which Wayne gracefully sidestepped. But it was true. Desmond was very black. He was the colour of ebony. It was something his friends often teased him about. By comparison, Wayne considered himself to be almost anaemic.

He pulled off his tie and shrugged himself out of his blazer. Tie and jacket were bundled into the top of his bag.

'That better,' he said. 'Now I feels like a 'uman bein' again.'

Desmond grunted and looked sceptical. 'It take more than that to make you a 'uman bein'.'

'Get off,' Wayne warned and swirled his bag in Desmond's direction.

The High Street was crowded. Women were strolling up and down in their summer dresses. Men wearing only shorts lounged at the street corners eyeing the passing talent.

Children in bathing costumes chased in and out of the crowd. It was like being at the seaside. Only the persistent patrol of policemen in their whiter than white shirts cast a shadow over the scene.

'They's everywhere,' Wayne muttered.

'Yeah,' Desmond agreed. 'Why can' they go an' do somet'in' useful?'

There was an ice-cream stand outside Woolworth's. Wayne and Desmond agonised over the placard showing what was available. They just couldn't make up their minds. Finally, they both plumped for ice-lollies and sauntered on, stripping away the wrappings and beginning to lick strenuously. The iciness froze their tongues. They stuck them out at each other and laughed at how the pink had been transformed into a lurid orange.

As he was biting into the last of the lolly and making sure it didn't drop off its stick, Wayne spotted a familiar figure on the other side of the road. It was his brother Colin. He was waiting for a bus. Wasn't that just like him? Waiting for a bus so he could go straight home and get on with his studying.

Wayne didn't want his brother to see him. Colin was so serious. All he thought about was doing his homework. The only time he went out was to go to the library and come back piled up with books. He didn't believe in having fun. It surprised Wayne, when he bothered to think about it, that they had the same mother and father.

He steered Desmond quickly along the High Street to a record shop to have a look at the new releases on show. Out of the corner of his eye, he kept a watch on what was going on across the road. A bus arrived, halted and went on its way again. Colin was no longer at the bus stop. Wayne felt he could relax once more.

'Hey, man,' said Desmond, and he began to shuffle his feet. Wayne knew what was coming. 'I'll 'ave to be goin'. My mum expectin' me, an' if I don' turn up, there'll be 'ell.'

Wayne curled his lip and gave his friend a contemptuous stare. Here was another one. He said wearily, 'OK. If that 'ow it is.'

'Sorry,' Desmond mumbled miserably. Then he added more hopefully, 'See you later?'

'Sure,' said Wayne without much enthusiasm. 'Later.'

He watched as Desmond scurried away down the High Street dodging in and out of the other pedestrians. Wayne was sorry to see him go. All the fun went out of the afternoon. How could you celebrate your last day as a schoolboy on your own? There was nothing for it but to cross the road and wait for a bus home.

Quite a few people were waiting there already. It was nearing the time when the buses were crowded and it was difficult to get on. Several buses went past without stopping. Even when they did stop, there was such a surge of people trying to board them that Wayne didn't even bother to try. He leaned against a shop window and waited.

It was all his parents' fault that he had to get a bus anyway. If they hadn't moved to Dukesbury two years before, all he would have to do was go along the High Street, turn down Balaclava Road and he would be home. Instead, he had to hang around here and depend on the goodwill of London Transport. Even if he got on a bus, it could take him half an hour to get home with all the stopping and starting of rush hour traffic. Not that it really mattered. There was nothing to hurry home for.

Another bus had just come and gone. Wayne was wiping the sweat off his forehead and deciding that he had better catch the next one, come what may, when the sunlight was suddenly blocked out.

Someone was standing in front of him, someone big. In fact, there were two of them. Wayne puckered up his face with annoyance and screwed up his eyes to try to make out who they were. Then his eyes shot open with shock and alarm. They were policemen.

'What are you up to, boy?' one of them demanded. His face was hard and suspicious, his voice cold and unfriendly.

The sweat broke out afresh on Wayne's face. He could feel it shivering down his spine. He looked about him desperately

5

for some way of escape, but he was hemmed in. The policemen's broad bodies had him trapped.

Wayne tried to pull himself together. What was the question the policeman had asked? What had he meant by it? What was it all about?

Before he could do anything or make any kind of reply, the second policeman broke in. 'We've been watching you. You've been at this bus stop for quarter of an hour now, and you haven't got on a bus. What's your game?'

So that was it. Wayne struggled to find his tongue. 'The buses was all full,' he stammered. 'I couldn't get on.'

The two policemen smirked unpleasantly. They exchanged glances and grunted as though they couldn't believe their ears.

'Come off it, blackie,' the first one said. 'We know what you're after. We get it all the time. You hang around bus stops and when you see your chance you grab a handbag from some poor old lady and make a run for it.'

'That ain't true,' Wayne spluttered as he tried to control his rising anger. He knew that wouldn't do any good.

'Don't give us any of that,' the second policeman said in a bored tone of voice. He turned to his colleague. 'They're very good at outraged innocence, aren't they?'

Then they swung into action. Before Wayne could protest or make any comment, he found himself being pummeled and manhandled. His bag was dragged from round his neck, and his ears were practically jerked off with it. He was turned round and thrust against the window of the shop, arms outstretched and legs apart. Hands were exploring his body and clothing, searching every crevice and lining, and being none too gentle about it.

Through the glass of the window, Wayne was aware of startled faces staring out at him. He could see them with a sudden clarity. There were two assistants and three customers. Two of them were Asians, two were black and one was white. He noticed as though for the first time that the shop was a newsagent's. He swallowed deeply and wondered anxiously if he was going to be sick.

Then the pressure was eased and the hands were removed.

'All right,' said one of the policemen, 'you can turn round.'

Wayne lowered his arms and drew his face away from the glass. The policemen were emptying the contents of his bag on to the pavement. Blazer, tie, books, ruler, pencil case spilled out. One of the policemen dug the toe of his boot under the blazer and rolled it over as though it were too contaminated for his hand to touch.

'You're clean this time,' the other policeman said, dropping the bag on the pavement. He sounded disappointed. 'But you watch it, blackie. We'll get you next time.'

There was a hard threat in the look the two policemen directed at Wayne before they nodded at each other and moved on. They strolled away down the High Street, gazing about them unconcerned, as though nothing had happened.

Wayne watched them go with hatred burning in his heart. Who did they think they were to treat him like that? Just because they wore uniforms, they thought they could do what they liked. Just because he was black, they thought they could treat him like dirt.

Some of the people at the bus stop were eyeing him with suspicion and distrust. Others were carefully looking away. Wayne felt ashamed and humiliated. It was as though he were standing there naked and defenceless. If he wasn't careful, he would be crying in a minute. The tears were inside his head ready to pour out.

To prevent them, he set about putting his scattered property back into his bag. A couple of pages of his file had come loose, and there was a dusty footprint on the cover of an exercise book where one of the policemen had stepped on it. He slung the bag round his neck again and joined the bus queue, trying to lose himself in the crowd.

He gazed out, unseeing, at the passing traffic, while inside his head he re-enacted the scene and allowed a torrent of emotions to rage through him.

He was furious that he had been suspected and manhandled the way he had been. What had he done to deserve that? He was innocent. He hadn't done anything except to mind his own business. And in the middle of the High Street too. To be shown up like that. He had seen how people had looked at him. He knew what they'd been thinking. And it wasn't true. It wasn't fair. He wasn't a criminal.

He ought to have protested or done something. But then it had been so sudden and unexpected. They had come out of nowhere and jumped on him without any warning. He hadn't had time to prepare himself or do anything.

But what a fool he was. Why was he surprised? This was the kind of thing that happened everyday. This was what had happened to Kingsley and Simon and Calvin and Willard and all the others. Except, they had it worse. They had been taken down to the station or had been beaten up. He ought to consider himself lucky.

But that was little consolation. All day he had been looking forward with excitement and anticipation to the end of school when he could be free. He almost laughed out loud. Free? That was a joke. How could he be free when there were people like that around?

Chapter 2

Colin sat on the bus and let the sweat pour out of him. He felt it trickling down his neck and along his thighs. His shirt and trousers were clinging to the fabric covering of the seat. When he eased his shoulders away, the clamminess of his shirt made him shiver. Even the light breeze curling in at the window was like a dank warm flannel against his face. It did nothing to make the heat more bearable.

All day, it had been heavy and oppressive. Dark clouds the colour of lead had weighed down on them, making everyone head-achy and bad-tempered. And then the sun had broken through with a blazing heat that was even worse. It was as though the sun had been stoking up its strength all day and the boiler door had suddenly been opened.

Wasn't that always the way? As soon as the exams began, the sun shone and the temperature shot up.

His exams were important to Colin. He had worked hard at school. He had done well at O Level. Now his A Levels were ahead of him. He had been offered a place at university if he got good enough grades, and he was determined to make it.

When the bus reached his stop, it was a relief to get off. It was no cooler, but at least the air had a chance to circulate between his body and his damp clothes. He walked away from the main road with its noisy traffic and dust and fumes down a side street and then took a turning off that. Already the atmosphere was quieter and cleaner. There were trees and gardens and a sense of space and being able to breathe.

That was one of the reasons they had moved to Dukesbury. His parents had wanted to get away from the crowded streets of Hillsden where they had been living and find somewhere more pleasant. It was only four miles further out in the London suburbs, but it made a world of difference.

One of the neighbours, Mrs Bloomfield, was watering the flowers in her front garden. She looked up as Colin approached and smiled pleasantly.

'Is it hot enough for you?' she joked.

Colin grinned back. 'Yes.'

'It must be just like home for you,' Mrs Bloomfield went on. She didn't mean anything by it. She was just being friendly.

Colin responded politely and walked on.

It was funny the way people always assumed that black people liked the heat. Colin wasn't any more used to it than anyone else. He had been born in London. The English climate was what he knew. Only his parents talked wistfully about the sun and the heat back home in Jamaica and dreaded the cold damp winters here.

Being the only black family living in Beechwood Crescent had been difficult at first. But their neighbours had got used to the idea. His parents had worked hard to save up enough money to buy the house. It was in what would be considered a very respectable area, Colin supposed. The next-door neighbour was a sergeant in the police. You couldn't get much more respectable than that. Now there were several other black people living there.

Colin wondered if there would be anyone at home. His younger brother Wayne never came straight home from school. His mother would probably be shopping on the way back from work. His father — well, his father didn't live there any more.

When he turned the corner, Colin was surprised to see the

car in the drive. His mother had got home before him after all. As he let himself in at the kitchen door, he made a bet with himself what her first words would be.

Mrs MacMorris was unpacking things from a shopping bag and putting them away. She stopped when she saw Colin and breathed out a great satisfied sigh.

'This more like it,' she said. 'Jus' like back 'ome.'

Colin smiled. He had been right.

'Not so good for studying though,' he said.

His mother became serious. 'Now don' you let that trouble you. Them exams is important. You jus' 'as to do well.'

'I know,' said Colin.

Mrs MacMorris went on chattering about how her day had gone. 'Ol' Mrs Nelson was 'streperous as always. Kept sayin' 'ow lonely she is an' 'ow no one ever visit 'er. "I visits you, don' I?" I says. An' she look at me wit' them bleary eyes o' 'ers an' say, "But you black. You don' count." ' Mrs MacMorris snorted though without any real surprise or indignation. 'Ain't that always the way? You does what you can an' don' nobody 'preciate it.'

Colin's mother was a district nurse. He didn't know how she managed to put up with her patients — they seemed so cantankerous and ungrateful. But she did. She was good at her job.

'Now don' you forget you Aunt Elma an' Uncle Neville comin' Sunday,' she went on. 'You knows 'ow much they likes you, so you got to find some time fo' 'em.'

'I think I can just squeeze them into my schedule,' Colin said with mock solemnity. 'I'll make a real effort.'

'You see you do,' said his mother seriously. 'I knows studyin' important, but so is family.'

Then she realised that Colin had been teasing her. She broke into a mighty squawk of laughter and playfully slapped his cheek.

'Get 'way wit' you,' she cried. 'I never knows when you playin' fo' real an' when you jus' 'avin' me on.'

Her face clouded over as other thoughts came crowding

in. 'You seen Wayne?' she asked, more out of habit than hope. 'That boy 'ave no sense.'

There was no need for Colin to make any comment. He left his mother in the kitchen beginning to slice up an onion and went to his bedroom. The sun was pouring in, and it was hotter than ever up there. He opened the window to let some of the baking air out. Then he took off his shirt and trousers and put on a T-shirt and a pair of sawn-off jeans.

His timetable for the next five weeks was fixed to the mirror on his chest of drawers. The days were marked out week by week, the actual days of the exams underlined in red, the rest of the spaces blocked out in three-hour sessions — so much for English, so much for history, so much for sociology.

Tonight's revision was English. He plumped up his pillow, took up his file and stretched himself out on the bed. He wiped away the beads of sweat that formed on his forehead and frowned in concentration over the tragic love story of the Moor and the fair Desdemona.

Did Shakespeare really think of Othello as a black man? Had he actually met one? It was just possible. More likely he had heard about them and thought it an interesting idea to explore. It was a kind of intellectual puzzle. If you take a black man and a white woman and make them fall in love, what would happen? The answer obviously was disaster.

It was all a bit silly, wasn't it? All that fuss over a lost handkerchief. And then there were all those comments about 'black rams' and 'sooty bosoms'. There were times when Colin suspected the examiners had chosen the play as a set-text simply to embarrass him.

He wondered if Jenny thought he had a 'sooty bosom'. At this very moment, she was probably hard at work next door concentrating on her revision, just as he was. Today was Friday, wasn't it? Tomorrow night they had promised themselves a night off. They were going to a disco. In just twenty-four hours he would be with her for a whole evening, close to her, holding her.

But then he snapped back to reality. He hadn't answered

his own question. Did Jenny think he had a 'sooty bosom'? Of course she didn't. She was an intelligent girl. There was nothing prejudiced about her.

It was an hour later that Colin decided the heat was too much for him. His throat was parched — as dry as sandpaper. He was just getting himself a drink of orange squash in the kitchen when the door burst open and Wayne appeared. His face was bright with excitement and enraged with fury.

'I been pick up by the police,' he announced.

Mrs MacMorris stopped in the middle of washing a lettuce as though struck by lightning. She stared horrified at her son while the water from the tap went on running over her hands.

'What?' she demanded.

'The police pick me up,' Wayne repeated, half proud, half angry.

'I 'ears what you says,' his mother went on, exasperated. 'Explain.'

Wayne gathered his patience together and began. 'I was waitin' in the 'Igh Street fo' my bus when these two policemen comes up to me an' starts searchin' me. They shoves me up 'gainst a shop an' feels me up an' down an' turns my bag out. It ain't right what they do.'

'They give any reason?' Mrs MacMorris asked. ' 'Ad you done anyt'in' wrong?'

'Course not,' Wayne retorted indignantly. 'I was jus' waitin' fo' my bus an' they treats me like a criminal.'

'But what did they say?' Mrs MacMorris persisted.

'They didn't say not'in'. They jus' does what they likes.'

Colin broke in. 'There've been a lot of police about lately. I think they're having some kind of drive against street crime.'

'Yeah,' agreed Wayne. 'You can 'ardly walk down the 'Igh Street wit'out you trips over the bull. But that ain't no reason fo' treatin' me the way they done.'

'I 'opes you didn' give 'em no trouble now,' said Mrs MacMorris. 'Was you polite to 'em?'

'Why should I be polite to them bullmen?' Wayne demanded.

Mrs MacMorris was patient but firm. 'That weren't the question I ax.'

'I didn' give 'em no mout',' Wayne conceded reluctantly. Then he burst out, 'But it ain't right they treats me like that. Who them t'ink them is?'

'The police 'as a job to do,' said Mrs MacMorris. 'I don' know as I always agrees wit' the way they does it, but they 'as to fight crime an' protect people an' property, an' if that mean one or two innocent folk gets inconvenience now an' then, well that the penalty we 'as to pay. So you jus' better accept that.'

'Why should I?' Wayne demanded.

His mother tried to explain. 'Look. If someone come an' t'ief you bike, you gonna report it to the police, ain't you? You gonna expect them to find out who done it an' get it back fo' you, ain't you?'

'I suppose so.'

'Well then. That what the police is fo'.'

'But I 'adn't done not'in',' Wayne complained. 'I 'adn't t'iefed no bike. They don' show no respect fo' nobody. Cha! They jus' lookin' fo' trouble, that's what.'

'Don' you talk that way,' warned his mother. 'You t'ank you lucky stars you still in one piece an' ain't been took down the station. I 'as 'nough trouble in my life wit'out that kin' o' t'ing.'

Wayne's anger subsided. He sucked his teeth slowly, but he didn't dare do more under this mother's watchful glare.

Mrs MacMorris sighed. 'I don' know. Perhaps you ought to 'ave change schools when we move out 'ere, then you wouldn' 'ave to get mix up in 'Illsden troubles.'

'That wouldn' be right,' Wayne protested. 'I don' wanna change schools. I'd lose all my friends.'

'Maybe that wouldn' be such a bad idea. But that ain't what I talkin' 'bout. I wants you 'way from that place so you don' get in no trouble.'

'I'm all right,' said Wayne. 'I don' get in no trouble so long as the police leaves me alone.'

Colin left Wayne muttering quietly to himself over his hurt pride and went back to his room. He agreed with his mother. The police had a difficult job to do. You couldn't expect them to go around wearing kid gloves all the time. In any case, his younger brother wasn't always as innocent as he claimed. There had been times when Wayne had been involved in things he shouldn't have been.

Scarcely had he settled himself on his bed and picked up his book again when the whole house was filled with the pulsating beat of soul music. He threw down his book and cursed. Wayne had turned on his transistor. With a bound, Colin was off the bed and at the door. He yanked it open and marched to his brother's room.

'Shut that noise,' he yelled.

Wayne was in the middle of the floor, swaying his hips in time to the beat. At his brother's words, his body froze, arms held loosely in the air, one leg jutting out. A look of bored disdain spread slowly across his face and stuck there.

'It ain't troublin' you,' he said coolly. He seemed to have fully recovered from his encounter with the police.

'Course it is,' Colin retorted. 'How can I study with that racket going on?'

'That all you ever t'inks 'bout,' said Wayne contemptuously.

'It's time you started thinking about it as well. You've got exams too, you know.'

'That's OK,' said Wayne grandly. 'I'm gonna do all right.'

'That's what you think,' said Colin. 'Now turn that off.'

The music was still pounding out, and they were having to shout at each other. Wayne made no move to do what his brother asked. With a snort of impatience, Colin advanced towards the chest of drawers and stretched out his hand to switch off the transistor. Wayne sprang into action. He grabbed his brother's hand and held on to it. The two glared at each other.

'You leave my t'ings alone,' Wayne warned.

Colin pulled his hand away. 'You turn it off then.'

'Naw, I won',' said Wayne stubbornly. 'Why should I?'

'I won't tell you again.'

'Naw. What you gonna do 'bout it?' Wayne narrowed his eyes and thrust his chin out defiantly.

Colin was saved from having to show his brother what he would do by their mother yelling up the stairs. 'You turn that trash off his minute. You 'ears me, Wayne? You get on wit' you 'ome-work. An' let Colin get on wit' 'is.'

Wayne glowered at his brother. 'Now look what you done. The mother always on your side. I t'ink this 'ouse jus' run fo' you.'

'Turn it off,' came Mrs MacMorris's voice again.

Wayne sucked his teeth angrily. He went over to the transistor and savagely slapped at the switches. There was a sudden silence.

'Thanks,' said Colin.

His brother turned round. 'That's all right,' he said coolly, and then went on as though speaking to himself. 'I t'ink I gets me a Walkman, an' then nobody know when I listens.'

'Good idea,' said Colin.

He went back to his bedroom and tried to continue with his revision.

He and Wayne had never got on. Things were better now that they each had their own room, but when they had shared, it had been unbearable. There had been disputes about when to put the light out, about who had been messing with whose clothes, about who was supposed to keep the place tidy. Frequently, they had sunk into brooding sullen moods of not speaking to each other. Then there were times when they hurled insults and jibes at each other endlessly.

Inevitably, the rows had spread to their parents, each of them taking a different side. There had been fierce explosions followed by smouldering silences that lasted for days on end before normal relations were resumed.

The trouble with Wayne, Colin decided, was that he was totally irresponsible. His attitude towards his exams was typical. He seemed to think the world owed him a living, that somehow success would come to him without his having to lift a finger. Well, he was in for a rude awakening.

With a shrug, Colin went back to his books. He wasn't his brother's keeper. He had more important things to worry about than that.

When his mother called him down later for his meal, Colin had completely forgotten about the row. But Wayne obviously hadn't. Colin could tell from looking at his brother's scowling face that Wayne was just spoiling for a fight. He was attacking his sausages and stuffing huge chunks of them into his mouth as though it were some kind of penance. Chewing them became an aggressive act, swallowing them a humiliation that he could scarcely bring himself to perform.

As he ate, Wayne kept shooting poisonous glances at this brother and mother. Colin was startled at recognising a sudden resemblance to his father when he was in one of his moods. There was the same downward thrust of the lower lip and the same fierce dark pin-points of the eyes.

But Colin wasn't prepared to encourage his brother's bad-temper. He paid no attention and went back to the problem of Iago. What part had he played in Othello's downfall?

His mother was behaving as she always did in such circumstances. She was placidly forking salad into her mouth and pretending that nothing out of the ordinary was going on.

'I 'opes this weather last,' she said conversationally. 'Summer really 'ere. 'Bout time too. Makes you glad to be out o' 'Illsden.'

Wayne scowled at her. Colin nodded in agreement, but his mind was still worrying away at Iago. Was his evil really unmotivated?

'The 'ouses there is so close together,' Mrs MacMorris continued. 'They jus' seems to 'old the 'eat in. I remembers

17

nights in summer when it so stiflin' you couldn' 'ave a sheet on the bed even wit' all the windows wide open. It jus' like 'ome.'

There was a mixture of reproach and regret in her voice. From where he was sitting, Colin could see the back garden. There was quite a large lawn with beds for flowers and vegetables. A high hedge provided a screen which hid the house backing on to theirs.

It was so different from the enclosed concrete slab they had had at their other house. Wayne didn't like it because he couldn't kick a ball around it, but their mother had fallen in love with it and devoted much of her spare time to looking after it. It reminded her of her childhood, she said, in the country where everyone had their own patch and grew their own food and had their own mango tree.

'I mus' water them tomatoes this evenin',' Mrs MacMorris said. 'They dry as dry. It won' be long 'fore we eatin' 'em. Ain't not'in' as good as you own grown tomatoes.' She gazed at the garden with satisfaction.

'I'll water them for you if you like,' said Colin. The thought of wandering round the garden with a hose-pipe as the evening began to cool was attractive.

'No, don' let that worry you,' said Mrs MacMorris. 'I can do it. You got studyin' to t'ink 'bout.'

' 'E never t'ink 'bout anyt'in' else,' Wayne muttered.

'Now don' you start that again,' his mother said sharply. 'An' what I tells you 'bout talkin' that way?' she asked, moving on to another familiar complaint.

'Why shouldn' I? You talks that way, don' you?'

'That's cause I don' know no better,' said Mrs MacMorris, half as a joke. But then she became serious again. 'But that ain't the point, an' you knows it. You ain't livin' in Jamaica, you knows. You livin' in England. Ain't nobody goin' respect you if you talks that way. Colin don' speak like that.'

'I ain't Colin,' Wayne retorted. 'I don' 'ave to do everyt'in' like 'im.'

'It'ld be better if you do.'

By now, Wayne and his mother were glaring at each other

across the table. Colin was struck again by how much Wayne resembled his father. The argument too was like those that had gone on between his parents before they broke up. It was as though Wayne had taken his father's place.

'Colin, Colin, Colin,' Wayne sneered. 'That all I ever 'ears in this 'ouse.'

He pushed his chair away from the table and stood up. He was clutching his knife and fork aggressively as though they were weapons.

'Sit down,' his mother said, remaining calm. 'You ain't finish you dinner.'

'I 'ad as much as I can stomach,' Wayne retorted. He threw his knife and fork down on the table with a clatter and stalked to the door.

'Where you t'ink you goin', mister?' his mother called sharply.

Wayne paused long enough to give her a withering stare. 'Out.'

'An' where's out when it at 'ome?'

'What that to you?'

Colin watched as his mother and brother tried to outstare each other in a battle of wills.

'You got studyin' to do,' said Mrs MacMorris. 'You got exams comin' up. You ain't goin' out.'

Wayne bared his teeth in a humourless smile. 'That what you t'ink,' he said, and he turned on his heel and went through the door.

Mrs MacMorris struggled to her feet and started to go after him, but the show she put on was half-hearted. Colin could tell that she already knew she had lost that round. She didn't bother to pursue Wayne any further. She came back again into the room, admitting defeat, and subsided into her chair again.

'Blast that boy,' she sighed. ' 'E got the devil in 'im at times.'

'He'll be all right,' said Colin, making light of it.

'You does you best fo' you children,' Mrs MacMorris

said, going into one of her philosophical moods, 'an' they don' 'preciate it. We took this 'ouse so's you'd be away from that bad influence in 'Illsden, but don' seem to make no difference to Wayne. 'E can' keep away. That street life like a drug to 'im. 'E jus' can' shake it off. One o' these days 'e gonna end up in real trouble.'

She shot Colin a sudden sharp look of suspicion. 'I bet 'e gone to the father. I bet that where 'e is.'

'Could be,' said Colin, trying to show an interest.

But his mind was already engaged with the problem of Iago. Perhaps jealousy was the motivation. He resented Cassio being promoted above him. He suspected Emilia of being unfaithful. He was bitter at seeing a black man like Othello being successful in love and war. It was something worth exploring.

'I'll get on with my revision,' he said as he left the table.

'You do that,' said his mother. She managed a bleak smile. 'You gonna be all right.'

Chapter 3

Wayne stormed out of the house in a furious temper. Nobody gave a damn about him. The police could beat hell out of him and lock him up in a cell for all his mother and brother cared about it. For all the sympathy he got, you would think it had been all his own fault.

Then all that talk about exams and having to study. Wasn't he allowed one night off, for goodness' sake? They seemed to think he was still a child, and he wasn't. He was sixteen — old enough to leave school, get a job, ride a motorbike, have sex (legally) — so why did they go on treating him like a child and expect him to do what they said all the time?

He was so absorbed in his own rage that he didn't notice Mrs Bloomfield in her garden until she stood up from her weeding and straightened her shoulders. She smiled at him. He scowled back. She was always pottering about in her garden spying on people coming and going, poking her nose into business that didn't concern her.

'Is it hot enough for you?' she called out cheerfully.

Wayne glowered at her. What a fatuous thing to ask. 'It's too flamin' 'ot if you ax me,' he snarled at her and passed on, leaving her puzzled and uncertain.

When he reached the main road, he was in luck. A bus

was just coming. He raced across the road, missing death from an oncoming car by inches. He leaped onto the boarding platform of the bus and scurried upstairs.

Half an hour later, Wayne was in Hillsden High Street, and he was happy again. This felt like home to him. It was like a village, especially now that summer was here. The shops were closed, but there were people in the street — black people — wearing T-shirts and jeans or thin dresses, sitting on the traffic barriers, leaning against walls, standing in groups, strolling up and down the pavements, talking and laughing, enjoying the warm evening air and the comp-anionship, taking life easy. It was what Wayne had missed since moving to Dukesbury. There, everyone kept to themselves. There was no mixing, no communication. And in any case, most of the people there were white. It just wasn't the same.

The other thing that made Hillsden High Street seem like a village was that everyone knew everyone. That was Winston's mother. That was Darryl's father who worked in a garage. That was Errol who had left school two years ago and who had been in prison. That was Julie who was what they called a single parent and who at seventeen was pregnant again.

But Wayne couldn't see any of his particular friends. They were probably at the Club or getting dressed up for a party somewhere. He wondered where it would be tonight. Nobody had said anything at school and he had forgotten to ask. But that was no big problem. He would find out easily enough. Word always went round.

First though, he would go and see his father. Perhaps he would show more sympathy.

Balaclava Road was a turning off the High Street. As Wayne rounded the corner, he noticed a group of girls sitting on the wall of the first house. They greeted him with good-natured shouts and shrieks.

'Look who 'ere,' cried one of the girls about his own age. 'The prodigal return.'

'Hi, Marlene,' said Wayne, grinning broadly. 'Ain't you married yet then?'

'Naw,' replied Marlene complacently. 'I'm choosy.'

'You mean nobody'll 'ave you,' said Wayne.

Marlene gave him a scornful look while her friends fell about laughing.

Wayne moved on before Marlene could think of an answer — and before she made up her mind whether or not to thump him. She was a big girl.

The familiar sounds of the street wrapped themselves round Wayne in a reassuring cocoon. Windows were wide open and televisions and sound systems were pumping out their messages. Someone was beating hell out of his drum kit at No 12. There were raised voices and angry accusations at No 16 — there always were rows there. On the other side of the road, someone was tuning his car, revving it up until it seemed that the engine was going to explode or else the car was going to take off. It was as though he had never been away.

Outside No 32, Mr James was lying underneath his car, the black blob of his head sticking out from beneath the exhaust.

Wayne stopped. 'Hi, Mr James,' he called. ' 'Ow it goin'?'

Mr James eased himself a few inches from under his car and peered suspiciously at Wayne. Then he opened his mouth in a broad grin. 'Well, if it ain't little Wayne. 'Ow you doin?'

'All right, I guess,' Wayne replied.

'It long time since I seen you,' said Mr James. He wiped the sweat off his forehead with the back of his arm.

'You big end broke?' Wayne asked with exaggerated seriousness.

Mr James looked puzzled for a moment. He frowned at the rear end of his car and examined it. Then he burst into laughter. 'I'll break you big end if you ain't careful.'

Wayne laughed back.

'You goin' to see you dad?' Mr James asked. He grinned knowingly. 'Say, 'e doin' all right.'

'See you,' said Wayne, moving on.

'Be good now,' called Mr James, and he slid himself under his car again.

Further along, some boys were playing football in the street. The ball bounced off a wall and landed in front of Wayne. He trapped it and began to dribble forward. Immediately, three or four boys were attacking with their feet, trying to gain possession. Wayne turned his back on them and went weaving up the street.

'Hey,' shouted one of the boys, 'it Wayne.'

Wayne pitched the ball into the air and caught it. The boys crowded round him.

'Hi, Wayne,' said one of them. Another shyly touched him on the arm.

'You all right?' Wayne asked.

'Sure.'

Wayne bounced the ball and kicked it down the road. The boys went chasing after it, whooping and yelling as they went.

It was strange standing outside No 42 having to ring the bell. For so much of Wayne's life this had been home and he had had a key.

When his parents split up, shortly after moving to Dukesbury, his father had gone back to Balaclava Road. The ground floor flat of No 42 had still been vacant, so that's where he'd ended up — back where he started.

Wayne had visited his father a number of times since then. The last time was some months before. Now he wondered whether he should have come. His father might be busy or getting ready to go out. Wayne knew he was home because his car with its L plates and driving school banner was parked outside. He was lucky to find his father in. He worked odd hours, and Friday evening was usually a good time for business.

Wayne pulled himself together and rang the bell. It was stupid just standing there when he had come this far.

The door was opened by a woman. Wayne wasn't sure if she was wearing a dress or an underslip. It was shiny and left great stretches of brown shoulder bare. He didn't like to look too closely. The woman was quite young, younger than his mother. Wayne had met her several times before. Her name was Helen.

She stared at him blankly for a moment or two before recognising him. 'Oh, it you Wayne. Come in. You dad in there.'

Wayne went into the front room. The curtains were drawn almost closed to keep out the heat, and it was dark. Mr MacMorris was sitting on the sofa in his vest and pants.

'Hi, son,' he greeted and held out his hand for Wayne to clasp. Then he pulled him down on the sofa beside him. ' 'Ow you keepin'?'

'Oh, all right,' Wayne mumbled. He was suddenly embarrassed at being there and wished he hadn't come. It was as though he were intruding and didn't really belong there any more.

'It sure is 'ot, innit?' his father continued. He chuckled. 'I decide it too 'ot to work so I cancel my appointments. You knows what they says — all work an' no play!' He chuckled again.

'An' it ain't the first time neither,' said Helen morosely. 'I surprised you got any pupils left.' She had come in and sat down at the dining table in the bay window. Mr MacMorris ignored her.

' 'Ow the mother an' Colin?' he asked.

'They're fine,' said Wayne.

'I must make a effort an' come an' see you sometime,' Mr MacMorris went on.

'Huh,' came a grunt from the window. Mr MacMorris appeared not to hear it.

'It long time since I sees Colin,' he said. ' 'E must be a man by now.'

'I'm a man too,' boasted Wayne.

'What?' cried his father. 'Why, you's still a pickney.' He laughed and punched Wayne playfully on the cheek.

Helen laughed too, a loud hurtful laugh that made Wayne lower his head and feel ashamed. He launched into his account of how he had been searched by the police. His father made sympathetic noises.

'That too bad,' he said. 'That ain't no ways to treat nobody.'

'You don' wanna go troublin' the police,' said Helen flatly.

'I wasn' troublin' nobody,' Wayne broke out defiantly. 'I was mindin' my own business. It was them was troublin' me.'

He glared at Helen through the darkness and sensed her shrugging her shoulders and turning away, withdrawing any slight interest she might have had.

'I 'ears the bull gettin' very active these days,' said Mr MacMorris. 'Word is they got a campaign on — 'gainst street crime they calls it. They bring in the Special Patrol. Least that what my pupils tells me.'

'I wasn' committin' no crime,' Wayne pointed out.

'I knows that,' comforted Mr MacMorris, 'but when there's criminals to be caught, sometimes the innocent gets caught wit' the guilty.'

Wayne was disappointed. It sounded just like what his mother had said. He had expected something better.

Helen stood up and straddled herself in front of Mr MacMorris. 'We goin' out or ain't we?' she asked.

'Yeah, yeah,' replied Mr MacMorris impatiently. He waved his arm at her. 'You go get ready.'

Helen gave a snort and went out of the room.

'Listen, boy,' Mr MacMorris said, taking hold of Wayne's shoulder. 'If you's ever in any trouble, you comes an' tells me. You knows I wanna 'elp you.'

Wayne lowered his eyes. He could make out his father's legs stretched out in front of him. They were skinny and hairy. The thighs had no shape at all and seemed wasted away. He realised suddenly that they were the legs of an old man.

'Sure, Dad,' said Wayne. He rose to his feet. He wanted to get away. 'I'll be seein' you then.'

'That's it,' said Mr MacMorris, slapping his son's bottom. 'You go an' enjoy yourself. That what life fo', ain't it? An' you forgets 'bout the bull. They ain't gonna trouble you no more — so long's you be'aves yourself.'

It had been a waste of time going to see his father. He had

been no better than his mother. People like them didn't realise what it was like to be stopped by the police and searched without any reason. They seemed to think the police were there for people's protection. They had no idea how the police hounded black kids and insulted them and harassed them. They were totally out of touch with what was going on. They had no idea what the real world was like.

Feeling bitter and let down, Wayne turned back into the High Street. If he wanted sympathy, he would have to find it in people of his own age. They were the only ones who could understand his indignation and knew what it was like. The Club was the best place to find people like that. Wayne strode out with a new sense of purpose.

Even if you didn't know where or what the Club was, you would have been able to guess by the sounds bouncing from the building. Wayne's steps quickened and his heart began to beat faster in time to the rhythm of the music pounding out into the hot summer evening.

He pushed through the door and immediately found himself in the midst of a scene of feverish activity. The air was full of scent and smoke and after-shave and sweat. The heat hit him like a fist. His shirt stuck damply to his back. The building was shaking with the vibrations from the sound system and the frantic movement of gyrating bodies. The lighting was alternately bright and murky. This was more like it.

It took Wayne a time to get used to the dazzle and the darkness. He pushed his way through the packed bodies towards the bar, greeting friends with a cheerful chuckle and a slapping handclasp, and making eye-contact with some of the girls, who pretended to stare hard-faced right through him, though he could tell they were interested.

At the bar, Wayne found Desmond talking to Mr Fernandez, one of the youth workers.

'I don' know 'ow I'm gonna do in the exams,' Desmond was saying despondently.

Wayne bought a Coke, unplugged it, and poured the cool

contents down his parched throat. Then he burst into the conversation and described what had happened to him.

'That dread, man,' responded Desmond, his mouth dropping open with shock and his face lengthening to show how appalled he was.

Mr Fernandez looked serious. 'That what I 'earin' all the time,' he said. 'I got so many cases I can' 'ardly keep up wit' 'em.'

Wayne was gratified that here at last was an adult who understood what the youth had to put up with.

'You was lucky,' said Mr Fernandez. 'You was let off easy.'

Wayne bridled at this suggestion, but he didn't say anything.

Mr Fernandez continued grimly, 'I 'as a whole 'eap o' cases that I investigatin'. Kids been take down to the police station an' charge wit' all sort o' t'ings. You don' know the 'alf o' what goin' on. An' it gettin' worse. They brings the Special Patrol in. They jus' ridin' rough-shod over everyone.'

Wayne suppressed his own personal anger. Perhaps Mr Fernandez was right. There was something about the solemn way he spoke that carried conviction.

There was a lull in the music. The fevered movement of bodies was gradually stilled and they flopped into attitudes of exhaustion like puppets whose strings were no longer being pulled. They wiped the sweat off their brows and faces. A buzz of excited chatter broke out.

Then there was a disturbance at the door. Someone had come in and was yelling his head off. Everyone stopped talking and turned to find out what was happening. But it was dark by the entrance, and all they could make out were the words, 'Rass, man. Leroy been drill up by the police.' They were shrieked out again and again in a frenzied voice that sounded terrifying as tearing cloth.

Wayne distinguished the figure of a man crouching there, his arms stretched wide, his eyes and mouth gaping with the horror and affront of what he was proclaiming. Around

28

Wayne, bodies stiffened and faces hardened as the information sank in. Then there was a surge towards the door as people felt impelled to move.

Wayne was carried along with the tide, his feet practically lifted off the ground, before the message of the man's words could fully penetrate his brain. Mr Fernandez was trying to stem the rush. 'Wait, wait,' he was shouting. 'What goin' on?' But no one listened. The man had stormed through the door out of sight, and the crowd followed him.

By now they were in the street. Wayne wasn't sure what was happening, but as he was pressed along he felt a mixture of rage and exhilaration. Here were the police at it again, harassing people like him, but now they were going to do something about it. They weren't going to get away with it this time.

Desmond was scurrying along breathless by his side. 'What is it, man?' he panted.

'Don' you ever learn?' Wayne retorted bitterly. 'It the bullmen. They got Leroy.'

'Who Leroy?' Desmond asked.

'I don' know,' Wayne replied exasperated. 'Do that matter?'

The crowd pounded down the High Street and into Rhodes Avenue. Startled passers-by stopped to watch, wondering what was going on. Wayne couldn't see the man who had burst into the Club but he was presumably leading the chase. About halfway down Rhodes Avenue, the crowd slowed down. Wayne pushed his way forward, followed by Desmond. There was a car drawn into the kerb. There was a policeman standing beside it. The back door was swung open. Inside, Wayne could see a black youth lying on the seat. There were two policemen beside him. The boy was lying with his head fallen back. His shirt was torn open, and it was stained with blood. Wayne felt himself go cold. Sweat broke out on his forehead.

The crowd was angry.

'What you doin'?' someone accused.

'Leave 'im alone,' demanded another.

A girl screamed hysterically, 'They killin' 'im, they killin' 'im.'

The policeman outside the car looked pale and tense. He tried to explain. 'There's been an accident. He's been knifed. We're waiting for the ambulance to arrive. We don't want to move him till then.'

He apprehensively surveyed the faces ranged around him.

'A accident! Huh!' someone roared, and a rumble of disbelief rolled round the crowd.

'You killin' 'im,' the girl screamed again, and her accusation was taken up by the others.

The policeman stood defensively in the open doorway of the car. He went on talking to try to pacify the crowd. 'The ambulance is on its way. We don't know how badly hurt he is. He musn't be moved until the ambulance arrives.'

But the crowd was having none of it. They were growing wild.

'Who say 'e mustn' be move?'

'We don' need no 'elp from them. We looks after our own.'

'They ain't waitin' fo' no ambulance. They waitin' fo' the bull van.'

'They 'restin' 'im.'

'They gonna kill 'im.'

Then the crowd was a screaming mob. It burst into frantic action.

Wayne was pushed forward. Hands stretched out to grab the policeman. He was shoved aside and thrown to the ground. The car rocked and groaned as people yanked open the other doors. Some of them were lifting it by the bumpers and trying to bounce it off the road. The policemen inside clung desperately to keep their positions. Hands reached in to seize arms and legs. They were dragged out and cast to one side. Leroy was carefully lifted out. He stared wildly about him. He was dazed and could hardly stand. His breath came rasping painfully through his open mouth. His shirt and jeans were soaked with blood. Two men arranged his arms round their shoulders, and they began to half run him, half drag him down the street.

More people started to attack the car, rocking it from side to side until it overturned and lay on its back with its wheels in the air like a beached turtle. There was an excited roar. The rest of the crowd followed the rescued Leroy.

It had all happened so quickly that Wayne could scarcely take it all in. He was still part of the jostling crowd with Desmond beside him. He wanted to make sure that Leroy was all right. He was full of murderous hatred for the police who had done this to a black boy. At the same time, he was high with pride that for once they had stood up for themselves and stood up for their own.

'We show 'em,' he cried exultantly.

'Yeah,' said Desmond, less elated. 'But what 'appen next?'

The crowd streamed into the High Street again. They were almost dancing. People raised their arms high and leaped into the air. They let out squeals of delight and cheers of triumph. They spilled over into the road. Cars shrieked to a halt, and the mob wove in and out, waving to the drivers and slapping the bonnets with their hands, to reach the other side. Leroy was still being helped along at the front by his friends.

The crowd ran round the Jubilee Clock Tower, scattering the pigeons that always settled there in spite of the traffic. With a great clapping of wings and clucking protests, the birds rose in a swirling cloud. Then the crowd was moving down Jubilee Parade. It came to a halt beside a parked car and gathered round as the back door was opened and Leroy was eased in. His eyes were closed and his breath was grating even more harshly than before. He slumped back in the seat.

'We done it our way,' cried one of the men joyfully. 'We take 'im to the 'ospital.'

'Yeah,' said the other. 'We look after our own.'

There were shouts of agreement and congratulation. The men got into the car, and it leaped out into the road with a violent screeching of gears.

People stood around, smiling and chatting, reluctant to separate. They had a sense of having achieved something and didn't want it to turn into an anti-climax now that Leroy had gone.

'The yout' sure stood up fo' 'emself this time,' Wayne whooped. 'They show us more respect next time.'

'You t'ink they really assaultin' Leroy?' Desmond asked dubiously.

'Course,' said Wayne defiantly. 'What else they got 'im in that car fo'? Where else 'e get that blood from? They got off light. We should 'ave lynched 'em.'

Desmond continued to be unconvinced.

'Look, man,' Wayne argued. 'You knows this is war. It them or us. It always been like that.'

'That ain't what you use to say.'

Wayne brooded. 'Well, perhaps I jus' feels more strong 'bout it since what 'appen to me.' Then he burst out vehemently. 'The bull the enemy. Don' you 'ave any doubts 'bout that.'

'Well,' said Desmond, 'one t'ing I knows is it ain't finish yet.'

At that moment, a police van came hurtling round the Jubilee Clock Tower into Jubilee Parade. It ground to a halt in the middle of the road. Ten policemen jumped down from the back. They ranged out across the road facing the crowd.

'What I tells you?' moaned Desmond.

'Shut you mout',' muttered Wayne. He was staring out grimly at the line of police. The mood of exhilaration had suddenly evaporated. A mixture of fear and bitter determination took its place.

The policemen were advancing slowly down the street towards them. They had taken their batons out and were fingering them nervously or brandishing them in the air. A murmur went through the crowd. For a moment, they backed off, afraid and uncertain what to do next. Then a bottle went hurtling through the air and crashed a few feet from one of the policemen, shattering across the road.

Someone had found a crate of milk bottles waiting outside a shop for the morning delivery. More bottles began flying. The police retreated to their van. A mighty roar of derision rose from the crowd, and they surged forward.

One youth went screaming ahead of everyone else. He threw a brick with all his strength at the window of the van. There was a loud crack as it made contact, and the window shivered into tiny fragments. The driver inside shielded his head with his arms and slid sideways. A loud cheer went up from the youth. Wayne joined in, but he wondered where the brick had come from.

The rejoicing was short-lived. The policemen had been issued with shields from the back of the van. They now advanced on the crowd with greater determination. A few bottles still smashed in the road in front of them, but the crowd was in retreat. Wayne pounded down the road with Desmond at his side.

'This is dread, man,' Desmond panted.

'It them or us,' Wayne reminded him.

Looking back, Wayne saw that the police were catching up on them. Three of them suddenly pounced and caught someone. It looked like the youth who had thrown the brick. The rest of the police slowed down, and the crowd slowed down too. The youth was struggling, but he was dragged back to the van and thrown inside. The other policemen withdrew to the van and surrounded it. The driver of the van revved up and backed it in preparation for turning round and moving off.

Someone rushed out from the crowd. The police were taken by surprise. The man ran forward, waving his arms and yelling unintelligibly at the top of his voice. He broke through the police and somehow climbed on top of the van. He began dancing and jumping there, thumping his feet into the roof. The van roared off towards the Jubilee Clock Tower, and the man, knocked off balance, clung on desperately. The van disappeared round the corner.

The policemen were moving forward once more, their shields held securely in front of them, their batons raised above them. The crowd turned and ran. But when they reached the end of Jubilee Parade, they found another line of policemen facing them. They were trapped.

There was a moment of confusion while they blundered about, wondering what to do next. It didn't last long. They wanted to get back to the High Street so that they could make it to their homes and safety. They turned once more and charged back the way they had come.

There was a desperate moment as they collided with the police. Wayne heard the whoosh of a baton as it swept past him within an inch of his ear. He saw a black boy on his left staggering from a blow on the head, and another on his right, grabbed by the shirt and struggling to get away. But then he was through and racing for dear life for the Clock Tower.

Desmond caught up with him and held on to his arm. They stood there for a moment panting and trying to regain their breath.

'Come on,' said Desmond eventually. 'We better go to my yard. It safe there.'

Wayne didn't reply. He allowed Desmond to lead the way down the High Street, but his mind was still reeling from what had happened. It seemed as though the world he knew had been totally transformed. They had let the police harass them and humiliate them, but now the worm had turned. They had shown that they weren't going to put up with that any more. They were going to fight back and carry the war into the enemy camp.

As he padded along beside Desmond, his breathing returned to normal. He found that he was smiling. It was about time something like this happened. It was time the police were taught a lesson.

Chapter 4

By ten o'clock that evening, Wayne had not returned home. Mrs MacMorris was growing worried. Colin had come down from his bedroom to keep his mother company and to be sociable, but he had brought his file of notes with him. Mrs MacMorris was knitting in spite of the heat — she couldn't bear to be idle. The television was quietly rumbling in the background.

'Where that boy gone?' Mrs MacMorris complained for the third or fourth time while Colin half attended. ' 'E should 'ave been 'ome a 'our ago. 'E know 'e suppose to be in by nine. I'll 'ave somet'in' to say when 'e do arrive.'

She was silent for a few moments, her attention caught by the advertisement flashing by on the television. It was funny, Colin thought, the way she always stopped knitting to concentrate on the adverts while during the actual programme her eyes scarcely ever rose from her work.

'I 'opes Wayne ain't in no more trouble wit' the police,' she said when the adverts had finished. ' 'E crazy 'nough fo' anyt'in'.'

Colin didn't comment. He was remembering another time when Wayne had stayed out. It all started with some trouble at school. Wayne had sworn at a teacher and had been sent home for the day. Their mother had read him the riot act and taken away all his privileges. Wayne didn't like that. Next day, he didn't come home from school. By nine o'clock their mother was frantic. She and Colin had gone out in the car to search the streets, but there was no sign of him. Their mother was getting more and more upset. She imagined all kinds of dreadful things — an accident, kidnapping, the police. Then when they arrived back home, there was Wayne, large as life and not a bit repentant, tucking into a huge plate of cornflakes. Their mother had been too relieved to tell him off, and so Wayne had got away with it.

Colin was sure it would be the same this time. There was nothing to get upset or alarmed about.

He turned over the page of his book. As he did so, his eye was caught by the image on the television screen. There was something familiar about it. With a jolt he identified it. It was the Jubilee Clock Tower in Hillsden High Street. Suddenly he was watching the changing pictures with anxious attention.

A great mob filled the screen. They were mostly young and black though there were some white people there too. Their faces were taut and angry. They were gesticulating wildly in the air with their arms. Their mouths were open wide as they yelled and shouted. Colin could hear a confused roar going on. A line of policemen came into view, standing shoulder to shoulder. They were holding batons and riot shields and were moving forward. The crowd turned and ran. The camera zoomed in on a black boy. He was bare-chested with his shirt tied round his waist. He twisted round and hurled something. For a brief moment, there was a close-up of his face — tense, determined, venomous. He couldn't have been more than fifteen. Then the police were charging down on the mob. Fights and scuffles broke out. The television picture wobbled as though the cameraman was caught up in the middle of it all and was having difficulty keeping his camera steady. Baton blows rained down. People fell to the ground. Three policemen were dragging a black man along the ground by his legs.

Mrs MacMorris too was staring at the screen, appalled and unable to speak.

Colin leaped at the set and turned the volume up.

'Fifteen people were arrested,' the news-reader was saying. 'Eight policemen were injured. Latest reports say that the area is now under control and all is quiet.'

He then moved on to the next item of news.

'That were 'Illsden,' Mrs MacMorris exclaimed, finding her voice. 'What the world comin' to? Now you sees why I wants you out o' there.'

'It looked pretty fierce,' Colin had to admit.

The naked violence of what he had seen shocked him. It was no game. That was real hatred on the faces of the crowd. Those were real blows the police had been dishing out, meant to crack someone's skull open. And it was happening in Hillsden. There would be people he knew involved.

'Fightin' in the streets,' his mother went on. 'Lawlessness everywheres. That it should come to this. People jus' don' 'ave no respect fo' what's right.'

'We don't know how it started,' Colin suggested cautiously. 'Something might have set it off.'

'That ain't no reason to go rampagin' 'bout the streets that way,' said Mrs MacMorris indignantly. 'The law is the law, an' it ain't right policemen should be 'urt doin' their duty.'

Then she clapped her hand to her cheek and opened her mouth wide with sudden fear. 'You don' t'ink Wayne mix up in this?'

The thought had already crossed Colin's mind. If there was anything going on, Wayne liked to be in the thick of it. He was sure to have made for Hillsden when he stormed out of the house. That's where all his friends were. He just couldn't keep away from the place.

Mrs MacMorris dropped her knitting with the row uncompleted on to the sofa and stood up. She was working herself into a state. ' 'E might 'ave been 'urt or 'rested. 'E crazy 'nough fo' anyt'in'.'

'He'll be all right,' Colin said, trying to reassure her.

But she wouldn't be comforted. ' 'Ow you knows?' she demanded aggressively. 'Anyt'in' could 'ave 'appen. I wants you to ring the father. See if 'e there.'

The idea didn't appeal to Colin. He hadn't spoken to his father since he had gone back to the old house. As far as he could make out, it was his father who had been in the wrong — starting rows, behaving unreasonably, and then going off with someone half his age. It was his mother who had been left to pick up the pieces and keep the family together. Colin didn't want anything to do with his father ever again.

But then he looked at his mother's face, troubled and drawn. 'Very well,' he said reluctantly. 'If that's what you want.'

He switched the television off and went to the phone in the hall. There was no need to check the number.

The phone went on ringing for a long time as though there were no one at the other end to answer. Mrs MacMorris waited, tense and impatient, at Colin's side.

At last, the receiver was picked up. ' 'Ello?' came a voice. Colin knew it was his father.

'Hello,' he said. 'It's Colin.'

'Oh,' said Mr MacMorris. ' 'Ello, Colin. 'Ow is you?'

As he listened, Colin analysed the tone of his father's voice. It was careful, guarded, suspicious.

'I'm all right,' Colin went on hurriedly. 'It's Wayne. Is he there?'

Mrs MacMorris nodded her head eagerly several times.

'No,' said Mr Macmorris. ' 'E were 'ere a couple 'o 'ours ago, but 'e ain't 'ere now.'

'D'you know where he's gone?' Colin asked.

'No. You knows Wayne. 'E 'ave friends. 'E could be anywheres.'

Colin wondered where to go from there. A strained silence descended. 'We saw about the trouble in Hillsden on television,' he said eventually, 'and we were worried in case Wayne was involved in it. He isn't back yet.'

'Yeah,' said Mr MacMorris. 'I seen that too, but I ain't 'ear not'in' 'bout it 'ere. I t'ink it must be all blow up. You knows what it like. These television people takes a little t'ing an' makes a big noise 'bout it so's they get a 'ole 'eap o' money fo' it.' He went on reassuringly, 'Ain't not'in' to worry 'bout. You knows Wayne. 'E turn up in 'is own good time like that bad penny they's always talkin' 'bout.' He chuckled.

'I hope you're right,' said Colin.

'Course I is,' said Mr MacMorris, growing more confident. 'When you ever knows me be wrong?'

Colin jibbed at that but he made no comment.

'Why don' you come visit me sometime?' Mr MacMorris asked. 'It long time since I seen you.'

'Well, I've got my exams coming up,' Colin explained evasively. 'I'll have to work hard at that.'

'Sure, sure,' said Mr MacMorris. Colin wasn't sure if there was a note of contempt in his voice. 'Well, I see you sometime. I 'opes Wayne back soon.' And his father put the phone down.

As Colin replaced the receiver, he realised that he was sweating — and it wasn't just the warm evening.

'What 'e say?' his mother asked, her voice heavy with disapproval.

'Wayne was there,' Colin told her, 'but that was two hours ago. Dad hasn't seen him since then.'

Mrs MacMorris wrung her hands and walked away. She turned and appealed to her son. 'What 'bout 'is friends? Could 'e be wit' one o' them?'

Colin was beginning to get exasperated. He agreed with his father for once. Wayne would turn up in his own good time. His mother was taking it all too seriously. It was just like the last time. Wayne was staying out and causing them worry simply to get his own back. And just like last time he would turn up looking all innocent, and his mother would be so thankful she wouldn't say a word of reproach.

His mother was looking at him with wide tragic eyes. 'Colin, take the car. Go an' see if you can find 'im.'

Here we go again, Colin thought. He was annoyed. He wanted to refuse. He had better things to do than trail round the streets searching for a younger brother whose sole aim was to exploit the situation. There was his studying to get on with. Had his mother forgotten about that?

But then he saw the appeal on his mother's face. 'All right,' he said. 'I'll go.'

As he turned the car into the main street, he brooded despondently on this wild goose chase. It was all such a waste of time. He didn't know who Wayne's friends were or where they lived. He didn't know what Wayne did or where he went in the evenings. All he could do was coast around the streets on the off chance of seeing his brother.

By now, he was in familiar terrotory. He was cruising through the streets he had grown up in. But there was something strange about them. At this time of night on a warm summer's evening, he would have expected there to be lots of people about, sitting on their garden walls or doorsteps, lounging about the street corners, chatting about the events of the day, waiting for something to happen, reluctant to go indoors. But the place was practically deserted. Colin had an eerie feeling that everyone was hiding behind locked doors and curtained windows peering out anxiously as he passed.

There were none of the party noises either that would be normal on a Friday night — no loud music throbbing out, or high-pitched voices laughing and shouting and enjoying themselves, or brightly-lit windows and doorways thronged with people jostling each other and jumping to the beat of blaring reggae.

He emerged into the High Street. It was strange to see how little traffic there was. The street was empty. It was like a ghost town. As he passed the Jubilee Clock Tower, he noticed that some of the shops had been boarded up. Perhaps the windows had been smashed in the disturbances. There seemed to be a lot of litter and rubble on the pavements — shattered glass, bricks, mangled waste-bins, fluttering sheets of torn paper.

Then he became aware of the police. They were every-where, standing vigilant in the shadows on the corners, or patrollling the pavements in pairs. A police car overtook him, siren screaming and for a moment he thought he was going to be stopped. But it passed on. He didn't dare drive too slowly in case he drew attention to himself.

Further along, there was the youth club Wayne sometimes went to. Colin knew one of the youth workers there, Mr Fernandez, but the place was in darkness, so there was no point in stopping. McDonald's still had its lights on, but there was no one inside except for an assistant at the counter bending over a newspaper.

He turned back and began to explore the side streets again. Eventually he found himself nosing down Balaclava Road. When he came to No 42, he paused. After two years, it still looked very familiar, but he was surprised at how shabby and dilapidated it now appeared. Once it had been home, and he had taken it for granted without actually seeing it. Now, remembering the more modern and airy house he had become accustomed to in Beechwood Crescent, he couldn't imagine how he had ever endured it.

The tiny front garden was a tangle of dank weeds. The gate was hanging off its hinges. the paint on the window sills was peeling. Where there were lights on in the house, they showed through curtains that were thin and frayed and sagging from their supports. The same picture was repeated by each of the terraced houses that swept on in an unbroken line up the street.

Colin wondered if he should get out and knock at the door. It was possible that Wayne had gone back there. But the thought of meeting his father face to face after all that time was too much. It had been bad enough speaking to him on the phone. He manoeuvered the car out into the middle of the road and drove on. It did all seem a useless exercise. Wayne was probably tucked up safe for the night on some sofa provided by a friend.

So as to be able to tell his mother that he had done a proper search, Colin slowly toured a few more of the back streets before returning to the High Street. There seemed to be more police there than ever. Colin didn't loiter. He followed the one-way system round the Jubilee Clock Tower, along Jubilee Parade and out past the blocks of council flats.

As he began to gather speed and set off for home, a figure wearing a track suit and a baseball hat darted across the road ahead of him. The face was turned towards him and was caught for a moment in the car's headlights. Colin recognised it. It was Herald. He had been at school with him. Colin pulled in sharply to the kerb. Herald might know something about Wayne. It was worth a try. He leaned over and wound down the window.

Herald approached slowly and suspiciously. When he was alongside, he looked as though he wasn't going to stop. Colin called out his name. Herald paused for a moment and then came up to the car and peered in. A slow smile spread across his face. Colin thought there was a rather contemptuous edge to it, but he couldn't explain why.

'If it ain't ol' Colin,' Herald said. He thrust his hand through the window and they shook hands. ''Ow you doin', guy?''

'All right,' said Colin.

'Yeah, I can see,' Herald went on, patting the roof of the car several times. 'A nice bit o' gear.'

'It's my mother's,' Colin explained.

Herald nodded and pursed his lips knowingly.

'How are you keeping?' Colin asked.

They had been in the same class but hadn't exactly got on. Herald had always been playing about, taunting the teachers, disrupting the work. There had been times when Colin had wanted to protest at the way Herald was holding the class back and preventing those who wanted to learn from learning. But he had never done anything about it. Herald had left school at the end of the fifth year, and Colin hadn't seen him since then. It was strange how you could know someone day in, day out at school, and then when they left you never saw them again.

'I gets along,' Herald said.

'Are you working?'

Herald stared at him sceptically. 'You crazy, man. Who got a job these days? I ain't 'ad a job since I left school.'

'That's bad.'

'I survives. 'Ow 'bout you? You still at school?'

'Yes, I've got my exams coming up.'

'Well, I 'opes there's a job fo' you when you finish.'

Herald's voice was filled with a weary cynicism that made Colin uneasy.

'Are you still living at home?' he asked.

Herald sucked his lips. 'You jokin'? Naw, I got threw out. The ol' folks don' see it the way the yout' does. We 'ad what you might call a disagreement. I's on my own now.'

'But how do you manage?'

'Oh, I gets by. I got somewhere to rest my 'ead, an' I got social security. That jus' 'bout keep the wolf from the door. When I ain't queuein' up at the Labour, I goes to the swimmin' baths or the library. They's free, you know. So I's gettin' myself a education. What that sayin'? A 'ealthy mind in a 'ealthy body. Ain't that the ideal we suppose to be strivin' towards?'

The mockery behind Herald's words unsettled Colin. There was something too about the scornful smile on Herald's face that made him turn away. He remembered why he was there. 'I'm looking for Wayne. Have you seen him?'

'What, you little brother? Naw, I ain't seen 'im. 'E probably down the bullstation.' He laughed unpleasantly.

Colin didn't like the sound of it. 'What was all that trouble anyway? It was on television.'

'Ain't not'in' unusual. It 'appen every day. It jus' that the cameras was there this time. You forgets what it like livin' in 'Illsden. The yout' an' bull is always 'avin' their little differences. Course, where you livin' now that kind o' t'ing don' 'appen. Dukesbury is so repectable. It is so law-abidin'. I surprise they lets black folks live there.'

Colin ignored Herald's jibe and went back to what he had seen on television. 'You were there?'

'Yeah. I was there. I seen it all. People can only take so

much. 'Ow d'you expect us to be'ave when we sees the bull actin' that way? They had Leroy in a car. I don' know whether they beat 'im up or not, but 'e was bleedin' an' we don' trust no bullman wit' one o' our own. Not any more. They says they takin' 'im to the 'ospital, but when 'ave we ever been able to believe what they says? So we jus' went in an' got Leroy out o' there. That's when all the trouble start.' Then he added with a sudden fierceness, 'An' it ain't finish yet. It jus' begin. There gonna be a explosion they ain't never gonna forget.'

Colin felt uncomfortable . He suspected that some of the hatred that burned so intensely in Herald's eyes was being directed to him. He wanted to get out of there.

'I'd better be going then,' he said.

'Yeah,' said Herald jeeringly. 'You'd better get back to you own yard where it's safe. There ain't likely to be any trouble up there. I 'opes Wayne all right.'

'Thanks. See you.'

'Laters.'

Colin wound up the window and checked his rear mirror. As he began to edge away from the pavement there was a thunderous thump on the car roof. Colin wasn't sure whether it was a friendly farewell or a warning shot. There was certainly something ominous about it.

It was after midnight when he arrived home. His mother opened the door to him. She must have heard the car. Her face dropped when she saw he was alone.

'There was no sign of him,' Colin told her. 'The whole place seemed deserted.'

Mrs MacMorris went into the back room and sank onto the sofa.

'He'll be all right,' Colin said, trying to comfort her. 'He'll come back when he wants to.'

His mother didn't respond. Her face was tired and drawn. Then she suddenly broke into a fierce cry, 'I'll give that boy lashes when 'e get back 'ome, upsetting us this way.'

But Colin knew she wouldn't. Her anger subsided and she sat staring miserably into space.

'Better go to bed,' Colin said. 'There's no point on staying up any longer.'

His mother sighed. 'All right. I'll go up in a minute.'

When Colin left her, she was making no move to get ready for bed. It looked as though she were preparing to sit up all night.

Chapter 5

Desmond lived in Mafeking Road, off the High Street. It was very similar to Balaclava Road where Wayne used to live, a parallel row of terraced houses built in the days when gentlemen had drawing rooms on the first floors and servants slept in the attics, and which were now split up into flats and bed-sits.

When Desmond's mother, Mrs Henry, opened the door at their ring, she was obviously surprised to see them. She had been comfortably settled in front of the television with a box of chocolates at her side. She led the way back to the living room and slumped in her seat again.

'What you doin' 'ere?' she demanded, eyeing them suspiciously. 'It ain't like you to be 'ome this early on a Friday night.' She paused and her eyes narrowed. 'You ain't been up to somet'in', 'as you?'

'No, Mum,' said Desmond wearily. 'We ain't done not'in'. We jus' tired, that's all . We jus' wants a early night.'

'Huh!' grunted Mrs Henry shoving a coffee cream into her mouth. 'A early night. That'll be the day. What 'bout you exams? Since you 'ome early, you can go do some studyin' fo' 'em.'

'Aw, Mum,' Demond protested. 'Ain't I allowed one night off in my life?'

Mrs Henry let that pass. A new programme had started, and she watched the opening credits critically. Wayne and Desmond sank back on the sofa. Mrs Henry absently passed the box of chocolates to them, and they helped themselves. Wayne was amazed at how delicious the chocolates tasted. It was as though he hadn't had food for days. He selected another one and popped it into his mouth. Mrs Henry quickly snatched the box back again.

Wayne let the television pour over him. If nothing else, it was a way of getting his breath back, so to speak, and catching up on the events of the past hour. He was exhausted. It was as though he had run a marathon or been through some kind of assault course. He wondered if he had fallen asleep when some time later he felt Desmond's elbow digging into his ribs.

'Hey, man, look at that,' Desmond was whispering.

Wayne blinked his eyes and focussed them on the television screen. Then he was suddenly wide awake. There was the Jubilee Clock Tower and the police charging down on a crowd of people. Batons were flashing and black youths were being grabbed and hauled away. Wayne watched horrified.

Somehow on television, it seemed more vivid and violent than he had remembered. A little glow of excitement began to grow inside him. Perhaps the cameras had photographed him. Perhaps he was on television. But almost immediately the thought appalled him. What would his mother say if she recognised him ? Even worse, the police might be able to identify him and arrest him.

He was still trying to come to terms with this terrifying idea when Desmond turned to him and asked, 'Say, man, 'ow come they gets there so fast?'

Mrs Henry was asleep, her mouth wide open and her breath rumbling in her throat, so it was all right.

Wayne pretended a cool indifference. 'When there bad news 'bout blacks, those cameras gets there in no time at all. When there good news, you never sees 'em.' But anxiety continued to gnaw at his inside.

He wondered if he should make for home. His mother would be worrying about where he was. It was long past the time when he was usually expected to be back. There would probably be a scene about it — not to mention the way he had stormed out of the house.

But then Desmond raided the kitchen and produced some Coke and cakes, so he stayed on to watch the movie on television. It was the same old stuff about spies and treachery and a double-dealing glamorous girl who turned out to be true in the end, but Wayne followed it engrossed, glad to be able to get away from his immediate worries.

As it finished, Mrs Henry snorted and woke up. She stared at Wayne as though seeing him for the first time, and then yawned.

'It way past my bed time,' she said. She frowned at Wayne. 'Ain't you got no 'ome to go to?'

'Yeah,' Wayne said, 'I better be goin'.'

Desmond saw him to the door.

'You take care now,' he said. 'The bull might still be around an' you don' wanna take no risks.'

'Sure, man,' said Wayne, pleased and amused at his friend's concern. 'I'll take it easy.'

The streets were surprisingly quiet. It was late, but even so Wayne knew that there were usually more people about than this, especially on a Friday night, rolling home from pubs or clubs, on the way to the next party. The emptiness of the streets was quite eerie.

He knew there was no chance of getting a bus at this hour, and he would have to walk. The prospect filled him with apprehension. It was not so much the effort involved in covering the four miles or so to home, it was more the thought of what could happen on the way. If the police were in the mood for revenge, he would be an obvious target.

Wayne had walked home before. It was nothing unusual. But this time it was different. He jumped at every shadow and watched warily every passer-by that approached him and every car that zoomed past. Twice, police cars passed him, cruising by slowly, giving him a cool scrutiny. It might even have been the same car that had come round a second time to give him a closer look. He couldn't be sure. All he knew was that both times his heart had leaped into his mouth at the sight. He expected the cars to screech to a halt and the policemen to jump out and drag him off to the station. When they didn't, and the cars sailed smoothly on, he was relieved.

It would take him another hour to get home. His mother would have given him up by then and gone to bed. No doubt there would be cold looks and hard words in the morning, but at least he could pretend he got in earlier than he actually did, and there would be no one to contradict him.

Wayne had reached the council flats beyond Jubilee Parade when he saw someone walking towards him. It was exposed here with a wide expanse of open land alongside the road with the flats in the distance. The figure was coming closer. Wayne was reassured to see that he was black. He was wearing a track suit and trainers with a baseball cap on his head. There was something familiar about him. Wayne was sure he had seen him at school, but he couldn't think of the name. So as not to seem unfriendly, he said, 'Hi!' as he passed. The boy returned his greeting. Wayne hurried on.

Then there was a call from behind him. 'Hey, man.' Wayne stopped and turned round. The boy was slowly advancing on him.

'Ain't you Wayne MacMorris?' the boy asked.

'Yeah,' Wayne replied, not sure whether it was something he should boast about or deny.

'I t'ought it were,' the boy went on. 'I jus' seen you brother. 'E been lookin' fo' you.'

This news shook Wayne. If his mother had sent Colin out to look for him then things must be serious. It might not be as simple as he had thought to slip back home without them knowing how late it was.

By now he had a clearer view of the boy. A faint memory began to take shape. 'It 'Erald Thompson, innit?'

'Yeah,' said Herald.

' 'Ow you doin', man?' Wayne asked becoming more cordial. They shook hands.

'All right, I guess,' said Herald. He took a slow and careful look all around him. 'Like I says, I jus' seen you brother. 'E worry case you involve in this bit o' trouble there been.'

'Oh?' Wayne asked, puzzled. Then he remembered the pictures on television. 'Well, I suppose I might 'ave been,' he went on evasively.

Herald looked all round again. 'You walkin' 'ome?'

'Yeah.'

'I don' t'ink it wise,' Herald warned. 'Not after what 'appen. You gonna get pick up 'tween 'ere an' Dukesbury fo' sure.'

Wayne weighed this up in his mind. He was so exposed walking along the deserted streets on his own. He remembered the police car that had cruised past him twice already. He might not be so lucky next time.

'I knows what you mean,' he said, 'but what else can I do? I gotta get 'ome.'

Herald hesitated for a moment. His face took on a brooding look. 'I could 'elp you,' he said at last. 'I 'ave a place. You could come wit' me. It ain't much, but it a roof over you 'ead.'

Wayne considered this offer. If he went with Herald, he would at least be safe for the night. It would be all right in the morning, in daylight. He could make it home then. He might even get home before his mother was up. She need never know that he had been out all night.

'OK,' he said. 'Thanks.'

'Don' expect no modern conveniences,' Herald warned him. 'I lives rough, man. But it all right.'

Herald led the way along the High Street and took the turning down Ladysmith Road. Wayne knew it, but it had changed since he had last been there. On both sides, the houses had been demolished. Fences of corrugated metal sheeting had been erected along the road. It was only at the end of the street where it backed onto the railway that a few of the terraced houses remained standing. Herald went up to one of them. Wayne noticed that the windows were boarded up. What remained of the small front garden was a mass of weeds. Herald pushed the front door open.

'Ain't no point in lockin' it,' he said. 'Ain't not'in' to t'ief.' He laughed.

It had been dark in the street, but inside the house it was pitch black. There was a click and a flash as Herald lit his paraffin lamp. It spluttered into action. Then he drew heavy bolts across the door at the top and bottom.

'Least that way I 'as warnin' when they comes to get me,' he explained. He laughed again.

The lamp cast flickering shadows around the hall. The plaster had crumbled or been kicked from the walls and lay in great piles on the floor, leaving ugly patches of bare lathes. Doors had been torn off their hinges. Floor boards had been ripped up. The bannisters on the stairs that led upwards were broken and shattered, but the treads themselves were still intact.

Herald led the way up. 'Keep to the wall,' he warned, and Wayne stumbled after him and the light. At the top of the first flight, Herald turned to the back of the house. The doors were still standing there. He pushed through one of them to the room beyond. It was lighter inside. Through the smashed window, where some jagged edges of glass still remained, Wayne could see the sky.

Herald put the lamp down on a wooden crate. He spread his arms out and gestured round the room. 'Welcome,' he said. 'It ain't much, but it 'ome.'

Looking about him, Wayne could make out a couple more wooden boxes and two battered kitchen chairs. On the floor were two bare mattresses with a few blankets and other clothes scattered over them. It was a bleak and desolate scene. Wayne couldn't help comparing it with his own comfortable room back home.

' 'Ow come you livin' 'ere?' he asked.

Herald grinned ruefully. 'Call it a temporary misunderstandin' wit' my people,' he said. 'They didn' like my life style, an' I got tired o' their naggin'. They says they put me out. I says I left.'

Would it ever come to this with his own family, Wayne wondered. If it did, he hoped he would find somewhere better than this to live in.

Herald must have sensed that Wayne didn't think much of the place. 'It ain't so bad,' he said. 'I ain't 'ere much except fo' sleepin'. I finds most o' what I needs outside. There's 'ot water at 'Illsden Station. There's launderettes. There's places to eat. There's friends who 'elps out when I wants it.'

Herald cleared the clothes off one of the mattresses. 'Rest you feet,' he said. Wayne stretched out on the mattress while Herald settled himself down on the other.

'What 'bout the bull, man?' Wayne asked. 'Don' they 'assle you?'

'Course they does,' said Herald. 'Fact o' life, innit?'

Wayne went on to describe his own encounter with the police. His indignation boiled in him afresh. When he had finished, Herald made no comment. He was looking at the younger boy coolly. There was a slight cynical twist to his mouth.

'You don' know you born,' he said at last. 'You ever been pick up by the police on a charge o' obstruction when all you do is standin' in the street? You ever been 'rested by the police an' made to strip to you pants while they stares at you an' laughs an' makes jokes?'

By now Herald's eyes were blazing. But he hadn't finished yet 'You ever get t'row in a bull van like a sack o' potatoes an' 'ave you 'air pull an' you 'ead bang 'gainst the wall? You ever get take to court on the say-so o' a bullman who 'ate you guts an' tell more lies than a weigh machine? When that 'appens to you, then maybe — jus' maybe — you might know the 'alf o' it.'

Wayne felt that he had been put in his place. Herald's outburst made his own experience seem insignificant. He knew that what Herald was talking about was true. He kept hearing similar things all the time from his friends. There was a whole dimension of police harassment that he had been spared.

'It the system, innit?' Herald went on. 'It the way white society keeps us blacks down. It make sure we knows our place — the bottom o' the 'eap.'

Wayne digested this. He had never thought of it that way before.

Herald was eyeing him again, speculatively. 'You tell me,' he said, 'when you ever sees a black policeman.'

Wayne considered for a moment and searched back in his memory. 'I t'ink I seen one,' he said very seriously. 'Must 'ave been a year ago down the market.'

They stared at each other solemnly and then simultaneously lost control and spluttered into a great burst of laughter. Herald slapped Wayne on the shoulder. 'Say, man, I t'ink you gonna be all right.'

Wayne went on for a while, quietly chuckling to himself, before subsiding. Then his thoughts went back to the way the crowd had rescued Leroy from the police. He didn't remember seeing Herald but he must have been there from things he had said earlier. It began to grow on Wayne that they had achieved something remarkable by their action.

He voiced his feelings. 'Say, man, we really done somet'in' tonight.'

Herald didn't need to ask what Wayne was referring to. 'Yeah, I t'ink we did.' His voice was full of a strange wonder. Then it hardened with resolution. 'But that jus' the beginnin'. We ain't scarcely started yet.'

He got up. 'Time we was asleep.' He went to the lamp and bent over it. 'Ain't no point in wastin' paraffin.'

For a moment, his face was lit up by the glare from the lamp. The hard lines of his face were revealed, the shiny skin stretched taut over the bone structure. Then the light went out and there was darkness. Wayne heard Herald shuffle back to his mattress.

'Let we sleep now,' Herald said. 'We gotta be fit fo' the fight when it come.'

But it was as though he were speaking to himself. And in any case, Wayne was already drifting into unconsciousness.

Chapter 6

When Colin got up next morning, he noticed that the door of his brother's bedroom was ajar. He pushed it open further and looked inside. The bed had not been slept in.

His mother was in the kitchen frying bacon. She was in her dressing gown, but from the signs of fatigue on her face she hadn't had much sleep. She glanced up.

'Look at the paper,' she said grimly.

It was lying on the table. The headlines blared out in heavy type right across the front page. 'BLACK RIOTS'. Underneath there was a picture of a policeman holding his head. Blood was running down his face. There followed an account of what had happened in Hillsden the evening before. Crowds of black youths had taken the law into their own hands. They had attacked the police with bricks and bottles and anything they could lay their hands on. Twenty policemen had been injured, and fifteen were still in hospital. That was more than the television had claimed. Ten black youths had been arrested.

According to the newspaper, the riots started when the police had tried to help a black youth suffering from a knife wound. They had been attempting to get him to hospital when they had been surrounded by a mob. The youth had been dragged away and the police car attacked and wrecked. The policemen called for reinforcements and then a pitched battle had taken place with rioters throwing bottles and other missiles, and the police making baton charges. In the end, the police succeeded in dispersing the crowd, and order was restored. But not until after a number of injuries and a lot of damage.

On an inside page, there were more pictures showing the police under attack, and an opinion column indignantly lambasted these black hooligans who had no respect for the law. It didn't quite say so, but it implied that hanging was too good for them and they ought to be repatriated to where they came from. Colin's stomach churned as he read through it.

'Now you sees why I wants you out o' that place,' Mrs MacMorris said. 'It jus' made fo' trouble.'

'It's probably exaggerated,' said Colin though he felt uneasy. 'You know you can't believe what you read in that fascist rag. It always tells lies.'

Mrs MacMorris prodded the picture of the bleeding policeman with a finger. 'You t'ink that a lie?' she asked.

'What about black youth with their heads split open by police batons?' Colin demanded. 'I notice they don't print any pictures of them.'

'They don' deserve no sympathy. If they breaks the law, they 'as to expect what comes to 'em.'

Colin didn't bother to continue the argument. To some extent he agreed with what his mother was saying, but he also knew that there was more than one side to any story. For instance, it was typical of the paper only to talk about black rioters. Whatever happened to those white faces he had seen on the television screen?

Mrs MacMorris busied herself preparing breakfast, and when she was ready, she sat down beside Colin to eat.

'I 'opes that boy know what 'e doin',' she murmured and settled into a kind of cold fury.

When Colin had finished his breakfast, he went into the back garden to get a breath of fresh air before continuing his revision. He had mapped out the work for the day, and he wouldn't be able to waste too much time outside.

It was still only nine o'clock, but the sun was already blazing down from a clear blue sky. At this hour most of the small garden was in sunshine. Later in the day it would be cooler when the sun had moved round to the front.

Colin didn't take too much interest in the garden. That was his mother's hobby. He went across to inspect the tomato plants that were her special pride at the moment. They really were doing remarkably well. She wasn't a particularly scientific gardener, and she had taken a risk by planting the tomatoes out so early, but it had paid off.

Colin was pleased for her. At least there was something that might cheer her up in her present worries. Wayne was being his usual irresponsible self. It was about time he started thinking about other people for a change. He just had no idea, that was his problem. No doubt he would roll up in the middle of the morning as though nothing had happened and wonder about all the fuss. That was his way — never any thought for anyone but himself.

Looking towards the fence, Colin noticed that the next door neighbour Mr Carter was busy in the small greenhouse at the bottom of the garden. He came out carrying a tray of plants.

'Hello there,' Mr Carter called. 'Just hardening these antirrhinums off.' He put the tray down and straightened up. 'It's going to be nice for the weekend.'

'Yes,' Colin agreed. 'It seems set.'

Mr Carter grunted. 'Not that it worries you much I suppose. The weather I mean. Not with your exams coming up.'

'No,' said Colin. 'I've got other things to think about.'

'Jenny's up in her room this minute working away,' Mr Carter said looking back to the house. 'She's taking it very serious I'm glad to say.'

'Well, so am I.'

'Yes, I'm sure.'

Mr Carter gave Colin a steady stare. 'I'm getting these

plants out now because if I don't I won't be able to later.' He paused before going on. 'I suppose you've seen the papers.' It was obvious what he was talking about. 'All police leave's been cancelled. So I'll have to be on duty this afternoon.'

Colin wasn't sure how he was expected to respond. 'Yes, I read about the riots,' he said at last.

'A bad deal,' Mr Carter commented.

He had this disconcerting habit of fixing you with his eye and holding your gaze until you had to look away. He did this now. Colin supposed it was part of his professional technique as a policeman. He looked away.

'I'm not talking about you, of course,' Mr Carter went on, 'but there's a hell of a lot of criminal black kids about. I know because I've seen it. Muggings, break-ins, drugs — you name it and they're up to it. We've been having a special operation to clamp down on street crime in Hillsden, and this latest trouble just proves how much it was needed. After all, the law's the law whether you're black or white. If they want to live in this country, then they have to behave like everyone else. That's reasonable, isn't it?'

· Colin felt uncomfortable under Mr Carter's defiant stare. 'Yes, I suppose so,' he murmured.

'Not that all blacks are criminals,' Mr Carter said, softening. 'I know that's not true — though it sometimes seems like it.'

Colin was beginning to sweat, though whether it was from the heat or from Mr Carter's conversation he wasn't sure. He was relieved when Jenny appeared from the house and came towards them.

'I thought you were supposed to be studying,' her father said gruffly, though he couldn't keep pride and affection out of his voice.

'I can't study all the time,' Jenny objected playfully. 'That would make me very dull.'

Mr Carter let that pass. With a quick look at Colin that was indecipherable, he went back to ferrying his trays of plants out of the greenhouse into the fresh air.

Colin was pleased to see Jenny. She was working for her A

Levels as well, though they went to different schools. They had seen a lot of each other since Colin had moved in and become friendly — though how friendly Colin couldn't be sure. They went out together and had a lot in common. But at the back of his mind, Colin was always conscious that he was black and she was white. Did she worry about that as well? If she did, she never said anything. Strangely, it was not something they had talked about, though Colin was well aware that her father didn't approve of their friendship.

'How's it going?' Jenny asked.

'I'm an hour behind with my schedule,' Colin replied.

'Is that all? You're lucky. I've just discovered a whole physics notebook I haven't looked at for months.'

They laughed. They were both very serious about doing well in their exams, but confident that they had everything under control and were on target.

'Don't forget you're having tonight off,' Colin reminded her. The disco in the West End was their one celebration and one concession before the examinations took over in earnest.

'I won't,' Jenny said. 'I'm looking forward to it.'

She smiled. Colin admired her white teeth and clear grey eyes. He liked the way her fair hair swept down over her forehead. He noticed her hand resting on top of the fence next to his own and felt suddenly shy and embarrassed. He drew his hand away.

'Right then,' he said. 'I'll see you at seven.'

'Right,' said Jenny. 'Don't work too hard.'

Colin grinned at her and turned back to the house.

Why did he always have to see problems where there weren't any? Jenny clearly liked going out with him. She was as excited at the prospect of going to the disco as he was. So why invent complications? He resolved only to think about the pleasure that lay ahead later that evening.

At one o'clock his mother called him down to have something to eat. There was still no sign of Wayne. Mrs MacMorris didn't mention him, but it was clear from her unaccustomed silence and her closed-in face that she was thinking about him and worrying about him.

At the end of the meal, she suddenly said, 'You t'ink 'e mix up in that?'

Colin dragged his mind away from *The Winter's Tale*. He didn't need to ask what his mother was referring to. 'Of course not. He's probably with some friends. All he thinks about is having fun. If he was in trouble we'd have heard.'

'D'you t'ink we ought to phone the police?'

'What for?'

His mother rounded on him angrily. 'To tell 'em Wayne missin' o' course.'

'But he isn't missing,' Colin insisted. 'He's just playing the fool as usual. Besides, the police have enough on their hands at the moment without being bothered about some kid who's had a night out. They just wouldn't be interested.'

'I suppose you's right.'

Colin left his mother wearily gathering the dirty plates together.

It was a couple of hours later, when Colin was in the middle of writing a practice essay, that the phone rang. Usually, his mother answered it after two or three rings, but this time it went on. She must have gone out shopping. With a grunt of exasperation, Colin got up and hurried down the stairs. It was probably the prodigal Wayne phoning up to make his peace or to find out if the coast was clear.

Colin picked up the receiver. 'Hello,' he said irritably.

'Hello,' said a woman's voice. 'Is that Colin?'

It was his Aunt Elma.

'I was jus' phonin' to see everyt'in' all right fo' tomorrow,' she went on.

'Yes, I think so,' said Colin.

' 'Ow you mum?'

'She's all right. I think she's out shopping.'

'Let's 'ope she buy somet'in' nice. Me an' you uncle sure lookin' forward to it.'

'It'll be good to see you too,' said Colin, doing his polite bit.

' 'Ow the studyin' goin'?' Aunt Elma asked.

'Not so bad.'

'That the idea. You stick at it now.'

'I will.'

Colin heard the car arrive. 'Hang on a minute. I think Mum's back.' He called out, 'Aunt Elma on the phone.'

Mrs MacMorris hurried out of the kitchen. As Colin was returning to his bedroom, he heard her saying, 'You see it in the papers? I worried sick 'bout that boy.'

Five minutes later, Colin was just getting his thoughts into shape once more, when his mother came into his room.

'I gonna ring the father,' she announced.

Colin was startled. It was over a year since his mother had spoken to his father, and she had sworn never to speak to him again.

'There gonna be more trouble, I jus' knows it,' Mrs MacMorris continued, 'an' I wants that boy 'ere where I can see 'im. It time the father took some of the responsibility.'

She went out without waiting for a reply. Colin followed her and leaned on the bannisters while she dialled. She held his gaze tensely as she waited for someone to answer. Then she blinked and concentrated on the phone. ''Ello,' she said.

There was a pause while she listened to a voice at the other end. Colin watched as her face grew cold and angry. 'I wants to speak to Mr MacMorris,' she said. She darted a look expressing contempt in Colin's direction and hung on to the phone.

Eventually there was some response at the other end. ' 'Ello,' said Mrs MacMorris urgently. 'That you, Gerry?' A stuttering greeting of some kind came through the phone, but Mrs MacMorris swept it aside. 'It Wayne. You 'ears 'bout this trouble there been in 'Illsden? Well, 'e there, I knows it. 'E ain't been 'ome since last night, an' I wants you to find 'im.'

The voice at the other end protested.

'I knows you seen 'im last night,' Mrs MacMorris continued exasperatedly. 'But what I wants you to do is find 'im now. I don' want 'im gettin' in no more trouble.'

Mr MacMorris seemed to be making soothing noises.

'Don' give me none o' that,' declared his wife. 'You go out this minute an' find 'im. Else somet'in' dreadful gonna 'appen. I jus' knows it. Now you the father. You acts like it.'

The phone was thrust down with violent force. Colin could imagine his father flinching under the impact. Then he would either shrug his shoulders and give a wry grin, or else puff himself up into a fury and burst out at anyone within shouting distance. Those were the ways he used to react to his wife's outbursts.

Mrs MacMorris was gazing up the stairs at Colin. 'If 'e don' find 'im by six o' clock, I'll go down there myself an' skin 'im alive. Call 'imself you father? 'E don' know what bein' a father is.'

She stalked into the kitchen and began to unpack her shopping with a great deal of unnecessary banging and thudding. Colin sighed and went back upstairs.

Why did all of this have to go on just as he was trying to get ready for his exams? The rows betwcen his parents had been bad enough before. He didn't want them to start all over again. He thought all of that was finished. Now it looked as though the disappearance of Wayne was going to start a new wave of arguments. It was almost as though everything was conspiring to make things as difficult as possible for him — the weather, Wayne's running off, the violence in Hillsden, and now this.

He went into the bathroom and ran the cold tap. He took his face cloth, wrung it out in the chilly water and passed it over his face. Then he returned to his bedroom and sat down with grim determination to get on with his revision. He knew it was the only way out.

Chapter 7

Wayne was glad when morning came. It had been a rough night. The mattress was so thin, he felt as though his body was pressing straight into the floorboards. He kept waking up to hear scratchings and scurryings. It must have been rats. Could rats climb up to the first floor of a house? Wayne didn't take time to find out. He wrapped his arms around himself, shivered under his sweat, and tried to get to sleep again.

When he finally opened his eyes, the room looked even worse than he had realised. Great swathes of paper had been ripped off the walls. There were gaping holes in the floorboards just waiting to trap your feet. The ceiling was so cracked and uneven it was in danger of collapsing on top of them and burying them alive under crumbling plaster.

But Herald had everything organised. When he woke up, he stretched his arms wide, yawned till Wayne feared that his jaw-bone was going to snap, and said, 'Let's get out o' 'ere.'

Outside, the sun was already shining. It was going to be another baking day. Herald wasted no time. They were off to wash up in the lavatory at Hillsden Station, and then have breakfast at the Island Café. Afterwards, they strolled about in the High Street basking in the warm air and chatting to friends and acquaintances. All the talk was of what had happened the night before.

'Say, man, we really show 'em.'

'Who say the black man done fo'?'

'We stood up fo' our own.'

There was a feeling of jubilation and excitement, of high spirits and celebration. Even the presence of large numbers of police on the streets couldn't dampen it. No one knew what had become of Leroy. It was assumed that he had been taken to hospital and been looked after, but no one was sure.

Wayne gloried in it all — in being with Herald, in being part of the life of the street, in being part of the chat and banter. He was amazed at how many people Herald knew. Wayne knew most of them by sight, but Herald knew them to talk to, greeting them and slapping hands with them.

During the morning, the thought crossed Wayne's mind that he ought to be making plans to go home or at least phone his mother and let her know that he was all right. He remembered that he had originally intended to leave early and get home before his mother was up. But that had been forgotten.

Herald's mind must have been working on the same lines because he asked, 'Ain't it time you was goin' 'ome?' He didn't sound as though he wanted to get rid of Wayne, more as though he were concerned for him.

'No problem,' Wayne declared. 'My mum won' worry. She know I come 'ome when my chip money done.'

Herald broke into a raucous laugh at this and punched Wayne on the shoulder. 'Man, I sure you gonna be all right.'

Wayne felt himself swell with pride under this praise. It seemed as though he had grown an inch taller. But at the back of his mind was the worry that his money would soon run out and he would have to go home whether he liked it or not.

He wasn't sure how long he had planned to stay away. It hadn't been planned at all. Nothing had been planned. He had gone to Hillsden in a fit of anger at his mother's attitude. He had stayed the night at Herald's because it seemed safer than risking being picked up by the police. He had intended going straight home in the morning.

But now he found he liked his independence. He was enjoying being with Herald, and Herald seemed prepared to tolerate him. Why should he rush back home just as life was beginning to blossom for him?

Still, it was a relief when Herald said, 'Come, we go eat. I treats you.'

For a moment, Wayne hesitated. After all, Herald was living on social security, squatting out in a derelict house. He didn't have money to throw away on a casual friend. But then Wayne decided there were all sorts of ways for someone like Herald to make some money on the side. And in any case, it so obviously gave Herald a kick to be magnanimous like this, that he felt he couldn't disappoint him.

They went back to the Island Café. The same people were there as when they had had breakfast. They looked as though they hadn't moved all morning and were still arguing over what had happened to Leroy.

'I 'ears it were a black guy what knife 'im,' someone said.

He was shouted down. 'Naw, naw. No black guy do a t'ing like that.'

'Yeah,' said Herald, joining in. 'That rubbish, man. That jus' a story the bullmen push around to confuse guys like you. You knows the bullmen drill 'im up. What else they gets 'im in their car fo'?'

'That true I guess,' said the man who had first spoken.

Herald pushed home his advantage. 'When you ever 'ears the bullmen 'elpin' black guys?'

The man thought for a moment and then said, 'You got me there.' He began to laugh at how easily he had been taken in.

His laugh was cut off abruptly as a man burst into the café. The newcomer was wild-eyed and in a state of great agitation.

'Leroy dead!' he yelled out.

There was a sudden hush and then a confused commotion of voices.

' 'Ow you knows?' someone demanded.

'I 'ears it from a friend. 'E say Leroy dead when 'e get to the 'ospital.'

People cried out in anger and shock.

'What I tells you?' Herald shouted bitterly above the noise. 'The bull does murder 'im. If they took 'im to the 'ospital straightaway 'e still be alive.'

'Yeah, yeah,' agreed some.

But others were more sceptical.

'I don' believes that,' said one.

'Ain't true,' shouted someone else.

Arguments broke out all over the café. People practically came to blows as they supported one side or the other. They yelled in each other's faces and raised their fists.

Herald gave up in disgust. 'Some people'll believe anyt'in',' he murmured to Wayne. 'Come on. Let we go down the market.'

The street was ablaze with sunshine and colour. On either side, stalls piled high with fruit and vegetables, bales of cloth and T-shirts, cosmetics and second-hand records, crowded the pavement, and boxes and crates spilled over into the road. The air was full of the contending voices issuing from numerous clangy transistors. Shoppers bandied words with the salesmen and bullied the tomatoes and avocadoes to make sure they were ripe. Idlers strolled and swaggered among them, seeing who they could see and watching for something to happen. Stall-owners tried to drown each other out with their cries. 'Ripe mango — flew in today.' 'Fresh patty — jus' bake.'

Herald knew everyone. He waved his hand, slapped palms, stopped to have words. Wayne felt proud to be with him.

A girl attracted Herald's attention.

' 'Ang on a minute,' he said, and he went over to chat to her.

Wayne couldn't help admiring his technique — the steady stare, the rueful pursed lips, the arm stretched out to hold the strut of a stall just behind the girl's head and block her escape. Not that the girl seemed to mind. She was pretending indifference, but every now and then her eyes would swing round to take in Herald's face before being lowered again.

Wayne smiled to himself and turned away. At the next stall, he spotted Desmond. His friend was working his way through the cassettes on sale. Wayne crept up on him.

'Gotcha!' he yelled as he threw out his arm and grabbed Desmond by the shoulder.

Desmond nearly jumped out of his skin. He stared panic-stricken at Wayne for a moment, his eyes wide with terror.

'I seen you t'ief those tapes,' Wayne continued ominously. Then he let go of Desmond and collapsed into a fit of laughter.

Desmond tried to pull himself together. He looked about him nervously and pleaded with Wayne. 'Don' do that, guy. You gonna get me in a 'ole 'eap o' trouble goin' on like that.'

'Sorry, man,' Wayne apologised, smothering the last of his giggles. 'I couldn' 'elp it. I jus' seen you there gazin' at all those tapes as though you was ready to swallow 'em all up.'

'I was only lookin',' Desmond protested.

'I'll believe you,' said Wayne, 'though the bullmen wouldn'.' He bubbled with laughter again. 'You should 'ave seen you face when I grabbed you.'

Desmond didn't seem to care for the joke. 'Ave you seen the papers?' he asked gloomily. 'I keeps lookin' at all those pictures to make sure I ain't in one o' 'em. I don' want the bull comin' round an' 'restin' me.'

'Yeah,' Wayne teased, 'but they must 'ave t'ousands o' pictures. Ain't jus' the ones in the papers. They got you on record sure 'nough.'

'You reckons?' Desmond asked with alarm.

'Probably,' said Wayne. 'But don' you worry. You safe. You know the bull t'inks we all looks alike.'

Desmond wasn't entirely reassured, but he let it pass. 'What you doin' 'ere any'ow?'

'I'm wit' 'Erald,' Wayne explained, cocking his head to

where the older boy was still chatting up the girl. He didn't seem to be making much progress.

'I didn' go 'ome' last night,' Wayne went on. 'I stayed at 'Erald yard.'

Desmond looked suitably shocked and impressed. Briefly, Wayne told him how his day had gone.

One thing seemed to puzzle Desmond. 'What did 'appen to Leroy then?'

Wayne became impatient. 'I don' know, do I? There all these stories goin' round. I can' tell which one right.'

Desmond's face puckered up as he thought. 'Say, man, who is this Leroy? I don' remember seein' 'im before last night.'

'So what? 'E black, inn'e? That all that matter.'

Really, Desmond was impossible at times, Wayne thought. 'What you doin' 'ere anyway?' he asked gruffly.

'I got to get out some time,' Desmond answered. 'I spent the 'ole mornin' cleanin' the 'ouse. Sweep, sweep, sweep fo' 'ours.'

'Ain't you got no vacuum?' Wayne asked.

'Yeah, but you knows my mum. She mean. She won' let me use no power. So it sweep, sweep, sweep.'

Wayne laughed. 'Life sure is 'ard,' he said as he put his arm round his friend's shoulders.

Herald had finished with the girl — or perhaps the girl had finished with him. Anyway, she had gone, but the satisfied look on Herald's face suggested that he was quite pleased with himself.

'I remembers you at school,' Desmond said in awed tones.

'Yeah,' said Herald, 'lots o' people do. I made quite a impact there.'

They moved on down the market street, and Herald seemed quite happy for Desmond to tag along. Stall-owners called out to them as they passed. One of them held up a bottle of shampoo. 'This'll make you 'air curl.'

'Yeah,' Herald quipped back, 'an' turn my face white an' all.'

Further on, a policeman and a policewoman were warily

making their way through the throng, their bright white shirts almost blinding in the sunshine. As they came abreast, Herald turned to Wayne and said loudly, 'Funny smell round 'ere, don' you t'ink?'

Wayne and Desmond sniggered appreciatively.

They left the market and sauntered along the High Street. It seemed to be hotter than ever. Wayne wiped the sweat off his brow and pulled out the tail of his shirt in the hope that some cool air would have the chance to circulate round his bare torso. Then he came to a full stop. There, ahead of him, was his father. Helen was with him, wearing a see-through blouse that showed her bra and had everyone turning to look.

Wayne didn't know why he stopped. Normally, he would have been pleased to see his father. But this time, he hesitated. Not that it mattered much. It was too late to do anything about it because his father had spotted him and was approaching fast.

'I been lookin' fo' you, boy,' Mr MacMorris declared with a disapproving glare. 'The mother jus' phone me. She sick wit' worry 'bout you.'

'I can look after myself,' Wayne retorted. His father's news surprised him. If his mother had really phoned him then she must be upset, and Wayne had a sudden prick of conscience that made him react more strongly than he might otherwise have done in order to justify himself.

'You better get 'ome to you yard straight'way 'fore there any more trouble,' Mr MacMorris continued. 'You 'ears what I says?'

Wayne didn't like his affairs being discussed in public like this. Helen was standing there eyeing the passers-by and pretending she had nothing to do with what was going on, but Herald was watching with cynical amusement, and Desmond was round-eyed with apprehension, ready to make a bolt for it should things get more heated.

'I 'ears what you says,' Wayne commented. 'But I don' see as it 'mount to much.'

Mr MacMorris was astounded. He looked as though he couldn't believe his ears.

'What you tellin' me, boy?' he asked. 'I you father, an' I got a right to expect you to do what I tells you.'

'Oh, no you ain't,' Wayne retorted. 'You give up that right two year ago when you walks out on my mum.'

Wayne hadn't known he was going to say that. He didn't even know the thought was there. It just came out. And now it was out, there was nothing he could do about it. His father's face was heavy with anger. He looked as though he was only just able to restrain himself from striking out at his son. Helen had stopped watching the crowd and was taking a sudden lively interest. Her eyes were bright and eager.

Mr MacMorris controlled himself. 'You gonna end up bad,' he muttered threateningly. Then he pushed Helen's arm and said, 'Come on. Let we get out o' 'ere.'

Helen gave a disdainful shrug, smiled at Wayne, and followed Mr MacMorris as he thrust his way through the last-minute shoppers.

'Wow!' sighed Herald with admiration. 'You sure told 'im.'

' 'E ain't got not'in' to do wit' my life no more,' Wayne said moodily.

Desmond licked his lips nervously but didn't say anything.

They moved on down the High Street. The shops were beginning to close. People were on their way home to settle down in front of television or to get dressed up for the evening.

Wayne wished he hadn't spoken that way to his father. He couldn't understand what had got into him. Did he really believe what he said? He would never have made a comment like that yesterday if someone had asked him. So what was so different today? Even if you thought it, it was the kind of thing that was better left unspoken. He knew that well enough. It was what Colin had said in those difficult days when their parents had been splitting up. But Wayne had never believed his brother was right — until now. And even now, he wasn't sure that was how he really felt.

Wayne's gloomy thoughts were interrupted by Herald. 'Hey,' he cried. 'What goin' on there?'

He was indicating a turning off the High Street. There were two policemen standing beside a parked car. The car had L signs on it and the name of a motoring school. For a moment, Wayne thought the car might have been his father's, but it belonged to a rival firm. But that moment had sent a pang of anxiety coursing through him.

As they approached the car, one of the policemen was speaking in at the open window. The driver, a man of about the same age as Wayne's father, was laughingly protesting.

'Ain't not'in',' he said.

'Look,' said the policeman, 'I saw you fold a piece of paper up and put it in your sock. I think you've got drugs on you.'

'Drugs?' the driver exclaimed, still smiling. 'I ain't got no drugs.'

Wayne and the others stood close to the car. Herald's face was hard and watchful. His eyes were fixed steady and unblinking on the policeman.

'Then you won't mind being searched, will you?' the policeman said.

The driver shrugged and climbed out of the car. He raised his arms in the air so that the policeman could feel inside his jacket and down his sides. He went on smiling as though that would somehow prove his innocence.

Herald grunted with disgust. 'You sees the way that driver smile?' he muttered to Wayne. 'It like that wit' all the ol' people. They aims to please. But I don' smile at no policeman. No way.'

The policeman had reached the man's feet. He had pulled up the trouser leg and was feeling inside the socks. When he stood up, he had three or four notes in his hand. He held them out to the man as though seeking an explanation.

'OK, OK,' the driver said. 'I puts my money in my sock. It safer there. That must 'ave been what you sees.'

By now, more people had gathered. Looking round, Wayne estimated there must have been about twenty people there altogether. They surrounded the car, blocking the pavement and spilling out into the road.

'What they doin'?' someone asked.

'Why don' they leave 'im alone?'

But the policeman hadn't finished yet. 'How do we know you didn't get this money selling drugs? It goes on all the time.'

'Ain't so,' said the driver. 'I gets that money from my last pupil.'

The other policeman had opened the back door of the car and climbed inside. He was lifting the seat up to search underneath.

'Don' let 'im do that,' someone shouted. ' 'E gonna plant somet'in' on you for sure.'

'Yeah,' agreed another. 'They can' search wit'out a warrant.'

The crowd had increased. It was filling the whole road now. People were jostling each other and straining their necks to get a better view. Wayne was pushed closer to the car. There were angry shouts and threats for the police to leave the man alone — or else.

The policemen looked round anxiously at the mob and tried to size up its mood. The one who had started it all spoke into his walkie-talkie. Then he took the driver to the back of the car, asked him some questions and wrote down the answers in his notebook. The other policeman went to the front of the car to check the road fund licence.

'You sees what they does?' someone yelled. 'If they ain't gonna get 'im for the drugs, they gonna get 'im for somet'in'.'

As the policeman came back, he found his way was blocked. A large black man was leaning with his elbow on the roof of the car and his body sprawling in the policeman's path. Wayne recognised the man. It was Fitzroy Jackson. He was about the same age as Herald and had been a good footballer at school.

'Out of my way,' the policeman ordered as he tried to get

past Fitzroy to join his colleague and the driver at the back of the car.

Fitzroy drew himself up to his full height. He was an inch or so taller than the policeman. 'Why don' you leave 'im alone?' he asked. ' 'E ain't done not'in'.'

'Yeah, yeah,' the crowd shouted in agreement. There were further jeers and insults.

'Get out of my way,' the policeman said grimly, 'or I'll arrest you for obstruction.'

Wayne wasn't sure what happened next. Someone in the mob shoved against him, and everything suddenly went wild. The policeman was hanging on to Fitzroy, and Fitzroy looked as though he had gone berserk. He was shaking his arms in the air and yelling right in the policeman's face. The policeman was shouting back.

Then it was difficult for Wayne to see any more. The crowd surged in, and Fitzroy and the policeman were swallowed up. It was all arms and legs and angry screaming faces.

Above the tumult, Wayne heard a warning cry. More police had arrived. They forced their way through the crowd and seized hold of Fitzroy. A police van came tearing round the corner and shrieked to a halt. More police jumped out. Fitzroy was dragged along the road and thrown into the back of the van.

The crowd began to chant, 'Bull! Bull! Bull!' The cry was taken up. It became louder and more threatening.

'They gonna drill 'im up!' someone yelled out.

'Get 'im out!'

The mob rushed to the van before it could start and surrounded it. People began pounding on the sides with their fists. Others pushed against it until it was rocking from side to side. The van revved up and shot away, leaving people staggering after it. Then a brick curved through the air and smashed into the back window. The door swung open, but the van went on going, lights flashing and siren wailing, round the corner into the High Street.

The crowd was huge by now. Wayne thought there must

be nearly two hundred people there, mainly black, though there were some white as well. They swarmed into the High Street. Wayne could see Herald and Desmond ahead of him. He had lost touch with them earlier on, and he now hurried to catch up with them.

'Blast them bullmen,' Herald breathed furiously. 'Why can' they leave us alone?'

'What's gonna 'appen to Fitzroy?' Wayne asked.

'Oh, they gonna beat 'im up a little an' then charge 'im wit' somet'in',' Herald said wearily. 'It always the same. They can do what they likes. They got the law on their side.'

The heavy irony in Herald's voice wasn't lost on Wayne. It did seem as though the police could do anything they liked, and there was nothing anyone else could do about it apart from throw the odd brick or make the odd protest. What had that driving instructor been doing for goodness' sake, other than go about his lawful business? He hadn't been doing anything wrong for the police to pick on him the way they had done. Blast, it could have been his own father.

'I don' know 'ow I gonna get 'ome,' Desmond moaned. 'My mum gonna raise 'ell.'

'Shut it,' commanded Wayne. 'This more important than you an' you mum.'

'Yeah,' Desmond agreed, 'but you don' know my mum. She gonna create somet'in' awful if I ain't there when she get back from work.'

There was no way they could get through the crowd. More people were arriving every second. They were hemmed in on all sides by the angry seething mob. Through arms and over heads, Wayne could see that a line of policemen had formed themselves across the road, armed with batons and shields. The traffic in the High Street had been stopped. More and more police vans arrived and policemen poured out ready for combat. Wayne couldn't believe there were so many policemen in Hillsden. It felt as though the police already outnumbered them.

There were higher officials and senior officers there too. Wayne could tell by the size of the pips on their shoulders and the braid on their peaked caps. There was a lot of discussion and conferring going on, and then a group of them stepped out into the narrow no-man's-land that separated the crowd from the police.

After a moment's hesitation, some of the crowd edged forward. Others followed, and then there was a rush. The police officers were surrounded by people screaming out angry accusations.

'Why you 'arass black yout' on the streets?'

'I seen a bullman wit' a steel bar. What 'e doin' wit' that?'

'They wearin' National Front badges, man. Ain't the police suppose to be neutral?'

The leading officer tried to make himself heard above the hubbub.

'You aren't doing yourselves any good,' he shouted. 'If you have any complaints, then we shall look into them.'

This was greeted with a roar of derision.

'Whenever the black man get justice?' someone asked contemptuously.

The officer went on, 'This street has got to be cleared. Go back to your homes now, and nothing will happen to you. We don't want any violence here.'

There were jeers and cat-calls at this. The crowd drew back and closed up again. Someone started to chant, and the call immediately spread through the whole crowd. 'Bull! Bull! Bull!' thundered out defiantly.

The police officers spoke among themselves and then began to walk back to their line of defence. Before they had gone more than a couple of steps, a bottle thudded to the ground at their feet and exploded into a hundred pieces. A shower of bricks and stones followed. The officers covered their heads and hurriedly retreated to safety.

An angry roar rose from the crowd, and suddenly they were moving in a great wave towards the police line. Wayne felt himself being dragged along in the wake. He was practically pulled off his feet by the rush.

The police were taken by surprise. There were one or two skirmishes as they tried to beat off the attack, and then they withdrew with the crowd chasing after them. They reformed, and the crowd came to a halt. They screamed insults at the police over the newly-formed no-man's-land.

In the course of the crowd's advance, a police van had been abandoned. It was set upon by some of the crowd. They rocked it over, and it sank with a crash on to its side. Someone undid the cap of the petrol tank. Petrol was bubbling out everywhere. The crowd scattered. There was a blinding whoosh. Yellow flames leaped out and clouds of black smoke billowed up. A triumphant cheer rose from the crowd. People started jumping and dancing with glee while others stood awed and hypnotised by the sight of the van being consumed by fire.

Then the crowd was in movement again. They turned and swarmed down the High Street. Boys with sticks and bricks ran down the length of the street, smashing window after window. Again and again, splintered glass flashed and crashed in jagged segments on to the pavement. Boys clambered into the shop fronts and began throwing goods out to their friends — transistors, records, hair-dryers, leather jackets, tins of biscuits, anything that came to hand. People jumped on the cars parked at the kerbside and beat a tattoo on the bonnets. They shattered the windows and kicked in the doors. Then some of them were set alight. Acrid black fumes belched out and swirled around the street. Wayne was soon coughing as the smoke caught at his chest.

They had reached the far end of the High Street. The crowd began to bunch together again and came to a halt. Wayne bumped into the people in front of him. Herald and Desmond were still with him. Then he saw why the crowd had stopped. Ahead of them was the Jubilee Clock Tower on its island. On either side of it, new lines of police had taken up their positions.

There were police behind them and police in front of them. They were trapped. Wayne searched anxiously around him, but there seemed to be no way to escape.

'This is it then,' said Herald grimly. 'Now it look like war really been declared.'

Chapter 8

Colin was getting ready for the disco. The evening ahead filled him with excitement. He was escaping from his revision for a while. He was going out with Jenny. The prospect was like a sudden and refreshing breath of fresh air.

He had had a bath and smothered himself in the cologne his Aunt Elma had given him for his birthday. He had to admit he smelled rather nice.

He put on his new silk shirt and studied himself in the mirror. The shirt was sky blue. It had cost a lot of money, but it looked good. Colin decided it had been worth the expense. He wiggled his hips at his reflection and mouthed the words of a song. He quite fancied himself. Jenny wouldn't be able to resist him.

He combed out his hair and was patting it into shape and making sure it was even when his mother called from below. Still humming to himself, he went downstairs.

Mrs MacMorris was standing in the middle of the back room staring at the television set. 'It start again,' she said in a despairing voice.

The pictures on the screen were similar to those of the evening before. A mob of mainly black youths was hurling bottles and missiles. A line of police, holding shields and wielding batons charged and started laying into the crowd.

Wrecked cars were belching out flames and smoke. The reporter was saying that the number of injuries and arrests was not yet known.

When the report was over and the newscaster had moved on to the next item, Mrs MacMorris switched the set off.

'An' that boy in the middle o' it all,' she moaned.

'You don't know that,' Colin said, irritated by the way his mother kept jumping to this conclusion.

She rounded on him with a sudden viciousness as though he had insulted her. 'Where else 'e is then?' she demanded. 'Course 'e there. Don' I know 'im? Don' I know that if there trouble, 'e bound to sniff it out, an' 'e bound to get mix up in it?'

Colin shrugged his shoulders. There was no point in arguing with her when she was in this kind of mood. She wouldn't listen to reason. It was almost as though she enjoyed tormenting herself by fearing the worst.

When he glanced at his mother again, her face had changed. The screwed-up expression of suffering had given way to an anguished look of appeal.

'You'll go an' find 'im won' you?' she begged.

Colin nearly exploded. She knew he had planned this one evening for his own enjoyment. She knew he was going out with Jenny. And here she was asking him to give up all that just because Wayne was being his usual thoughtless self. It was too much.

The resentment boiling inside him must have shown on his face because his mother went on to plead, ' 'E you own flesh an' blood. 'E too young to know what 'e do. 'E could be lying somewheres beat up an' 'urt or 'rested in some cell. We got to 'elp 'im. You got to find 'im.'

For a moment, Colin thought of storming out of the house as Wayne had done. Why should his pleasure be spoilt because of his brother's selfishness. He wasn't responsible for Wayne. If Wayne wanted to play the fool and get into trouble, then that was his lookout. Why should he get involved simply because he was Wayne's elder brother. He had his own life to lead, and here was Wayne getting in the way again.

His mother was gazing at him anxiously. Her eyes were wide, and her lips were trembling. She would be crying in a minute. Colin went on hesitating. He almost turned on his heel, but he knew he couldn't. He couldn't let his mother down when she needed him. All his fury collapsed like a burst balloon.

'All right,' he said with a bad grace. 'I'll have to tell Jenny first.'

When he rang the door-bell, it was Jenny's mother who answered. 'Oh,' she said with a squirm of distaste that Colin knew she felt for him, 'it's you. You'd better come in.'

She held the door wide open so that he could enter and ushered him into the front room. She stood for a moment, flustered, seeming not to know what to do, twisting her hands, her face pinched and sour.

'Sit down,' she said at last. 'Jenny should be ready in a minute.' Then she went out as though eager to escape.

Colin wondered whether she were afraid to be alone with him. That was the impression she gave. But there was no time to worry about that. The door was thrown open, and Jenny burst in. Colin sprang to his feet at the sight of her.

'It's lovely to be going out,' Jenny exclaimed. 'It's bliss to get away from all those boring books for a while.'

Her eyes and cheeks were bright with excitement. Her face was elaborately made up. She was wearing a loose dress of some kind of white crimply material through which could be seen the vague outline of her body. Colin felt the pulse in his temple begin to throb. He pulled his eyes away.

'I can't go,' he said.

There was no immediate reply. The remark seemed to drop into a bottomless pool of silence. When he ventured to look at Jenny's face again, her bubbling eagerness had gone. In its place was a puzzled and pained expression.

'But we've planned it for so long,' she protested. 'It was our special treat. What do you mean you can't go?'

Colin cursed his brother's stupidity and his mother's absurd anxiety. He felt utterly miserable, but there was no going back now. He mumbled his apologies.

'I'm sorry, Jenny. It's Wayne. He hasn't been home, and Mum thinks he might be mixed up with this trouble in Hillsden. She wants me to go and look for him.'

Jenny slumped down in one of the armchairs and wrapped her dress around her knees. She was pouting with disappointment.

'There was something about it in the paper this morning,' she said, 'but I don't see what it has to do with us. If they want to riot against the police, that's their business.'

Colin tried to explain. 'It's nothing to do with that really. It's Wayne. He didn't come home last night and Mum's worried.'

Jenny gave him a hard stare. 'But that's just Wayne, isn't it? Because he didn't come home doesn't mean he's involved in this riot rubbish does it?'

'That's what I think too,' said Colin. He went on trying to explain. 'It's Mum. She's concerned about him.'

Jenny glared at him. 'Why? He can look after himself, can't he? No reason for you to go chasing all over the place looking for him.'

'Well,' said Colin desperately, 'he is my own flesh and blood.' He cringed inwardly as he realised he was using his mother's argument.

But it had no effect on Jenny. She suddenly flared up. She shot to her feet and stood tense in front of him. 'Isn't that just typical,' she burst out. 'I should have known. It's what my father's always saying about you people. Just can't rely on you.'

Her eyes were blazing, and her lips closed into a hard line. Colin had never seen her like this before. He felt his mouth drop open in astonishment. He tried to recover himself, tried to find something he could say to make her see reason. But he wasn't quick enough. Before he could work out the right words, Jenny had swept past him and out of the room. It was so sudden that all he noticed was the swirl of her white dress and the lash of her fair hair. He could hear her feet thudding up the stairs. She left behind her in the air all around him the overpowering scent of her perfume.

Before he could pull himself together and decide what to do, Jenny's mum came in. She must have been lurking outside the door.

'Oh,' she said as though surprised at finding him still there. 'Is everything all right?'

'Yes,' Colin answered. 'I was just going.'

Mrs Carter eased backwards to make sure there was plenty of room for Colin to get past her without brushing against her, and he let himself out of the front door. He was aware of Mrs Carter hovering in the hallway, tight-lipped and disapproving.

Once outside, he drew himself up and wiped the sweat off his forehead. What did she mean by 'typical'? He had never let Jenny down before. Typical of what? Then the full horror of what she had said rushed in on him. She believed that you couldn't rely on black people, that was it. They couldn't be trusted to keep their word.

Colin snorted with anger and amazement. He wished he had slammed the door. He strode across the lawn that connected the Carter's house with his own, climbed into the car and banged that door behind him instead.

The main road was busy. The frantic search for Saturday evening fun was on. But not for Colin. He cut recklessly across the traffic and turned right, ignoring the horn beeps of irate motorists. All his plans were going wrong.

If only other people hadn't got in the way — Wayne, his mother. If Wayne hadn't gone off, and if his mother hadn't pleaded with him to go in search of his brother, then the quarrel with Jenny need never have happened, and she would not have said what she said.

There was that other remark of hers as well. Perhaps she was right. Perhaps what was going on in Hillsden had nothing to do with them after all. If people wanted to rampage in the streets and attack the police, then that was their lookout. There was no reason why he should get involved. That was why his parents had moved to Dukesbury — to get away from things like that.

Now here he was going back into the thick of it. And it was

his mother who was sending him. He would murder Wayne when he found him.

That was another problem. Where was his brother likely to be? The fool could be anywhere, and there were bound to be police all over the place. Colin's last attempt to find his brother had been useless. There was no reason why he should be more successful this time.

He was aware that he was driving too fast. Cars swerved out of the way and gave him a wide berth. But as he approached the High Street, he had to slow down. There was a blockage of some kind at the entry to the one-way system and cars were forming a queue. When he got nearer, Colin saw that a barrier had been erected across the road. There was a great crowd of policemen there. Colin couldn't remember ever seeing so many of them in one place before. They were directing the traffic round the triangle in the road, away from the High Street, sending it back the way it had come.

Some drivers tried to protest, but the police were having none of it. They shouted angrily, banged on the bonnets of cars and looked as though they would use brute force if the drivers didn't do what they were told. It was clear the police didn't want anyone to get into the High Street.

Colin followed the column of vehicles round to the right and wondered what to do next. He would have to find somewhere to park the car as near to the High Street as possible and continue his search on foot. Clearly finding Wayne was going to be even more difficult than he had feared.

As soon as he could, he cut off the main road and began to double back along the side streets. He knew the area well and had no difficulty worming his way right and then left through the terraced streets. For a moment, he considered stopping at Balaclava Road to see if Wayne was there or whether their father knew where he was. But he continued past. Meeting his father again would have to be a last resort.

There were small knots of people standing at the corners, wary and watchful. They gave him hard stares as he went past. Others in groups, **mainly young**, were hurrying along the streets. Colin sensed something furtive and fearful about the way they moved, but he didn't have time to stop and check.

He reckoned the best place to start his search for Wayne would be the Club. There might be someone there who had seen him. He could park in the back street behind Woolworth's, then walk up to the High Street past the Jubilee Clock Tower and on to the Club.

Finding a parking space was easy. There were scarcely any cars around. Colin thought this was strange at first until he remembered the police barriers. No cars were being allowed in.

It took him only a few minutes to reach the High Street. What he saw there appalled him. The devastation was staggering. It was as though the place had been hit by a tornado. Doors of shops had been ripped off, windows smashed, goods strewn and scattered all over the pavement. Great jagged sheets of shattered glass, drunken piles of boxes and cartons, squashed tomatoes and battered cauliflowers made it an obstacle course.

Some shop-keepers were trying to sort through their goods and calculate the damage. Others were just standing in the midst of the ruins, lost and bewildered. They looked as though they were about to burst into tears. A lorry had been allowed into the area, and workmen were hard at it boarding up the gaping windows. A cynical thought swam into Colin's mind. The rioters had succeeded where the government hadn't. They'd provided some new employment.

Police cars and vans were parked all along the road. Bunches of policemen were huddled together in earnest conversation.

As he crunched through the broken glass littering the pavement, past the Jubilee Clock, Colin suddenly felt very exposed. With a shock he realised that he was the only person moving along the street, and he was the only black person in sight. He began to walk faster.

He was within sight of the Club and crossing a side street, when two policemen emerged. At first, Colin thought he was going to be able to get past them without any problem, but then one of them yelled out, 'Hey, you!'

Colin's heart thumped violently against his chest. He considered going on as though he hadn't heard, but then he decided against it. After all, he had nothing to hide. He stopped and turned around to face the policeman.

'Come here,' the same policeman ordered.

Colin moved towards them, but he obviously didn't do it fast enough for the liking of the policeman. One of them stepped forward, grabbed him by the arm and threw him against the wall of the corner shop.

'When I say come here, I mean come here,' he snarled. He looked questioningly at his colleague. 'Is this one of them?'

'I don't know,' the other policeman replied. 'Could be. All these black bastards look the same to me.'

'Let's nab him then. It'll even up the numbers. What are you doing here anyway?'

Colin stammered out an explanation.

'A likely story,' jeered the first policeman. 'Pull the other one.'

'Better search him. Just to make sure.'

Their hands pulled Colin about roughly as they checked up and down his body.

'Whew!' said the first policeman, catching a whiff of Colin's cologne. 'He pongs of perfume. Don't he smell sweet!'

'Well, that makes a change,' said the other sourly.

'Do we take him?'

'No. Let him go. We've got enough of them fouling up the cells as it is.'

The first policeman patted Colin familiarly and sharply on the cheek. 'You're lucky this time, sweetheart. But my advice to you is to get the hell out of here. If your kid brother's one of these thugs on the rampage, we'll get the little bastard, don't you worry.'

Colin realised that he was free to go. He staggered across

the road towards the Club on legs that seemed made of water.

So that was what it was like. He tried to pull himself together, to stop his body from shaking and his mind from bursting out with anger and outrage. Who did they think they were, talking to him and treating him like that? He was a human being with rights and feelings like anyone else. Yet they had behaved as though he were a dog or a block of wood. No one had ever spoken to him or manhandled him like that before — not his parents, not his teachers, not any stranger he had ever met in the street or any public place. So why did they?

All right, they had a difficult job to do. They had a difficult situation in Hillsden to control. But was that any excuse? He was a law-abiding citizen going about legitimate business. He didn't deserve to be humiliated like that. He wanted to go home and change his clothes to get rid of the contamination of those hands and those words. He felt unclean.

As he pushed through the doors of the Club, he was still seething with bitter resentment. His legs were steadier now, but inside him was a steaming anger he hadn't known he was capable of.

The Club had a strangely subdued atmosphere. For a start, there was hardly anyone there — unlike the usual loud and rowdy crowd Colin remembered on Saturday nights in the times when he used to go there. Some boys were playing pool. Others were at the bar or sitting talking in corners. But all the talk seemed to be in undertones. There was none of the joking and play-acting and larking about that there usually was.

Wayne wasn't there — that was soon clear. Nor was there anyone that Colin recognised. They were all younger than he was. He had recovered sufficiently to think ruefully that at eighteen he was too old for the Club.

The only person he knew was Mr Fernandez, the youth worker, who was in tense argument with a group of boys.

'I knows they's 'arassin' you,' Mr Fernandez was saying,

'stoppin' an' searchin' you an' tryin' to make you 'ide in you own yard an' keep off the streets as if you didn' exist. I knows all that. But what you doin' jus' make it worse.'

'Aw, you talks jus' like my momma,' said one of the boys, his face twisted into a sneer.

Mr Fernandez spread his hands wide in entreaty and tried to continue, but the boys had had enough. They signalled to each other with their eyes, shuffled to their feet and drifted towards the door.

'If you can' be good, be careful,' Mr Fernandez shouted after them.

But the boys walked on as though they hadn't heard.

The youth worker sat for a moment, shaking his head. Then he looked up and saw Colin. A smile quickly spread across his face.

'Well, if it ain't ol' Colin,' he said with pleasure, and he went across to him, slapping his palm affectionately into Colin's and gripping his hand firmly. ' 'Ow you keepin'? I ain't see you in such a time.'

'I'm all right,' Colin answered. He wondered if he should tell Mr Fernandez about what had happened. But he decided against it. The youth worker clearly had problems of his own. Instead, he said, 'I'm looking for Wayne. He didn't come home last night. Have you seen him?'

Mr Fernandez's broad brown face became thoughtful, and he pulled slowly at the hair of his beard. 'Let me see now. 'E were 'ere yesterday evening' — 'bout eight o'clock.' Then he looked serious. 'You don' t'ink 'e mix up wit' this business?'

'I don't know,' said Colin. 'He could be.'

Mr Fernandez let his exasperation burst from him suddenly. 'I don' know what the yout' comin' to, be'avin' this way.' Then he shook his head sadly. 'No, that ain't true. I knows exactly why they doin' it. They put up wit' it an' put up wit' it for so long they jus' can' put up wit' it no more.'

Colin felt as though he was beginning to understand what the youth worker meant.

'But there's got to be other ways than this violence,' Mr

Fernandez said. 'We got to talk to people an' tell 'em. We got a meetin' wit' the police this evenin' — me an' a couple o' the people o' the community. We gonna tell 'em 'bout our complaints. They gotta listen.'

Mr Fernandez snorted in an embarrassed sort of way. 'Sorry 'bout that. I gets carried away times. 'Bout you brother, I'll keep my eyes open case I sees 'im. I can' do not'in' now. Like I says, there's this deputation to the police.'

A thought suddenly seemed to strike him. He eyed Colin speculatively. 'Say, why don' you come wit' me? A good sober representative o' the yout' like you might impress 'em. Show 'em they ain't all good fo' not'in' criminals like they t'inks.'

Colin wasn't sure that he liked Mr Fernandez's description. He wasn't sure after his recent experience that he wanted to have anything more to do with the police. But then he caught the expression on the youth worker's face. It was suddenly drawn and haggard and old. What age was he, Colin wondered. Forty? Fifty? He couldn't tell. But in the lines around the eyes and the anxious set of the mouth, Colin could read a whole history of striving and rejection, of effort and rebuff, of optimism and disillusion. There was an almost naked appeal for support and approval.

'Come on,' Mr Fernandez pleaded. 'You intelligent an' educated. You ought to be good wit' words. You could 'elp.'

'All right,' Colin found himself saying. 'I'll come with you.'

Chapter 9

Wayne couldn't believe that he was still in one piece. It wasn't just the danger from the charging police. It was also the pummelling and jostling of the crowd as people bumped and crashed into him in the advance and retreat, and colliding with walls and tripping over pavements as he fled, looking half over his shoulder at his pursuers. Now, lying on the mattress in Herald's room, he found even that inadequate clapped-out lining a comfort to his weary limbs and had a chance to regain his breath and his strength.

The noise of it all was still pounding and reverberating in his head — the taunts and shrieks of anger, the chanting of 'Bull! Bull! Bull!', the crashing of bottles and the thud and crunch of bricks as they burst on the roadway, the splutter and whoosh as another car was swallowed up in flame and smoke, the creepy heart-stopping whine of sirens as fresh police made their attack, the jeers and cries of pain and screams of fear and panic as the crowd turned and ran.

It had been a real battle all right with the enraged mob facing the line of police. Each time, the pattern had been the same. The crowd slowly moved forward. One or two of the braver spirits — or more incensed — advanced a step or two in front, yelling their defiance and hurling a missile. The crowd pushed forward to back them up and join them. Then the police charged, striking out viciously with their batons, seizing a straggler here and there to pull behind their lines, driving the crowd back. They could see their comrades, now prisoners, being set upon, booted and clubbed and dragged along the road. The crowd's fury erupted once more, and threats and anger and bricks were flung at the police. They would advance again, and the police would counter-charge.

Sometimes, one of the policemen got too eager and found himself stranded in the hostile mob, away from the protection of his colleagues. Then the crowd was on him like wild animals. his helmet was knocked off, his shield kicked away, his baton wrested from him, and all weapons were used against him — fists, nails, knees, feet. Wayne had never seen faces so distorted with hatred and the desire for revenge. In the few blows the crowd were able to land before the policeman, bloody and staggering, was rescued, were packed the bitterness and resentment of years.

In the middle of it all, Wayne wondered how long it could go on. Backwards and forwards they went, and there seemed to be no end to it. At times he lost contact with Herald and Desmond, and then they would reappear, Herald cool and determined, Desmond desperate and trying hard not to show how petrified he was.

Then there was a sudden surge from behind, and the crowd was propelled straight at the police cordon. It gave way, and there were cheers and exultant cries as the mob broke through and scattered into the network of streets beyond. On the way, police cars and vans were smashed and set on fire while the police stood helpless to stem the flood that engulfed them.

In this way, Wayne and Desmond were able to follow Herald through the back streets to his squat.

As soon as they arrived, all three of them collapsed on the mattresses, exhausted and unable to speak. Now, Wayne felt more relaxed. It was like emerging from a dream or a nightmare. He felt he could breath again. Desmond was sharing the mattress with him, and he gave his friend a kick.

'Hey,' Desmond yelped. 'That 'urt.'

'Well,' said Wayne, 'you shouldn' take up so much o' the bed.'

Desmond roused himself and looked about him, 'I gotta get 'ome,' he said. 'My mum'll go spare.'

Herald stirred himself on the other mattress. 'You can' go 'ome yet. It ain't safe. The streets'll still be crawlin' wit' bullmen.'

Wayne noticed that Herald's arm was bleeding. There was a jagged cut on his forearm, and the blood was trickling down, bright scarlet against the dark skin. Herald examined it, puzzled and curious.

'I don' know 'ow that 'appen,' he said. 'I didn' feel not'in'.' He stuck his tongue out and licked the blood tentatively. 'That the blood o' the revolution.' He licked the blood again and smiled slowly and appreciatively. 'Taste good.'

Wayne laughed, but Desmond just shuddered. 'I wants to go 'ome,' he said.

'Well you can',' said Wayne, turning on him. 'You 'ears what 'Erald say. It ain't safe.'

Desmond hunched his shoulders up and withdrew within himself.

Wayne gave a sigh and contemplated his own problems. What must his mother be thinking? He hadn't been in touch, and she had no idea where he was. She would guess he was in Hillsden, and she would have heard about the trouble there. He wouldn't half get a lashing when he eventually reached home. It didn't bear thinking about.

His meditations were interrupted by a 'Shoosh' from Herald who had suddenly become upright and alert. Wayne hadn't heard anything, but he listened intently. He became aware of a faint tapping.

Herald moved towards the door. He turned to Wayne. 'If there any problems, use the window,' he said. Then he was gone.

Wayne looked at the window, but he couldn't see how that was going to help. They were on the first floor, weren't they?

But it seemed to be all right. There were voices coming up the stairs.

When Herald came back into the room, there were two other people with him. One of them was a tall gangling white man who looked a few years older than Herald. The other was a black girl with close cropped hair wearing a T-shirt and jeans. When Desmond saw her, he suddenly became all attention, and Wayne had to kick him again.

Herald introduced them all. The white man was called Alan, and the black girl Stella. The girl seemed familiar, but Wayne couldn't quite place her.

He wondered what the white man was doing there. Something of his suspicion and doubt must have got through to Herald because he said, 'It's all right, guy. Alan is a friend.'

Alan smiled in an encouraging way. 'It's not just black people the police harass you know.'

Wayne accepted this statement. In any case, if he was a friend of Herald's, he must be all right. He tried to work out some words of welcome, but Alan had already turned back to Herald. There were obviously more important matters to be dealt with.

'We've got some petrol bombs,' Alan said.

Herald was filled with a mixture of wonder and appreciation. 'Great, man.'

Alan continued. 'The plan is to attack the Queen's Arms. You know how racist they are. Now we're going to show them what we feel.'

'I knows the Queen's Arms,' said Herald with feeling. His face had become heavy with resentment. 'If you black, you don' get served.'

'Yeah,' agreed Stella, 'an' you knows 'ow they 'as these special meetin's for National Front supporters there.'

'Well,' said Alan, 'this is our chance to get even with them.'

'We're tryin' to round up a bit o' support,' Stella explained.

'Not that it's necessary,' Alan said. 'The gang's already

on its way. We just thought you and your posse would hate to miss out on the fun.'

He grinned at Herald, and Herald grinned back. They slapped hands delightedly.

'Bet you life man,' Herald cried. 'I wouldn' miss it fo' anyt'in'.'

Wayne's heart sank. They weren't going out into the fray again were they? He felt he was suffering from — what did they call it? — battle-fatigue. He wasn't sure he could take his place in the front line and go into the attack once more. He had regained his breath, but he had lost his will to fight.

Not that he was asked his opinion or given any choice in the matter. From the way the others were going on, it was assumed that they were all eager and frantic to get back to the battle. It was left to Desmond to voice his feelings.

'I wanna go 'ome,' he protested miserably.

Stella rounded on him. 'Look,' she said. 'This is important. It them or us. We got to fight fo' the right to be black an' free. Don' you understand that?'

The expression on Desmond's face suggested that he didn't.

Stella went on. 'You gotta stick up fo' you rights. You ain't a child no more. You a man.'

That did the trick. Desmond perked up amazingly. He braced his shoulders back with pride.

And so Wayne found himself following the others down the precarious vandalised stairs.

He knew the Queen's Arms well by sight and reputation. It stood on the north side of the High Street, about halfway along. It was a large rather grand building clad in pale green tiles. It took up the whole of the frontage between two side streets. Wayne had heard that blacks were not welcome there. They couldn't refuse to serve them, of course, but they weren't encouraged. When it came to taking orders, the barmen somehow only managed to see the white customers.

In any case, it was a predominantly white pub and attracted mobs of National Front supporters from all over London wearing their fascist badges and handing out leaflets and loud-mouthed insults. They seemed to run special coaches for them.

Local people had protested, but that hadn't done any good. Some of them had taken the law into their own hands, and there had been outbursts of fighting on a number of occasions which the police had had to break up. Now it looked as though accounts were going to be settled once and for all.

The news had spread fast. There were groups of people emerging from the side streets and making their way up to the High Street. Wayne noticed that some of them were carrying sticks and staves — the kind you put on pick-axes — and tins of petrol or paraffin. There was a subdued intensity about them that was frightening.

The reports were that the police had cordoned off the High Street at both ends and were patrolling it to keep it free from rioters. Their idea was to pen the rioters into the criss-cross of roads between the High Street and the railway and prevent them from breaking out and escaping to other parts of the area. But it was impossible to keep a guard everywhere in that warren of streets with its closely-packed houses. Barriers had been placed across every entry to the High Street, but not all of them were manned.

The crowd was increasing in size and momentum. The murmur of excitement and rumblings of revenge were growing louder. A police van screeched to a halt on their left, and half a dozen policemen scrambled out. There were scuffles and screams, but the main body of the crowd pushed on towards the High Street. The murmurs and rumblings rose into howls of anger and frustration as the barriers came into sight. The crowd forced a way through them, buckling them and banging them aside, and poured into the High Street like water from a burst main. Wayne and the others were swept along in the flood.

The handful of police near the scene retreated along the High Street, pursued by the enraged mob. The whole roadway was a mass of people, yelling, gesticulating, congratulating each other, dancing. Some of the small panes of glass in the windows of the Queen's Arms had already been broken, but now whole window frames were splintered and staved in. The various entrances were rammed and kicked until they gave way. There was a great cheer from the crowd as they rushed through. Others clambered in at the windows.

Wayne stayed outside. Heads were raised as a figure appeared at a first floor window. It was pulled up and the white face of a man was thrust forward. Wayne assumed it must be the landlord. He looked furious and terrified.

Alan cupped his hands and yelled, 'You better get out, you fascist bastard, if you don't want to fry.'

Wayne doubted whether the man could have heard Alan above all the other jeers and screams and shouts, but the general message of the words must have got through. The window shot down and the man disappeared with amazing speed.

The crowd didn't have much time to waste on him because the next moment there was a flash and the pub was alight. The interior was bright with yellow flames. Another jubilant roar rose into the sky. The people inside scurried out, and the crowd drew back to escape the sparks and smoke and heat that spewed out from the windows. Wayne began to cough and splutter and moved away. All round him were cries of triumph and rejoicing.

'Great, man!'

'That'll show the fascist pigs.'

'Wow! Just think — all that booze goin' up in smoke!'

'Down wit' the National Front!'

But the joys of victory were short-lived. Even as they gazed in wonder at the flames catching hold and licking higher, and heard the creak and crash of beams collapsing inside, the police were mobilising their forces and advancing on them.

The crowd reformed ranks, and the flow of bricks and bottles and sticks resumed. This time, there were petrol bombs among them, smashing on the road in front of the police and spurting up in flashes of flame that caused the police to panic and pull back. One of them was too late. His clothing was alight. He began to beat frantically at the flames. His colleagues rushed to his assistance. While rocks and missiles landed all around them, they tried to extinguish the fire. They dragged him to safety behind their lines.

Watching, Wayne was suddenly sickened. He felt his stomach turning and rebelling. It was all going on too long. It was all getting out of hand. He wanted to go home.

But there was no escape from the press of the crowd. He was hemmed in on all sides. His friends were still beside him. Desmond was holding on to his arm as though for support. Herald and Alan were laughing at some joke or other. Stella was staring with awe at the blazing pub. Wayne could see the flames reflected in her brown eyes.

Then his attention was diverted by a shrill clanging at the end of the High Street. The police lines divided, and a fire engine came thundering through. Before it had come to a halt, men in bright yellow helmets and trousers leapt off and were busy unrolling their hoses with frantic haste.

At first the crowd was taken aback. They watched as though stunned. Gradually, they came to and began to murmur among themselves. There were shouts of protest and outrage. All their efforts were going to be spoilt. Their gesture was going to be cancelled out.

Some people moved forward and started arguing with the firemen and shouting at them. The firemen ignored them and went on with their preparations. A young black man seized one of the hoses. Some of his friends helped him. There was a tussle, and the firemen fell back. Others in the crowd advanced, and the fire-engine was surrounded. A ladder was dragged from its rack and disappeared into the crowd. The hoses were slashed.

The firemen abandoned their appliance and made for the police lines. As they reached them, another fire-engine arrived. This time, it came forward slowly under police guard. The crowd hurled bricks and abuse at them, but they were forced to retreat. The fire-engine was able to get into position, and the hoses were unloaded.

But as the water rushed through them, they were seized by policemen and directed at the crowd. The column of water as it swept through the crowd was like a body-blow. People were knocked off their feet and went slithering along the ground.

Wayne was hit in the chest and went flying. The suddenness and the force of the water took his breath away. A voice called out, 'Hey! They ain't suppose to do that!' Then a hand was stretched out to him, and he was hauled to his feet. It was Herald.

The hoses were now turned on to the burning public house, but under cover of the disorder, the police line had closed in. It was bearing down on the crowd, shields thrust out, batons on high. It was within grappling distance.

There was a mad panic as the crowd tried to disperse and find places of safety. Wayne felt himself being dragged along by Herald. He looked back at the advancing police with their shields and protective helmets. They were like robots from some space age epic.

Then his eye caught a figure beyond them. It looked like his brother Colin. But it couldn't be. What would he be doing there — and behind the police line too?

He was just trying to take a second glance at him, almost ready to shout out and warn him, when a heavy blow struck him on the back of the head, and he went falling, falling into a dark emptiness.

Chapter 10

The police kept the deputation waiting.

It was the first time Colin had been inside a police station. He was reassured at least to discover that the police were not expending vast quantities of tax-payers' money on luxurious premises. The waiting room where the deputation had been parked was little more than a corridor. There was a continual stream of police officers passing to and fro. Colin wilted under the constant barrage of suspicious and hostile stares. It was difficult for him to meet all those eyes with their open contempt burning into him.

To avoid them, he gazed down at the ground and tried to guess the sizes of the various boots that stomped along the corridor. That gave him some comfort. He wondered whether the two policemen who had abused him in the High Street were among them. He wouldn't recognise them if he saw them. All policemen looked the same to him — and he smiled wryly at the thought. Then he quickly stifled the smile before any of the policemen could catch sight of it and suspect he was laughing at them.

He had the feeling that the other members of the deputation were in no way intimidated by this parade of police strength. They were probably used to police stations. Mr Fernandez was sitting next to him with a glum face, twirling the hair of his beard, staring into space. By leaning forward, Colin could see the others. One of them was the local vicar, the Rev. Sampson. The other two were councillors — Mr Padmore and Mrs Daley. The Rev. Sampson and Cllr Padmore were waiting patiently — indeed, they seemed to have abstracted themselves totally from the scene as though they weren't there. But Cllr Mrs Daley, who was black, stormed and fumed at the delay.

'Why they keepin' us waitin'?' she demanded. 'They got somet'in' to 'ide?' She didn't wait for an answer. 'I knows they busy puttin' away the evidence in lock drawers an' movin' our black boys on to the next station so's we won' see 'em.'

'Keep cool, Hazel,' said Cllr Padmore. 'You know that won't achieve anything.'

'I ain't keepin' cool for nobody,' retorted Mrs Daley, stoking herself into a greater rage. 'What there to keep cool 'bout? When the police keeps cool an' leaves our black boys alone, that the time I keeps cool.'

Mr Fernandez nodded his head in agreement while Cllr Padmore sank back into his private thoughts and the Rev. Sampson continued whatever complicated prayer was going on in his head. At least that was what it looked like to Colin. When they were eventually ushered into Superintendent Cross's office, he was to find that he had underestimated them.

Superintendent Cross was sitting behind his desk, a stiff-looking man with a gaunt face and grey hair. He rose, shook hands with the members of the deputation and indicated where they could sit. Then he resumed his place behind his desk, clasping his hands on the uncluttered surface in front of him. The expression on his face was one of polite attention. He reminded Colin of his headteacher, Mrs Howard. That was the kind of pious look she put on for assembly — but heaven help any pupil who misbehaved or reacted the wrong way.

'I am very pleased to have this opportunity to meet members of the community,' the superintendent began, very official. 'I can understand your concern about the present situation. It is distressing for all of us.'

'But what cause it?' demanded Mrs Daley. 'It this police 'arassment o' the black yout' — that what cause it. We been tellin' you time an' time again 'bout that, an' you don' pay a blind bit o' notice.'

'I have to agree with Mrs Daley,' said the Rev Sampson, coming in surprisingly strong. 'I have had so many of my parishioners coming up to me worried and upset because their sons have been stopped and searched by the police. It just creates bad feeling. It does no good at all.'

'And what about the Special Patrol and its activities?' asked Cllr Padmore, joining the attack. 'This Operation Purge as you call it — though I can't say I think much of the name. What do you hope to achieve by flooding the place with police? All you do is stir up resentment when innocent people can't walk the streets without being stopped and manhandled. I don't remember the Police Committee being told about the Special Patrol being brought in. Were they consulted? I certainly intend to bring it up at the next meeting.'

The superintendent remained cool. 'We have a job to do and that is to maintain the law. This is one of the worst areas in the whole country for theft and street crime. We have to combat it by every means at our disposal.'

'Street crime,' snorted Mrs Daley. 'What you doin' is treatin' every black person in the Borough as a criminal. Honest people can' walk down the street wit'out they be 'arassed an' assaulted by the police an' treated like criminal.'

'I don't think that's true,' said the superintendent. 'There is a large black population in this area, so obviously many of the people my men stop and search are black, but that's only to be expected.'

'That ain't the way we sees it,' said Mrs Daley.

'Yeah,' agreed Mr Fernandez. 'You ask anyone. Take Colin 'ere. 'E ain't no criminal. 'E sittin' 'is A Levels. 'E a respectable black boy. Ask 'im what 'e t'ink.'

All attention was suddenly directed at Colin. Even the

superintendent was gazing at him with polite interest. Colin felt himself going hot and cold. What was he supposed to say?

'I know a lot of my friends have been stopped and searched,' he began, 'and they hadn't done anything.'

His mouth was dry. He didn't know how to go on. They were still staring at him. He remembered what had happened to him in the High Street. Now here he was in the police station itself. Would there be more trouble if he mentioned it? He licked his lips. He felt scared, but he had to say it.

'I was stopped myself an hour ago. I think what Mrs Daley said is true. It makes you feel like a criminal, even though you aren't one. If I had been white, would they have treated me the way they did?'

It was feeble. He knew that. But it was the best he could manage.

Mr Fernandez broke into the silence that followed Colin's words. 'There, you see? The police is racist I tells you.'

'Of course they're not racist,' retorted the superintendent, a touch of resentment beginning to appear.

Mr Fernandez pursued his point. 'Then all these stories I does 'ear 'bout black people bein' abused an' insulted ain't so?'

'I've had a lot of complaints as well,' said the vicar.

'The police are not racist,' maintained the superintendent. 'At least no more than any other section of society.'

There was a roar of derision at this from Mrs Daley and Mr Fernandez.

For a moment, the superintendent was almost flustered. He continued. 'In any group of people there are bound to be a few who are racist. In this respect the police are no different from anyone else. But if we find anyone expressing racist views or behaving in a racist way, then we take action.'

'I can't accept that,' said Cllr Padmore. 'Given the position of trust and power the police are in, there shouldn't be any racists among them.'

But it was more an aside than a statement he wanted to develop there and then.

Mr Fernandez burst in, 'An' what 'bout those policemen wearin' National Front badges? What 'bout them?'

'I don't know anything about them,' said the superintendent. 'If they were wearing such badges, then that is quite improper. I'll investigate that allegation.'

'What 'bout the way they insults our black boys,' demanded Mrs Daley, 'callin' 'em black bastards an' niggers an' I don' know what.'

'I think complaints like that are invented and exaggerated,' said the superintendent. 'I have never heard any of my officers use expressions like that.'

'Yeah,' said Mrs Daley, 'but what 'bout when you ain't there?'

For a moment, it looked as though the superintendent was going to blow up. He held himself very still, and bright red patches burned on his haggard cheeks. Then he relaxed and bent forward confidentially over his desk.

'You know, a lot of this ill-feeling is manufactured by people out to create trouble. There are a lot of extremists out there who want to see law and order break down so that they can take advantage of it. And then there are all these race relations people. It's a new growth industry. They have a vested interest in creating bad feeling between the black community and the police, don't they? If they didn't do that they'd be out of a job.'

It was the wrong thing to say — even Colin knew that. Mrs Daley and Mr Fernandez burst out in angry protest. The Rev. Sampson looked shocked. It was left to Cllr Padmore to restore order. His expression was grim, as though there were things the superintendent had said that he wouldn't forget in a hurry, but he bulldozed over the voices of the others and won the attention of the meeting.

'This is not the place to go into all that,' he said. 'What we are here to discuss is the present situation and how to deal with it. Though I must say,' he added, 'that I can't help feeling that police action in the past has had a lot to contribute to it.'

There were loud murmurs of agreement from the others. The superintendent held himself very stiff in face of this criticism but he didn't say anything.

'Yeah,' cried Mrs Daley, 'what 'bout this black boy what were knife by you men. That what start it all.'

'That isn't true,' said Superintendent Cross. 'My report is that two of my officers found a young black man lying in the street. He had been attacked and wounded by a number of black youths. My officers were trying to get him to hospital when they were set upon by a crowd of people.'

'But 'e dead, inn'e?' said Mrs Daley.

'That is absolute nonsense. As yet, we do not know the whereabouts of the injured man, but if he were dead it would have been reported to us.'

'Well, that the story goin' round,' said Mrs Daley, sounding dissatisfied with the superintendent's version of events.

'Look,' said Cllr Padmore impatiently, 'let's get back to the purpose of this meeting. What do we do about the situation? There has been looting and rioting in the streets out there. It's quite possible there will be more. How do we stop it?'

The superintendent opened his mouth as though about to tell him, but Cllr Padmore was in the middle of his speech and didn't want to be interrupted.

'Now I have been talking to a lot of people and listening to what they say, and what they say is important I think. As far as I can gather, the police have gone at this thing like a bull in a china shop. They've over-reacted. They've brought in the big battalions to smash a nut, when if they'd kept their cool and treated people reasonably and decently, none of this would ever have happened.'

It was clear that the superintendent wasn't enjoying this. His hands had disappeared under the desk, and Colin wondered if he were tapping the wood to restrain himself and keep his patience. But the others were nodding their approval.

'The press and the television haven't helped any,' Cllr Padmore went on. 'But I suppose it's their nature to build up any little snack into a feast. What we have to do is to defuse the situation. You have hundreds of men out on the streets. What you have to do is withdraw them.'

The superintendent was suddenly alert. 'Do you realise what you're asking me to do? If I withdraw my men, there will be even worse rioting. And it won't be confined to a small area of Hillsden, it will spread right through the whole Borough. I have a responsibility to see that the streets are safe, and if that means having hundreds of men patrolling them, then that's what I'll do.'

'But don't you realise?' exclaimed the Rev. Sampson. 'Having all those police on the streets is acting as a provocation.'

'Why should it be?' the superintendent asked. 'Law-abiding citizens have nothing to fear.'

'You just don't understand,' the vicar continued nearing despair. 'Those young people feel trapped with cordons of police all around them. If the only way to escape is to fight, then that's what they'll do.'

'Law-abiding citizens have nothing to fear,' the superintendent repeated.

The members of the deputation exchanged glances. There was a general feeling that the meeting had achieved nothing.

'Then what are you going to do?' Cllr Padmore asked.

'I shall keep my men in the streets until order is restored,' the superintendent said.

'What 'bout all those black boys bein' beat up an' thrown in the cells?' demanded Mrs Daley.

'What about all my officers being injured and ending up in hospital?' retorted Superintendent Cross. The fierceness of his stare made even Mrs Daley flinch.

The tension in the room was broken by a knock at the door. A constable entered.

'Sorry to interrupt you, sir,' he said, 'but we've just had a report that the Queen's Arms public house has been set on fire.'

'Thank you, constable,' the superintendent said. 'I'll be with you in a minute.'

The members of the deputation were stunned by the news. Mrs Daley clasped her hands to her head and rolled it round and round. Colin wasn't sure, but he thought he saw a sudden gleam in the superintendent's eyes. If it was there, it was soon gone, and the superintendent became very brisk and business-like. He stood up.

'I'm sure you'll appreciate that I must attend to this new development,' he said.

'Of course,' said Cllr Padmore.

The deputation prepared to leave. There was an air of despair and defeat about them. As they made their way down the corridors of the police station to the exit amid the frantic noise and activity, no one paid them any attention.

'That was a waste of time,' said Mr Fernandez when they were standing on the steps outside.

'Well, we've made our gesture,' said Cllr Padmore. 'We'll just have to see how things develop.' He said it in a way that made Colin suspect that as far as Cllr Padmore was concerned that wasn't the end of the story. There might yet be some political advantages to be made out of the meeting. 'Come on, Hazel,' he added. 'There's nothing else to be gained here.'

He and Mrs Daley said their goodbyes and went off. The Rev. Sampson hesitated for a moment and then he too tripped quickly down the steps and away. Mr Fernandez and Colin were left alone.

Across the road a crowd of people had gathered. They were waving banners and chanting and protesting at the police arrests. Colin could hear their calls of 'Bull! Bull! Bull!' and 'Let our people go!' They were being kept in check by traffic barriers and patrolling policemen.

A man rushed up to Mr Fernandez. He had a microphone in his hand, and there was someone else behind him with a TV camera on his shoulder.

'We're covering the riots,' the man explained. 'Have you any comments you want to give us?'

'Plenty,' snapped Mr Fernandez, 'but I ain't givin' 'em.'

'What's wrong?' the man asked. 'Why not?'

''Cause I don' know what use you people'll make o' 'em,' Mr Fernandez replied calmly.

'What?'

Mr Fernandez went on, 'Excuse the expression, but you people could make black white.' He fixed the man with a hard stare.

The man with the microphone blinked for a moment and then shrugged his shoulders. 'All right. If that's the way you feel. Come on, Vic. Let's find someone else.'

They began to move down the steps in the direction of the crowd of protesters.

'Yeah, that the way I feels,' Mr Fernandez bellowed after them.

There was frenzied activity in the yard behind the police station. There was a constant coming and going, and cars and vans hurtled in and out. But Colin scarcely noticed.

The meeting had been a disappointment to him, and he was disappointed with himself. What had Mr Fernandez said? 'You ought to be good with words.' Well, he had been useless. He might as well not have been there.

Mr Fernandez suddenly spoke. 'Thanks fo' comin' along. It were good to 'ave you support.'

Colin couldn't believe him. Did he really mean it? Before he had a chance to question the youth worker, Superintendent Cross appeared on the steps, resplendent in his official braided cap. He acknowledged Mr Fernandez and Colin with a curt nod, and then marched down the steps, followed by a retinue of other officers.

As they reached the pavement, Mr Fernandez called after him and ran down the steps. Colin hurried to join him.

'There still a chance,' Mr Fernandez was saying earnestly. 'I knows them guys. If I could jus' talk to 'em, perhaps I could persuade 'em to see sense.'

Superintendent Cross seemed irritated at being interrupted in his progress, but he listened patiently and considered Mr Fernandez's suggestion seriously.

'Well, it's a possibility,' he said. 'You'd better come along.' And he set off again down the road.

Colin kept pace with Mr Fernandez as they covered the hundred yards or so to the Jubilee Clock Tower and turned into the High Street.

'Will it do any good?' he asked.

Mr Fernandez shook his head. 'I don' know, do I? But it wort' a try. Anyt'in' to stop this trouble goin' on.'

Smoke and the smell of burning drifted down the street. At the far end black clouds were swirling and spiralling into the sky from the Queen's Arms, followed by showers of sparks and spurts of flame. There was a tremendous hubbub of voices bouncing off the cliff-faces of the shop fronts. It seemed like the rumbling of thunder. A fire engine careered past them, its blue light whirling round and its warning signal clanging. Superintendent Cross and the others had to jump to one side.

There were policemen and police vehicles everywhere. A line of police several deep spanned the whole width of the street near the Queen's Arms. Beyond them Colin could see the wild churning mass of the crowd. The noise was deafening.

At one end of the police cordon there was a sudden flurry of activity. The line broke up as a figure burst through. It was a policeman. His clothes were on fire. He was beating at the flames with his hands and stumbling along the road. A confused mass of people crowded round him — policemen and ambulance-men — and he was lost from sight. The next thing Colin saw was a stretcher being rushed to an ambulance. The policeman was on it, wrapped in a blanket.

'He'll be all right,' an officer reported to Superintendent Cross. 'He's not seriously injured.'

'That's something at least,' the superintendent replied. He was looking grim.

Another fire engine hurtled past. The line of police parted to let it through and then moved forward as though to protect it. Superintendent Cross and his party advanced to be closer to the action, and Mr Fernandez and Colin followed them.

Beyond the police line Colin could make out individual faces in the crowd. There was an angry roar as the firemen began to unroll their hoses. Then suddenly a gush of water shot across the road and into the crowd. There were shrieks and frantic movement as people panicked and tried to get beyond the reach of the powerful jet.

Colin watched as yet another black boy was caught by the thrust of the water and was knocked off his feet. Someone helped him up. The boy turned to stare at the police. His face was filled with terror and despair. With a shock Colin recognised his brother.

He shouted out and lunged forward to try to reach him. Even as he did so, he saw a policeman's baton crash down on Wayne's head and a wave of horror swept over him. Wayne dropped to the ground.

At the same moment. Mr Fernandez grabbed Colin's arm and held him back. 'Take it easy, man,' he warned.

Colin glared wildly at him and threw him off. 'That's my brother,' he screamed. 'I've got to help him.'

But it was too late. The crowd was on the run with the police in hot pursuit. Wayne was nowhere to be seen.

Chapter 11

Wayne was on fire. His clothes were alight. Flames were climbing up his body. He beat at them with his hands, but it was no good. His skin was being scorched, his flesh was melting away. His hands in front of his eyes were flaring torches. The flames had reached his face. They were licking at his cheeks and hair. He screamed out in agony.

Then he was suddenly awake. Sweat was running down his body and he was shivering. Had he actually screamed or was it just part of his nightmare? He wasn't sure. He opened his eyes.

He was back in Herald's squat. He couldn't remember how he had got there. Desmond was sitting hunched up at the bottom of the mattress. On the other side of the room, Herald was lying fully stretched out, his hands behind his head. Near him were Alan and Stella, sitting on the floor with their backs against the wall. His long legs were splayed out in front of him, and she was hugging her knees to her chin. The light was fading, and it was very quiet. It was as though they were each absorbed in their own thoughts.

Then Desmond glanced over his shoulder and saw that Wayne had come to. He slid up the mattress until his face was close to Wayne's. 'You all right?' he asked anxiously.

'Yeah, I t'ink so,' Wayne answered, none too certain. He felt weak and dazed. He just wanted to lie there and do nothing. The idea of getting up or moving was impossible.

It occurred to him to wonder why Desmond was still there. 'Ain't you suppose to be 'ome?'

'Aw,' Desmond replied, as though embarrassed. 'I guess my mum can go on waitin' fo' a bit.' He called across to Herald. 'Wayne come round.' Then he turned to his friend again and laughed at the back of his throat with relief. 'Hey, man, we sure was worried 'bout you.'

They were all clustered round him now. Wayne examined one face after another and thought hard. What had happened? He couldn't remember.

' 'Ow did I get 'ere?' he asked.

It was Herald who explained. 'You got 'it on the 'ead an' we brought you back.'

'Yeah,' burst in Desmond, seeming to become light-headed now that everything was all right, 'we 'alf drag, 'alf carry you.'

'You safe 'ere,' Herald concluded.

Now that it was mentioned, Wayne felt an ache at the back of his head. He stretched his hand up and there was certainly a bump there under the close crinkly hair. Touching it sent waves of pain through his body, and he felt dizzy.

Then it all came back to him — the assault on the Queen's Arms, the roar of the flames as they caught hold, the petrol bombs, the policeman alight like a walking inferno, the image of his brother's face, the sudden darkness.

'I seen Colin there,' he said.

Herald's eyes narrowed. 'You mean you brother?'

'Yeah, he was there. I seen 'im. 'E was wit' the police.'

Herald looked dubious. 'I know I don' 'ave no 'igh regard fo' you brother, but I don' believe 'e join the police 'gainst us.'

Wayne became agitated and rose on his elbows. ' 'E were there I tells you. 'E were standin' be'ind the police line.'

'All right, all right,' soothed Herald. 'Take it easy, man.' He eased Wayne back into a horizontal position.

As his head touched the mattress, Wayne thought he was going to black out again. There was a buzzing in his ears, and his whole body felt as though it were fading away into nothing. He heard Desmond ask, 'What we gonna do 'bout Wayne?' He sounded worried.

Herald said, 'Perhaps I could go an' look fo' Colin. 'E might be able to get Wayne back 'ome again.'

Then the billowing clouds and smoke and mist descended, and Wayne was being dragged under them. For a while, he resisted, but the effort was too much for him. He gave up the struggle and surrendered himself to the tug and sway of the clouds, letting himself float weightless at their will. He sank deeper and deeper until he wasn't aware of anything any more.

When he surfaced again, the sky through the window was dark. In the room itself there was a glow of light in one corner from the paraffin lamp. The others were still there, except for Herald, crouched round the lamp as though for warmth in spite of the hot oppressive atmosphere. It might have been night, but it was certainly no cooler. There was the murmur of voices, though Wayne couldn't make out what was being said.

Very carefully, he patted the bump on the back of his head with his fingers. It still hurt when he pressed it, but otherwise the pain seemed to be less. He was still weak. He could no more think of moving or standing than he would of flying. There was a new ache in his body as well — caused by the hardness of the floorboards thrusting up through the thin mattress. He wished he were at home in his own comfortable bed.

Herald had said something about going to find his brother. He didn't know how long Herald had been gone. He didn't give much for his chances of coming across Colin in the crowds and chaos that were sure to be continuing outside.

And even if he did, what use would that do? What help

could Colin be? In his depressed state, it seemed to Wayne that there would never be any end to the warfare that was raging and that he was doomed to be trapped in this squalid room for the rest of his life.

It was a surprise then when there were footsteps on the stairs and the door burst open and Herald entered leading Colin. Desmond must have been having the same gloomy thoughts because he asked Herald, ' 'Ow you find 'im?'

'Easy,' Herald replied casually. 'I jus' went to the Club an' 'e were there.'

Colin went across to Wayne and looked down at him. 'Are you all right?'

'Yeah,' Wayne said, subduing the relief and joy that welled up inside him. 'Ain't not'in'.'

He tensed himself and waited for his brother to tell him off for staying out at night and getting mixed up with the riots and worrying his mother sick. But there were no angry words.

Instead, Colin said, 'Good. We'll soon have you back home.' He even put his hand out and gave his brother a pat on the head. Wayne couldn't believe it.

'Shouldn't he be in hospital?' Colin asked Herald. 'He could have concussion.'

'I ain't goin' to no 'ospital,' Wayne protested, some of his old spirit returning.

'It ain't safe,' said Herald. 'Even if we gets 'im there, the bull is sure to be keepin' watch. 'E'll be all right.'

'We'll have to take the risk then,' said Colin, but he sounded unhappy about it.

Herald turned towards the others. 'You knows Stella, don' you?'

Wayne watched as his brother swung round to take in the girl. He sensed that Colin was put out. His air of composure and being in command of the situation slipped.

'Yeah,' said Stella before Colin could reply, 'we knows each other from long time back.'

'An' this is Alan an' Desmond,' Herald went on, but it

was clear that Colin wasn't listening. He was still staring at Stella. He looked as though he were seeing a ghost.

'How you doing?' he managed to get out at last.

'Oh, as well as you can expect,' Stella replied, 'when you female an' you leave school an' there ain't no job fo' you.'

She was smiling as though amused, but there was no mistaking the bitterness in her voice.

Wayne suddenly remembered why Stella seemed familiar to him. She had been one of Colin's girlfriends when she was at school.

'I'll get the car,' Colin said. 'Then I can take Wayne home.'

'Better leave it a while,' Herald advised. 'You knows the bullmen is still pretty active out there.' He laughed and explained to the others. 'We 'ad a couple o' close shaves gettin' 'ere. It were like playin' 'ide an' seek.'

Colin agreed to wait. Wayne wanted to urge him to go now. He was angry with himself for being so feeble, but he was scared too. He had never felt so weak and helpless before. Was it just tiredness, or was he really ill? Whichever it was, it was frightening. He wanted to go home. But he couldn't summon up enough energy to argue.

'Better sit down,' Herald said.

Colin looked round the room as though there were no space left for him.

'I knows it ain't what you use to,' Herald went on, 'but this the way some o' us 'as to live.'

'Yeah, the floor good 'nough fo' us,' said Stella.

Colin squatted down in front of the window. For a moment there was silence as they seemed to size each other up. Wayne felt a tension growing in the room.

'How long is this going to last?' asked Colin, making conversation.

'Ain't never gonna end,' Herald replied calmly.

'What d'you mean?' Colin demanded.

'What I says,' Herald explained. 'It ain't never gonna end. The only t'ing they understands is violence. So we

111

gonna fight. One way or other it gonna continue till we gets our rights.'

Stella joined in. 'You seems to 'ave forgot what it like when you black an' you lives in 'Illsden.'

Herald laughed. ' 'E forgot what it like to be black. Period.'

Wayne couldn't quite make out what was going on, but he knew from the tightening of the muscles in Colin's face that his brother was getting rattled. It seemed to be some kind of game Herald was playing so as to embarrass Colin. Desmond too appeared to be puzzled. He caught Wayne's eye and pulled a face and shrugged his shoulders.

Alan said, 'This isn't just a black problem. There are whites involved as well. It's a question of who has the power. And while the power is in the hands of a few privileged people, then the majority of the working class, whether they're black or white, are going to be exploited, and if they want a say in their own destiny, then they have to fight for it.'

'Aw, spare us the political speeches,' said Herald with some contempt. Alan looked quite hurt. 'You ain't understood what I sayin'.' He lowered his eyes and shook his head and sighed as though he wondered whether he had the energy and the words to get his meaning across.

He raised his head again, and his eyes were bright and piercing. 'Look at 'im,' he said.

The others obeyed his words. Colin seemed to flinch under the onslaught of all those eyes, but he met them without turning away.

' 'E look like a black man, don' 'e?' Herald went on. 'But when you black, you oughta be'ave like you black. An' 'e don'.'

'That's absurd,' Colin protested.

'That's absurd,' said Herald, mimicking Colin's voice. He laughed bitterly. 'Listen to 'im. 'E even talk like a white man.'

Colin definitely flinched this time. His head jerked back

and his eyes narrowed. But before he could reply, Alan butted in. 'Hey,' he said, 'that sounds racist to me.'

Herald turned a cool glance on him. It was as though he were weary of having to go through all these arguments again and again. 'I ain't got not'in' 'gainst white people who ain't prejudice. But they don' 'mount to many. What I's sayin' is that black people ought to be black an' not pretend they's white.'

'But I don't pretend to be white,' exclaimed Colin. Wayne could tell that he was having difficulty keeping his temper.

'All right,' said Herald, prepared to be generous, 'perhaps you ain't doin' it deliberate. Perhaps you jus' ain't aware o' what 'appenin'.'

His voice became darker and more serious. 'They trainin' you. They trainin' you to be one o' they meek little lap dogs. They givin' you a education so you can be someone they can show off. They can trot you out an' say, "Look, 'ere we 'as a success story. 'Ere we 'as a black man what made it. 'E 'as intelligence. Now don' that surprise you? Well, not all black men is thick animal brains. An' see 'ow good we is. We 'llows 'im to go to university an' get a degree. You ain't gonna call us prejudice when we 'llows that, is you?"'

The mockery in Herald's voice cut right through Wayne. Why was he giving Colin such a hard time? Because it was obvious that he wanted to show Colin up and hurt him. Why was he needling him like this?

Colin wasn't prepared to let him get away with it. He came back to the attack. 'That's rubbish and you know it. You're just jealous. Because you wasted your time at school and didn't get anywhere, you think everyone else should do the same. And when they don't, when they work hard and try to make a success of their lives, all you can do is sneer.'

'Oh, I admits I didn' do much at school,' Herald agreed, 'but that kind o' education is white man education. Like I said.'

He fixed Colin with a questioning stare. 'You ever look at the books they use? They tells you all 'bout 'ow great the white man is an' what wonderful t'ings 'e done. But what 'bout the black man? What 'bout me? The only black folks I ever 'ears 'bout in school is slaves an' starvin' peasants an' wild savages.'

Colin was about to say something, but Herald carried on. 'No, I tells a lie. That ain't so. They show us a film once. It were 'bout this black general, except 'e weren't black. 'E were a white man wit' a 'eavy sun tan. I guess they couldn' find a black man wit' enough intelligence to learn the lines. I thought it were interestin' at first. But what this general do? 'E strangle 'is white girlfriend. Didn' I tell you all black people was savages?'

'But that's *Othello*,' Colin exclaimed.

'Yeah,' agreed Herald slyly, 'I believes that what it call.'

'Who's making speeches now?' Alan asked.

'I ain't never 'eard you speak as much as this before,' said Stella. 'What get into you, man?'

But it was clear that the contest was between Herald and Colin. The others had become mere spectators, sitting on the sidelines.

'There more than one way o' gettin' a education,' Herald continued. 'I seen 'ow black people treated. I experience it myself. I learn all kinds o' t'ings 'bout society they never tells you 'bout in school — not from books but from real life. Course, I 'as plenty o' time to t'ink an' read too. But I finds my own books to read now — not that white propaganda they dishes out in school.'

Herald paused to study Colin before going on. 'You know, you reminds me o' a book I read once. It call *Invisible Man*. Not that kid stuff by H.G. Wells. This by a black man. Ralph Elliston 'is name. 'E show 'ow the only way white society gonna accept a black man is if 'e so goody-goody, they don' even notice 'im or 'is colour. 'E become invisible. That what you is, boy. You's become invisible.'

Colin had taken as much as he could stand. He got to his feet. 'I'd better go and get the car now,' he said.

Herald rose too. He seemed suddenly to lose his cool detachment. He prodded Colin in the chest with a finger.

'What you name?' he demanded.

Colin appeared to be bewildered. 'What?'

'What you name?' Herald repeated.

Colin was becoming impatient. 'Don't be stupid. You know perfectly well what my name is.'

'Well, say it,' Herald commanded.

Colin sighed as though deciding he might as well humour Herald and give in to his peculiar request. 'Colin MacMorris.'

'MacMorris? MacMorris?' Herald queried. 'What kind o' name is that fo' a black man?'

Colin tried to move away, but Herald grabbed him by the shirt.

'That you slave name, boy,' he hissed venomously, his face an inch away from Colin's. 'That the name you slave master give you ancestors not so very long ago. An' it been pass down till it reach you. An' you know what? You still a slave, an' you jus' don' know it.'

They stared at each other for a moment, the hiss of Herald's words still reverberating in the air. Then Colin broke away and seemed to shake himself free from Herald's dominance.

'You crazy, man,' he cried.

Herald erupted with a roar of triumph. 'At last. That more like it. That sound like a black man talkin'.'

For a second, Wayne thought his brother was going to strike Herald. Then he seemed to get himself under control and turned to Wayne. 'I'll go and get the car. I'll be back as quick as I can.'

'Right,' said Wayne.

On the surface, Colin appeared calm and confident again, trying to convey to Wayne assurance and brotherly concern, but underneath Wayne sensed that Colin was feeling hurt and battered.

He couldn't understand why Herald had treated his brother that way and said the things he had said. Wayne was very sorry for him, and then was surprised at himself for having that feeling. He had never imagined he would ever feel that way about his brother.

Perhaps Stella was experiencing something similar because she said, 'Take care now. Them streets is dangerous.'

'I will,' said Colin, and then he was gone. Herald followed him out to bolt the front door behind him.

'That was a bit strong, wasn't it?' Alan commented when Herald returned.

'Well, 'e got a lot to learn,' Herald explained. ' 'E 'ad it so easy all 'is life. 'E t'ink 'e know everyt'in', an' yet 'e don' even know 'e born. I jus' want to shake 'im up a bit. 'E too please wit' 'imself fo' 'is own good.'

'There's times when you don' sound none too 'umble,' Stella pointed out dryly.

Herald grinned. 'OK. I takes that. Is true. But at least I knows what I sees when I looks at myself in the mirror, an' I knows first-'and what this society do to someone like me. Them's my credentials. You got any better?'

Stella didn't reply.

After a moment, she said, 'You t'ink 'e gonna be safe out there?'

Herald gave her a mocking smile. 'What you concern 'bout 'im fo'? 'E ain't you boyfriend no more.'

Stella flushed. 'That got not'in' to do wit' it, an' you knows it.'

'OK, OK,' said Herald, laughing. 'I were jus' jokin'. But Colin a big man now — least 'e t'ink 'e is. 'E won' want no woman chasin' after 'im to 'old 'is 'and.'

Stella ignored this jibe. She got up. 'I t'ink I goes an' make sure 'e all right jus' the same,' she said stubbornly.

'If that what you wants,' said Herald. He rose wearily to his feet. 'I'll let you out.'

When they had gone, Desmond went across to Wayne. 'You gonna be 'ome soon. You gonna be all right.'

'Yeah,' said Wayne and he grinned.

He gave up worrying about Colin and Herald and the argument that had gone on between them. He even forgot about his head and the weariness of his body. The idea of home grew warm inside him. His brother had gone to get the car. How long would it take him? Half an hour at the most. Then another half an hour for the journey — or less. He would be home within the hour. Wayne hugged the thought to him. Within an hour he would be safe.

Chapter 12

Colin blundered into the street. He stood for a moment staring with anger at the block of houses with their boarded-up windows silhouetted against the night sky. Who did Herald think he was, talking to him like that?

Then he turned and strode through the darkness, past the walls of corrugated metal sheeting, back to civilisation. Though even here, in the streets where the houses were still inhabited, many of the street lights had been smashed, and the roadway was littered with rubble as if a flood had swept through abandoning its debris in its path.

His mind was in turmoil. He felt bruised and insulted. It wasn't true that he was trying to behave like a white man or that he had the mind of a slave or any of the other things Herald had said. What was wrong with working hard at school, going to university and getting a good job? It was fine for Herald to sneer — loafing about on social security, living in that beat-up house. Well, that wasn't the life Colin wanted for himself.

All right, it was true that Colin had stuck to his books, and Herald had learned the hard facts of life through his own experience. But that didn't mean that Colin was totally ignorant. He knew about black men trying to be white and about slave names. He knew about racism and prejudice. It was all part of his sociology course. Just because he didn't make a great fuss about it didn't mean he didn't know they existed. Herald thought he was so superior, but what had he achieved? Nothing.

All this time, Colin had been easing his way steadily but cautiously through the streets. As he came to each corner, he slowed down and edged round, keeping a close look-out for lurking policemen or cruising panda cars. The streets weren't empty. There were people scurrying to get to the safety of their homes. There were groups of youths, urgent and intent on their own business, prowling in the shadows.

He started and became wary every time a figure approached him or a shape emerged out of the darkness. He had to admit he was afraid walking through the streets like this alone. A shiver ran through him in spite of the warm evening air. He felt the sweat on his back and his shirt sticking to it — his new silk shirt that he had put on specially for Jenny.

What a long time ago that seemed, he thought bitterly. How had he got himself into this mess? He had seen how angry and violent the police had become. It wouldn't just be a case of stopping and searching him if they caught him now.

There was a shout behind him, and he heard his name called out. He felt a sudden jab of fear. He stopped and turned round, puzzled and apprehensive. Then Stella caught up with him, smiling and out of breath.

'I wasn' sure if I'd find you,' she said. 'I thought I'd better come wit' you in case there were any problem.'

Colin couldn't decide if he were pleased or not. He was grateful for her company, but did it mean they thought he wasn't capable of walking through the streets on his own? He mumbled something and they set off together.

It had been quite a shock seeing Stella again after two years. She had changed a lot. Then, she had been dumpy with puppy fat. But she had fined down, and now as he cast furtive glances at her, Colin had to admit that she had grown into a rather attractive young woman. When he had moved to Dukesbury and she had left school, their paths hadn't crossed again until now. That hadn't been her fault. Colin remembered with some embarrassment the phone messages she had left that he had ignored. He wondered if Stella remembered them as well. It wasn't something he wanted to talk about.

'I don't know why 'Erald didn't let me get the car on the way back to his place,' he muttered, allowing some of his resentment towards Herald to come out. 'It wouldn't have taken much longer, and it would have saved this walk back.'

Stella gave him a look, and it seemed to Colin that she understood the feelings that lay beneath his words because she said, 'You know, you mustn' blame 'Erald fo' what 'e say. 'E 'ad a 'ard time o' it. It weren't 'is fault 'e get turn out by 'is folks. They jus' belong to a different generation. They don' understand what life like fo' the yout' today.'

Colin listened, but he didn't make any comment.

'An' 'e 'ad it 'ard wit' the police too,' Stella continued. 'I knows 'e treats you rough, but 'e been t'rough it all, so that make 'im feel 'e 'as a right to speak the way 'e do, don' it?'

She looked at him questioningly, but Colin refused to meet her eyes and stared straight ahead.

' 'Erald's changed,' he said. 'At school he was always getting into trouble for not doing any work and playing about. Now he's more serious. I never knew him to read a book.'

' 'E change in some ways an' not in others,' said Stella. ' 'E jus' a natural rebel. 'E not prepare to accept what people tells 'im jus' because they says it.'

'You're different too.'

Colin remembered a time when Stella had become all tearful and petulant because some of her friends told her — incorrectly — that he was going out with another girl. He couldn't imagine her behaving like that now.

'That ain't so strange,' Stella said, turning to him with a smile whose meaning was difficult to decipher. 'It what they calls growin' up, innit?'

By now they were coming dangerously close to the High

Street. They could see it brightly illuminated at the end of the narrow road into which they had emerged. There was a blur of traffic — police cars and vans with their lights whirling and their sirens wailing. Colin didn't want to get involved in that.

They turned down a side street running parallel to the High Street and crab-like, moving up and then left, edged their way to where he had left the car.

Thinking about it later, Colin realised that he should have been prepared for what he found. There had been signs and warnings all along the road that he had noticed but ignored.

Now, standing beside the car, all he could do was gaze at it with horror. The windows had been smashed in, the tyres had been slashed, and it looked as though someone had been dancing on the bonnet and the roof in hob-nailed boots.

'Blast man,' Stella said. 'I'm sorry.'

She put her hand on Colin's arm, but he shrugged it away.

What would his mother say when he told her? It was her car. She needed it for her work. She would murder him when she found out. He tried to comfort himself by assuming that the car was insured and she would get the money for it. But was it insured for this kind of thing? It wasn't as if this were an act of God. It was the act of hooligans out to destroy.

He fingered a piece of jagged glass still fixed to the window frame and worked it loose. He felt near to tears. He looked inside. They had even ripped out the car radio. With a sob, he kicked savagely at the hub on one of the wheels and slumped round with his back against the bodywork. Why had they done this to him? He was on their side against injustice and police harassment, wasn't he?

'Ain't not'in' we can do 'bout it,' said Stella sadly.

Colin rounded on her. 'It's easy for you to talk, isn't it? It's not your car.'

Stella stiffened, and her voice became harder. 'All right,

so you car been mash up, and I's sorry 'bout it, but that ain't no reason to take it out on me.'

Colin mumbled an apology,

'Look, Col,' Stella went on more urgently, 'you don' know the world you livin' in.'

She paused for a moment. 'I remembers once seein' a Rolls Royce parked by the kerb, an' I looks at it an' I t'inks, God that's beautiful. It was a shiny gold colour an' 'ad 'uge leather seats inside. Then a crowd o' other kids comes along — poor kids jus' like me – an' starts gawpin' at it, an' one o' 'em takes out a nail-file an' runs it 'ard an' deep the full length o' the car. I was 'orrified at the time an' yells out to 'im to stop it. But now, I understands why 'e done it. Don' you?'

Frankly, Colin didn't. He saw no connection between Stella's story and what had happened to his mother's car. All he knew was that the car was a wreck.

'What am I going to do about Wayne now?' he asked.

'Ain't you father still in Balaclava Road?' Stella asked. 'You could take Wayne there.'

The idea did not appeal to Colin, but there seemed to be no alternative unless they were to walk back to Dukesbury, and he was sure that Wayne wouldn't be up to that.

'We better go back an' tell the others,' said Stella.

With a final despairing look at the car, Colin turned and followed Stella back the way they had come.

There seemed to be more people in the streets now. They were moving with a greater furtiveness and urgency. There was a tension and a sense of danger brewing. An ominous rumbling like distant thunder filled the air. It was getting louder and then going soft again like someone playing with the volume control of a transistor.

'I t'ink it start again,' said Stella. 'We better 'urry.'

By the time they reached Ladysmith Road, the noise was all around them. Running figures bumped into them and shoved them out of the way. The top end of the road, in the direction of the High Street, was dark with people.

Stella grabbed a boy by the arm as he passed. The boy

turned on her, snarling, and pulled back, but before he could break away, Stella was able to ask him what was going on.

'The bull movin' in,' the boy explained, gazing back anxiously up the street. 'They brung in reinforcements. They tryin' to clear the 'ole area. I'd get back to you yard if I was you.' Then he was off again down the street.

Yes, Colin thought, that was fine advice. But how did he get back home?

Not all of the people were running for it. A crowd of people had gathered alongside the corrugated sheeting that lined the derelict street. They were jumping at it, climbing it, dragging it down. Whole sections of it gave way underneath their efforts. They were carried away to be used as shields or to be thrown at the police.

The area thus exposed was a treasure trove of bricks and rubble. There were whoops of delight and triumph as this new supply of ammunition was raided. Some of the boys scurried backwards and forwards accumulating piles of broken masonry in conveniently sited places. Others marched in purposefully, lifted a brick in each hand, and turned back to the battle.

But it was not going well. Colin could sense this as the mob was pressed back towards them. More people were breaking away and making their escape. Over the heads of the crowd, he could see the shields and helmets of the police and beyond that the flashing lights of their vans. The boys behind their corrugated sheets with their hoardes of missiles would delay the advance for a while, but it wouldn't be long before the police reached Herald's squat.

'We better warn 'em,' said Stella.

'We've got to get Wayne out,' said Colin.

They joined the increasing number of people fleeing down the street. But then as they reached a turning to the right, Stella came to a full stop in the middle of the road so suddenly that Colin collided into her. The crowd was pouring into the side street. The last section of Ladysmith Road lying straight ahead of them was empty.

'I jus' remembers,' Stella cried with horror.

Colin remembered too. Ladysmith Road ended as a cul-de-sac. Beyond it was the railway. If they went down there, they would be trapped.

For one desperate moment, Colin wanted to seize Stella by the arm and drag her along with the others down the side street to safety. But there was Wayne. He couldn't just leave him there.

'We've got to get them out,' he yelled. 'There's no time to lose.'

They broke away from the mob and raced to Herald's house. As they banged violently at the door, Colin stared anxiously back up the road. The police were advancing. There was no doubt about it. Before long they would have pushed the crowd round the right turn or have them cornered in the cul-de-sac. They would be certain to search the houses to make sure no one was hiding in them. They would know they were derelict.

Colin battered on the door again. He was getting frantic. What was the matter with them? Why didn't they answer? Had they all gone to sleep? He didn't want to be caught by the police, did he?

But then the idea flashed into his mind that it was probably already too late. By the time he got Wayne out, the police could have reached the corner, and there would be no way of escape. As this despairing thought sank in on him, he heard the bolts being pulled back.

Herald's face appeared. With a hurried look, he took in Stella and Colin and the confused fighting going on higher up the street.

'You gotta get out, man,' Stella cried.

'Get Wayne,' Colin said. 'Bring him down. While there's still time.'

But Herald seemed not to hear them. He took Stella's arm and drew her into the house. Then Colin felt himself being pulled in as well. He was so surprised that he made no resistance. But when he realised what was happening, he began to protest. 'Are you crazy, man? I don't want to be trapped.'

124

Again Herald paid no attention. He was busy ramming the bolts home. What light there was in the street was blocked out. He hadn't brought the lamp with him. Out of the blackness came his voice, calm and decisive. 'Ain't no use gettin' mix up wit' that mob. We get caught fo' sure.'

Colin felt Herald's hand on his arm as he moved round him and then heard the pad of his trainers on the stairs followed by Stella. He began to climb after them as best he could, blundering forward and feeling his way until he reached the stairs and then inching himself upwards on all fours. It was just typical, he fumed to himself — Herald, certain of himself as ever, knowing his way round from long habit, striding up with confident step, while he, Colin, struggled in the dark, groping with his fingers to prevent himself from falling headlong through one of the gaps the vandals had made in the house.

And all the time, the noise from outside of the crowd and the police was growing louder. It was getting nearer.

A door opened upstairs, and a weak sliver of light aided Colin up the last remaining steps. The others were still there. By now, they too had heard the rumbling and the roaring like the groundswell of an earthquake. Colin was amazed that the whole house wasn't shaking with it. Alan and Stella were looking anxiously at Herald for a lead as to what to do next. Wayne and Desmond were sitting together on the mattress as though to protect each other — though from the worried and frightened expressions on both their faces, it was difficult to tell which of them was supposed to be doing the protecting.

Before anyone could say or do anything, there was a thunderous thudding at the door downstairs. They all froze. Only their eyes moved, searching each other out anxiously and questioningly. There was no way of knowing whether the knocking was an appeal for refuge from a desperate rioter or the police.

Then, as the banging on the door was repeated even more urgently, Herald acted. He picked up a shoulder bag — Colin wondered cynically if he kept it ready packed for just such an emergency. He strode to the window and yanked it open.

'Come on,' he said. 'We go this way.'

He threw his leg over the sill, twisted round and grasped the sill with his hands, and then vanished into the darkness. Colin watched aghast. He waited to hear the shriek as Herald hit the ground and broke his ankles. But there was no sound. Instead, Herald's head bobbed back into view just above the sill.

'There's an out'ouse 'ere,' Herald explained. 'Once on that it easy to get to the ground. Come on.'

Alan and Stella prepared to follow him while Colin went over to his brother.

'Are you all right?' he asked.

'Yeah,' Wayne replied.

Colin wasn't so sure. His brother's face looked drawn and exhausted. When he tried to get up, he staggered, and Desmond had to help him. Colin hoped that whatever escape route Herald had planned for them wasn't going to prove too much for Wayne.

Alan and Stella had already disappeared through the window. The noise from downstairs was continuing, but now it was rhythmic and repeated. It sounded as though they were trying to ram the door down.

Colin put his arm round Wayne and drew him to the window. If he hadn't done that, he felt that Wayne would have collapsed. A strange tenderness for his brother swept through him — a tenderness he hadn't experienced before. He was concerned for him, worried about how ill he was, determined to get him to safety. Perhaps there was something in what his mother had said after all. Wayne was his flesh and blood, but he was realising it now as though for the first time.

'I'll 'elp 'im,' said Desmond, sitting astride the window sill. 'I'll guide 'is legs.' Then he was gone.

Colin leaned Wayne against the sill and hooked one of his legs over. It was as though Wayne had no power over his own limbs. It was as though he were drunk. Colin eased

Wayne's other leg over and began to lower him, holding on to his waist.

'It all right,' Desmond called from outside. 'I got 'im.'

Colin felt the weight of Wayne's body taken from him and heard a kind of scrunch below. His brother must have landed safely.

He was just about to follow when he noticed the lamp. If it were the police trying to break in below — and it sounded more and more like it from the determined thudding that was going on — they would know from the lighted lamp that someone had been there recently. He strode across the room and turned the wick down. The light gave a few feeble spurts and then went out.

At the same moment, there was a shuddering wrench from below and what seemed like a cheer of triumph. The door must have come off its hinges.

Colin made a bolt for the window. He blessed Herald for not having any furniture that could trip him up. He swung himself over the sill and stretched himself down until his feet touched the roof of the outhouse.

The others had already reached the ground. Colin worked his way along the roof and shinned down a pipe at the end to join them.

'Say, man,' Herald observed. 'You good at this. I forget 'bout the light.'

Colin could sense that Herald was smilling. For a moment, he was absurdly pleased by the praise. He almost said, 'Ain't not'in', man', but he refrained. Before he could explain to himself why, Herald was talking again, telling them what they were going to do next.

'The railway down there,' he was saying, pointing to what was presumably the bottom of the garden, 'so that ain't no good. What we gotta do, we gotta go cross country, climb t'rough every garden in 'Illsden till we reaches a nice quiet road where there ain't no police.'

Without waiting for anyone's opinion on the plan, he turned and led the way. So the long trek began.

They went down to the bottom of the garden — or what

had once been the garden. Now it was a jungle of long tangled grass that made them lift their feet at each step and sway from side to side as though wading through water. Colin was last and followed in the wake left by the others. Wayne was just ahead. Desmond had his arm around his waist to support him. There were noises from the house, but Colin didn't look back.

At the end of the garden, they came to a fence. Over it, Colin could see the sheer drop to the railway line. Herald was already working away at the fence to the next garden. The wooden slats were rotten and uneven. Some had already collapsed or disintegrated. It was easy for Herald to drag enough away to make a gap. He thrust his way through.

The next garden was even more overgrown. Bushes and creepers fought with each other for every inch of space. Herald beat a path through. Even so, Colin felt fronds and branches pulling and plucking at his clothes and slapping against his head. Something caught his arm. There was a sudden sharp needle of pain and the sound of tearing. A briar had ripped the sleeve of his shirt and scratched his arm. Colin cursed and struggled to keep up with the others.

He lost count of how many gardens they crossed, pulling holes in the fences or clambering over them, hacking and ploughing their way through undergrowth that had been left to run wild for years. Was this what the world was like before man, Colin wondered, as he staggered on. Wayne seemed to be coping all right with Desmond's help, so that was something.

Eventually, they came to the gardens of houses that were still occupied. Here the problem was not trailing through long grass that tried to trip you up or avoiding brambles that tried to lacerate you or throttle you or branches that tried to poke your eye out. It was making sure that your presence and your advance remained secret from the people in the houses. The fences were in better condition here too and sometimes there were dividing brick walls. They had to give each other a bunk and a hand over. Colin, being last, always seemed to have to clamber over as best he could.

There were other hazards too. Although no dogs actually sniffed them out and attacked them, they seemed to sense the presence of intruders and set up a yapping and a yowling that spread from house to house as the group passed.

In one garden, they were halfway across when Herald suddenly turned round, collided with the others and sent them all sprawling into the shadows. There was the gurgling of an outside toilet being flushed, and then a shaft of light as a man emerged, zipping up his trousers, A second beam of light spread out into the garden as he opened the kitchen door. When it had closed, they went on.

Another time, a woman at a lighted first-floor window must have noticed some noise or some movement. She jerked up the window and leaned out. 'What you doin' there?' she yelled. 'If you don' clear out, I calls the police.' She stared threateningly out at the garden.

Colin heard Herald splutter with laughter and then his mock terrified voice calling, 'Don' do that, man, please. I goin'.'

And so they climbed yet another fence.

Colin began to wonder whether Herald knew what he was at. Did he have any idea where he was going? Perhaps he ought to have brought his compass for this night safari. Or did he have one in his ready-packed shoulder bag?

At one point, Colin was able to have a quick word with his brother. He was looking tired and bleary, but he was bearing up well.

' 'E doin' all right,' said Desmond encouragingly.

And then they climbed another wall and unexpectedly found themselves in a street. Colin was taken aback by the suddenness of it. He had become so used to the routine of struggling over fences, skulking through gardens, that he was expecting it to go on for ever. Now that it was over, he was puzzled about what they were going to do next.

The street was quiet and dimly lit. From the distance came the steady chanting of voices and the whining of police sirens. But it seemed a long way off. There was no one else in the street. Colin vaguely recognised it as one of those leading to the Club.

The others seemed as lost as Colin. They gazed about them curiously, trying to take their bearings, and then they broke out cheerfully with their congratulations to Herald.

'Great,' said Alan, slapping him on the back.

'Yeah,' said Stella with a big smile, 'a great operation.'

Colin knew he should add his praise as well. If it hadn't been for Herald, they would probably be sitting bruised and battered in the police cells right now. But he couldn't bring himself to do it. It rankled with him that it should be Herald who was the leader, that it was Herald who was getting all the congratulations — Herald who had left school with nothing and who had no prospects. Mingled with his resentment was an unexpected jab of envy.

Instead, Colin began to tidy himself up, brushing some of the grass seed and dirt off his trousers.

'What do we do now?' he asked. It came out almost as a challenge.

Herald held him with a steady gaze. 'I don' know. You suppose to be the brains.'

Colin looked away first. He had the feeling that Herald was taunting him. 'I could take Wayne to the father,' he said, bringing up the idea he had been trying to avoid.

'In Balaclava Road?' Herald asked contemptuously, as though he could scarcely believe that Colin was so stupid. 'Don' you 'ear that noise?' he went on, jerking his head in its direction. 'That where that come from — all round Balaclava Road. It swarmin' wit' bull. No way you gonna get t'rough that lot wit'out you get in more trouble.'

Colin felt put in his place.

'You can come back to my yard,' said Desmond. Then he added, 'Though I don' know what my mum gonna say,' as though suddenly regretting his generous impulse. 'I gonna get it anyway fo' stayin' out so late.'

'Where that?' Herald demanded.

'Mafeking Road.'

'Yeah, that OK. That ought to be quiet.'

There seemed to be nothing else for it. 'All right, Wayne?' Colin asked.

'Sure,' his brother replied. He looked as though he were asleep on his feet.

Herald turned to Alan. 'What you gonna do?'

'I can doss down with a friend,' Alan said. 'Don't you worry about me. How about yourself?'

Herald pondered a moment. 'I jus' 'ang around fo' a while an' then I goes back to my yard.'

'Will it be safe?'

'Yeah, later.' He added with a smile, 'All I needs to do is get a new door.'

'I'll come wit' you,' said Stella quickly.

'Sure, man, if that what you wants. You welcome any time.'

For an instant, Colin caught Stella's eye. He wasn't sure what expression he saw there. Whatever it was, he hurriedly turned away before she could observe the jealousy that he knew for sure was burning in his own eyes. And even as he turned away, he acknowledged that he had no right to such feelings. That right had been surrendered two years before, and there was no point in regretting it now.

Herald was gripping Alan's hand firmly in his own. 'Take care, man.'

'Sure,' said Alan, 'You too. See you.'

'Yeah. Later.'

Alan waved to the others and sauntered casually down the street as though there were no possible dangers and all was right with the world.

Herald studied Colin steadily for a moment. 'You better be goin' too case the bullmen changes their mind.'

'Yes, well,' Colin began and struggled with himself. 'Thanks for everything,' he eventually managed to force out.

'Ain't not'in',' commented Herald. There was no false modesty about the statement. It described exactly the way Herald felt.

There were mumbled goodbyes, and Desmond set off down the road with Colin and Wayne in tow. Colin had a last fleeting impression of Herald and Stella together, standing close, sharing an intimacy that he couldn't enter into.

There were no problems getting to Desmond's house. The streets in this part of Hillsden were deserted. If there had been any disturbances, they were long over, though the signs of them were still strewn everywhere — shattered glass, bricks and rubble, wrecked cars.

Outside the door, Desmond apologised in an embarrassed way for having to ring the bell. His mother wouldn't let him have a key, he explained.

Her first words when she opened the door were, 'Where you been?' in a voice that would have sunk a battleship. Then she saw the others and stopped.

'Wayne an' 'is brother can' get 'ome,' Desmond pleaded. 'Can they stay 'ere the night?'

Mrs Henry softened immediately. 'Sure they can. Come on in.'

Desmond shot Colin and Wayne a look of relief and they followed Mrs Henry into the house. Meanwhile, she maintained a stream of complaints. 'I don' know what the world comin' to. There been gangs o' kids rampagin' up an' down the street an' police an' God knows what. They been 'urlin' rocks at each other an' fightin' an' 'busin' each other a way it ain't fit fo' a God-fearin' person to 'ear.'

She fixed her son with a stern look. 'You ain't been mix up in all this, 'as you?'

'Naw, mum,' Desmond replied as though shocked that she should even think such a thing.

'That all right then,' said Mrs Henry, satisfied that her son was innocent. And she made no further references to the disturbances.

Colin sank into one of the armchairs in the living room and felt the relief flowing through his limbs. Without being asked, Mrs Henry made them some coffee and produced some home-made cake. Colin discovered he was famished, and ate three slices before realising it. Desmond and Wayne devoured the rest.

When Mrs Henry was clearing the things away, she eyed the empty cake plate with interest. 'Hm,' she observed. 'Nice to know you still got appetites.'

Colin suddenly remembered his own mother. He ought to ring her and let her know everything was all right. She would be worried sick. But when he asked Mrs Henry if he could use the phone, she rounded on him. 'Phone?' she exclaimed, scandalised. 'Ain't got no phone. I 'as it disconnect. I ain't payin' no bills so's other folk can use the phone all day long.' She cast an accusing stare at her son. Desmond shrivelled up in his seat.

So that was that. His mother would have to go on worrying until the morning. He ought to be able to make contact with her then and let her know all was well.

'Desmond,' Mrs Henry commanded. 'Time you was in bed.'

'Yeah, mum,' Desmond responded, resigned. He said his goodnights and slunk off to his room.

'Now I don' know 'ow you boys gonna manage,' Mrs Henry continued in a gentler tone. 'Ain't got but two beds. There the sofa 'ere an' the chairs. I guess you won' need no blankets in this 'eat.'

Colin remembered his responsibilities as the older brother. 'That's fine, Mrs Henry. Don't you worry. We'll manage all right.'

When she had gone, Colin went and sat on the sofa beside his brother. 'How are you feeling?' he asked.

'I'm all right,' said Wayne, 'I'm jus' feelin' tired.'

'How's your head?'

Wayne touched the bump gingerly with the tips of his fingers. 'It don' feel too bad.'

'Good,' said Colin. 'Stretch out on the sofa. What you need is some sleep.'

Wayne did what he was told and closed his eyes. Before turning out the light, Colin took a last look at him. It wasn't like him to be so meek and docile. He must still be suffering from the effects of the blow. Somehow, he looked smaller, sunk into the hollow of the sofa — so young and helpless. He seemed to be already asleep, his chest heaving evenly, his face relaxed. His mouth had dropped open, and Colin noticed as though for the first time the rim of pink that showed inside his lower lip.

He switched off the light and groped his way to an armchair. He tried to settle himself into a comfortable position so that he could sleep. But his mind was choked and clogged with impressions of the evening's events that he couldn't absorb — the deputation to the police, the clubbing down of his brother, the argument with Herald, the wrecking of the car, the escape through the gardens.

All of them whirled round and round in his head as he attempted to make sense of them. What did he think? What was his position? Where did he stand in all this? It was as though he had been scooped up on a great tidal wave out of his safe secure existence and cast down amid chaos. Once, he had known where he was going and his whole life was planned ahead of him. Now, he didn't know where he was or what to think.

But amidst the turmoil of thoughts and impressions and memories that flooded and confused his mind, one conviction grew stronger and stronger. He wasn't sure that Wayne had been right, but at least he had tried. At least he had stood up and been counted, part of the crowd who screamed their protest at the police and at society for their treatment of people who were black.

Colin felt a sense of shame sink into him at having left it to his younger brother. It suddenly came to him that he had been wrapped up in his own little world, blind to what had been going on all around him. He thrust his back into the armchair and pressed his lips firmly together. Now it was up to him to do something about it.

Suddenly, he was sleeping.

Chapter 13

When Wayne woke next morning, he couldn't understand at first where he was. He expected to be back at home in his own bed, but when he opened his eyes it was obvious that that wasn't the case. From the dim light seeping through the curtains, he gradually made out the furniture and recognised it. He was at Desmond's. But why was that? Colin was supposed to get the car and take him home. Why hadn't that happened?

Then bit by bit, it all returned to him — the hammering on the door, the climb from the window, the trek from garden to garden, the arrival at Desmond's. It was all like a dream. He could remember all these things happening and yet he couldn't remember actually being physically involved. It was as though he had floated through them.

He examined the bump on the back of his head with his fingers. It felt all right. In fact, he had slept well, and the sleep had done him good. His head was clear, and something of his old vitality had come back to him.

That was a relief at least. Feeling so weak and shaky had been a shock to him. It had been scary. There had been times when he had wondered if he was going to survive. Now it looked as though it was going to be all right.

But there was still one mystery. What had happened to the car? Why hadn't Colin brought it as he promised?

There was Colin, sprawled out in an armchair, his legs spread out and his head bent at an awkward angle. He looked very uncomfortable, but he was still asleep.

The sound of movement and the smell of coffee drifted into the room. Wayne discovered that he was extraordinarily hungry. There had been Mrs Henry's cake the night before, but that seemed to have had no effect in filling the gap in his stomach. He was delighted when the door opened and Mrs Henry came bustling in.

' 'Ow you sleep?' she asked cheerfully as she drew the curtains.

'Fine,' Wayne replied.

Colin was just beginning to come to, stretching his legs and pulling a face as though every muscle in his body had become stiff.

'Breakfast ready soon,' Mrs Henry informed them with a smile as she went out again.

Wayne stole a quick glance at his brother and then looked away. He felt he ought to apologise for getting him into this mess. What was more, he realised that he genuinely wanted to apologise.

'I'm sorry fo' stayin' away like that,' he mumbled. 'If it 'adn't been fo' me I don' suppose you would 'ave been mix up in all this.'

'That's all right,' said Colin, and Wayne was suprised at how mild his voice was. 'We'll soon get you back home, and it will be as though nothing had ever happened.'

Wayne wasn't so sure about that. He had a feeling that nothing would ever be the same again.

'Yeah,' he said, 'this time you can get the car, an' we be 'ome in no time.'

'I can't get the car,' Colin explained sombrely. 'Someone wrecked it. It's a write-off.'

Wayne gazed horrified at his brother. Here was something else he would get the blame for.

'I don't know what Mum's going to say when she finds out,' Colin continued gloomily.

The mention of their mother suddenly pricked Wayne's conscience. ' 'Ow is she?'

Colin put on one of his deliberately pompous voices. 'At the last time of contact, she was in a state that could be described as bordering on the hysterical because of lack of information about the whereabouts of her younger son.' Then he resumed his normal voice and said with relish, 'God, she's going to give you lashes when she gets you.'

Wayne giggled happily. He knew his brother was joking — at least he was almost certain he was. That was something that was different. He couldn't remember them talking in this familiar and friendly way before. The sense of rivalry and resentment between them was gone.

Mrs Henry called them into the kitchen to eat. They had bacon and eggs, and then Wayne had four slices of toast smothered in butter and marmalade. Mrs Henry watched him eat with chuckling delight and pressed another slice on him. Wayne thought he had better refuse.

'Nice to know someone appreciate you momma food,' she said with a sniff towards her son.

Desmond blew out his lips and raised his eyes to the ceiling, but he was careful to do it when his mother had turned away.

They thanked Mrs Henry and Desmond for their help and said their goodbyes. Desmond went with them to the door.

'I gonna get down to some studyin' today,' he said. 'Those exams ain't gonna go away, you know.'

Wayne had forgotten all about the exams. There would be so much to catch up on.

Then they were out of the house and walking along Mafeking Road.

Colin had it all planned out. There was no point in going to get a bus home. Quite likely the High Street was still blocked off and no buses were running. There was no point in going to a phone box and ringing their mother to let her know they were all right. They would all have been vandalised, and anyway she no longer had a car she could use to get them home. The only thing to do was to go to their father's house. They could phone their mother from there, and their father could drive them home.

Wayne knew what Colin's feelings about their father were. He wasn't exactly looking forward to meeting him again himself. The last time, in the market, hadn't been particularly friendly. But there seemed no other way.

It was Sunday morning, quiet and dozy like most Sunday mornings, but otherwise utterly different. For the first time, Wayne saw clearly the debris and destruction left behind by the riots — the smashed windows, the rubble in the streets, the burnt out skeletons of cars. Instead of strolling casually in vests and slippers to get the Sunday papers, the people they saw were gazing in awe at the damage. They looked like sight-seers or reporters from the way they were ogling the wrecked shops and calculating the cost.

There was no need to go by the High Street, but they did so out of curiosity. Most of the shop fronts had been boarded up, and men were already at work providing protection for others. The Queen's Arms was blackened with smoke. The roof was still on, so the firemen must have done a good job, but inside, it was a shell of charred beams.

Gazing at it, Wayne couldn't tell whether he felt appalled or elated. He had been there when it had been attacked and set on fire. He had been one of those fighting against racism. Perhaps it would be something to remember.

There were still plenty of policemen around, standing in groups, keeping a wary eye on everything around them. Wayne thought they looked nervous and jittery, expecting another attack and not quite knowing where it would come from. But they paid little attention to him and his brother, and nobody tried to stop them.

There were the same signs of destruction all the way down Balaclava Road — bottles and flower pots smashed in the gutter, rocks strewing the pavement, cars with their windows shattered or their tyres slashed, or both. Nothing seemed to have been spared, though whether all the damage had been done by the rioters or by the police it was impossible to tell.

In spite of it all, it was still a relief to be there and to be standing in front of that familiar door waiting for their father to answer their ring.

When the door was eventually opened, it was clear that their father was not exactly pleased to see them. He scowled at them as though they were strangers and barked at them, 'What you want?' Then before they could answer, he sucked his teeth impatiently and said, 'Aw, come in, come in.'

They followed him into the kitchen where Helen was still sitting at the table over a cup of tea. She gave them a bored look which become more pained as Mr MacMorris went on.

'I don' know what goin' on las' night, but all 'ell break loose. What wit' kids bawlin' they 'eads off an' chasin' up an' down the street an' police breakin' the door down an' demandin' to search the place I didn' get no wink o' sleep. A man can' call 'is 'ouse 'is 'ome no more.'

'I 'ears you sleepin' plenty,' Helen remarked complacently. 'You was snorin' loud 'nough to wake the 'ole street.'

'I don' snore,' Mr MacMorris retorted indignantly.

Wayne knew these moods of his father's. When he was in them, he was angry with the whole world and no one could do or say anything right. They couldn't have picked a worse time to call. Even as he heard his brother explain why they had come, he knew there was going to be trouble.

'That right, innit?' Mr MacMorris sneered at Colin. 'I notices you only comes to you Dad when you wants 'elp. Well, I ain't gettin' no car out. It in the garage, an' it stay in the garage. 'Ave you seen what 'appen to 'em cars in the street? 'Ave you seen 'em? All mash up an' wort' not'in' even as scrap. Well, I ain't riskin' that wit' my car. I needs that car fo' my livin' an' it stay in that garage till I knows it safe to to bring it out.'

'How are we going to get home then?' Colin asked, his voice becoming more belligerent.

' 'Ome! 'Ome!' Mr MacMorris demanded. 'Ain't this 'ome too? There a place 'ere you can sleep. An' if you don' like that you can walk.'

139

Helen began to shift uneasily in her seat at the suggestion that Colin and Wayne should stay there. She opened her mouth to make some protest or objection, but before she could get any words out, Mr MacMorris had rounded on her.

'An' don' you poke you nose in my family business. You keep you mout' shut.'

They glared at each other for a moment, and it was Helen who looked away with tight lips.

'Is it all right if we phone Mum then?' Colin asked. His voice was calm, but Wayne knew it was taking a lot of effort for him to restrain himself.

'Sure, if that what you wants to do,' said their father airily. 'I won' make no charge.'

Wayne felt his own anger mounting. What kind of father was it that could make a sneer like that when his sons needed help? Colin was still in control. Without making any reply, he went into the hall to phone.

Wayne knew his father's eyes were burning into him, but he kept his own eyes averted. He could hear part of what Colin was saying on the phone. He tried to imagine how his mother was taking it. She was probably in tears. He wanted to laugh at her weakness, but instead he felt tears welling up in his own eyes. It was the frustration of it all, he told himself. To have come so near the end of the journey and then to land smack into the wall of his father's obstinacy.

Phoning their mother wasn't going to solve things either. There was still the problem of transport. Perhaps she would be able to get a taxi or a mini-cab. If she couldn't, then Wayne was quite determined to take up his father's suggestion and walk. He would rather do that than stay here.

He was growing nervous and sullen under his father's piercing scrutiny. If he wasn't careful, he wouldn't be able to hold out and he would erupt with some unforgivable insult. If only Colin would hurry up and come back. What was keeping him? But then he supposed his brother had a lot to tell, and his mother would want to know everything straightaway.

140

At last there was the tinkle of the receiver being put down, and Colin returned. His first words dispelled Wayne's worries about how they were going to get home.

'Aunt Elma and Uncle Neville are coming in their car,' he announced.

Their father's reaction was to snort with contempt. 'Huh! I might 'ave knowed they'd come interferin'. That Elma t'ink she know everyt'in' 'bout everyt'in'. She so sure-sure. An' that Neville press down under 'er t'umb so 'ard 'e can' 'ardly move. 'E ain't no man no more. 'E can' even give 'er no child.'

Colin didn't respond to the baiting. He just sat down and stared blankly in front of him as though he had more important things to think about. Wayne could see that this infuriated their father even more than any defence of Aunt Elma and Uncle Neville could have done.

The waiting was awful. It was all right for Colin. He had already made it clear what his position was. But Wayne could remember how often his father had been kind to him, and what fun he had been to be with. He hated to see his father like this. The only thing to do was to pretend he wasn't there, like Colin, and to make sure he didn't catch his father's eye.

Mr MacMorris went on making comments about Aunt Elma and Uncle Neville, but nobody was listening, and gradually he gave up. He seemed lost without an audience that would stand up and fight him.

The phone rang. Mr MacMorris knocked his chair back with a curse and went to answer it. They could hear his voice in the hall raised in heated argument. When he returned, he complained resentfully, 'There another pupil gone an' cancel 'is lesson. An' it all the fault o' you an' the yout' fo' causin' this trouble. 'Ow you expects me to make a livin' when my pupils cancels they lessons all the time?'

'But you says you ain't takin' the car out o' the garage,' Helen pointed out.

'That different,' said Mr MacMorris. 'That my decision. If I cancels a lesson, that one t'ing. But if one o' my pupils cancel it, that quite another. Anyways, I t'ought I told you to keep you nose out o' my business affairs.'

Helen rose slowly to her feet. 'Family affairs, business affairs — I don' wanna know 'bout none o' 'em. This Elma an' Neville comin' 'ere, so I t'ink I goin' fo' a walk case I gets accuse o' pokin' my nose in.' Then she gave Mr MacMorris a withering look and said with emphasis, 'I might jus' come back.'

When she had gone, the silence in the kitchen was deafening. Wayne excused himself and went to the lavatory just to get away from it. He took as long as he could. When he returned, there was no change in the atmosphere. He risked a quick glance at his father. He was still sitting with a disregarded cigarette in his hand. His face was clouded and brooding, and his eyes were staring blankly into space. Wayne hurriedly looked away.

It was a relief when the doorbell rang. Their father went to answer it, and there was a sudden explosion of noise and voices.

Wayne watched the door, waiting for his uncle and aunt to come through. But when the door opened, it was his mother who burst into the room. He was taken completely by surprise. He hadn't expected her to come. He wasn't prepared. He hadn't worked out his story. He hadn't decided how to respond to her anger and recriminations.

But everything seemed to be all right. She was smiling and laughing, although her eyes were gleaming with tears.

'So you all right?' she asked, putting her hand round his neck and stroking his hair.

'Yeah, Mum,' he mumbled. He felt like a baby again and embarrassed about it, but it wasn't altogether unpleasant.

'My, you give us all a fright,' his mother went on. 'Jus' you wait till I gets you 'ome.' But the threat didn't have much force behind it.

She stretched across and patted Colin's head. Then she gave a long drawn out sigh of contentment, sank into a chair and wiped away the tears that were spilling from her eyes.

Aunt Elma and Uncle Neville came in with Mr

MacMorris, and the kitchen was suddenly very crowded. Aunt Elma and Uncle Neville themselves were so big that they took up the space of four people. Then they were all talking at once, and the walls were bouncing with their loud voices. Wayne could only make out the half of it.

'I seen it on television,' Aunt Elma was saying, 'an' I was so shock.'

'I didn' get no wink o' sleep,' Mr MacMorris was claiming.

'I sure is glad I took Elma advice an' move out,' Uncle Neville boomed.

His mother leaned urgently across to Wayne, her face inches from his. 'You wasn't mix up in that trouble, was you?' she demanded.

'No, Mum,' Wayne answered. 'I was wit' Desmond.'

She seemed satisfied. 'That all right then.'

Wayne was relieved. His brother must have given a very edited version of the events of the previous night.

His mother stood up. 'Well, mister,' she said, 'it time we gets you back to you own yard.' She smiled at him and took his arm to lift him to his feet.

Then her manner changed. She turned stiffly to her husband and said, 'Thanks, Gerry. I grateful fo' what you done.'

She put her hand on her husband's shoulder and pecked him on the cheek.

Mr MacMorris laughed. 'Ain't not'in',' he said. 'Them's my boys as well, you know.'

She looked at him very solemnly and nodded her head. 'I know.'

Then she walked with great dignity and with a very straight back out of the room.

The others followed. There was much confusion and argument at the car as to who was going to sit where, and in the end Uncle Neville sat in the front with Aunt Elma who was driving, and Wayne and Colin sat in the back with their mother.

'You got it right this time,' Mr MacMorris called to

Uncle Neville. 'The man always sit in the front.'

He seemed to have recovered his spirits. But as they drove off, Wayne saw him turn back into the house, and the rounded shoulders and the drooping head reminded him that his father was becoming an old man.

On the journey, there was much eager conversation. Colin told about his visit to the police station with Mr Fernandez. Aunt Elma described the terrible things she had seen on television for a second or third time. Uncle Neville wondered what the youth was coming to.

'I'm sorry about the car,' Colin said.

'So am I,' said their mother grimly. Then she softened. 'Well, I guess that jus' life. I can check up on it tomorrow an' see what the insurance situation is. I reckons I can use the bus like everyone else till that problem sorted out.'

She turned to her other son. 'You very quiet, Wayne.' He was sitting in the middle between her and Colin.

'I t'inkin',' he explained.

His mother smiled at him as though she understood what he meant, and he smiled back.

It suddenly struck him that it was the first time he had given his mother a real smile for years — a genuine smile that spoke through the brightness of his eyes and the yielding of his lips and came directly from his heart. His mother didn't seem to notice anything particularly different, but the realisation made Wayne feel sorry for the way he had behaved in the past.

He had told the truth. He was thinking. As the car sped up the main road towards home, all kinds of thoughts and feelings went racing through his head. There was relief, of course, that he would soon be back in the comfort and safety of home. There was nothing like a couple of nights on a makeshift bed wondering where the next meal was coming from to make him appreciate that.

But there was more to it than that. Somehow Herald's way of life and the life of the street didn't seem quite so glamorous and desirable as they had been. Did he really want to spend the rest of his days living from hand to mouth and having no object but passing the time without too much hassle? There had to be more to life than that.

Then there were the other experiences he had been through — the police harassment, the mob fury, the setting fire to the Queen's Arms, the sight of that policeman in flames. He shied away from the last image, but it went on burning in his mind. Sure, black people had their rights and ought to stand up for them, but was this the way to do it? Sure, the police were prejudiced and allowed their prejudice to show in how they treated black people, but did anyone deserve to be set on fire like that policeman? These were questions that it was going to take him a long time to work out.

He remembered what Desmond had said about studying for his exams. They were one of the hard realities of life. They wouldn't go away. They hung over him like a terrifying dark thunder cloud ready to burst and drench him.

And yet, looking at them in another light, wasn't that a way out? Herald had rejected school and exams and qualifications, and look where it had got him. There was no guarantee that if he worked hard and gained some good results that life would turn out any differently for Wayne. He might have already left it too late. But it was worth a try. Wasn't it?

Chapter 14

Colin decided his mother really was amazing. In spite of all the worry she must have had over the past couple of days, first with Wayne and then himself, she had been able to prepare everything for the Sunday family lunch. There it all was in the kitchen waiting for the finishing touches — the roast chicken portions, the rice and peas, the daintily arranged salad, the avocado.

'Food on the table in quarter o' an 'our,' she announced cheerfully.

Colin went upstairs to brush his teeth. He had been able to wash his face at Desmond's, but his mouth felt as though it were lined with that nasty fur that grew on stale cheese. He scrubbed at his teeth until they were fresh and sparkling.

Then he changed his clothes. It was too bad about the silk shirt. He examined the tear in the sleeve hopefully, but there was no way it could be repaired without showing. He dropped the shirt on the bed and sighed. Perhaps that was just part of the price he had to pay.

When he came down again, it was clear that Uncle Neville had had time to prime himself with several glasses of rum. Aunt Elma was looking at him disapprovingly and fanning herself delicately with a folded handkerchief and dabbing at the sweat on her upper lip. Inevitably, the heat reminded her of back home, and she was going into long nostalgic reminiscences that no one was listening to.

The Sunday papers were lying on a side table. Colin picked them up and skimmed through the front pages. There were the same headlines as before screaming about 'Black Rioters'. Was Alan black, or the other white people he had noticed in the crowds, he wondered.

Ah, but the papers explained that later on. Yes, there had been some white people there, but they were extremists leading the blacks on to overturn law and order.

All right, they were extremists. So what? Didn't they have as much right to their point of view as anyone else? And they weren't all extremists, and the blacks didn't need anyone to lead them. They had their own grievances and their own sense of injustice to fire them with anger. They had their own leaders.

There were the same emotional pictures of wounded policemen, holding their heads and lying on stretchers looking bewildered and confused. Was he supposed to feel sorry for them? They got paid well, and they must have known they might have to face hazards like this when they joined up, mustn't they? So why was he supposed to give them his sympathy as well? They must expect a few bumps and bruises. It wasn't as though anyone had been killed or seriously injured.

Anyway, they weren't his police. They weren't there to protect him. They were there to protect 'the fabric of society' and to preserve 'law and order'. Fine phrases. What they meant was to protect and preserve the top people against the masses — and especially against the blacks because there weren't many blacks among the top people. They had seen to that.

At the end of the reports, there were statements about an 'uneasy truce' in the streets and calls for a government inquiry into the disturbances.

Colin threw the papers down. He was surprised at how bitter and angry his reactions were. Had he thought like that yesterday?

Over luch, Aunt Elma went on with her reminiscences.

'D'you remember when we first come 'ere, Rose?' she asked. 'Oh, them was 'ard times.'

'There was good times too,' Mrs MacMorris reminded her.

'Oh, I don' mean between you an' me. I means the difficulty o' findin' a place to live an' the ways folks treats you.'

'I remembers that all right,' said Uncle Neville. 'Won' never forget. Those cards in lodgin' 'ouses sayin' "No Blacks". An' gettin' a friend wit' a white voice to phone up an' arrange a room. Then when you arrives an' they sees you, they all o' a sudden full up. An' goin' in a bar room an' askin' fo' a drink an' the bartender he say yes an' smile an' bring you a drink an' break the glass on the counter. Oh, yes, I won' never forget them days.'

Colin had probably heard it all before, but he was listening now with a newly-awakened alertness. This was what his own parents must have had to put up with as well.

'But times is changed,' his mother said. 'That kind o' t'ing don' 'appen now.'

'On the surface maybe,' Aunt Elma conceded, 'but it jus' the same underneath. Take that trouble in 'Illsden. I was shock by what I seen on television. Shock I tells you. It ain't jus' our black boys an' the way they treats the police, it the way the police treats 'em. The police needles 'em an' chases 'em and persecutes 'em so much, 'ow else they gonna be'ave? What else can they do?'

'But the law is the law,' protested Mrs MacMorris.

'Yeah,' agreed Aunt Elma, 'the law's the law. But if the law's the law, then it got to be the same fo' blacks as it is fo' whites. An' it ain't.'

Aunt Elma picked up a drumstick and examined it to see which part she would sink her teeth into first. But then she put it down and fixed her sister with an accusing stare. 'You says times is changed? You seen the papers? What they sayin'? "Send 'em all back to Jamaica" — that what they all sayin'. "We don' want no blacks 'ere. Give 'em some money so's they can go back to where they belongs an' we can be rid o' 'em".'

'Is true,' said Uncle Neville, shaking his head. 'When I remembers wit' what 'igh 'opes I comes to this land. Why, it were like a dream come true to set foot on the earth o' the Mother Country. An' then to t'ink o' the welcome we gets. Welcome? Huh!'

'Well, they can keep their money,' Aunt Elma continued. 'They don' need give us no money fo' us to go back 'ome. We goin'.'

'But you always says that,' protested Mrs MacMorris. 'Long as I can remember.'

'We means it this time. Don' we, Neville.'

'Yeah, guess that so,' Uncle Neville agreed.

'This country finish as far as I concern. It all mash up. An' what 'ope is there fo' the young people? There ain't no jobs fo' 'em, an' they treated like criminal. If you ax me, this country doin' it best to turn 'em into criminal the way they treatin' 'em. I don' know what kind o' future you boys 'as, but times it make me glad me an' Neville ain't got no children.'

'Hush, Elma,' Mrs MacMorris said. 'Ain't no need to talk that way.'

Uncle Neville studied his plate and forked over the remains of the salad on it. Mrs MacMorris looked from one to the other of her two sons and sighed. Aunt Elma finally selected the fattest part of the drumstick and dug her teeth into it.

As usual on these occasions, Colin and his brother contributed little to the conversation. In these matters, their mother was strict and believed in the old adage of 'speak when you are spoken to'.

Now that attention had been directed on them, Aunt Elma and Uncle Neville went through all the familiar questions about school and exams and what they hoped to do when they left. It was as though his aunt and uncle couldn't remember from one visit to the next what their replies had been. It was kindly meant, but Colin found it embarrassing. And in any case, he had more important things he wanted to think about.

When Wayne had finished eating, he asked his mother if he could leave the table. That surprised Colin for a start. His brother usually got up without asking and had to be told to sit down again.

'I wanna get on wit' my revision,' Wayne explained.

That was another surprise. Colin wondered if he had heard right. Was it just an excuse to get away from Aunt Elma and Uncle Neville? Or had the bump on the head affected him more than he thought? Their mother was also staring at Wayne as though she couldn't believe her ears. Here he was suggesting studying without a word of nagging or insistence from her.

'Yes, of course,' she said at last.

Shortly afterwards, Colin too excused himself and went to his room. There were no sounds coming from his brother's bedroom — not even his transistor at its lowest volume. Colin put his ear to the door to make sure. There was something there. A faint grunting sound. He carefully opened the door and peered round.

Wayne was lying on the bed. His eyes were closed and his chest was rising and falling rhythmically. Every now and then, his breathing thickened into a quiet snore. A book lay abandoned by his side.

So much for good intentions, Colin thought. And yet, he couldn't help smiling with affection. After all, it wasn't surprising. Wayne had had a rough time, and big helpings of their mother's cooking had finished him off. The sleep would do him good. There was plenty of time to catch up later. He had his whole life ahead of him.

Colin slipped out, closing the door behind him.

In his own bedroom, his books were spread out on his table as he had left them. He studied the revision time-table taped to the mirror. He wasn't too far behind. He had only missed that morning's session as the previous evening had been reserved for going to the disco with Jenny.

The thought of her hurt him as he remembered their last

conversation, but the pain was beginning to fade — he was amazed at how quickly. He was sure once she had got over her outburst, she would have spent the evening on some extra revision. There was something cold and ruthless about her, he realised. She had the kind of determination that nothing could deflect or interfere with. If he were to go across to her now and say, 'I'm sorry about last night. Why don't we go to the disco tonight instead', she would probably reply, 'No, thank you. It's not on my schedule.'

He sighed and turned to the books he had planned to revise that morning. For some time, he read the words and referred to his notes, but after a while he became aware that nothing was going in. He was seeing the words, even saying them to himself, but they made no connection in his brain. They were meaningless.

Instead, there flashed before him the events of the previous evening, and the people he had met. Had it all taken place in one evening? It seemed as though a whole lifetime had been packed into that space of time.

And dominating it all was the figure of Herald. His words went on reverberating in Colin's brain, and there was no escape — Herald accusing him of trying to behave like a white man. Herald denouncing him for still being a slave.

There was Mr Fernandez too, praising him for being good with words, and needing his support. Well, if he was good with words, why wasn't he using them to help fight prejudice and injustice for his own people?

He couldn't believe that throwing petrol bombs and setting fire to the Queen's Arms was the answer. There had to be other ways. And yet he felt he was so ignorant and had been so sheltered that he couldn't be entirely sure. His own experience of the police counted for nothing against what Herald and the others must have had to put up with.

There were the things Aunt Elma and Uncle Neville had been saying over lunch as well. If people like them felt that nothing had really changed, then wasn't it time someone did something about it? If they had no hopes for the future, if all they saw was unemployment and black youth being turned into criminals, then wasn't it time someone did something about that as well?

But what? Perhaps people had tried words already and they hadn't suceeded. Perhaps after all it needed a few petrol bombs and a few Queen's Arms set on fire for society to take notice. Was it true that violence was always wrong? He just didn't know. There was so much he didn't know.

The teachers at school had helped him as much as they could — he was sure of that. He suspected that one or two of them were racist — secretly or without being aware of it. But most of them had been sincere, sympathetic and encouraging. They had told him that the world outside was prejudiced. They said that what he had to do was to work hard and get good results and prove he was just as good as anyone else — even if he was black.

But had they been right? Hadn't they in fact lulled him into becoming a passive conformist following the white road to success? That was what Herald believed. Shouldn't they rather have urged him to stand up for his rights and the rights of his people? If they knew there was prejudice and injustice in society, shouldn't they have incited him to climb to the rooftops and yell his defiance to the whole world at the top of his voice. Shouldn't they have stood up and yelled themselves?

He remembered how in earlier days when he used to get into trouble at school, Mr Elliston, his year head, would punish him even though he hadn't done anything. If there was a fight in the playground or a scene in the dining room, he would be picked out as one of the pupils involved. When he protested his innocence, Mr Elliston would say, 'But you were there. If you don't want to get punished, stay away from where the trouble is.' Colin had gone on complaining about the unfairness, but it hadn't made any difference, and he had had to accept his punishment.

Now, he wondered whether it had been right to accept it. Wayne had been hit on the head by a policeman, not because he had done anything wrong, but because he was there. All right, the policeman didn't know, and in his panic to restore order had hit out at anyone within reach. But that didn't make it fair, did it?

And it was no good saying life wasn't fair and you just had to put up with it — another of Mr Elliston's regular comments. That was no answer either. There was no point in having a society if justice wasn't available to every single member of it.

And there was something else about what Mr Elliston had said. Didn't it tie up with the feeling that the school had tried to subdue his anger and make him an amenable member of society? When Mr Elliston said, 'But you were there. If you don't want to be punished, stay away from where the trouble is' wasn't he also saying, 'But you are black. If you don't want to suffer injustice, then be a good meek member of society'? Become the invisible man as Herald called it.

Colin closed his book with a thud. His teachers might have been right when they drummed into him that exams were important. But after what he had seen and heard the previous evening, he was no longer entirely convinced. There might be other things that were more important.

He went downstairs. From the living room came a burst of laughter. Aunt Elma must have been telling one of her stories. He opened the door and interrupted them. His mother's face was turned towards him, still bright with laughter.

'I'm going out,' he announced.

His mother became serious — even anxious. 'But what 'bout you studyin', you exams.'

'I need some air,' Colin persisted.

'Yeah, a man can' study all the time,' said Uncle Neville in support.

' 'Ow you know?' Aunt Elma demanded with a cutting edge to her voice.

'I'll be back,' Colin said casually and went out.

His mother came after him into the hall. 'Where you goin'?' she asked, her face troubled and unhappy.

'Like I said, I need some air. I need to walk and do some thinking.'

'Don' give up now, son,' his mother pleaded. 'The exams is so close, an' you jus' gotta do well in 'em.'

'Don't worry about it,' said Colin.

' 'Ow can you say that? Course, I worries.'

Colin sighed. 'It's like Uncle Neville said, a man can't study all the time.'

'You don' know 'bout that. You ain't a man yet.' There was a touch of scorn in his mother's voice.

Colin replied as gently as he could though he knew that his mother was still going to be hurt. 'But I am a man, Mum, and I make my own decisions.'

She looked at him for a moment as though she were drowning and all the events of her past life were flashing desperately past and out of reach and all her hopes were fading.

Colin turned away from her and went out.

In the open air, the atmosphere was fresher. A breeze was getting up, stirring the leaves and clearing the mugginess. It looked as though the spell of hot weather was coming to an end. Colin breathed in deeply and felt invigorated.

As he turned into the street, he saw Jenny approaching. She had that absurd dog with her — a Yorkshire Terrier, wasn't it? — on a lead. It might as well have been a toy on wheels. She stopped and smiled.

'I was just taking Timmy for a walk,' she explained unnecessarily. 'I needed a break. Is Wayne back?'

'Yes,' Colin replied. 'Everything's fine now.'

'I'm glad.'

Colin wanted to get away. He had other things on his mind. But he lingered a moment longer to be polite. 'How's the studying going?'

'Oh, I'm up to schedule. I'm even a little bit ahead.'

Her face was animated and excited, and her eyes were shining. But Colin couldn't respond to her enthusiasm. It had lost its savour — at least for the moment. And Jenny too — she didn't move him at all. She no longer seemed to have anything whatsoever to do with his world.

'Good,' he said. 'Keep at it.'

'Yes, I will.'

He moved past her and began to stride purposefully down the street. The dog yapped hysterically after him, but he didn't turn round.

At last, he was on his way. At last, he was getting involved. His mother had no cause to worry. He wasn't going to abandon his studying. He would go back to it and make sure he did well in his exams. Because that would prove the kind of person he was and give him the confidence of mind to be able to speak and make people listen.

But first he had to find Herald. There were so many questions he wanted to ask, so many answers he needed to have. And he knew now that Herald was the person who would be able to give them to him. Herald who had left school with nothing. Herald who had experienced injustice at first hand. Herald who was proud to be black. Together, they could really do something.

A tingle of excitement ran through his whole body. He quickened his step. He had the feeling that for him the battle was just beginning.

Getting it Wrong

Rhodri Jones

Chapter 1

Half-term and nothing to do.

Donovan roamed moodily round his bedroom. It was the year of his exams. There would be the mocks in January, in just over two months, and then the real exams in June. He ought to be doing some studying, but he didn't feel like it.

He sat down at his drum kit and beat out a rhythm. But it was half-hearted. What was the point of beating out a rhythm when there was only you there?

Anyway, it didn't sound right. He knew all black men were supposed to have rhythm, but it sounded nothing. It really needed a guitar or a keyboard to provide a melody. Then he could really get going with a bass and a rhythm. You couldn't play a tune on the drums. Well, you could actually, but it came out a bit monotonous.

He could practise, of course, but what was the point of that when there was nothing to practise for? Anyway, Mum wouldn't like it.

He tried another roll just for the sake of it, and sure enough, Mum's voice came calling: 'Ain't you got not'in' better to do?'

'I were just practisin',' Donovan yelled back.

'Well, practise some other time,' Mum cried. 'I got a 'eadache already. I don' want you makin' it no worse.'

She was probably doing the ironing, and that always made her bad-tempered. She was a cleaner at the hospital, but she was on the late shift this week. She wouldn't be going out until after one o'clock.

Donovan got up and wandered about the room again. He couldn't go round to Sandra's. She wouldn't be there. She was working. He wouldn't be able to see her until the evening. The thought made him feel more discontented. He was longing to see her again. To be with her. The evening seemed so far away.

So what else was there to do? He picked up one of his school books and thought about that again. But no, this wasn't the moment. He just couldn't put his mind to it.

He filled his lungs and let out a long slow stream of air. Of exasperation. Of boredom. He opened the door and went into the kitchen.

Sure enough, Mum was ironing. She looked up as he came in and gave him a beady stare.

'What you moochin' round fo'?' she asked. 'Can' you find somet'in' useful to do?'

'Like what?' Donovan asked in return.

'I don' know, do I? Perhaps you could do some studyin'. That'd make a change.'

'I ain't in the mood.'

'When is you?' She glared at him for a moment and added darkly, 'I wish I'd never bought you that drum kit.'

Then she went back to her ironing. She thumped the iron down violently on the shirt she was doing as though she was stamping out devils.

'You don' 'alf go through some shirts in a week.' she muttered. 'I seems to spend my 'ole life keepin' you in shirts.'

Donovan didn't listen. He put the kettle on and made himself a cup of coffee.

Mum banged away at her ironing.

'My,' she said. 'It's all right fo' some folks. Lazin' 'round an' drinkin' coffee. I sure wish I 'ad the time to do that.' She gave Donovan another stare.

But he ignored her. He stirred his coffee and took a sip. He spooned some more sugar in.

'Why don' you go an' see one o' you friends?' Mum suggested. 'You at a loose end. You don' seem to know what to do wit' you'self.' She grunted. 'At least it get you out o' my 'air.'

Donovan thought about it. It was possible. He could go and see Clive. He might have some ideas about what they could do.

He finished his coffee and got up.

'See you, Mum,' he said.

Mum narrowed her eyes and smouldered at him. 'I suppose you be back at feedin' time?'

'I reckons,' Donovan said airily, and he went out.

Clive lived on the other side of the High Street. It didn't take long for Donovan to stroll across there. The house was one of a row of terraced brick houses, old but neatly done up. There were even a few late chrysanthemums in the tiny front garden. Clive's dad prided himself on his skill as a gardener.

Donovan rang the bell and waited.

No one answered.

That wasn't unusual. Clive's mum didn't always answer the door. She was afraid badmen might get in, Clive had said. And Clive himself, if he was in, was too lazy to answer the door unless it was somebody he was expecting.

Donovan rang again.

After a while, the door opened an inch. It was Clive's mum. She peered at him suspiciously through the crack, and then drew the door wider.

'Clive's up in 'is room,' she said. She didn't seem particularly pleased to see him. Perhaps she was busy with the ironing as well.

She moved back so that Donovan could get in and then shut the door with a bang and bolted it. It gave Donovan quite a start.

'You can' be too careful,' Mrs Miller said. 'Wit' all them t'iefs an' muggers around. Ain't safe in you own 'ome these days.'

Funny, Donovan thought as he climbed the stairs. He'd never been mugged in all his almost sixteen years. But then Clive had said his mother was going a bit weird. Taken to religion as well. That was a bad sign.

When he pushed open the door of the bedroom, Clive looked up. He was lying on his bed with his arms folded behind his head.

'Hi,' he said. But his face was glum, and he didn't look particularly pleased to see him either. He was probably in one of his moods.

' 'Ow's it goin'?' Donovan asked.

'It's borin',' Clive replied. 'My mum keep gettin' at me. I never thought I'd be glad to get back to school. But I will be. It's moan, moan, moan all the time.'

'Same 'ere,' said Donovan. He sat down on the edge of the bed.

'There ain't not'in' to do,' Clive complained.

'Yeah, I knows what you mean, I tries practisin' on my drums, but it didn' seem worth it.'

Clive showed a gleam of interest. 'Yeah, I thought o' doin' a bit o' practisin' too, but I ain't got a keyboard. You knows I plays real well.'

Donovan remembered. During music lessons at school, Clive was always tinkling away on the piano. Mr Greenaway, the music teacher, used to get mad and yell at him to stop that infernal row. But Clive fancied himself. And he had some talent.

Donovan remembered something else. His Aunt Elsie had a portable organ. Why hadn't he thought of that before? She wasn't his real aunt. She had come over from Barbados with Mum years ago, and they had stayed close.

She had bought the organ quite recently. She sang in the choir at church and used it when she was learning new hymns and songs. Not that she was the holy type. She liked

4

her fun too. She'd never married, but she was never short of boyfriends.

Perhaps she would lend him the organ for a few days, and then he and Clive could practise together.

'My aunt got a organ,' he said.

Clive looked at him as though he'd gone mad. 'What? She peculiar or somet'in'?'

Donovan sucked his teeth and kept his patience. 'No. A portable organ. One you can play. She might loan it us.'

Clive began to show interest.

'Yeah?' he said. He eased himself up on the bed.

'We could go an' ax 'er. She might be 'ome 'bout this time.'

'Oh, all right,' Clive said, pretending a show of reluctance. 'It might be worth a try.'

He got off the bed and stood there for a while yawning and stretching his body. He was playing it cool, but Donovan could tell that he was hooked.

He was sure of it when Clive turned on him as though it was all his fault and said, 'Well then. Let's go if we're goin'.'

Aunt Elsie lived in a small block of flats not far away. They were there in ten minutes. Her flat was on the second floor. They climbed the stairs and Donovan rang the bell.

Aunt Elsie was a big woman. Her fat round face lit up when she saw Donovan. He was a favourite with her. The way she looked at him with pleasure as though proud that he was growing into a fine young man always boosted his ego.

'Come in, come in,' she cried. 'I only got a minute. I just come 'ome fo' a early lunch. I got to get back to work quick quick.'

Donovan saw the organ as soon as they entered the living room. It was standing against the wall with its case beside it.

' 'Ow you mum?' Aunt Elsie was asking. 'You tell 'er I comes round soon soon to visit wit' 'er.'

'I'll do that,' said Donovan. 'Aunt Elsie,' he began.

'I knows that voice,' she said, looking at him with

5

pretended suspicion. 'You wants somet'in'. I can always tell.'

'Well . . .'

'An you knows you nearly always gets it too.' She was beaming at him. 'You knows you can twist me round you little finger.'

Donovan put on a show of modest embarrassment. But he was well aware that what she said was true.

'You see, me an' Clive 'ere wants to do some practisin', an' we was wonderin' if you could loan us you portable organ.'

Aunt Elsie glanced at the instrument doubtfully. 'Well, I don' know. That cost a 'ole 'eap o' money. You sure you knows 'ow to look after it?'

'Sure,' said Donovan, putting on one of his best smiles. 'Clive 'ere play real good. Show 'er.'

Clive went over to the organ and began to finger out a beat. Then he superimposed a melody, and the two went bouncing along together. Donovan was surprised. It did sound good.

Aunt Elsie was surprised too. ' 'E can play all right. Though I can' say I cares fo' that kind o' music.'

She thought about it for a moment and then looked at her watch. Her face filled with horror.

'Wow! 'Ow time do fly. I gotta scoot.' She decided. 'OK, you can 'ave the organ fo' a few days. But I gotta 'ave it back by Saturday, an' you gotta take care o' it.'

'Don' worry, Aunt Elsie,' said Donovan. 'We will. An' thanks.'

They put the organ in its case and locked it up. It was quite a weight.

'Thanks, Aunt Elsie,' Donovan said again.

'Yeah, thanks, Miss Benson,' said Clive. 'I'm real grateful. It's real good o' you.'

Donovan gave him a nudge to stop. Clive always went over the top.

'That's OK, boys,' Aunt Elsie said, and she saw them to

the door. 'Now I gotta 'urry.' She closed the door behind them.

Donovan carted the case down the stairs. It was worse than the time he met his cousin Hazel from Barbados and had to carry her case all the way from the tube station.

After they had gone a few yards along the street, he dumped the case on the pavement.

' 'Ere,' he said to Clive. 'You gonna play it, you can carry it.'

Clive pulled a sulky face. 'Hey, man, I thinks you should carry it. I don' wanna take no responsibility fo' damagin' it.'

They argued about it for a while, and then Donovan noticed that someone had come up to them. There was a man standing there looking at them.

'What are you doing with that case?' the man asked.

Donovan couldn't see what it had to do with him. He examined the man more closely. He was about twenty, big, solidly built. There was something at the back of Donovan's mind that said 'police'. It had to do with the man's square shut-in face, the hard steady eyes, the short hair. He had a thin blond moustache.

But the man wasn't wearing uniform. And he hadn't said he was a policeman. So what was he interfering for?

'Ain't not'in,' Donovan said.

'I asked you what you were doing with that case?' the man went on. His voice was harder and more threatening as if he was only just managing to keep his patience.

'What it got to do wit' you?' Clive asked, giving the man an angry stare. He was always quicker to get riled than Donovan.

'I asked you a question,' the man said, his eyes narrowing in on Clive.

'Yeah, yeah, man,' Clive cried. 'An' I ax you a question as well.' He began to throw his arms around. He moved a step or two away and stood muttering to himself.

The man turned back to Donovan. 'What's in that case?' he asked.

More and more Donovan's suspicions were growing that this was the police. But the man still hadn't said so. Even so, Donovan thought perhaps he ought to cooperate.

'It's a organ,' he said.

The man gave him a vicious look. 'Don't play games with me.'

'But it is,' Donovan insisted. 'It's a portable organ.'

'D'you think I'm stupid?' the man said.

'Yeah, yeah,' shouted Clive jeeringly.

The man's face went red.

People were stopping to see what was going on. Donovan was conscious of faces staring and people talking. He wished he wasn't there.

'Open it,' the man said.

'Why should we?' Clive retorted.

'It's locked,' said Donovan.

'Then unlock it.'

'Why?'

The man gritted his teeth and stiffened his mouth as though trying to keep his temper in.

'How do I know you haven't stolen it?' he asked.

Donovan was stung by the accusation. 'It ain't stolen,' he cried. 'My Aunt Elsie loan it me. She live just up there.' He pointed back to the block of flats.

The man didn't bother to look. He didn't take his eyes off Donovan's face.

'Cha,' said Clive with contempt under his breath. He made to pick up the case.

'Leave it there,' the man ordered.

'Who you tellin' what to do?' Clive demanded.

Two men were hurrying across the road towards them. One of them was in a police uniform.

'You having trouble?' the policeman asked.

The two newcomers fixed the boys with the same hard unblinking stare as the first man. They were older. Maybe thirty, thirty-five. And they were big too. A good six feet, and broad with it. Donovan began to feel afraid.

'These boys are being awkward,' the first man said. 'I asked them to open the case, and they won't.'

'It's my Aunt Elsie's,' Donovan cried, making a last desperate effort. 'You can go an' ax 'er.'

But one look at their faces, solid as stone walls, was enough to tell him they weren't in any mood to do anything he suggested.

He gazed around in the hope of finding some way out, and there was Aunt Elsie. It was like a happy ending to a nightmare. She was just coming out of the entrance of the flats. She was cutting across the pavement to the road. She looked right and then left to see if there was any traffic coming and caught sight of the small crowd. She seemed to hesitate a moment, then walked towards them to find out what was going on.

At last, Donovan thought. Here was someone who could clear up the whole situation. Help was at hand. They would listen to her. He felt a great wave of relief.

He wasn't sure if Aunt Elsie had seen him yet. Her view was probably blocked by the three big men. But at least she was on her way.

The three men were going on with their questioning. Nothing Donovan or Clive said could convince them. Then Aunt Elsie was there. Donovan saw her anxious face between two of the men. She realised the men were talking to Donovan.

'How d'we know you haven't stolen it?' the man in uniform was saying again.

'It's mine,' Aunt Elsie cried. 'I loan it 'em.'

But it might just as well have been a bee buzzing in the air for all the attention the three men paid her. Just a slight shift of the eyes in her direction and then back to bore through Donovan and Clive.

'You stole it, didn't you?' the first man accused.

'It's mine,' Aunt Elsie repeated. 'I got the receipt. You wants to see the receipt?'

Again the men ignored her.

9

'I think we ought to take them down to the station,' the policeman said.

'Come,' Aunt Elsie shouted. 'I'll show you the receipt.'

The three men crowded her out and moved in on the boys.

A great surge of memories flashed through Donovan's mind. Stories friends at school had told of being harassed by the police. Being picked up for no reason at all. Being moved on without cause. Being threatened and called insulting names. Being beaten up.

It hadn't happened to Donovan before. But it looked as though it was going to happen now.

He looked around him desperately. Aunt Elsie was still shouting, but the men weren't listening to her. They were closing in.

Suddenly Donovan was running. He broke past the men. His feet pounded the pavement. Clive was running too. People scattered out of their path.

Donovan didn't know where he was running to. All he knew was that he wanted to get away from those men. But where was he to go? The entrance to the flats was near. He made for that. Clive followed him.

He took a quick look over his shoulder. The three men were after him, lumbering down the street.

He shot into the entrance to the flats with Clive just behind him. Even as he did so, he knew he'd made a mistake. There was no escape through the flats. All he could do was go up the three flights of stairs and jump off the roof.

But it was too late now. As he raced up the stairs, panting and feeling that his chest would burst, he heard the front door crash open. He heard the clatter of heavy feet behind him.

There were shouts too. Donovan couldn't make out the words. And he didn't stop to try.

They were on the second floor by now. The door of one of the flats opened, and two little black girls peeped out, round-eyed and frightened.

10

Donovan grabbed the rail and forced himself up the next flight of stairs. As he already knew, that was the end of the line. They were cornered. He could hear the clash of leather on stone getting nearer. In desperation, he began banging on one of the doors. Someone might help him. Someone might hide him. But no one answered.

The men were there now, red-faced and breathing heavily. They glared at the boys and then advanced towards them. Their bodies filled up the whole width of the corridor.

The one in police uniform grabbed Donovan while the other two went after Clive. Donovan tried to draw away, but his back was to the wall, and there was nowhere he could go. He was yanked forward, and then swung round as his arms were twisted behind his back. The policeman pressed upwards, and Donovan let out a yell. Pain shot across his arms and shoulders. He thought his arms were going to snap.

Gripping both arms in a fierce lock, the policeman pushed Donovan towards the stairs. He wasn't sure what was happening to Clive. He could hear his friend shouting, and the other two men were shouting as well. There were a lot of scuffling noises going on.

Donovan was propelled down the stairs with the policeman hanging onto his arms. The two girls were still there.

'Leave 'im alone,' one of them cried defiantly.

And then their mother came and dragged them inside.

By the time Donovan reached the ground floor, he felt as though his arms had been ripped out of their sockets. The policeman thrust him with his face against the wall with his arms up. His legs were kicked apart, and he almost fell. The policeman began padding up and down his body, with his hands. Then he put his head very close and said menacingly, 'Don't you try that again.'

The blow took Donovan's breath away. The policeman's fist had smashed right into his ribs. Donovan gasped. It felt as though his ribs were broken. He wanted to curl up with pain. But he kept his hands high and gritted his teeth.

11

The front door burst open and more policemen bundled in. Donovan couldn't tell how many there were, but it must have been four or five. He was dragged away from the wall and pushed outside.

'Lie down,' one of the policemen said.

Donovan was bewildered. He didn't understand what the policeman meant.

'Lie down on the pavement when you're told,' the policeman barked.

Donovan knelt down and stretched himself out face-down. A policeman pulled at his hands and placed them on top of his head.

As his cheek ground into the grimy stone of the pavement, Donovan flicked his eyes around. All he could see were highly polished black boots moving around. They were like giant beetles.

He could hear a voice shouting, almost screaming. 'What you doin'?' It was angry and confused. It was Aunt Elsie. But the voice became more distant. She must have been moved back.

Donovan's body was aching. He still hadn't had a chance to check on his ribs. There was a burning sensation down there that worried him. But he didn't dare investigate.

There was a noise from the entrance to the flats. Donovan took the risk. He lifted his head slightly off the ground and squinted round. Clive was being brought out by the man who had first stopped them.

The man was having a job. Clive was struggling. Somehow, their legs got entangled, and they both fell to the ground in an undignified heap. The man got up first. His face was blazing with fury. He lashed out with his foot and kicked Clive in the back. Then he seized him by the arm and jerked him to his feet, pinioning his arms behind him.

Donovan couldn't bear to watch any more. He lowered his head to the pavement and pressed his cheek against the cold stone. He felt numb. He felt as though all he wanted to do was drift into sleep and escape. Forget that any of this was happening.

He came back to reality with a shock. There were hands grabbing at his arms and legs. He was being lifted into the air. A police van had arrived. He was thrown into the back like a sack of potatoes. He crashed on the floor in a crumpled heap.

As he picked himself up, he felt a wave of amazement run through him. No, it wasn't the humiliation or the indignity or the pain. It was something else. One of them had been a woman. The one who had got hold of him by the left arm and helped to catapult him into the van had been a policewoman.

Clive came next, shoved in with such force that he banged against the side of the van. Then the policemen climbed in.

As the doors were being shut, Donovan heard a voice crying out, 'Where you takin' em?' It was Aunt Elsie again.

'None of your business,' someone said curtly.

The doors banged shut.

The engine started, and they were off.

It was eerie inside that enclosed space with those hulking men who were his enemies. He could hear them breathe. He could smell them. The stifling air of the van was filled with their hostility and anger. There was a feeling that anything could happen.

The man who had first stopped them was there. He suddenly shot out an arm and seized a handful of Clive's hair.

'My God, you made me look a right fool,' he hissed.

He screwed the hair tighter and crashed Clive's head against the metal of the van.

'You black bastard,' he snarled.

'That's right,' someone else growled.

Donovan felt his own hair being grasped. His face went banging against the van.

'You black bastard.'

Tears sprung to his eyes. Was it the blow or the insult?

He didn't know. All he knew was that he wanted to get out of there. Blot it from his mind. Pretend it was just a bad dream.

But he couldn't. All around him were these men. He could smell the sweat on their bodies. He could smell their hatred.

Or was it the smell of his own fear?

Chapter 2

Sandra was exhausted. It had been a heavy day. The queue at the check-out desk had been never-ending. What was that line from the play she had done for her exam? 'Will the line stretch out to the crack of doom?' That was it.

And there had been all the usual problems. Goods with no price labels on them. People forgetting to get their fruit and vegetables priced. People accusing you of charging them twice. Old-age pensioners who scraped about in their purses and paid with all their small change — or got confused and gave you 20p instead of a pound. They could never get the hang of the new coins.

Actually, Sandra felt sorry for the old people. What they bought seemed to be so meagre — a few rashers of bacon, a pork pie, a small tin of beans, a packet of digestive biscuits. Some of them tried to stop for a chat. Sandra smiled at them brightly and asked how they were. She was probably the only person some of them spoke to all day.

But it took it out of you. Being cheerful all the time and making sure you didn't make any mistakes. There were times when she regretted getting the job. It was much harder than school.

She could have stayed on. Her teachers said she was intelligent. She could have gone on to the sixth form.

But the chance of the job came up, and with all the unemployment about, she was lucky to get it. And Mum and Dad could do with the money. So could she. It was a good feeling to know that you could buy something nice now and then if you wanted to.

She took a quick look at her watch. Half an hour to go. As she picked items out of a basket and rang them up, she thought about Donovan. He would be coming round that evening. It made the day seem not so bad when there was something like that to look forward to.

Her friends used to tease her about going out with a boy who was younger than she was. But he was only nine months younger actually. Besides, she didn't care what they thought. She liked Donovan. She liked being with him. He could be loud and full of himself. But when he was with her, he was soft and gentle. That was the picture she had of him. She only just realised that. Now wasn't that strange?

She didn't know how serious it was — her and Donovan. There had been other boys before him. There were other boys now who were interested in her. Errol, for instance. He worked in the same supermarket.

She raised her eyes from the till for a moment and immediately caught sight of him. He was only a couple of yards away. He was pretending to unpack a case of tins and put them on the shelves. But it was obvious that he had been gazing at her. Waiting for her to lift her head. Willing her to look at him. He always seemed to be hanging around like that.

Now, his face lit up in a big grin. He winked at her and pushed out his lips in a kind of kiss. Sandra smiled back briefly and began to attend to the next customer.

Errol was older than she was — twenty or twenty-two. He was big with a broad face and wide shoulders. And he was sure of himself. He seemed to think he only had to whistle and any girl would go running to him.

Well, she wasn't going to go running. She didn't really like him. He made her feel uncomfortable. She didn't like the way he looked at her. The way his eyes glowed and went up and down her body as though he was undressing her. It was enough to make anyone shudder. Donovan didn't look at her like that.

And yet, at the same time, she couldn't help being flattered. Errol was attractive. There was no denying it. Sexy, too.

She went back to thinking about Donovan. If it ever did become serious between her and him, she was sure of one thing. She wouldn't wash and scrub after him the way his mum did, waiting on him hand and foot. No way. He would have to pull his weight in the house.

That was probably what came of being an only child — and being a boy. Sandra had two younger sisters and a brother. There wasn't much chance of being spoilt with all of them around.

And there was only his mum as well. Donovan had told her that his dad had walked out on them when he was four. He'd gone to America. They hadn't heard from him for years. So Donovan was the man of the house. Sandra smiled quietly to herself at the thought.

That was why his mum pampered him so. She pretended to nag and grumble, but she worshipped the ground he walked on. She was like a slave to him. Perhaps she'd been like that to Donovan's father. Perhaps that was why he'd left her. He wanted someone who would put him in his place more often.

Well, if it ever came to anything, Sandra was quite clear about one thing. She wasn't going to be anybody's slave. Donovan would just have to accept that and play his part. He wasn't any better than she was, after all, just because he was a man. They were equal, and he'd have to treat her as an equal.

At last, the supermarket was closing. Sandra sighed with relief and tiredness. She cleared her till and handed the money over to the supervisor. Then she hung up her overalls, put on her coat and said goodnight to the other girls.

Errol was waiting for her just outside. She was sure he was waiting for her, but she smiled and nodded at him quickly and hurried past. Errol took hold of her arm and walked along beside her. The grip of his hand on her arm was strong.

'Say, when you gonna give me a date?' he asked.

Sandra only came up to his shoulder. She had to lift her head to meet his eyes. He was smiling down at her, but from his voice, Sandra couldn't tell whether he was trying to coax her or threaten her.

'Sometime,' she said. And then added, 'Maybe.'

'I got my car now you knows,' Errol boasted. 'We could be real mobile. Go up the West End. Take in a disco. 'Ave some fun.'

'Thanks,' said Sandra. 'I'll think 'bout it.'

'Don' you leave it too long,' Errol warned her. 'You may be too late.'

'I'll remember that,' Sandra promised, hoping that that was the end.

But Errol was still hanging onto her arm and striding along beside her.

' 'Ow 'bout tomorrow night?' he asked.

'No, I can't.'

'Then when?'

'I lets you know.'

Errol stopped suddenly and pulled on Sandra's arm. She had to stop too. His face had taken on a hard look, but then it softened into a self-satisfied smirk.

'You don' know what you missin',' he said.

'Maybe,' she said as though agreeing, though she was quite sure Errol didn't have anything she wanted. 'Now I gotta get my bus. They expectin' me.'

Errol let go her arm.

'One o' these days you gonna give in,' he said confidently. 'Just you wait an' see.'

He winked at her and pushed his lips out at her and ran his eyes up and down her. Sandra felt like something up for sale. As if Errol was having a good look to judge whether she was worth the price. She didn't like it. He was always doing it. She was glad when Errol turned and strolled down the street away from her and she could go and catch her bus.

As she waited at the bus stop, she thought about him. He really did fancy himself a lot. God's gift to women. Well, there was no way he was going to get her to go out with him.

She waited impatiently as first one bus and then another went past. It would have been just as quick to walk. She was anxious to get home. Already, she could feel the buzz of excitement inside her at the thought of seeing Donovan.

When she eventually got on a bus, she had to stand all the way. And then there was the walk through the estate and the climb up all those stairs.

How she hated the estate. Those vast concrete blocks of flats. The lifts that never worked. The dark smelly stairwells. The draughty walkways.

But then, she supposed Mum and Dad were lucky to live there. It wasn't easy to find somewhere when you had four children.

Dad was getting ready for work. He was on the night shift again.

'You sure you ought to go?' Mum asked.

'I'm goin',' Dad said. 'Don' fuss.'

He was looking tired and worn. His face had that glazed look about it as if he wasn't quite awake.

'You ain't well,' Mum went on. 'You ain't 'ad no sleep.'

'I'll manage,' he said. Then he grunted and added, 'Somebody got to.'

He put on his coat and cap, kissed Mum and Sandra, and went out.

Mum gave a sigh and set about preparing Sandra's meal.

She was looking tired too and weighed down. She had a hard life of it, bringing up that family. It was half-term as well, so the other children would be home all day — or out playing and back late for meals.

They were in now. Robert was in his bedroom. Sandra could hear his transistor blaring out. Debbie and Angie were in the living room, shouting and screaming at each other. They were supposed to be watching television.

Had she been as noisy as that when she'd been their age, Sandra wondered. Probably. Funny really, but all she wanted now was quiet. And Donovan. She must be getting old, she thought, and smiled to herself. When she married — *if* she married — she wasn't sure that she wanted to have children.

Mum put the plate on the table. She sat down beside Sandra and poured herself a cup of tea.

'What kind o' day today?' she asked.

'Oh, so-so,' Sandra told her.

'Like that?' Mum gave her an understanding smile. 'I knows what that mean.'

She talked about her own worries. 'The father weren't feelin' well. 'E couldn't sleep. I wish 'e'd stayed at 'ome. But no, 'e 'as to go to work, well or not. That way 'e is. I'll be glad when the children is back at school,' she went on. '' 'E might get some sleep then.'

Sandra sympathised.

She helped Mum clear away the plates and wash up. Then she went upstairs to her bedroom. Donovan would be arriving soon. She had to change and get ready.

It was half-past seven when she came down again. Donovan was usually there by then. But there was no sign of him. She was disappointed. She felt let down.

Mum was seeing Debbie and Angie to bed. Robert was still in his room. She sat down alone in the living room and stared glumly at the television.

A while later, Mum joined her and took up her crochet. She gave her daughter a searching look, but Sandra kept her eyes fixed on the screen.

'Donovan comin' round?' Mum asked.

''E suppose to,' said Sandra. 'But I don' know where 'e is.'

She had a sinking feeling inside. And then told herself not to be silly. There was probably some good reason.

But what good reason could there be? Donovan had said he would come round. And he hadn't come round. At least not yet.

Perhaps he had gone out with one of his friends. Lester or Barrington. The thought didn't please her.

Or Clive. That was worse. She didn't like Clive. She didn't know what it was about him. He was sly and underhand and moody. He only thought about himself. She hoped Donovan wasn't out with Clive.

But what was he doing out with anyone anyway? When he said he was coming round. It was too much.

It wasn't like him either.

She suddenly became worried. What if something had happened?

She jumped up. 'I think I go phone 'im.'

Mum looked at her with concern. 'You be careful,' she said.

There had been a number of muggings on the estate recently. Many people were afraid to go out at night. The police didn't seem to be doing anything about it.

'I'll be all right,' Sandra said.

There was a phone box on the corner. But when she pulled the door open, she found it had been vandalised. The coin box had been staved in and the receiver wrenched out by the roots.

There was another telephone on the other side of the estate, but it would take her five minutes to get there. It was dark. A lot of the street lamps had been smashed. There were some youths lurking in one of the car park areas. Sandra didn't like the look of them.

She regretted the day Dad had had the telephone disconnected because he said he couldn't afford it any more.

But she had to phone Donovan. She had to make sure he was all right.

She pulled her coat around her, put her head down and set off briskly across the estate. Her footsteps rang sharp and echoing on the pavement. Her eyes kept a wary watch in all directions. The gang of boys didn't pay her any special attention, and there didn't seem to be anyone else out.

Luckily, the other phone was working. She dialled Donovan's number and listened to it ring. She had the coins in her hand ready to insert them as soon as Donovan answered.

But the dialling tone just went on and on.

'Answer it,' Sandra muttered impatiently.

After it had rung twenty times, she put the receiver back.

Perhaps she had made a mistake. Perhaps she had dialled the wrong number. She tried it again.

Once more, the tone went on buzzing in a vacuum. She gave up.

The thought came to her that he might have arrived while she was out. She hurried back to the flat.

He wasn't there.

She suddenly felt sick. She couldn't explain it, but she had an ominous feeling that something was wrong.

Chapter 3

Donovan lay on his back, his head resting on his clasped hands. The cell was cold and comfortless. Beneath him was the hard bench, in front of his eyes the bare wall. He stared at it as though trying to pierce a way through.

They had said they wouldn't let him loose on the streets until his mother came to collect him. They said they were trying to contact her.

Donovan didn't know how long he had been there. They had taken his watch away from him. It seemed to have been hours.

He groaned out loud and then suddenly stopped and held his breath in case someone might be listening. His cheek felt swollen where it had been banged against the side of the van. His ribs hurt when he touched them.

The last few hours had been a nightmare. He wanted to forget them, but what had happened went round and round in his head.

He had been photographed, finger-printed, stripped of his possessions. He had been questioned, put in a cell, and then questioned again. He had been urged to make a statement, to confess to his guilt. He had been told it would be all the worse for him if he didn't.

23

But although he'd been afraid, he'd been determined as well. He stuck out for what he knew to be true. He wouldn't admit that he'd done anything wrong.

They hadn't liked that. They had tried to intimidate him, brow-beat him into submission. Oh, they hadn't beaten him up or called him names again or anything like that. They had just stared at him with their hard faces. Stood close to him and towered over him. Warned him of what the consequences would be.

But Donovan hadn't given in. That was why he was in the cell now. They had left him there and forgotten him.

They were going to charge him with resisting arrest, they said. Was that serious? He didn't know. All he knew was that he didn't think it was fair or right.

He wondered how Clive was surviving. He hadn't seen him since they arrived at the station.

Divide and rule. Wasn't that what they called it? Keeping them apart so that each would worry about what the other was saying. Keeping them apart so that they couldn't give each other moral support.

Well, he hoped Clive was all right.

Then suddenly he remembered. He lifted his arm to see what the time was and then let it fall back. Of course, they'd taken his watch. But he was supposed to go round to Sandra's that evening. Was it that late already? What would she think when he didn't show up.

He began to worry. She wouldn't think he'd forgotten, would she, or hadn't bothered? Seeing Sandra was important. It wasn't something he would overlook or brush aside. She must know that. If he didn't turn up, she would know that something beyond his control had prevented him.

Wouldn't she?

He hoped so, but he wasn't sure.

She was the first girlfriend he'd ever had — the first real girlfriend. He'd admired her for a long time before he plucked up courage to talk to her and ask her out. And he'd been so surprised when she'd said yes. He'd tried not to show it, of course. That would have been bad for his image. But he'd been over the moon.

They'd been seeing each other for over six months now. And yet he still wasn't sure that he knew her. When he was with her, he felt warm and loving. There wasn't anything he wouldn't do for her. And she seemed to like him a lot too.

But when they were apart, he was assailed by all kinds of doubts. She was so quiet and sensible. How could she care for him with his big talk and showing off? He squirmed with shame as he remembered some of the things he'd said and done.

And now? When he hadn't turned up? Would she forgive him? Would she understand?

Donovan rolled over onto his stomach and buried his face in his hands.

Some time later, he heard the door being opened. He swung his head round to look. A policeman had come in.

'Your mother's arrived,' he said. 'You're being released.'

Donovan got up off the bench. He suddenly felt dizzy. He nearly fell over.

The policeman grabbed him by the arm to steady him. 'You all right?'

'Yeah, yeah,' Donovan said. He pulled his arm away. He knew the policeman was only showing concern, but he couldn't bear the thought of being touched by him.

Mum was waiting in reception. When she saw him, she rushed to him and swallowed him up in her arms. One hand patted his back and the other stroked the hair at the back of his neck. He was embarrassed, but at the same time he couldn't prevent his eyes from watering with relief.

Mum held him away from her and examined his face. She gasped with shock. She turned to the desk sergeant.

'What you do to 'im?' she demanded furiously.

The sergeant remained cool and uninvolved. 'We haven't done anything to him,' he said. 'He probably bumped into a wall.'

He emptied Donovan's possessions out of a plastic bag onto the counter. Watch, gold chain, ring, wallet, keys. Donovan picked them up.

'You better check it,' the sergeant said. 'We don't want to be accused of stealing.'

'It's all 'ere,' Donovan said.

'Right. Sign on the dotted line.'

'Did they question you?' Mum asked.

'Yeah,' said Donovan .

Mum rounded on the sergeant angrily. 'I thought you wasn't suppose to question 'im wit'out me bein' there?'

The sergeant stared at her blandly. 'I understand we tried to contact you, and you were unavailable.'

'Unavailable,' Mum muttered. 'Unavailable.' But she didn't take it any further. 'Can 'e go now?'

'Yes, he can go now,' the sergeant said. 'You'll be hearing in due course.'

Mum put her arm round Donovan. 'I've got a mini cab waitin' outside. We'll be 'ome in no time.'

They moved towards the door. As they reached it, two policemen burst through.

'We've got another one here, Sarge,' one of them cried. He sounded almost jubilant.

Between them, they were half carrying, half dragging a man. He looked dazed. A trickle of blood was running down his forehead into his left eye. He was black.

Mum sucked in her breath and looked horrified. She drew back to let the policemen past and then pushed Donovan in front of her out of the door. She bundled him into the mini cab.

'Ain't no use relyin' on buses this time o' night,' she said as the car started off. 'Anyway, it sound like a emergency, so 'ang the expense.'

Then she turned on Donovan with a show of anger and demanded, 'What all this 'bout? Aunt Elsie tell me somet'in'. She say she been ringin' an' ringin', tryin' to get me at 'ome an' at the 'ospital. But it weren't till 'alf a hour ago when I reach 'ome that she get through to me. They never bother to pass on the message at the 'ospital. So what you been doin'?'

Donovan sighed wearily. 'Aw, Mum. I'll tell you when we gets 'ome.'

He sank back on the seat. Great waves of tiredness swept over him.

And anyway, he didn't want the driver to hear.

As soon as they arrived home, Mum put some ointment on the bruise on his face. He told her about his ribs. She had the shirt off him in no time and began applying ointment there too. Donovan yelped as her cold fingers probed the hurt.

'First t'ing tomorrow,' Mum said, 'I takes you to the doctor an' gets that seen to.'

She sounded matter-of-fact and business-like, but Donovan could tell that she was deeply disturbed.

'Now what all this 'bout?'

Donovan told his story in fits and starts as Mum attended to the bacon and eggs she was frying for him. He was suddenly ravenously hungry. Every now and then in the story, Mum exclaimed with horror and amazement.

When he had finished, she turned round and faced him solemnly, with the perforated spoon she was using raised in the air like a banner. There were tears in her eyes.

'Fourteen year I been livin' in this country,' she said. 'Fourteen year. An' I never been in no trouble wit' the police. Why they wants to go treat you this way? You never done not'in' wrong far as I can see. It seems now you can' walk down the street wit'out bein' arrested if you black. It make me sick it do. Resistin' arrest indeed! What 'bout what they done to you?'

Then she sniffed and pulled herself together. Her eyes burned with determination. 'First t'ing tomorrow I gets you a solicitor.'

'Mum,' Donovan pointed out, 'the bacon's burnin'.'

But he was grateful for her support.

She was just serving up when the phone rang.

'I'll get it,' Donovan cried.

He had a sudden hope it might be Sandra. But it wasn't.

'Is that you, Donovan?' came Aunt Elsie's voice. 'You all right?' She sounded anxious.

'Yeah, Aunt Elsie, I'm fine.'

'I were so worried 'bout you,' she went on. 'I didn' know what to do. I tries ringin' the police station, but they just wasn't interested. I tries ringin' you mum. I rings an' rings but I just couldn't get through to 'er till a hour ago. You sure you all right?'

'Yeah, Aunt Elsie.'

'I were 'orrified by what I sees. Just 'orrified. They wasn't interested in what I 'ave to tell 'em. They was just out to get you boys.'

'Yeah, it look that way.'

Mum came into the living room. 'Who's that?' she asked in a whisper.

'Aunt Elsie,' Donovan told her. ' 'Old on,' he said into the mouthpiece. 'Mum want to speak to you.'

He handed the receiver over.

While he knifed into his bacon and eggs in the kitchen, he could hear Mum wailing and moaning on the phone. Part of him was making fun of her for getting so worked up about it. But that was only because most of him knew she loved and cared for him.

When she had finished, Mum came back and slumped down in the chair beside him and watched him eat. She seemed to enjoy it. Then she gave a sigh.

'It's times like this,' she said, 'when I wishes there were a man 'bout the 'ouse. If only you father were 'ere. 'E'd know what to do.' But then she had second thoughts. 'I don' know though. I doubts whether you father would 'elp any after all. You father just like a man. When the goin' get tough, 'e go.'

She sighed again.

In bed, Donovan thought about what she had said. It was

a long time since she'd mentioned his father. He himself couldn't remember much about him. He'd walked out on them when Donovan was four. Gone to America. Occasionally, postcards would come from him with a few words of greeting meaning nothing. But that was all.

Donovan often wondered about him. What he was like. Whether life would have been different if he had stayed. He supposed Mum must have missed him. Perhaps even felt it was her fault he had left. She must have been lonely at times. It must have been difficult for her bringing up a child on her own. Perhaps he hadn't always shown her the gratitude and love he ought. Where would he have been tonight if it hadn't been for Mum?

As the memory of what he had been through flooded his mind, he shuddered, and pushed it away. He tried to think of other things.

What kind of father would he be? He knew if he had a child, he wouldn't abandon it and forget it ever existed.

He thought of Sandra. He felt his body grow tense with longing for her. If they had children, he would give his life to see that they grew up strong and healthy and cared for.

But that was absurd. They hadn't reached that kind of understanding yet. Perhaps they never would.

Then he remembered. He hadn't gone round as he said. What would she think?

Again, the horrors of the day swirled in on him. The man stopping him in the street. The attempt to escape. His arms pinioned behind his back. The punch in the ribs. Lying flat on the pavement. His head banging against the side of the van. The policeman hissing those words.

He struggled to escape from these nightmarish images. He turned this way and that in the bed. And then he suddenly stopped. He opened his eyes and stared into the darkness. What about Clive?

He had forgotten about Clive. Was he all right?

Chapter 4

Clive was walking home. It was seven o'clock in the morning. Nobody had come to collect him, so the police had just let him go. It was very considerate of them. Or perhaps they just needed the cell for another victim.

It was just like Mum and Dad, wasn't it? They didn't worry what happened to him. For all they cared, he could have stayed in that cell until he rotted.

The night had been cold, the bed had been hard, and he had had no food. But it wasn't any of those things that he brooded over as he put one foot in front of another and floated like a zombie down the street, scarcely seeing or noticing people or shops that he passed.

He was thinking about the police and the way they had treated him. In particular, one image kept recurring. He was racing up the stairs of the block of flats. He reached the top floor. The corridor came to a dead end. There were doors, but they were all shut. There was no way out.

He turned. There were two men closing in on him. He put up his hands to defend himself. To protect his face. But the men's fists broke through. They were pounding into his head and body. He could feel the impact as the blows landed, the jagged edges of pain that shot through him. The men were grunting with the effort as they ploughed into him. They called him names that were just a blur.

Then he was hurtling down the stairs, driven by one of the men hanging onto his arms. By the time he was outside, he was scarcely conscious. His feet could hardly support him. He was staggering. He gave way. He fell to the ground. The man holding him fell as well.

Lying on the pavement came as a merciful release. He just wanted to sink through the stone. But a sudden sharp blow in his back made him yell out in agony. He was dragged to his feet. There were people all round him, grabbing at him and pushing him. He was being propelled towards a police van. He felt himself flying through the air. He crashed into the side.

The van filled up. He was jerked onto the bench and hemmed in. The van was moving. Someone put his face close to him so that he could feel the breath against his cheek.

'My God, you made me look a right fool,' the man said.

There was a searing pain as his hair was yanked back. His face went crashing into the side of the van.

'You black bastard,' the man said.

He could hear the vicious hatred in the voice.

Why, he asked himself. Why?

But he didn't say anything. He huddled inside himself with his hurt and his misery until they arrived at the station.

It was the worst moment. Nothing afterwards had been quite as bad. Now the sheer horror of it swept through him again.

He tried to blot it from his memory. He tried to concentrate on walking. Putting one foot in front of the other.

He didn't mind walking. He was used to it. He spent hours walking about the streets, going around with his friends.

No, it wasn't walking that worried him. It was something else that had come into his head and caused him to hesitate and break the rhythm of his steps. It was the thought of what lay at the end of it that worried him.

Mum and Dad hadn't bothered to collect him from the police station, but they would be waiting at home for him. What would their reaction be? What would they say?

He had been in trouble with the law before.

It was more than two years ago. He was caught stealing. Nothing much, just a pair of trainers. He fancied them, but he didn't have any money. So he lifted them and tried to get out of the shop with them under his shirt.

He was crazy of course. They might not even have fitted.

The shopkeeper saw him, grabbed him and got him in a corner. Someone else phoned for the police. He was taken down to the station. It wasn't as bad as this time, but it was bad enough.

He had to appear before the Juvenile Bureau. Him, Mum and Dad. The policeman there was stern-faced. He tried to frighten him by telling him what would happen if he was caught stealing again. He was let off with a warning.

But the policeman's threats had been nothing compared with Mum and Dad's. It was nothing to the way Mum and Dad carried on from the moment he'd been caught. And they carried on after they'd been to the Juvenile Bureau as well. They made his life a misery. They nagged him, yelled at him, punished him. They never let him forget it.

And if they'd been like that then, what would they be like this time?

Clive plodded despondently along the streets.

Then he plunged his hands into his pockets and thought, to hell with it. Why should he care? They could shout at him as much as they wanted to. He hadn't done anything wrong. It was those pigs. Beating him up like that. Charging him. Putting him in a cell all night. He hated them.

He was nearing home by now. Dad probably hadn't set off for work yet. That made it worse. He thought he could manage Mum. But the two of them together.

Well, it couldn't be helped. Of course, he could hang

around until Dad was off the scene. But what was the point? He'd have to face him sometime. It might as well be now.

He turned in at the gate and rang the bell. They wouldn't let him have a key. Not since he brought a girl home and they found her with him. There'd been a row about that too. Wasn't that just like them?

Not that it made much difference. He just went round to the girl's place instead.

Nobody bothered to answer, so he rang again. He stood there, feeling like a dog waiting to be let in.

After some time, the door opened a crack.

'Yeah?' came a voice.

It was Mum. She really was getting weird. She didn't even recognise him.

Eventually, she did and pulled the door open wider.

'I didn' know you was out,' she said, staring at him.

'I been out all night,' Clive said.

How could she not have noticed? She really was living in a dream world.

But there was no point in making an issue of it. There was no point in trying to get away with some put-up story either.

Mum let him in and gazed crazily after him as he walked into the kitchen. Dad was there, stuffing a slice of toast into his face. He stopped with frozen jaw and blinked stupefied at Clive.

He swallowed what he had in his mouth and demanded, 'Where you been?'

Clive came straight out with it. 'I been arrested. I spend the night at the bull station.'

'You what?' Dad roared as if not believing his ears. Mum was in the kitchen too by now. She was gazing at Clive with horror.

Dad opened and shut his mouth a couple of times before he finally got some words out. His eyes were blazing. 'What I tells you 'bout gettin' in trouble wit' the law? You a disgrace, you is.'

'But it weren't my fault,' Clive tried to explain.

Dad wouldn't listen. 'Course it you fault. It always you fault. You does not'in' but bring trouble on this family.'

He threw the rest of his toast down. He was getting into his stride. 'I works all the hours God give to keep you, an' what thanks does I get? None. You ain't got no gratitude. All you does is mess around an' make trouble.'

'What the matter wit' you face?' Mum asked when Dad had paused for breath, and she could get a word in. 'It's all puffy.'

'The bull mash me up,' Clive told her.

'That rubbish,' Dad cried. 'Been in a fight more like. I don' know what thanks we gets fo' bringin' children into this world when all they does is let we down. I sure knows where I goes wrong wit' you. I never beats you enough. That were my mistake.'

Clive wondered how much more of this he could take, but he tried to stay cool. 'I tells you I got mash up. The bull arrests me fo' not'in'.'

'Yeah,' Dad taunted him. 'Like the last time.'

Clive knew it was useless to argue. He turned on Dad bitterly. 'You didn' even come an' get me. That show 'ow much you cares. The bull says they inform you I were there.'

' 'Ow I comes an' gets you?' Dad retorted. 'I didn' know not'in' 'bout it till you comes walkin' through that door.'

Mum was hovering in the background. She made a funny croaking noise in her throat. Dad swung round to stare at her in annoyance.

'That must 'ave been what it were,' she mumbled.

'What you on 'bout?' Dad demanded irritably. 'Speak up, woman.'

'The police,' Mum said. 'There were a ring at the door. 'Bout five o'clock. I peeps through the window an' seen it were the police. So I didn' answer it. That must 'ave been what it were. Comin' to tell us Clive were at the station.'

Dad fumed impatiently. 'I don' care if it were the police. I ain't goin' near no police station no'ow. It were bad enough the last time. I warns you what I do if it 'appen again.'

Clive thought he had better get it all over with in one go. 'They gonna charge me. I gotta appear in court.'

'What!' Dad nearly went through the roof. 'My name bein' drag through the court? This more than I can take.'

He thrust his chair back and stood up. He looked about him as though for some instrument he could beat his son with. He would start throwing things in a minute. It wouldn't have been the first time.

Clive stood his ground. 'Ain't you gonna 'elp me?' he asked. 'What am I suppose to do?'

'What are you suppose to do?' Dad yelled back. 'You can get out my 'ouse, that what you can do.'

His eyes were practically coming out of his head with rage. His beard was positively bristling with anger.

Mum was turning her face from husband to son as though not quite sure what was going on.

Clive was boiling inside. He wanted to strike out at Dad just as Dad seemed to want to strike out at him.

Then he suddenly became extraordinarily calm. He felt quite detached from what was going on. He was standing outside himself, looking down at Dad breathing fury, at Mum blinking with bewilderment, at himself being pushed into a corner.

He heard himself shout, 'Stuff you 'ouse.'

He didn't bother to wait for a reply. He walked to the door. He threw it open and stalked out.

Chapter 5

When Sandra woke up, the first thought in her mind was Donovan. Why hadn't he come round as he promised? What had happened to him?

At work, the worry was still there. There weren't many customers to start with. She had time between each one to brood over her disappointment and her anxiety. Even when she was ringing up the prices, the hurt was still there at the back of her head like an aching tooth that wouldn't give her any peace.

She got things wrong and had to alter bills. It was a long time since she'd done that. Not since the first week.

Errol noticed. He came across and leaned against the till.

''Ow come you makes all those mistakes?' he asked. Then his eyes narrowed and his lips twisted into a smile. 'I reckons you's thinkin' too much 'bout me. I reckons I excites you too much.'

'Could be,' said Sandra, trying to make a joke of it.

'Say, 'ow 'bout comin' out wit' me tonight? I got the car.'

He made his voice sound eager and urgent. Would he never give up?

'No,' Sandra told him. 'I already got somet'in' on.'

Errol gave a show of disappointment and sighed. 'One o' these days I gonna be lucky.'

To Sandra's relief, the supervisor appeared at that moment, and Errol scooted off down one of the aisles and began earnestly examining the shelves.

When her break came, she didn't bother about coffee. She went straight to the telephone and dialled Donovan's number.

Donovan's mum answered the phone. 'That you, Sandra? Just 'old on a second. I gets 'im.'

Sandra could hear her heart beating fast as she waited. So he was there. Her anxiety eased a little, and she was surprised to find resentment taking its place.

' 'Ello, Sandra,' came Donovan's voice.

Sandra blurted out her hurt and anger at him. 'Where you been?' she demanded. 'Why didn' you come round last night like you promise? I were expectin' you.'

'I couldn't 'elp it,' Donovan replied. 'It weren't my fault. I were pick up by the police.'

Sandra's stomach gave a lurch. Her anger evaporated in a moment, and she was suddenly filled with fear.

'You all right?' she asked anxiously.

'Yeah,' said Donovan. 'I got take down the station. That were why I couldn't come. Didn' get 'ome till eleven o'clock.'

Sandra was frantic to know more, to be reassured. 'But why? What you done?'

'I 'adn't done not'in',' Donovan told her.

Sandra had a sudden sense of foreboding. She remembered things she had been told by friends. 'They treats you all right?'

'Well,' said Donovan. She could hear the hesitation in his voice. 'I tells you when I sees you.'

'You sure you all right?'

'Yeah. Don' you worry.'

Donovan's words were bland and soothing. If he had been there, Sandra was certain she would have hit him. Not hard, but enough to show her exasperation. How could she not worry when he hadn't told her anything?

'I'll be round tonight,' Donovan said. 'I tells you all then.'

Sandra wanted to know more. She wanted to know now. But she had to get back to work. In any case, Donovan wasn't saying any more. She would have to be satisfied with that.

'I sees you tonight,' she said.

'Yeah, I'll be round 'bout seven.'

She rang off. She was filled with relief. At least Donovan was safe. At least there was a reason for him not showing up.

But what a reason! Now she had something else to worry about for the rest of the day.

When the front door bell buzzed, Sandra jumped up.

'I gets it,' she said to Mum. 'It's Donovan.'

She opened the door. There he was, smiling in that shy way he had when he was with her. She threw her arms round him, pulled him close and kissed him.

'Ouch!' Donovan cried.

Sandra leaned back and studied his wincing face. She was put out. 'What's the matter?'

Donovan took one of her hands in his while he stroked his side with the other.

'It's my ribs,' he explained. 'It still 'urt.'

Sandra looked at him with alarm. 'Did they beat you up?' she asked.

'I tells you later,' Donovan said.

He waited until Sandra's mum went upstairs to put the girls to bed, and then he told her everything.

Sandra was appalled. That they should treat her Donovan that way. She felt sick at what he had gone through. She felt sick just listening to it.

'But you 'adn't done not'in',' she protested. 'Why they do this to you?'

Donovan gave her a wide-eyed unblinking stare. 'Don' you know?'

'No,' she said. But she did.

'It's 'cause I'm black. 'Cause they prejudice. D'you think they would 'ave done that if I'd been white?'

She knew it was true. There were the things she'd been told by friends about what had happened to them. She had even seen it for herself, in the supermarket. Oh, nothing much, but enough. When people took one look at her and then joined another queue even though the one at her check-out desk was shorter.

But you just accepted that sort of thing. You just put up with it. What had happened to Donovan was something else altogether.

He was sitting there brooding, his face bitter and angry.

Sandra put her arm round his shoulders and pressed against him to comfort him. No wonder she didn't want any children, she thought, when she had Donovan to care for and console. He was still in so many ways like a child who needed someone to look after him and soothe him. Though what he had been through was truly appalling. No one had a right to treat anyone that way. Least of all her Donovan.

He was still lost in thought, a thousand miles away from her, reliving what he'd been through. His eyelids flickered. He shot her a sideways glance and then looked away.

'An' there another thing.' He hesitated and licked his lower lip before going on. 'I were so afraid. My insides was like jelly. I never stood up fo' myself.' He sounded as though he wanted the ground to swallow him up.

'That ain't not'in' to be ashamed of,' said Sandra, drawing him closer to her. 'Anyone would 'ave felt the same.'

But Donovan didn't seem to be reassured.

She looked up at him. 'You get you ribs seen to?'

'Yeah. Mum took me to Dr Aziz this mornin'. She examine me an' say it all right. Just a bruise. Not'in' broken. But it still sore. She say dab my cheek wit' cold water so the swellin' go down.'

Sandra peered at his face.

Donovan patted his left cheek-bone. 'It were there.'

She tenderly stroked both cheek-bones to see if she could feel the bruise.

'Oh, yeah,' she said. 'I sees it now.' Though she couldn't. Both cheeks seemed the same size to her.

Even so, she went on doing it. It was an excuse — if she needed one — to touch his face and to look at him. His skin was so soft. Like silk. And his eyes were round and dark and glowing at her.

She watched as the tip of his pink tongue licked his heavy lower lip. Then he put his arms around her and was kissing her. She wanted it to go on forever.

'Sandra,' he said at last, 'you's so good fo' me.' He began to smile, a slightly mocking smile. 'It were almost worth it to 'ave you make a fuss o' me.'

'Don' say that,' Sandra scolded him. Though she wasn't too severe. 'It ain't over yet. Didn' you say they was gonna charge you?'

She regretted saying it. Regretted seeing the light of happiness fade from his eyes.

'Yeah,' he said moodily. 'It ain't finish yet. Wouldn't be so bad if it were. I could just forget 'bout it. Put it down to life an' 'ard luck. But no, they gonna 'ang it out. They gonna take me to court. Resistin' arrest, they says.'

'What you gonna do?' Sandra asked.

'Mum's fix me up to see a solicitor tomorrow.'

'Won't that cost?'

'Yeah, but I gotta 'ave somebody to speak fo' me. Anyway, I'll probably get legal aid.'

His eyes were suddenly blazing. 'An' I gonna tell 'im everyt'in'. I don' see why I should keep quiet. I don' see why the bull should treat me that way an' get away wit' it.'

Sandra stroked his arm to calm him down.

'Sorry I explode at you that way on the phone,' she said. 'But I were upset when you didn' come round last night. An' I worried 'bout you.'

'That's all right,' said Donovan. He narrowed his eyes

and gave her a slow smile. 'It's nice to 'ave someone that worries 'bout you.'

Was he laughing? Was he making fun of her? She didn't care.

Chapter 6

It was nearly twenty-four hours since Clive had stormed out of the house. He was lying now on the settee in Leroy's front room, watching the morning light seep through the curtains. The settee was lumpy and the springs were creaky and broken. He had spent the night there, uncomfortably, tossing from one side to the other. What he wouldn't give to sleep in a real bed again. Not the one in the police cell. Not this settee.

Still, he supposed he was lucky to be there. To have had a shelter over his head for the night. For a moment, it had been touch and go. He thought he was going to have to doss down under a hedge in the park, or find someone's garden shed to break into.

And then he had met Leroy and had coaxed him into taking him home with him.

He had no shame about it. What were friends for, if not to help you when you were in need? It wasn't as if it was the first time he'd had to scrounge. He was used to it. He'd spent the whole day doing it.

When he left the house, he wandered about the High Street for a while, wondering what he was going to do, feeling more and more desperate for something to eat. And then he saw Carlton going into the Paradise Cafe. Carlton was three years older than he was, but Clive had helped him out on his stall down the market a couple of times, so he reckoned the older boy owed him a favour.

He followed him inside and sat down at the same table.

'Hi, Carlton,' he said with a friendly smile.

Carlton looked up without saying anything and gave him a hard suspicious stare. It was almost as though he knew what was coming.

Clive put on his hangdog look. 'Say, I'm out o' funds. Can you buy me somet'in' to eat?'

Carlton pursed his lips and blew his breath out long and steady. As though he was trying to decide whether to agree or whether to slap him round the head. Clive looked down and tried to appear even more pathetic.

At last, Carlton called to Jeff behind the counter, 'A cup o' coffee. An' give this one somet'in' to eat.'

'What you want?' Jeff asked.

'Sausage an' egg,' Clive said quickly. 'An' a cup o' coffee.'

Carlton widened his eyes at him as though horrified by the expense that was being incurred. Or aggrieved at being taken advantage of. Clive pretended not to notice. He was a man of few words was Carlton. Perhaps it was just as well.

With his stomach full again, he spent the morning hanging around the High Street, passing the time of day with friends, catching up on the latest news. He told them what had happened to him and Donovan. They were shocked, but not surprised. That sort of thing happened every day.

When lunch time came round, he latched onto Dennis.

'I'm goin' 'ome now,' Dennis said.

'That's OK,' said Clive. 'I come wit' you.'

'But I'm goin' fo' my meal.'

'That's OK.'

Dennis didn't look too pleased. He was probably thinking there'd be less for him. He was greedy about his food.

When Clive got to Dennis's, they couldn't very well turn him away.

Dennis's mum had to go out that afternoon, so Clive and Dennis stayed in and played records. She seemed surprised to see Clive still there when she got back. She had no option but to let him share their tea.

But when Dennis's dad arrived home from work, Clive knew from the look on his face that it was time to go.

He spent the evening at the Club. Harold bought him a Coke. And Sylvester. But neither of them could offer him a roof over his head for the night.

Then he met Leroy, and here he was seven hours later, turning over on the battered settee in Leroy's front room.

It wasn't the first time he'd slept away from home. It wasn't the first time there had been a row and Mum and Dad had thrown him out. Though he wasn't sure if that was right. He remembered the old joke — did you fall or were you pushed? It was a bit like that. Had he been thrown out or had he just left?

Those other times, he'd found somewhere to sleep, someone who would take him in. Then after a couple of days, he'd crawled back with his tail between his legs, and Mum and Dad had let him in.

But he wasn't so sure this time. It seemed more serious, more definite somehow. He knew Dad's bark was worse than his bite. He'd stopped beating him years ago. But this time he seemed to mean it.

Anyway, Clive thought, he wasn't sure if he wanted to go back. If Mum and Dad didn't have any sympathy for him, didn't want to help him, then why should he?

But Leroy's wasn't satisfactory. It wouldn't do. And it wasn't just the lumpy settee. Leroy's mum had made it quite clear that it was just for the one night. She wanted him out of there in the morning. She wasn't having him messing up her front room longer than that.

Clive wasn't too worried. He'd got through one day and one night all right. He'd manage somehow. And if the worst came to the worst, well, there was always the park or someone's garden shed.

Then he had a sudden inspiration. What about Donovan? After all, it was because of him that he was in this fix. If Donovan hadn't come round and wanted him to play the keyboard and got him to go to his Aunt Elsie's for the organ, none of this would have happened.

Yes, that was a good idea. He would try Donovan. Try a bit of moral blackmail.

When she came to get him up, Leroy's mum was quite surprised at how cheerful Clive was.

Donovan was just getting ready to go to the solicitor's when the door bell rang. He opened the door to find Clive standing there. He was looking down in the mouth.

'Hi, Clive,' Donovan greeted him. 'Come on in.'

They went into the living room. Mum glanced in briefly to see who it was and then hurried upstairs to get her coat.

'I were worried 'bout you,' Donovan said. 'I went round yesterday afternoon to find out 'ow you was, but nobody answer the door. You all right?'

'I been thrown out,' Clive told him.

'No, man,' Donovan cried. 'That's grim. What they do that fo'?'

Clive pulled a long face. 'They says they don' want not'in' to do wit' me now I mix up wit' the law.'

'But it were the law what mix up wit' you,' Donovan exclaimed indignantly.

'I knows that,' said Clive. 'But my mum an' dad don' see it that ways.'

'When did they throw you out?'

'Yesterday mornin'.'

'Well where did you sleep last night?'

'Leroy let me sleep in 'is front room. But it were only fo' one night. I don' know where I gonna sleep tonight.' He shot Donovan a pleading glance. 'Will you mum let me sleep 'ere?'

Donovan thought about it. They had a spare room. Cousin Hazel had slept there when she visited. Mum would have to move her sewing machine out. But she'd done that last time.

He felt a surge of anger against the police. Here they were again. It was all their fault. Picking on him and Clive for no reason. Turning Clive's parents against him. Making him homeless.

He was lucky. He had a mum who cared. He ought to do something to help his friend.

'I go see,' he said.

Mum was in the kitchen now. Donovan explained about Clive.

'But 'ow long 'e plannin' to stay?' Mum asked in a loud whisper. The walls in these houses were so thin.

'Don' know,' said Donovan. 'Till 'e fix up I guess.'

'An' when that gonna be?'

'I tells you I don' know.'

'An' I reckons 'e expect me to wash an' iron 'is shirts too.'

' 'E only got the one 'e stand up in far as I can see.'

Mum gave in grumpily. 'Oh, all right. But only fo' tonight though. I don' like to see a boy turn out into the streets wit' nowheres to go.'

Clive was overjoyed when Donovan told him.

'Thank you, Mrs Bailey,' he exclaimed. 'That sure is a load off my mind. I were that worried 'bout what I were gonna do. I were worried sick. I don' know 'ow to thank you.'

'That's all right,' Mum said coolly. She didn't seem to like Clive going on about it.

She changed the subject. 'That were a bad thing what happen wit' the police. A bad bad thing. I just can' get over it. It just go on round an' round in my 'ead. That they should treat young boys that way.'

Another thought struck her. 'What you doin' 'bout it?' she asked Clive.

'Ain't done not'in' 'bout it yet,' Clive said. He dropped

his head, and his face went all miserable. 'Don' know what I can do 'bout it if my mum an' dad don' wanna 'elp me.'

Mum brooded on it. 'We's off to see the solicitor now. You better come as well. I don' see why 'e can' settle both o' you at one go.'

'Thanks, Mrs Bailey,' said Clive, gleaming up at her. 'That's good o' you, Mrs Bailey.'

Donovan wished he wouldn't go on so. He always overdid it.

Chapter 7

Mr Abbott knew before he entered the classroom that something was up. Usually after half-term, the pupils were quiet and subdued. As if they'd exhausted their energies during the holiday and needed a few days' rest at school before they could build up steam again.

But today, there was a bubbling and an excitement that was different. He heard voices raised in anger, cries of indignation. What could be the matter with them?

As he went in, Donovan was speaking — or rather protesting. 'I 'adn't even done not'in'.'

'That's dread, man,' Mr Abbott heard Lester say.

He walked to the front of the room and put his books on the desk. Nobody seemed to have noticed he'd come in.

Then Barrington saw him and said, 'Hey, sir. D'you think it's right the police should take you in an' beat you up when you 'aven't done not'in'?'

'Of course not,' Mr Abbott said immediately. He didn't need to think about it. 'Why? What's happened?'

'It's Donovan,' said Lester. ' 'E were pick up last week by the law.'

'Yeah,' said Barrington. 'An' they beats 'im up.'

Mr Abbott looked across at Donovan who was trying to shrink behind his desk. 'Is that right?'

Donovan gave an embarrassed smile. 'Yes, sir. Me an' Clive.'

Clive, sitting across the room, had his hard-done-by look on.

'Why?' Mr Abbott asked. 'What had you been up to?'

'Not'in',' said Clive. The word came out like a bark.

'Come and tell me at break,' Mr Abbott said. After all, he was their year head. If something like this had happened to them, he wanted to know about it.

He picked up his textbook, sat on the edge of his desk and looked at the class, ready to begin the lesson.

But the class didn't respond. The pupils didn't fall back quietly into their seats and gaze up at him awaiting his words of wisdom. He was an experienced teacher, so he could tell it wasn't because they were being awkward or difficult. It was because they were still full of what they had heard about Clive and Donovan. Mr Abbott let them go on.

'The police is always like that,' Barrington was saying. He had his eye on Mr Abbott and clearly wanted to make sure the teacher heard. 'They always treats black kids like dirt.'

'Yeah,' agreed Lester. 'You remembers what 'appen to Fitzroy? 'E were just standin' in the street, an' they arrests 'im fo' obstruction.'

'What 'bout Desmond?' Susie put in. ' 'E were taken in 'cause 'e 'ad a Afro comb. Offensive weapon they calls it.'

'An' Kenton down the 'Igh Street,' said Janine. 'Loiterin' wit' intent. 'E were only waitin' fo' 'is mum.'

Even the white pupils agreed with what was being said.

'It's right,' said Steven. 'I was somewhere where I shouldn't 'ave been. With Clinton. Down the back of the old factory. The fuzz comes along an' catches us. They lets me go. But they takes Clinton in an' gives 'im a good goin' over.'

Mr Abbott felt it his duty as a teacher to try to keep some kind of balance.

'All right,' he said, 'some policemen are prejudiced. It's

49

only human nature, I suppose. You can't expect them all to be perfect, can you? It's the same in any group of people. You'll always find some who are racists. But you can't say that all policemen are prejudiced. Can you?'

He was almost knocked over by the 'Yeah' that came thundering from the class.

He rallied himself.

'But isn't that just as bad? If you really think that, then you are just as bad as you claim the police are. You are just as prejudiced.'

He had the feeling though that his words didn't cut any ice. Barrington for one wasn't prepared to accept them. He went back to take up a point Mr Abbott had made earlier.

'What you said 'bout you can' expect all policemen to be perfect. Why not? What they paid fo'?'

He looked calculatingly at the teacher for a moment before going on. Barrington was always one for an argument, and Mr Abbott respected him for it.

'What would 'appen if a teacher was to call me a black bastard?'

The insulting words lay in the air like a nasty smell. Mr Abbott could see where Barrington was leading.

'Well,' he said, 'he would probably be severely reprimanded.'

'Told off, you mean,' said Lester.

'Yes.'

'Would 'e lose 'is job?' Barrington asked.

'It's possible,' said Mr Abbott. 'If he did it again.'

'Then why don' that 'appen to the police?' asked Barrington, arriving triumphantly at his conclusion. 'I been called a black bastard dozens o' times, an' I still sees those police *officers*' (he loaded the word with withering contempt) 'on the streets goin' 'bout their duties.'

'Yeah,' agreed Lester. 'Ain't the police suppose to be there to protect everyone? 'Ow can they do that if they racist an' pickin' up black people all the time? They didn' ought to 'ave no racist feelin's. An' if they does, they ought to be throw out.'

'There is a complaints procedure,' Mr Abbott pointed out, 'if the police behave improperly.'

'Yeah,' said Barrington. 'But look who deal wit' 'em. The police does themselves. You ain't gonna tell me that's fair?'

'It's the best we've got,' said Mr Abbott.

The anger and despair of the pupils was beginning to get to him. He tried to respond calmly.

'Look,' he said. 'You've got to remember what I've told you before when you get caught up with the police. You've got to stay cool and polite, even if you think they're in the wrong. Then if they do anything improper, you tell your parents or you tell me, and we try to sort it out. Make an official complaint if necessary. But respect at all times is the keynote. No matter what the police say or do. No matter how angry you are inside. Then perhaps we can act. But if you lose your temper or put yourself in the wrong, then it makes it more difficult to complain or to get justice.'

'Ain't no justice anyway,' Lester muttered. 'Not if you're black.'

'I don't think that's true,' said Mr Abbott. 'There's a lot of injustice and prejudice about, I know. But things are improving. There are people fighting to improve things. The picture isn't all black.'

He knew as soon as he said it that he'd said the wrong thing. Barrington pounced on the word.

'Black,' he exclaimed. 'There you are. You always tellin' us 'bout 'ow words we use 'elps keep prejudice goin', an' you use 'em yourself. If things is bad, you says they's black, don' you? All things black is bad.'

Mr Abbott blushed. He became flustered. He stuttered an apology.

'You see how easy it is,' he said. 'You see how ingrained it is. I'm sorry. I didn't mean it.'

The pupils jeered at him, but it was good-natured. His credentials had been established a long time. They knew where he stood when it came to racism. He was sure of that. At least he hoped so.

'Perhaps we ought to get on with the lesson,' he suggested. Though he was well aware that more real education had gone on in the past ten minutes of discussion than from anything he had to teach them.

There was a girl waiting for him at his office at break. Linda. He knew what she was there for. Bunking off school again. Well, he would see her later. Donovan and Clive were more important.

'I've got something else to deal with now,' he told her. 'Come again at lunch time.'

'Yes, sir,' Linda said. She didn't seem to mind one way or the other.

Mr Abbott ushered Donovan and Clive into the office and told them to sit down. He gave them a steady look.

He had known them both for more than four years, watched them grow up and develop. Donovan was a thin wiry boy with a fine bony face and a halo of Afro-styled hair. He came from Barbados — or his parents did — and he was proud of the fact. He could sometimes get carried away in arguments with his friends, and he was not the kind of boy to stand any cheek from them.

But to Mr Abbott and to other teachers, he was unfailingly pleasant, friendly and polite. He always had a ready smile. He'd never been in any serious trouble in the school. Mr Abbott couldn't imagine him doing anything that could bring the police down on him.

He was less sure about Clive. He was plumper and had a podgy unformed face. He could be surly and quick to take offence. He became aggressive when he didn't get his own way. Mr Abbott could remember a number of times when he'd had to step in and calm Clive down to keep him from getting into serious trouble. There was also a deviousness and slyness about him which prevented anyone from feeling he could really be trusted.

'Now then,' Mr Abbott said. 'What's this all about?'

Donovan did most of the talking. He had it off pat. No, that wasn't fair. He told it with burning conviction and anger. As though he was living it all again. As though the whole terrifying degrading experience was being re-enacted. He was not normally the most articulate of boys, but he related the events with a kind of bitter intensity that gave fluency and the ring of truth to his words.

Mr Abbott listened with a growing sense of horror. If only half of what Donovan said was true, it was bad enough. He was disturbed and upset to think that pupils of his should have been treated like that. They were only fifteen.

He tried to imagine what he would have felt like if it had happened to him at their age. He couldn't think how he would have coped.

There was no doubt in his mind that Donovan was speaking the truth. He knew the kind of boy he was. Honest and truthful.

In any case, some of the details he gave were not the sort of thing anyone would invent.

'Tell me,' Mr Abbott asked when Donovan had finished. 'Why did you run away when the policeman stopped you?'

'I don' know,' said Donovan. 'I got it wrong. I were just scared. I panicked.'

'And why did you run into the block of flats? You must have known the police would follow you, and you would be trapped.'

'I couldn't think of anywheres else to go.'

Mr Abbott could understand.

He had had a number of cases involving black pupils and the police, but this was the worst he had had to deal with. As far as he could tell, Donovan and Clive had tried to follow his advice. But fear had made them panic and try to escape. It was almost as though that was what the police wanted. As if it gave them an excuse to behave the way they did. Surely it was wrong that the police should inspire that kind of fear?

He was still sure that his advice was right. Respect at all times as far as the police were concerned. Then any complaints could be dealt with later. But he was beginning to think, in spite of all his experience, that he had underestimated the kind of restraint and control his black pupils needed when faced with this kind of situation. It was something he would have to think about.

And the police? The way they had acted? Well, they certainly seemed to have exceeded their authority.

'How's your mum taken it?' he asked Donovan.

'She's all right.'

'And you, Clive?'

Clive hung his head. 'I been thrown out,' he mumbled.

'What?' Mr Abbott exclaimed. 'But why?'

'They blames me fo' gettin' mix up wit' the law.'

Mr Abbott sighed. That was always the way with problems like this. You turned over one stone and discovered more nasty things underneath.

'What are you doing? Where are you sleeping?'

'Oh, it's OK,' Clive told him. 'I'm stayin' at Donovan's at the moment.'

Mr Abbott supposed that was all right. He returned to the problem of the police.

'You say they're charging you?'

'Yeah,' said Donovan. 'Wit' resistin' arrest.'

'Have you got a solicitor?'

'Yeah, my mum got me one.'

'Good. Let me have his name. I'll ring him up and see if there's anything I can do.'

Donovan took out his wallet and handed Mr Abbott a card. The teacher made a note of the name, Spence, and the telephone number.

'Now, look, both of you,' he said. 'I know this has been an unpleasant experience. It's not something I would like to have been through myself. But it's behind you now. There's still the court case, but you'll have people on your side there, and we'll do everything we can to help you. Understand?'

Clive nodded his head and said thanks in that effusive way he had sometimes.

Donovan began to smile for the first time since he'd come into the office.

'Right then,' said Mr Abbott. 'Don't you worry about it.' Then he added, 'Sorry to take up your break.'

'That's all right, sir,' said Donovan.

When the boys had gone, Mr Abbott sat for a moment. The last thing he saw was the back of Donovan's head as he went out of the door. Yes, you could certainly grab a good handful of that hair if you wanted to smash his face against a wall. He gave a shudder.

He still retained some respect for the police. He tried to be fair to them. They had a difficult job to do. It was hardly their fault that there was so much crime on the streets and social deprivation and unemployment. Yet they were the people who had to deal with the results of problems like these face to face. No wonder there was so much hard feeling against them.

He remembered how they had been when he had crashed his car on the motorway a couple of years before. They couldn't have been more helpful. Taking him back to the service station. Giving him a cup of tea. Arranging for the break-down van. Organising transport for him.

But then, he was middle-aged, wearing a suit and tie. He spoke with a polite accent. And he was white.

It was different if you were young and black.

Other cases before this had sorely tried his respect. Now it was beginning to crumble.

Why had they gone on that way with Donovan and Clive? They were just being stupid. That's what it amounted to. Throwing their weight about. Acting big. Causing bad feeling.

They must have known they had made a mistake, but they just hadn't had the guts to admit it and climb down gracefully. They just carried on and made it worse and then left someone else to try to repair the damage.

But you couldn't judge the whole police force by one incident, or even a few. That wouldn't be right. In spite of what he'd just been told, it was possible that his original view that there were bound to be a few rotten apples in any barrel was still correct. Wasn't that what the Police Commissioner himself had said?

And it was those rotten apples that gave the whole police force a bad name and made it even more difficult for the decent ones.

He reached for the phone and asked for a line. He was able to get through to Mr Spence straightaway.

'I understand you're dealing with Donovan Bailey and Clive Miller,' he said after he had introduced himself. 'I've just heard about this trouble with the police.'

'I'm glad you phoned,' said Mr Spence. 'What can you tell me about the boys?'

'Well, Clive can be a bit awkward at times, but Donovan is a very decent kid. I believe what they say.'

'Yes, so do I. I've had years of listening to people telling their stories, and if ever anyone's telling the truth, Donovan is.'

He went on, seeming to welcome the chance to let off steam. 'It really upsets me to think of kids like that being treated the way they were. It's time something was done about it. I've had so many cases like this where the police have acted improperly. No wonder relations between the police and black kids stink.'

'What are their chances?' Mr Abbott asked.

'Depends what the police say,' Mr Spence told him, 'and whether the magistrate believes them. It's probably their word against Donovan and Clive's. But really,' he exploded indignantly, 'when you think it took six or eight policemen to deal with a couple of boys, it makes you furious. It certainly sounds like operation overkill to me.'

'Is there anything I can do?'

'Would you be willing to appear as a character witness?'

'Of course.'

'That's great. It might help if their year head is there in court to speak for them.'

Then Mr Spence burst out again in a great flood. 'I'm fed up to here with the police. The way they behave I sometimes think they must all be racists. There are so many cases. Racial abuse. False charges. Planting of evidence. Then I have to pull myself up short and remind myself that not all the shrieks of "Prejudice!" are true. Quite a few of my clients try it on in the hope of getting away with it. It's a handy excuse sometimes.'

Mr Abbott made sympathetic noises.

'Not that I believe that's the case here,' Mr Spence went on. 'There's absolutely no doubt about it. There's no justification for what the police did. They're supposed to be the upholders of the law, yet they seem to be the biggest law-breakers of them all. Take this case. Don't caution the boys in the proper way. Beat them up. Use racial abuse. Question them without their parents being there. You name it, they did it.'

'They certainly do seem to have acted badly,' agreed Mr Abbott.

'You can say that again,' Mr Spence retorted. Then he seemed to become aware of how he had been letting rip. 'Sorry to blast your head off with it all like that. But it's a relief to get it off my chest.'

'That's all right.'

'I'll contact you again nearer the time. And thanks again.'

When Mr Abbott put the receiver down, he felt himself overtaken by a feeling of despair. Even Mr Spence — a solicitor — found it difficult to keep a free and open view of the situation. Even he felt at times that the whole police force was racist. Wasn't that exactly what the class had said?

It couldn't be true. Could it? Mr Spence only thought that way when he was harassed and overworked.

Even so, Mr Abbott realised that the last vestiges of his faith in the police were beginning to slip away.

But there was no more time to worry about that now. He had done the best he could for Donovan and Clive for the moment. He would let them know he had phoned Mr Spence and agreed to be a character witness. Then they would just have to see how things turned out.

The bell had already gone for the end of break. As he began to get his books together, he remembered the organ that had started the whole thing off. What had happened to it? He would have to ask Donovan.

But then thoughts of his next class took over. He was going to be late.

And he hadn't even had a cup of coffee.

Chapter 8

'Mr Abbott gonna be a character witness,' Donovan told Mum that evening as they sat round the kitchen table having their meal. ' 'E gonna speak up fo' us in court.'

Mum glanced across at him. 'That good news. I 'opes it 'elp.'

She sounded low and tired.

'Course it'll 'elp,' Donovan reassured her, though he wasn't too confident.

'I worries 'bout what gonna 'appen,' Mum went on. She gave a sigh. 'That it should come to this.'

'It'll be all right,' said Donovan. 'Like Mr Abbott said, we got people on our side. There's 'im an' Mr Spence.'

'I don' know what Mr Abbott gonna say 'bout me,' Clive put in. 'I ain't exactly one o' 'is favourites.'

'You ain't been in no bad trouble,' said Donovan encouragingly.

Clive didn't seem so sure.

'What 'bout that time I 'ad a row wit' Desmond in the dinin' room an' throw the custard all over 'im?'

'That were over a year ago.'

'An' that time I chuck a chair leg out the classroom window an' just miss Mr Lewis. Old Abbott weren't too pleased 'bout that. I got suspended. 'E ain't gonna say much good 'bout me.'

'But you didn't mean to 'it Mr Lewis.'

Mum was listening with growing disapproval. Her eyes were fixed on Clive and her mouth had stopped chewing.

Donovan hurriedly assured Clive before he could reveal any more of his dubious past. 'It'll be OK. You see. 'E's on our side.'

Mum began to eat again.

' 'Ow long you plannin' on stayin'?' she asked Clive after a while.

The question came out casual like. It didn't sound too loaded to Donovan.

'I don' know,' Clive replied gloomily. 'I can' say.'

'Ain't you gonna see you folks an' ask if they'll take you back?'

'Ain't no point. They make up their mind. They ain't gonna change it.'

Mum thought about that.

'What 'bout you clothes, then?'

' 'E can loan some o'mine,' Donovan said.

'That what 'e been doin',' Mum pointed out, a touch sharply. 'They gonna be wore out.' She turned to Clive. 'Can' you go 'ome an' collect some? You mum'll let you do that, won't she?'

Clive burst out angrily. 'I ain't goin' round there. I ain't gonna beg.'

There was an uncomfortable silence round the table. Donovan stole a quick glance at Mum. She was looking at Clive as though she was seeing him for the first time. Clive must have sensed he had spoken too abruptly.

'You knows I'm grateful,' he said humbly, 'fo' the way you 'elps me out.'

Mum grunted. 'Then you can show it by givin' me a 'and wit' the washin' up.'

Clive pulled a face, but he did what he was told.

Afterwards, he suggested to Donovan that they should go

to the Club. Donovan wasn't seeing Sandra that evening. He'd told her he had to stay in and do some revision for his exams. But Clive's idea sounded better. Somehow, he just couldn't settle down to his books.

'Ain't you got no studyin' to do?' Mum asked when she saw Donovan was getting ready to go out.

'Aw, Mum,' Donovan pleaded. 'I can' study all the time.'

'Yeah,' agreed Clive. 'You gotta 'ave some fun while you're young.'

From the look on Mum's face, Donovan didn't think that went down very well. They got out quick.

As they turned into the High Street, Donovan asked, 'D'you think we should 'ave done what Mr Abbott said? Stand and take it?'

'I reckons that what we done,' countered Clive. 'It were only when you start to run that t'ings went wrong.'

It sounded as though Clive was blaming Donovan for everything that had happened.

'You start to run too,' Donovan reminded him.

'Only 'cause you did.'

'So it were all my fault, were it?' Donovan demanded angrily.

'Naw, naw,' said Clive, soothing him down. 'It would 'ave 'appen anyway whatever we done. They was just out to get us any way they could. We just give 'em a 'elpin' 'and.'

Well, whatever the truth of it, it was too late now, Donovan thought. The police had had their fun, and there was still the court case to come.

'What d'you reckon to Mr Spence?' he asked.

'I don' know 'bout 'im,' said Clive. ' 'E sure ask enough questions.'

'That 'is job,' said Donovan.

He remembered the interview with Mr Spence. The solicitor had been pretty aggressive, asking them again and again about this detail and that. Going over their story three or four times to make sure he got it right.

Donovan had to admit the first sight of Mr Spence hadn't

impressed him. The solicitor was small and slight with a tired lined face and a bald head. He wasn't what Donovan had been expecting. Perhaps he'd been watching too much television.

But there was no doubt that the solicitor was thorough. He went on and on. By the end of the interview, he knew everything that had happened. And Donovan's estimation of him had gone up.

'I think 'e don' believe us,' Clive said, still considering Mr Spence. ' 'E strike me like the kind o' guy what don' like black people.'

'Why you say that?' Donovan asked.

'You gets a feelin' 'bout guys like that. The way 'e go on. All those questions.'

' 'Ow else you expect 'im to find out what 'appen?'

Donovan felt exasperated. Really, there were times when he wondered why he bothered with Clive. He had a chip on his shoulder as big as a boulder.

'You only sayin' that 'cause 'e's white,' Donovan accused him.

'No, I ain't,' Clive retorted, though he sounded rather defensive.

Then Donovan remembered that Clive had been thrown out by his parents. That he was living with them. One of the family.

'It gonna be all right,' he said. 'Mr Spence gonna try 'is best.'

'I sure 'opes 'is best is good enough then,' Clive grumbled.

The Club was crowded. Donovan and Clive greeted friends and pushed their way through to the bar. They bought themselves Cokes and stood watching the girls.

'I could 'ave anyone o' them I likes,' Clive said smugly.

'Listen to the big man talk,' jeered Donovan.

'Naw, it's true. Chat 'em up a bit, flatter 'em, an' they're yours fo' the takin'.'

He went on eyeing the girls. 'Which one d'you fancy?'

Donovan was suddenly disgusted. He rounded on his

friend. 'I don' fancy none o' them. I got Sandra. Remember?'

'Oh, yeah,' Clive said as though it had just come back into his mind. 'What's she like?'

There was a suggestiveness in his voice that Donovan found hard to take. Sandra was special. He wasn't going to let anyone say anything cheap about her.

'You watch you mout',' he muttered menacingly.

'OK, man, OK,' Clive protested. 'I didn' mean not'in'. I didn' know that 'ow you feels 'bout 'er.'

'Well, you knows now.'

Donovan settled into a deep depression. Having somebody staying with you like Clive brought with it responsibilities. Going out with him tonight, for instance. He was his friend after all. He couldn't just abandon him.

But when he said things like that about Sandra, Donovan felt angry. Clive just didn't understand. Sandra meant everything to him.

He let his eyes roam round the crowded hall. He took in Clive beside him jigging up and down to the beat of the music that was belting out. The girls giggling among themselves in one corner. The boys playing pool and arguing.

He wished he was with Sandra.

Chapter 9

Mrs Bailey decided it was time she saw Clive's mum. Clive had been staying with them for over two weeks now, and he looked as though he was becoming a fixture. Something would have to be done about it. Apart from everything else — the extra washing and ironing and cleaning — he was eating her out of house and home.

She wasn't sure about the influence he was having on Donovan either. They went about a lot together. Went to the Club. Stayed out later than she liked. Seemed to have lost any interest in their school work.

That was natural, she supposed, to some extent. After what had happened and with the worry of the court case to come. But still.

She couldn't quite put her finger on it, but there was something about Clive that wasn't quite right. For one thing, he was so full of thanks and gratitude for what she was doing for him that it wasn't natural.

Then there were those things he let drop about how he behaved in school. And little bursts of temper. And refusing to go and see his parents. That was why she was going. She sighed. That Clive sure was a worry.

Now Sandra was a different matter altogether. She was a

really nice girl. Sensible and considerate. Donovan was lucky to have found her. Mrs Bailey felt herself glowing warmly as she thought of her.

Of course, it was still just a little boy, little girl thing. But you never knew. Something might come of it.

She remembered the time when Donovan's father had been courting her. It had been good then. He'd been so kind and loving. Wasn't anything he wouldn't have done for her then.

They'd got married and had Donovan. Then he'd gone to England and got a job. Two years later, he sent for her.

But it wasn't the same. He'd changed. Perhaps she'd changed too. Whatever it was, it just wasn't right any more. There'd been rows. There'd been other women. He'd gone off to America and left her.

Well, at first she hadn't been sorry, the way he treated her. Then, she began to miss him, to feel lonely, to feel the need of a man about the house. Now, it didn't matter one way or the other. She'd got used to it. Except sometimes.

Donovan was very like his father. There were times when she caught sight of him unexpectedly and her heart turned over, he was so like. And not just his looks. There were ways he had. Raising his chin and looking at you through narrowed eyes as though you'd insulted him. Turning his lower lip down when he disapproved. Making his eyes glow like two suns when he liked you.

He couldn't have learned those from his father, imitated him. His father had left when he was four. They were in the blood.

It hadn't been easy. Bringing up a boy on your own in a strange city. But she'd worked hard and stayed respectable. She'd made a home for them.

And Donovan had been good. Oh, there'd been little things. As he got older, Donovan liked to be the man. He liked to have his own way. Think he ruled the roost. Well, that was only natural. And he hadn't been too bad. Not like some. And she'd known how to handle him so he thought he was getting his own way — and wasn't.

Would he turn out like his father later? You couldn't tell. She hoped he would be good to Sandra if anything came of it. Make her happy.

Now there was this business with Clive and the police and the court case. Why couldn't they be left to lead their own lives in peace and quiet?

Mrs Bailey had decided to visit Clive's mum on the way home from the hospital. She was on early shift, and the afternoon seemed the best time. She would catch Clive's mum on her own. His father wouldn't be there.

She knew Mrs Miller slightly, the way she knew a lot of the mums and dads. She met her at the shops, at church, at the school on parents' evenings. But she couldn't say she knew her well. She wasn't sure what kind of a welcome she was going to get. She wasn't exactly looking forward to it. But it had to be done. Something had to be settled about Clive.

She rang the bell and looked about her as she waited. It was a well-kept house. The doorstep was swept, the letter-box and bell polished, the door brightly painted, the pointing in the brickwork recently re-done.

It reminded her that it was time she had some work done on her own house. Certainly the paintwork needed doing. It was beginning to crack and peel. But where was the money to come from? Especially with Clive costing so much.

Perhaps she could sell that drum kit she'd bought Donovan. That had cost a lot of money. He hadn't touched it for days and days now. Not since what happened with the police. He seemed to have completely lost interest in it. He seemed to have lost interest in everything.

She rang the bell again.

She heard the bolt being undone, but she had to look carefully to make out whether or not the door had actually been opened. Then she saw a sliver of a face in the crack.

'Good afternoon to you, Mrs Miller,' she said.

The door opened wider.

'Oh,' said Mrs Miller, her face guarded and uncertain. 'Good afternoon to you, Mrs Bailey.'

They shook hands.

'I've come to talk to you 'bout Clive,' Mrs Bailey said.

She took it for granted that Mrs Miller knew that Clive was staying at her house. Word of that kind of thing soon went round.

'I sees,' said Mrs Miller, going all thoughtful. 'I reckons you better come in.'

Mrs Bailey stepped into the house, and Mrs Miller shut the door, but not before she'd taken a quick squint up and down the road as though afraid someone might be lurking there.

She led Mrs Bailey into the front room.

'Sit yourself down,' she said. 'I'll make us some tea.'

While Mrs Miller busied herself in the kitchen, Mrs Bailey gazed round the room. It had been newly decorated. The paper on the walls was bright and clean. A cocktail bar in one corner glittered with bottles and glasses. There were holy pictures above the fireplace, and doilies and dishes on all the little tables. The furry rug in front of the gas fire was new too.

It looked as though Clive's father was doing all right. And here was she having to keep his son. She felt a fury rise up in her, but she pushed it back. She was determined to stay cool.

Mrs Miller came back with a tray of tea things. There was a plate of fancy cakes and banana bread.

'Made it myself,' she said, indicating the banana bread. 'It real good even if I does say so myself.'

'Then that I must taste,' said Mrs Bailey.

Mrs Miller poured out the tea and helped her visitor to load her plate. Then she sat down opposite.

It was she who broached the subject of Clive.

' 'Ow is 'e?' she asked, licking her finger where some icing had got stuck.

'So so,' Mrs Bailey replied. ' 'E got a 'ealthy appetite.'

'Yeah,' Mrs Miller agreed. ' 'E always did like 'is food.'

She spoke as though Clive was in his grave.

Then she seemed to feel that some kind of thanks were due.

'Good o' you to take 'im in. May the good Lord bless you fo' that.'

'Well,' said Mrs Bailey, 'I don' like to interfere in family matters. What go on 'tween parents an' their children ain't none o' my business. But I couldn't very well see the boy starve or walk the streets all night. I feels I 'as a duty to my own people.'

'Yeah, well, I knows 'ow you feels,' said Mrs Miller. 'But I didn' want 'im to leave 'ome that way. It were the father. 'E were so vex at Clive gettin' mix up wit' the law the way 'e done. You knows what men is like. 'E so proud o' 'is name, an' the thought o' it bein' drag through the court were just too much fo' 'im.'

'Yeah,' agreed Mrs Bailey with feeling. 'I knows what men is like.'

Tea seemed to have the same effect on Mrs Miller as rum did on some men. It loosened her tongue. She couldn't stop talking.

'I tries to argue wit' 'im,' she went on. 'After Clive left. I tells 'im it weren't right. But 'e just wouldn't listen. I tries an' tries to make 'im change 'is mind. But it were no good. 'E say Clive 'as made 'is bed an' 'e just 'ave to lie on it.'

'That one o' the troubles,' Mrs Bailey said pointedly. ' 'E don' make 'is bed. Expect me to run after 'im all the time.'

' 'E were always like that,' said Mrs Miller. Again, she made it sound as though he was dead. 'I always 'as to do everyt'in' fo' 'im. An' if somet'in' weren't ready or weren't on time, 'e use to go into such a tantrum.'

She smiled fondly as she remembered.

'That's men again,' said Mrs Bailey.

'Too true,' said Mrs Miller. She gave a sigh. 'I sometimes

think if there weren't any men this world would be a easier, better place.'

At least they were agreed on something, Mrs Bailey thought. But she had to turn the talk back to what she had come about.

'You don' think Mr Miller would 'ave Clive back?' she asked.

'I don' reckon so,' Mrs Miller said, her eyes large and worried. 'You see 'e 'as trouble wit' Clive before. An' 'e warn 'im not to get mix up wit' the law again. Or else.' She pounded the arm of her chair to give emphasis to her words. 'Or else. That what e' say. So you sees when this thing come up, 'e already give 'is word. 'E couldn't go back on it.'

'But 'e 'ave a duty, don' 'e?' said Mrs Bailey. 'Under the law. To look after Clive till 'e sixteen.'

'Oh, the law,' said Mrs Miller scornfully. ' 'E don' care not'in' 'bout the law.'

'But who 'e expect gonna look after Clive?' Mrs Bailey demanded. 'An' feed 'im an' clothe 'im an' give 'im shelter?'

Mrs Miller raised her arms in the air like a dog begging and pulled a bored indifferent face in imitation of her husband's reaction.

'An' you feels the same?' Mrs Bailey asked.

Mrs Miller put on a concerned expression. ' 'Course not. I worries 'bout that boy. Same as any mother would. 'E mine after all. 'E my flesh an' blood. I prays the good Lord to 'elp 'im.'

Mrs Bailey felt she wasn't getting anywhere. She decided she would have to try another approach.

'Do the Social Service know Clive gone?' she asked.

Mrs Miller eyed her warily. 'No. I ain't told 'em. Why should I?'

'Well, you knows you can' go on claimin' child benefit if the child ain't livin' 'ere no more.'

'It ain't my fault 'e ain't livin' 'ere,' Mrs Miller cried in her own defence.

'That ain't the point I were makin',' Mrs Bailey told her. 'The t'ing is you's gettin' the money, an' I's 'avin' the expense. 'Ow 'bout you gives me some money fo' Clive's upkeep?'

Mrs Miller stared at her. 'Money?' she said as though it was a dirty word.

'Well,' Mrs Bailey argued. 'I'm keepin' 'im at the moment, an' you can' pick food off the trees fo' free. Somebody gotta pay fo' it. An' I findin' it rather difficult. You 'is mum. You responsible fo' 'is maintenance till 'e sixteen.'

Mrs Miller thought about it. 'Well,' she said grudgingly. 'I suppose I could give you five pound a week to 'elp out.'

'Five pound!' Mrs Bailey cried contemptuously. 'That ain't 'ardly gonna keep 'im in school dinners.'

'Well, I gets confused these days,' Mrs Miller defended herself, 'by 'ow much t'ings goes up an' 'ow much t'ings costs.'

She lowered her eyelids and gave Mrs Bailey a guarded sideways glance. ' 'Ow much was you t'inkin' of?'

'Ten pound at least,' said Mrs Bailey, 'an' even that ain't much, the way 'e eat.'

Mrs Miller sighed. 'Well, I suppose I can' see the boy starve.'

She got up and stepped across to the sideboard. She opened a drawer and took out her purse. She counted out the money and handed it to Mrs Bailey.

'An' there another t'ing,' Mrs Bailey said. 'What 'bout 'is clothes? 'E only 'ave the t'ings 'e stand up in when 'e come to me. 'E been wearin' some o' Donovan's clothes since then. An' wearin' is the word. 'E been wearin' 'em out. You could maybe let me 'ave some o' 'is clothes so 'e got somet'in' to put on.'

'What kind o' t'ing does you want?' Mrs Miller asked.

Mrs Bailey stared at her in disbelief. Was the woman feeble-minded or something? Fifteen, sixteen years she'd been looking after Clive, and she didn't even seem to know what clothes he needed.

'I can give you a list,' Mrs Bailey said, deciding she would have to spell it out. 'Shirts, vests, pants. Another pair o' jeans an' a sweater. Shoes an' socks. Oh, an' pyjamas. 'E's gone right through the old pair o' Donovan's 'e's been wearin'.'

Mrs Miller gave a weary sigh. 'I'll go see what I can do,' she said, and she went out.

Mrs Bailey tapped her fingers impatiently on the arm of her chair and waited. She was annoyed that she was having to undertake this business. Clive should have come himself. But no, he was too proud. As usual, it was left to her to do the dirty work.

Eventually, Mrs Miller returned. She was carrying a small hold-all. Mrs Bailey eyed it coolly. It didn't look big enough to contain all the items she had mentioned, but she could hardly unpack it there and then and go through it to check. She would just have to hope for the best.

'I'm glad you come,' Mrs Miller said. 'Really, I were so worried 'bout that boy. I feels easier now I knows 'e all right.'

She became thoughtful. 'I don' know 'ow it is 'e turn out this way. 'E were ever such a pretty baby. Everyone say so. An' good as gold. An' then somet'in' just 'appen.'

'Growin' up more difficult fo' some than others,' said Mrs Bailey.

'I reckons,' Mrs Miller agreed reluctantly.

She pressed her visitor to have some more banana bread, but Mrs Bailey declined.

'I gotta get back an' cook a meal,' she said as she struggled out of her chair. 'I got two growin' boys to feed,' she added.

But Mrs Miller didn't seem to take the point. 'Yeah,' she said. 'That's right.'

As she walked home, Mrs Bailey's mind was busy. She didn't notice the other people in the street. She hadn't got all she went for. She hadn't persuaded Mrs Miller to take her son back. But at least she'd got something, little though it was.

'Huh!' she exclaimed aloud. 'Some women don' deserve to 'ave children.'

A woman hurrying past her was startled. She turned round to look. The remark wasn't meant for her, was it?

Chapter 10

Sandra felt hurt and annoyed. Donovan had brought Clive with him. It wasn't the first time. Didn't he realise that having Clive there spoilt everything? She wanted to be with Donovan. Not with Donovan and Clive.

She understood why Donovan brought Clive with him. He meant well. He felt he had a kind of duty. But Clive had plenty of other friends. Donovan didn't need to look after him like a nursemaid all the time.

Mum was busying herself in the kitchen. Dad was on the night shift again. The other children had gone to bed. Sandra was sitting on the settee with Donovan, but she couldn't get close to him. Not with Clive there.

' 'Ow you exam go today?' she asked.

It was after Christmas. Donovan was back at school. He was just beginning his mocks.

'All right, I guess,' he said. He sounded a bit doubtful.

'Maths, weren't it?' Sandra asked.

'Yeah.'

'It were easy,' said Clive. 'If I don' pass that, there ain't no justice in the world.'

Sandra couldn't help feeling that the word 'justice' was unfortunate. The court case was coming up in just over a week. She looked anxiously at Donovan, but he didn't seem to have noticed anything.

'What you got tomorrow?' she went on.

'English.'

'Shouldn't you be doin' some studyin' fo' it?'

'Ain't no revision you can do fo' English,' said Donovan.

'Yeah,' agreed Clive. 'You just 'as to go in there an' sit it.' He laughed and said to Donovan, 'She sound just like you mum.'

Sandra felt her resentment at Clive's presence burst afresh within her.

'But studyin''s important,' she said to justify herself.

'Yeah,' Clive conceded. 'But there's plenty o' time fo' that.'

Sandra frowned but held herself back from saying anything. They watched television in silence for a while.

She hadn't seen much of Donovan over Christmas, what with the family and visiting. Mum had a sister living in Leicester, and they had gone up there for one of the days.

Donovan had given her a gold pendant. Well, gold-plated actually. But that was just as good. And anyway, it was the thought that counted. She was wearing it now. She hoped Donovan noticed. She had given him a pair of leather gloves.

She had only had a few days off for Christmas, and then it was back to work.

Thinking of work reminded her of Errol. He was still being persistent, still pestering her with his attentions and pressing her to go out with him. Well, it might be more fun than sitting here with Donovan and Clive. She suddenly grew hot and reproached herself. What an idea! She wasn't sure that she even liked Errol, whereas Donovan . . . She sometimes wondered if she liked him too much.

Oh, she knew that she kept telling herself that if anything serious came of it, she would make sure Donovan pulled his weight and took his share of responsibilities. Treat her like an equal, not trample all over her. Yet there were other times when she felt she didn't care how he treated her so long as he loved her.

No, it was just having Clive there that turned everything sour and made her think things she wouldn't have done otherwise.

'There ain't not'in' on telly worth watchin',' Clive announced after having gazed at the screen steadfastly for half an hour. 'Why don' we go down the Club?'

'Yeah,' said Donovan. 'Why don' we do that?'

He turned eagerly to Sandra, but she didn't respond. It was not so much that she didn't want to go to the Club. It was more that she didn't want to go there with Clive tagging along. No doubt they would separate once they got there, go their own ways. But he would still be around. What was it about him that she didn't like?

In any case, there'd be a lot of people there. She wanted to have Donovan to herself.

'No,' she said. 'I don' want to. I been workin' all day. I feels too tired.' Then she added, 'But you go if you wants to,' hoping that this would persuade him to stay.

'Come on,' coaxed Donovan. 'It'll do you good to get out.'

'No,' Sandra burst out. 'I told you I'm tired.'

She spoke more harshly than she had intended. She looked hurriedly at Donovan. He and Clive were exchanging glances, as if confirming with each other that girls were beyond them, just too peculiar for them to understand. Sandra fixed her eyes on the television screen and boiled inside. They just didn't want to understand. That was their trouble.

Donovan cleared his throat as though about to speak, but Sandra didn't take her eyes off the screen.

'Well,' he said hesitantly, 'if it's all right wit' you, I think I'll go to the Club wit' Clive.'

'That's all right,' said Sandra. 'You go.' She knew her voice sounded tight and cold, but she couldn't help that.

Donovan put his arm round her and gave her a hug and

an awkward kiss on the cheek. Then he was on his feet, and he and Clive were moving out of the room.

'See you,' Donovan said.

'Yeah, see you,' said Clive.

'Yeah,' Sandra replied without looking at them.

They let themselves out.

Sandra sat and glowered at the television. How could Donovan do that? Just go and leave her like that? Didn't she mean anything to him? How long had they been going out together now? Nine months? Didn't that make any difference? Didn't that amount to something? Or was he just tired of her? He just didn't seem to care.

She blamed Clive. He was no good. He had too much influence over Donovan. Ever since that trouble with the police, ever since Clive had gone to stay with Donovan, things had been going wrong. It was all Clive's fault.

But it was Donovan's too. He was too soft. He was too easily taken in.

Oh, she could understand. They had both been involved in that nasty business. And she could feel sorry for Clive. Being turned out of his home and all that. But that was no reason why Donovan should hang around him all the time and feel he ought to look after him.

Mum came in from the kitchen. She looked round in surprise.

'They gone already?'

'Yeah. They gone to the Club.'

'Didn' they ax you?'

'Yeah, but I'm just too tired.'

'I were just gonna make some tea fo' them. You like a cup?'

'No thanks, Mum. I think I'll just go to bed.'

'But it early yet,' Mum protested.

'Yeah, I knows. But it were a 'ard day.'

Sandra stood up. She knew Mum would be lonely with Dad at work, but she couldn't help it.

Mum was eyeing her shrewdly. 'Everyt'in' all right?'

'Yeah. Sure.'

For a moment, Sandra had a sudden urge to throw her arms round Mum, lean against her and sob her heart out. But it was only for a moment. Instead, she forced her face into a quick smile and kissed Mum goodnight. She felt Mum's hands patting her back.

As she undressed, she found herself remembering Errol again. The way his eyes glowed and ran up and down her. A shiver went through her.

Then she pulled herself together. She told herself not to be silly. She held herself straight and looked at her reflection in the mirror. Why shouldn't someone look at her that way? It was only natural. She was an attractive girl. She had nothing to be ashamed of.

She thought about Donovan. He would be at the Club by now. No doubt he would be talking to the girls there. Chatting them up. Flirting with them.

Well, she didn't care. If that was what he wanted, let him.

She put the light out and climbed into bed. She tried to go to sleep. But the muscles of her face and her whole body were clenched tight with resentment. She rolled over and made a conscious effort to relax.

Again, Errol came into her mind. What would it be like to go out with him? He was older than she was. He was big and good-looking. No doubt he'd had lots of girlfriends.

But would it be fair to Donovan?

She felt her jaw harden once more. What did fairness have to do with it? Was Donovan being fair to her? Just possibly, she decided, when Errol asked her to go out with him again, she might say yes.

Chapter 11

The English exam was harder than Clive expected. Writing a story was easy. He never had any trouble in making things up. It was the comprehension that was the problem. It was one of those multiple-choice things. There was a long piece of writing and then forty questions, each of which was supplied with five possible answers labelled A to E. What you had to do was choose the right answer in each case and write down the appropriate letter.

Just looking at it was enough to put Clive in a panic. For a start, it covered eight sides of paper. He turned over the pages to the end, skimming down the print, and then went back to the beginning. He glanced across at Donovan who was sitting at the desk next to him and let his mouth drop open in a droop of despair. Donovan replied with a similar grimace.

The whole hall had been filled with desks, line upon line of them, two feet apart, for the mock exams. All around, other pupils were frowning furiously at the paper or gazing around them in bewilderment or staring into space with bored expressions on their faces. Teachers patrolled up and down the aisles between the desks to make sure no one cheated and to hand out extra sheets of paper when required.

'You may start,' Mr Lewis announced. He seemed to be in charge. 'You have one hour to complete this part of the exam.'

Clive began to read. The passage being examined was about football hooligans and what ought to be done about them. He got that much. But there were a lot of big words and long sentences that he couldn't make head or tail of. He struggled his way through to the end and studied the questions. They had practised something like this in class, but this was far more difficult.

The first question said, 'All of the following are correct except' and gave five possibilities. Clive read them all, but he was already lost. He put down a D and hoped for the best.

He squinted across at Donovan. He seemed to be getting through them all right. It was a pity his desk was so far away.

Even so, Clive thought, it was worth a try. Donovan wouldn't mind. And Mr Abbott was always saying intelligence was not knowing the answers, but knowing where to find the answers.

Clive opened his eyes wide in an effort to increase his range of vision and beamed in on the letters Donovan had written down. It wasn't much help. The letters were still blurred. He concentrated harder. He was almost certain that the first letter was an E.

Then Donovan turned the page.

Clive blinked and cursed to himself. He brought his eyes back to his own paper. They felt quite strained. He looked around to see if anyone had noticed and found Mr Lewis staring at him strangely. The teacher was only a few feet away. There was a kind of shocked expression on his face. There was no doubt he was gazing fixedly at Clive. Could he suspect something? Clive hurriedly concentrated on the paper in front of him.

It was baffling. 'The writer says the sale of drink at football matches should be banned because A, B, C, D, E.' But which one? They all seemed possible. They all made some kind of sense.

Clive's eyes strayed across to Donovan's desk again. He leaned over slightly in that direction. He located the place on Donovan's answer sheet that he wanted and tried to get the letter into focus. He had just decided it looked like a B when he became aware of someone moving rapidly up the aisle towards him. He hooded his eyes and swung them back to his own paper.

The person had stopped. Clive stayed still for a moment and then glanced up quickly, pretending surprise. It was Mr Lewis. His face was stern and unfriendly.

'Leave your paper on the desk, Miller,' the teacher said. 'I want a word with you.'

Clive put on an expression of bewilderment and incomprehension. Then he shrugged his shoulders, got up and followed Mr Lewis. As he walked up the row of desks, heads and eyes were raised in question.

In the foyer outside the hall, Mr Lewis turned to Clive and said quietly but intensely, 'You were cheating.'

'What?' Clive cried. He screwed his face up into an angry scowl of disbelief. 'What you sayin'?'

Mr Lewis had always had a down on him. Ever since that chair leg went through the window and nearly hit him.

'I saw you,' the teacher went on. 'You were trying to look at Bailey's paper. Twice I caught you at it.'

Clive sucked his teeth in disgust. 'You makin' it up. I weren't doin' not'in' like what you say.'

'I tell you I saw you. You know what happens if you're caught cheating. You were warned. I'll have to cancel your paper.'

'But I weren't cheatin',' Clive protested.

'Look,' said Mr Lewis. 'I saw what I saw. I'm not going to argue.' His lips closed in a determined line.

Clive let himself go. 'That's always the way, innit? You always accusin' me. You always pickin' on me.'

His voice was loud now. He was sure they could hear him in the hall. 'Well, I tell you, I ain't takin' it. No way you gonna stop me sittin' my exam.'

'That's what you think,' retorted Mr Lewis. His voice was loud too.

Clive made to go back into the hall. Mr Lewis put his hand on his arm to stop him. Clive jerked his arm into the air and threw Mr Lewis's hand off.

'Don' you touch me,' he snarled.

Then Mr Abbott was there. He looked anxiously at teacher and pupil. 'What's the matter?'

Clive got in first. He went into a frenzy before Mr Lewis had a chance to explain. He repeated what he had said earlier. ' 'E accuse me o' cheatin'. 'E say I can' take my exam. My paper cancel. Cha! 'E always pickin' on me.' His voice was angry and aggressive.

Then he suddenly stopped.

'I'm not having him speak to me like that,' Mr Lewis said grimly.

Clive lowered his head and looked away. He had seen the look on Mr Abbott's face. There was shock and surprise and doubt there. Clive felt he knew the thoughts that were going through his year head's mind. He was thinking about what happened with the police. He was thinking about the story Clive and Donovan had told him. About how they hadn't got angry or behaved threateningly. He was wondering whether they had told him the truth.

Clive decided he'd better be careful.

'Leave it with me, Mr Lewis,' Mr Abbott said. 'I'll deal with it.'

Clive heard the swing door into the hall open and shut. Mr Lewis must have gone back inside. He risked a quick look at Mr Abbott. His year head was waiting for him to do that. They held each other's eyes for a moment. There was disappointment on Mr Abbott's face.

'Why did you have to do it?' Mr Abbott asked.

'But I weren't cheatin',' Clive protested, though less violently this time.

'Mr Lewis said you were.'

'Well, 'e would, wouldn't 'e? 'E just tryin' to get me into trouble. 'E imagine it. Like the last time.'

'Oh, yes,' said Mr Abbott, remembering.

Clive realised he had made a mistake. He should have kept quiet about it.

'So Mr Lewis just imagined a chair leg came through the window and missed his head by inches?'

'Naw,' Clive admitted reluctantly. 'That were real enough. But it weren't meant fo' 'im.'

'Just as well,' said Mr Abbott drily.

'But this is different,' Clive argued. 'I weren't cheatin'.'

'Mr Lewis said you were.'

They were back there again.

'An' I suppose you believes 'im,' Clive said.

'Yes, I do.'

What else could you expect, Clive thought. Teachers always stuck together. He resigned himself.

What was all the fuss about anyway? Most of the people in the hall would have cheated given half a chance. And most of them probably were. It was just his hard luck to get caught. Just his hard luck that Mr Lewis always kept his eye on him, hoping to catch him out.

'So you're going to have your English exam cancelled,' Mr Abbott went on.

'Yes, sir.'

'It's for your own good. It's better that you learn your lesson this time. If you are caught cheating in the real exams in June, you'll have all your exams cancelled. Now you don't want that to happen, do you?'

'No, sir.'

'And another thing. The way you were behaving to Mr Lewis when I came in. Shouting and arguing. They must have heard you all over the school. And especially in the examination hall. Remember what I've said to you about that kind of thing?'

'Yes, sir.'

Stand and take it, that was it. Just like he was doing now.

'I thought you'd have enough sense to keep out of trouble. Particularly with your court case so near.'

Clive knew Mr Abbott would bring that up sooner or later.

'Yes, sir.'

'You know I want to do the best I can for you, but I can't say good things about you if you keep getting into trouble.'

'No, sir.'

Mr Abbott seemed to have come to an end. 'Right, there's no point in going back to finish your exam. I think you'd better go home for the rest of the day.'

'Yes, sir.'

He might as well do as he was told. Though Mr Abbott seemed to have forgotten that he didn't have a home to go to. At least not one he could call his own. He began to walk towards the door.

'And Clive,' Mr Abbott called after him.

Clive turned to look. The teacher's face was creased up with pleading.

'Please don't get into any more trouble,' he begged.

'No, sir. Thanks, sir.'

Mr Abbott meant well, Clive supposed as he went down the drive. At least he was prepared to listen to you. Not like Mr Lewis. Not like the police.

Clive grew gloomy at the thought of the police and the court case. He wasn't looking forward to that. Not one little bit.

He turned at the gate and made for the High Street. He might as well go to Donovan's house. Mrs Bailey would be there. She'd give him something to eat. He didn't have enough money to buy anything. He could say he'd finished his exam early, it was so easy.

But when he came to the High Street, he had another idea. Perhaps Mr Abbott telling him to go home put it into his head.

He cut off the High Street and down the street that was most familiar to him, the street in which he had grown up.

He didn't think there was any danger of meeting Mum and Dad. Dad would be at work, and Mum would be hiding behind the safety of the bolted door.

And yet, he wouldn't have minded bumping into one or other of them.

He passed the house at an easy pace, not hurrying, but not slowing down either. He glanced up at it. The polished windows. The neat brickwork. Dad's pride and joy. He would have to make his peace there sometime. Stand and take it.

But not yet.

There were other things to think about and get out of the way first.

Chapter 12

Sandra had said yes. She had agreed to go out with Errol. When he had caught her in the staff canteen, at the table in the corner, and sat down in front of her so that she couldn't escape, he had asked her for the twentieth or thirtieth time. The broad bulk of his body blocked her way. His eyes gleamed and glowed and burned through her. His lips curled and smiled and seemed to want to kiss her.

And she had said yes.

Straightaway, Errol had looked pleased. Not so much pleased that she was going out with him. More pleased that at last he had pulled it off. He had won a kind of victory. He was pleased with his own attractiveness and charm. This new proof that he was irresistible.

Now, as she rang up items on the till, Sandra remembered that self-satisfied smirk that had been on his face. In less than an hour she would be with him. He had suggested they go for a meal and then take it from there. He made it all sound very sophisticated. She had warned Mum that she wouldn't be home from work.

But she was dreading it. She didn't know why she had agreed. But no, that wasn't true. She knew perfectly well why she had said yes. Her mouth tightened as she thought of it. It was Donovan. He was so wrapped up with Clive that she might as well not have existed. Well, she would show him. He wasn't the only fish in the sea.

She tried to raise some enthusiasm within herself for the evening ahead. Errol was a good-looking young man. He had a car and knew his way about. He was a man of the world. It would give her status to be seen out with him. She knew some girls who were desperate for the chance.

Still, as the minutes ticked past and closing time drew nearer and nearer, she felt a chill creep over her. What had she done? What had she let herself in for?

When the last customers had gone, she hurried to hang up her overalls. She went into the toilet and examined herself in the mirror. She cooled her face with cold water, freshened up her make-up and tidied her hair. She was wearing a new dress that showed off her figure to advantage. Perhaps it showed too much. She felt her face grow hot again at the idea.

She looked herself resolutely in the eyes and pulled herself up straight. She was going to go through with it. She put on her coat.

Errol was waiting for her. He was wearing a jacket and trousers, a shirt and tie. Sandra had never seen him with a tie before or in anything other than jeans. He looked really smart. He was clearly making an effort to impress. She ought to have been pleased. But somehow it only made her feel more uncertain. Was she doing the right thing? Well, only time would tell.

Errol greeted her with a wide smile. He eyed her up and down.

'You looks good enough to eat,' he said, and he sucked his teeth with appreciation.

Sandra pulled her eyes away from his. She knew she was blushing. It was embarrassing to be stared at like that. And yet it was flattering as well. It was only too obvious what Errol was thinking, and she couldn't repress the quiver of excitement that ran through her.

Errol led the way to his car. It was a big shiny red cadillac, more American than British. It was probably quite old, but Errol obviously lavished a lot of care on it. The bodywork and chrome were polished and glowing. It was just the sort of car he would have. But how could he afford it, Sandra wondered. Was it really his?

Errol opened the door for her to get in. He really was trying to be a gentleman, Sandra thought. Then she noticed the way his eyes slid down to take in her legs as she swung them in. She drew her skirt and coat down over her knees and tried to still the urgent throb in her stomach.

Errol drove fast and flashily, showing off the car. The engine had been tuned, and the car could put on sudden spurts of speed to overtake, swinging and swaying its way through the traffic. All the time, Errol talked, laughing and taking his eyes off the road to look at Sandra. She scarcely heard what he was saying and made only brief replies.

They went quite a distance, to an area Sandra hadn't been to before.

'We use to live round 'ere,' Errol told her, 'till two year ago when Dad change 'is job an' we move.'

They were going to an Italian restaurant Errol knew. He made it sound as though he was a connoisseur of restaurants and this one was something special.

When they got there, Errol parked the car immediately outside though Sandra noticed there was a yellow line. It wasn't half-past six yet.

Errol seemed to know the waiters. They had a joke together and laughed. The restaurant was almost empty. Errol chose a table in the window where they could watch people passing by outside — and where they could be seen. He recommended one of the range of pizzas they did. He ordered a bottle of red wine. When the waiter brought it, he poured a little of it in Errol's glass for him to taste. Errol took a sip and rolled it round in his mouth like an expert before indicating that it was all right. The waiter filled their glasses.

Sandra had had wine before. But only a glass at a time,

not a bottle. She would have to be careful. She worried too about how much it was costing. Ought she to offer to pay her share? But then perhaps Errol wouldn't like that. He wanted to be the big man and show off.

She sipped the wine. It tasted thick and fruity.

'Good, innit?' Errol said. 'It'll warm you up an' make you glow.' He grinned.

As they waited for their pizzas, they talked about people they knew at work. Errol grumbled about the supervisor.

'She always watchin' me,' he complained. 'Ready to pounce on any little t'ing I gets wrong. I don' know 'ow I stands it so long. Maybe it's time I looks fo' somet'in' else. Somet'in' better.'

He didn't seem to realise how lucky he was to have a job at all, Sandra thought. To be able to run a car and afford meals like this.

The pizzas when they came looked delicious. They were huge, practically dropping off the plates. The pastry was crisp and thick with melting cheese and tomato and mushroom and anchovy and olives and heaven knew what else. It was nothing like any of the pizzas Sandra had had before.

'They got a special oven,' Errol explained. 'These is real Italian pizzas. Not them plastic things you gets in other places.'

Sandra cut into her pizza. The cheese stretched like elastic as she lifted a piece on her fork. It tasted good. She took another sip of wine. She began to feel more relaxed.

The restaurant was filling up. Around them, people were chatting and laughing. They seemed to be enjoying themselves. The waiters bustled about taking orders and serving. One of them refilled their glasses from the bottle. Perhaps it was going to be all right after all.

Errol was gazing at her with those liquid eyes of his. There was a slightly amused twist to his lips.

'Tell me,' he asked. 'Why it take you so long before you comes out wit' me?'

'I thought you was just playin' around,' Sandra countered.

'Oh, no,' said Errol. 'When I ax a girl out, I's serious.'

He seemed to want her to drown in his eyes. She lowered her head and concentrated on her pizza.

'You ain't got a boyfriend, do you?' Errol asked.

Sandra hesitated for a moment and then said, 'No.'

'Good. I didn' think you 'ad.'

'An' you? You got a girlfriend?'

'I's sort o' between at the moment,' Errol confessed. Then he gave her another of his wide stares. 'But I could 'ave my eye on a suitable candidate right now.'

His leg under the table brushed against hers. Sandra moved her leg away quickly. But not before a shiver had gone through her body at the contact. She held herself stiff and still and hoped that Errol hadn't noticed.

When they had finished their pizzas, Errol ordered ice-cream. It came in tall glasses, layer upon layer of it, all different colours, with fruit in between.

'This one o' their specialities,' Errol boasted.

Sandra dug into it with her long-handled spoon. The ice-cream was cold and smooth and sweet.

Afterwards, they had coffee. Sandra felt slightly hazy. It must have been the wine. She had had less than half the bottle, insisting that she had had enough and that Errol should finish it. But even so, it was having its effect.

'We could go an' see a movie,' Errol was saying. 'Or go to a disco. Or just go fo' a drive.'

Sandra couldn't think.

'I don' mind,' she said.

'Let's go for' a drive first,' Errol suggested. 'Then we can decide.'

His leg was pressed up against hers under the table. She could feel the muscle of his thigh pumping in and out. Her own leg was trembling.

Errol signalled to the waiter and asked for the bill. When it came, he examined it carefully and checked that it was correct. He took out his wallet and placed some notes on the plate on top of the bill. Sandra's eyes opened wide with shock as she saw how much money Errol put down. Mum would have been horrified.

Again, she wondered whether she should offer to pay half. She knew Errol lived with his parents and didn't have the expense of a bed-sit or a flat or anything like that. But even so. She always paid her way when she went out with Donovan.

She was suddenly hot all over. The thought of Donovan burned through her. She looked around her wildly. What was she doing here? And with Errol? She had a desperate urge to get up and race out of the door.

But then she calmed herself. She was being silly. It was probably just the wine. After all, she wasn't doing anything wrong. Why shouldn't she go out with Errol for a meal? He was someone she knew at work, a friend. It was a perfectly civilized thing to do.

And if Errol did try to take advantage, did try to push it too far, then she was old enough to look after herself.

She glanced quickly at Errol. He was taking his change from the waiter. She didn't think he had noticed her moment of panic.

'Right, let's go,' he said.

He left most of his change on the plate as a tip.

In the car, Sandra worried about Errol's driving. He zoomed out from the kerb without signalling and was hooted at by an approaching car. Errol just laughed. Was it safe for him to be driving after so much wine, Sandra wondered.

'That were a near thing,' Errol said, still grinning. 'If I mash up the car, Dad would —'

He didn't finish. So, Sandra's suspicions had been right. It was the family car, not Errol's at all.

She worried too about where he was taking her. Just for a drive, he said. They seemed to be going north, further out of London. Houses began to give way to what appeared to be countryside. Beyond the street lights, there was darkness.

'Where we goin'?' Sandra asked. She tried to sound casual.

'You sees soon,' Errol replied. He turned and winked at her. 'A nice quiet spot I knows.'

Sandra didn't feel too happy at this news, but Errol didn't seem to notice.

'If only I 'ad my own place,' he went on, 'it would be different. But till then, we just 'as to find some other way.'

He slowed the car down and took a turning off the main road. This road was much narrower, more a lane than a road, with grass verges and hedges on either side. There was no street lighting. Soon Errol slowed the car down again. He swung it off the road onto the grass verge. It bumped and bounced a bit and then came to a halt.

Errol shifted round in his seat to look at Sandra. She could tell that he was smiling.

'Ain't nobody gonna disturb us 'ere,' he said softly.

He leaned forward and switched off the car lights. Then his arm was round Sandra's shoulders and his head was moving towards hers. His lips touched her cheek and worked round to her mouth.

Sandra didn't respond. She held herself stiffly. She could feel her body tingling and yet tense.

Errol's tongue was pushing her lips apart. She felt as though she was suffocating. His hand was moving over her body inside her coat, firm and smooth, stroking and exploring. She could feel her blood stirring. A shudder ran through her.

She pulled her head away. Errol left his hand resting on her thigh.

'Relax,' he whispered. 'Let yourself go.'

His hand began to move again, his finger tips going round and round. She tried to control herself.

'It's better in the back,' Errol said. 'More comfortable. Come on.'

He opened his door and stepped out.

Sandra made an effort to subdue her trembling. Her legs

were weak and shaky. She pushed the door. She put her feet on the ground and stood up. The night air blew chill against her face. She drew her coat about her. Her mind was suddenly clear.

She had been a fool. She had guessed how it would all end and yet she had gone along with it. She had thought she could handle any situation that might arise, but now she wasn't so sure. It was obvious what would happen if she got into the back of the car. She wouldn't be able to stop him. She didn't know if she would be able to stop herself.

But she didn't want to find out. Not with Errol.

She knew what she had to do.

Errol was already climbing into the back. She slammed the door and started to walk, stumbling over the tufty grass and onto the road. Her heels clicked on the asphalt.

Errol called after her. 'Hey! What you doin'?'

She didn't look round. She just kept walking.

'Come back,' Errol yelled.

Then he came pounding after her. He grabbed her arm and swung her round.

'What you think you doin'?' he demanded.

She could see the angry scowl on his face.

'I ain't gettin' in the back o' no car wit' you,' she said.

She was surprised at how firm her voice sounded.

'Come on,' Errol urged, his voice softening. 'Why can' we 'ave some fun?'

' 'Cause I don' want to.'

She pulled away from him and tried to go on, but he caught her arm again.

'Ain't that just like a woman,' he exploded. 'You leads a man on, an' then 'olds out on 'im.' He was really furious now. 'Well, you don' think I spends all that money fo' not'in', do you?'

He dragged her to him and wrapped his arms round her. He pressed his mouth on hers. She struggled, but he was big and strong. She could feel his body hard against her.

She was suddenly terrified. Here, on this lonely road, he could do anything he wanted to.

Fear gave her strength. She pushed against his chest with her hands. She drew her foot back and struck out with all her force. She was lucky.

Errol gave a yelp and let her go. He hopped up and down on one leg and bent down to rub his injured shin. Then he straightened up. They glared at each other.

'Right,' Errol said finally. 'If that the way you wants it. You can walk 'ome.'

He turned on his heel and marched back to the car. Sandra watched as he switched on the lights and the engine. There was an angry grinding of gears as he swung the car out into the road, reversed and shot round to go back to London. The lights and the roar of the engine disappeared into the distance.

It was suddenly very quiet. She was alone in the darkness.

Somewhere, a bird let out a shrill squawk, and there was a rustle of leaves. For a moment, Sandra was startled, and then she recovered herself. She couldn't stand here all night.

She tried to take stock of her situation. She didn't know where she was. She was in the countryside somewhere, dumped and deserted. She would have to get home somehow. But how? Walk, Errol had said.

Very well then, that was what she would do. She set off towards the main road.

It was eerie. She listened to her footsteps while her eyes tried to pierce the darkness all around her. She kept imagining all kinds of things watching her and preparing to leap out at her. It was a comfort when the lights of the main road came into sight.

At the junction, she stood for a moment. She knew she had to turn right. There was quite a lot of traffic. Cars swept past at frequent intervals. Surely there would be buses on a road as busy as this? Perhaps she wouldn't have to walk so far after all. With renewed hope, she hurried on.

She was right. After five minutes, she came to a bus stop.

The notice giving details of the service had been vandalised. There was no way of knowing which buses ran on this route, how often or where to. She would just have to wait and see. But at least there was a chance.

It was cold. Sandra shivered and huddled inside her coat. She felt very conspicuous standing there. As cars passed, she could see heads turn to examine her. She remembered stories she had read in the papers. Errol had been bad enough. If a stranger tried to pick her up, she didn't know what she would do.

And she wouldn't try to hitch a lift either. That was far too dangerous. If no bus came, she'd rather walk.

She shivered again. She moved back from the bus stop to the shelter of the hedge and hoped that no one would notice her.

She waited and waited. She almost gave up. Then she had another idea. If she walked back to civilization, she might be able to find a taxi. It would be worth the expense.

Then at last she saw a bus come trundling towards her. She never thought she would be so glad to see that old familiar red shape. She almost cried for joy.

The sign board said 'Oxford Circus'. That would take her a long way into the centre of London. But she didn't care. She could work out on the journey how to get home from there. She stuck out her hand, jumped on board and found a place. A wave of relief swept through her.

At first, she gazed out of the window, interested in where the bus was taking her. The countryside was soon left behind, and houses and shops crowded in. She even thought she recognised the restaurant where she and Errol had eaten. She congratulated herself. It was going to be all right.

But gradually, reaction began to set in. She remembered what had happened, and her cheeks burned.

What was it Errol had said, 'Ain't that just like a woman?' Well, wasn't it just like a man? Thinking he could buy her with a meal. The arrogance of it. It might have worked with some girls, but it hadn't worked with her. What did he take her for? She wasn't that kind of girl. She wasn't his just for the asking.

And why had she gone out with him in the first place? Because of Donovan. If it hadn't been for him, none of this would ever have happened. She wouldn't have had to put up with Errol's kisses and gropings. She wouldn't be sitting on this bus now wondering how she was going to make her long journey home.

She felt bitterness and resentment swell up inside her.

But underneath, she couldn't prevent a sense of shame and guilt from stirring as well. What else was it Errol had said? 'You leads a man on an' then 'olds out on 'im.' Was that true? She had known the kind of person Errol was. She had known what he wanted. She had known what to expect if she went out with him.

And if she was honest with herself, hadn't she felt a thrill at Errol's touch, his lips on hers, his hand on her body? Hadn't she almost enjoyed it? Part of her had enjoyed it.

That was the most shaming thing of all. How could she ever face Donovan again after that? She could never forgive herself.

She sat hunched on her seat and stared blindly out of the window.

Chapter 13

Donovan was on his way to Sandra's, threading through the late shoppers in the High Street and people scurrying home from work.

Next day, he and Clive were to appear in court. It was three months since they had been arrested outside Aunt Elsie's flat.

It had been a long wait. The thought of the court appearance had been in his mind every minute of the day — and quite a few of the night as well. He was dreading it.

He wasn't quite sure what it would be like. Mr Spence had tried to give him some idea, but he wasn't reassured.

What if the prosecutor asked him awkward questions and tried to trip him up? What if he got things all mixed up and contradicted himself? It was all so difficult.

Mr Spence had done his best. Donovan had liked him better the second time he saw him. He felt sure that the first time — all those questions, going through the story again and again — had just been to test him. There was no doubt that Mr Spence believed him and was on his side. Well, that was something.

Mr Abbott had been good too. He hadn't said much. Just asked when the case was coming up and said he'd be there and he wasn't to worry. But Donovan had got the feeling that he was behind him and would do all he could to help.

No, it had been the waiting that had been the worst bit. Day after day after day of it. Having that hanging over your head and not being able to shake it off.

Mum had worried as usual. Nagged and grumbled at him. He knew it was for his own good, but he still resented it. The way she treated him you'd think he was still a little boy.

It was partly because of the exams. He'd had his mocks, and judging by the results he'd had so far, he hadn't done very well. How could he, when he had this thing like a dark shadow over him all the time? He hadn't been able to do his revision properly. Hadn't been able to settle to it.

But it was partly also Clive. He was still staying with them. And Donovan had to admit he had been going out with Clive quite a lot. To the Club, to see friends, just to wander round the streets. Well, you couldn't act unfriendly, could you? Especially when the person was staying in the same house as you.

He felt sorry for Clive. How could his mum and dad just cast him off like that? They didn't seem to care what happened to him. They hadn't even sent him a Christmas present.

But Mum hadn't liked it. He could tell.

Sandra hadn't liked it either. She hadn't said anything direct, but every time Clive's name came up in talk, she had put on this distant disapproving look. Whenever Clive was with them, she hardly had a word to say. Donovan couldn't understand her. What was wrong with going out with Clive? He was his friend, wasn't he?

Could Sandra be feeling jealous? But that was stupid. Perhaps he hadn't seen her quite so often lately because of Clive. But that didn't mean he didn't care for her any more. It was only natural that he and Clive should stick together. After all, they had something in common. They had gone through an unpleasant experience together. And there was more unpleasantness to come. Couldn't Sandra understand that?

But he didn't want to think about things like that any more. He was on his way to see Sandra. She was waiting for him. The idea of it made him feel warm inside. He quickened his step.

Sandra opened the door. She looked tired and bad-tempered. There was no smile of welcome.

'You're late,' she said.

Donovan was thrown.

'Am I?' he said. 'I didn' mean to be.'

But at the back of his mind he was thinking, 'What have I done? Why's she getting at me like this?'

They went into the living room and sat down on the settee. Sandra's mum was there, half watching television and half concentrating on her crochet.

She looked up. ' 'Allo, Donovan. All right?'

'Yeah, thanks, Mrs King.'

Sandra was staring at the screen. It was some detective series. The criminal was being brought to justice. The defending counsel didn't look anything like Mr Spence. The court set-up looked frightening. All those officials, all that fuss. He hoped it wasn't going to be anything like that tomorrow.

He took a sideways glance at Sandra's profile. The hair drawn back. The smooth curve of her forehead. The long curling eye-lashes. The wide eyes. The jut of her nose. Her lips slightly open. The chin held high.

She seemed to be totally absorbed in what she was watching. And yet he was sure she knew he was looking at her.

Was there something wrong? Wasn't she speaking to him, or something? Was it something he'd said? He'd hardly opened his mouth.

Then Sandra said without taking her eyes off the television, 'Ain't seen you fo' a week.'

So that was it.

'Well, I were out wit' Clive,' Donovan began by way of explanation.

But Sandra interrupted him. 'Oh, that Clive,' she cried. And there was real venom in her voice.

Even her mum was startled. She looked across at her over her spectacles in surprise before going on with her crochet.

'What's wrong wit' that?' Donovan asked.

Sandra turned and fixed her eyes on him. 'You an' that Clive,' she said in an intense whisper. 'That's all I ever 'ears 'bout.'

Donovan couldn't understand her. 'But 'e stayin' wit' me. 'E my friend. 'E mix up wit' the same trouble as me.'

Sandra seemed to soften a little. 'Oh, I knows that.'

'Then why don' you like 'im?'

'I don' know. I just don'. That's all.'

' 'Ow's work?' Donovan asked, changing the subject and hoping that would bring back the old Sandra. She liked chatting about things that happened at work.

But her answer was like a slap in the face. 'What you wants to know 'bout that fo'?' she snapped.

Her eyes were glaring at him. He held them for a moment and then looked away. What had he seen there? Anger? Alarm? A strange defensiveness? It was as if she had something to hide.

What had got into her? He just couldn't make her out at all.

Sandra was gazing at the screen again. She seemed to have cut herself off from him completely.

It was the news now. Donovan had missed how the court case ended.

He watched the newscaster, but he couldn't really take in what she was saying. He was worrying about Sandra. She seemed suddenly to have gone cold and unfeeling. He tried to make light of it, pretend it was nothing important, but inside he knew he was deeply unhappy. He was hurt. Why should Sandra treat him like this?

There was some discussion programme on next, but

Donovan wasn't interested. His eyes began to water. He knew if he didn't get out of there quick, he'd be crying.

'I've gotta go,' he said suddenly, jumping to his feet.

'So soon?' said Mrs King, surprised.

'Yeah. Gotta get ready fo' the big day.' He pretended a brightness he didn't feel.

Sandra saw him to the door.

'I 'opes it go well tomorrow,' she said, her face solemn and serious.

'Yeah,' said Donovan with a forced grin. 'Me too.'

He turned his back on her and strode along the walkway.

She hadn't touched him or kissed him or anything, he thought. He bit his lips to prevent the tears from coming. What had it all been about? She didn't care for him at all. Here he was, up in court, having to relive that horror, and was she worried? Oh no. She'd said she hoped it went all right, but that was only being polite, wasn't it? It didn't mean a thing.

As he went down the stairs and turned the corner, he thumped the wall with the flat of his palm.

Well, if that was the way she wanted it, she could have it. But he knew he didn't mean it.

When he reached the bottom, he paused for a moment and pressed his head against the concrete wall. It was cold against his face. He screwed up his eyes, and his mouth went into a contorted grimace. He held his breath.

Then he relaxed. He pulled his face away from the wall and let out a deep sigh. He turned and walked through the estate towards the main road.

He walked like a dummy, putting one foot in front of the other, but not really seeing where he was going. His mind was miles away, thinking of Sandra. Thinking of Sandra and him. Had it all been a mistake? Had he just imagined that she liked him?

He crossed the High Street, getting nearer to home, and thoughts of the next day began to return and intrude.

What if he were found guilty?

The possibility must have been at the back of his mind some time. Mr Spence must have mentioned it. But somehow it had never made an impression. He was innocent. How could he be found guilty? It was the actual appearance in court that was the ordeal, not any worry over the verdict.

But now, the thought was suddenly up front, pounding in his forehead. It couldn't happen, could it? Hadn't he been through enough? They wouldn't do that to him on top of everything else.

He tried to convince himself. Told himself that that wouldn't be right. It wouldn't be justice.

But no matter how hard he tried, a chill struck deeper and deeper into his bones.

And it wasn't the chill of the night air.

Chapter 14

They were told to be at the Juvenile Court at ten o'clock, and they all turned up promptly. But there were two cases before theirs, and they had to wait.

More waiting, Donovan thought bitterly. Presumably they were all asked to arrive at the same time because no one knew how long a particular case would take.

'Don't worry,' said Mr Abbott. 'It'll be all right.'

Clive smiled, but Donovan was less certain.

'Mr Watson's appearing for the police,' Mr Spence told them. 'I know him slightly. Met him a couple of times. He's quite sound.'

The information wasn't very reassuring.

They waited in a small ante-room. Policemen kept walking past, looking in and giving them a steady neutral stare.

Donovan felt Clive nudge him urgently. He raised his head in time to see a young policeman with a square face and a thin blond moustache.

Mr Spence had noticed too. 'Was that him?' he asked.

'Yeah,' said Clive with a sneer. 'That's 'im. I've been askin' my friends. 'E's well known. Always throwin' 'is weight 'bout an' makin' out 'e's Mister Big.'

Donovan's mum and Aunt Elsie vented their shared indignation.

'Why don' they go lookin' fo' real criminals?' Mrs Bailey wanted to know. ' 'Stead o' 'arassin' our boys?'

'Why they didn' want to see the receipt?' Aunt Elsie demanded. 'That what I keeps askin' myself. I offers it an' they just ignores me. Seems to me they just out to cause trouble. They out to get those boys. Ain't interested in not'in' else.'

They went on for a while, grumbling and complaining, before subsiding.

Clive chattered about this and that. But Donovan gave him only mumbled replies. And then even Clive was silent.

A feeling of gloom descended on them. It was almost more than Donovan could bear. All this hanging around. Why didn't they get on with it? It was almost as though they were doing it deliberately as part of the agony, as part of the suffering and punishment.

A sudden flurry of activity in the corridor announced that the first case was over. A white boy went past, talking to his solicitor. He was smiling. Whatever he'd been up for, he must have got off.

Was that a good sign? Donovan wasn't sure.

He sank back on his chair and tried not to think about it. He tried to make his mind a blank so that he wouldn't brood on the ordeal to come. But his anxiety kept rising to the surface. Would he be able to answer the questions? Would Mr Watson try to trick him? Mr Spence had said he was 'quite sound'. What would the police say? Would the magistrate give him a fair hearing?

He would be glad when it was over.

He must have managed to blot out some of the time because the next thing he knew was Mr Spence saying, 'We're next.'

The second case had been short. It had been adjourned so that the defendant could get legal representation. Donovan wished it had gone on longer. He suddenly felt he wasn't ready. His body was tingling. He had the feeling he was shaking all over. He wouldn't be able to speak. But when he looked down at the hand lying on his thigh, that seemed to be steady enough. All the turmoil was going on in his mind.

Clive gave him a quick look. 'This is it,' his eyes said. Donovan returned the glance grimly. They got up and went out into the corridor.

The courtroom was small and dark. The walls were panelled with wood. There was a witness box and a raised bench with the magistrate's seat behind it and above it a huge coat of arms. The atmosphere was heavy and solemn. Like being at a funeral. Donovan sat down and tried to stop his heart from beating so fast.

They had to stand up when the magistrate came in, and then Donovan and Clive had to stand up again on their own as the charge was read out. They were asked how they pleaded.

'Not guilty,' said Donovan.

His voice came out louder than he intended. Somehow he had been afraid that if he didn't make an effort no sound would have emerged at all.

'Not guilty,' said Clive in more of a mumble.

They sat down once more, and Donovan felt his body begin to tingle and tremble again. He tried to get a grip on himself. At least it's started, he told himself. At least it'll soon be over.

But the thought didn't comfort him. There was something about the magistrate that he didn't like. Something about him that seemed to say he wasn't on their side. The magistrate was about sixty with a bald head and a grey face. Donovan couldn't tell whether the expression on his face was one of boredom or disapproval.

Mr Watson stood up. He had shiny rosy cheeks like apples that had been polished. He made a brief statement in a bored self-satisfied voice. He sounded as though he couldn't quite understand what all the fuss was about, why the defendants hadn't pleaded guilty when the case against them was so obvious. It would have saved them all so much bother.

He said he would call witnesses to show that the two defendants were guilty of the charge of resisting arrest. The first witness was PC Logan — the young policeman with the fair moustache who had first stopped Donovan and Clive.

Helped by questions from Mr Watson, PC Logan gave his version of what had happened. He spoke flatly and without emotion.

Donovan listened with growing disbelief. How could the policeman say such things? It hadn't been like that at all. The policeman was making it up. He was telling lies. Donovan wanted to jump up and shout at him, shout at the court and tell them.

But he had to sit there and hold back his anger.

What was more, the policeman had a notebook in front of him. He kept referring to it when Mr Watson asked him questions. He had it all written down. That wasn't fair either. Donovan had only his memory to rely on.

According to PC Logan, he had been off duty when he saw the two defendants acting in a suspicious manner. They had been carrying a suitcase, and he had approached them. He had told them he was a police officer and enquired whether the case was theirs. The two defendants had become abusive and had started to swear at him. He cautioned them that if they continued to carry on in this way, he would have to arrest them. They became more abusive and began to behave in a threatening manner.

At this point, PC Logan had been joined by two colleagues, PC Bedford who was in uniform and PC Ward who was off duty. The defendants had again been warned that if they continued to be uncooperative, they would be arrested. It didn't make any difference. The defendants went on swearing and acting threateningly.

Then the defendants had thrown the case to the ground and tried to escape. They ran into a block of flats. PC Logan and his colleagues followed them. PC Bedford arrested Bailey, but when PC Logan had tried to arrest Miller, the defendant had resisted and had attacked him. It was only with difficulty that the defendant had been restrained.

A police van had been called, and the defendants were taken to the station for questioning.

As Donovan watched PC Logan's impassive face and listened to his statement, he grew more and more angry. It wasn't right that he should tell lies like that.

The magistrate was watching carefully too. He kept his eye firmly on PC Logan as he gave his evidence, but in a tired sort of way. As though he was doing it out of a sense of duty rather than because he found the case of any great interest. He jotted down notes of what PC Logan said.

Donovan felt his anger begin to merge into despair.

Mr Spence stood up and began to ask PC Logan some questions.

'Can you tell the court why you first became suspicious of the defendants?' he asked.

'They were carrying a suitcase,' PC Logan replied.

'I imagine lots of people carry suitcases,' Mr Spence said, 'and you wouldn't think of stopping them all. Was there anything particular about the way the defendants were carrying this suitcase?'

'They were behaving suspiciously.'

'Can you be more precise?'

PC Logan searched his mind for the right words. 'They were looking furtive.'

'I see,' said Mr Spence. 'You say the defendants became abusive and threatening. Can you give a more exact account of how they behaved?'

PC Logan referred to his notebook. 'They swore at me and threw their arms about in the air.'

'And this you construed as threatening?'

'Yes, sir.'

'You don't think it could have been an expression of their surprise at being stopped?'

'No, sir.'

'I see,' said Mr Spence. He thought for a moment and then asked suddenly, 'What was in the case?'

'I don't know, sir,' said PC Logan. 'The defendants said it was an organ.'

'So you stopped the defendants because you considered they were behaving suspiciously, but you did not personally investigate what was inside the case?'

'No, sir. The defendants tried to escape before I had an opportunity to do so.'

'Were there other people around at the time that you stopped the defendants?'

'Yes, sir. A number of people had gathered to see what was going on.'

'Did one of those people tell you that the case was hers and that she had lent it to the boys?'

'I do not recollect that, sir.'

'When the defendants were finally arrested, what happened to them?'

'They were taken to the station in a police van.'

'Did you accompany them in the van?'

'Yes, sir.'

'Did anything improper happen on the journey?'

'No, sir.'

'The defendants were not mistreated or racially abused?'

'No, sir.'

During the questioning, PC Logan's face had grown progressively redder and grimmer. By the end, he was gripping his notebook tightly and glaring stiffly ahead of him as though getting more and more annoyed that his word was being doubted.

Donovan didn't know what effect Mr Spence's questioning would have on the magistrate's decision. The magistrate had looked across impatiently a couple of times as though weary that the cross-examination was going on so long and so unnecessarily.

Donovan remembered that Mr Spence had said that it

was a bit tricky bringing in allegations of police mistreatment. It was only their word against that of the police, and magistrates didn't like it. Presumably, they thought our police were wonderful and didn't take kindly to the idea of them being smeared.

But it was a risk Mr Spence felt he had to take. You didn't always win a case by telling the truth, but in this instance, he had decided that the truth ought to be told.

The second witness was PC Bedford, the policeman who had arrested Donovan. He was older than PC Logan, more experienced. He gave his evidence in a much more relaxed way.

He stated that he had been on duty patrolling the area. He stopped to talk to a colleague, PC Ward, who had been in plain clothes, when he noticed a disturbance on the other side of the street. As he and PC Ward crossed to investigate, he recognised PC Logan. He too was in plain clothes. The defendants were acting in an abusive and threatening manner.

PC Bedford heard PC Logan caution the defendants, but the defendants went on swearing and behaving in an aggressive way. Then PC Logan had told them they were under arrest. The defendants had pushed past him and tried to escape.

PC Bedford gave chase and caught up with the defendant Bailey inside the block of flats. Bailey had tried to resist arrest, but he (PC Bedford) had managed to restrain him and took him outside. Later, PC Logan brought the defendant Miller out. The two defendants were put in a police van and taken down to the station.

'Did you know what the dispute was about?' Mr Spence asked him.

'I understand the defendants refused to tell PC Logan what was inside the case they were carrying,' PC Bedford replied.

'Did someone in the crowd explain that the case was hers and that she had lent the case to the defendants?'

'I do not recollect that, sir.'

'You say the defendant Bailey resisted you when you arrested him inside the block of flats?'

'Yes, sir.'

'What did he do exactly?'

'He turned and faced me. He threw his arms about and tried to punch me.'

'What did you do?'

'I got hold of his arms and pinioned them behind his back.'

'Did you punch the defendant Bailey?'

'No, sir.'

'Did you accompany the defendants to the station?'

'Yes, sir.'

'Are you aware of any mistreatment of the defendants on the journey?'

'No, sir.'

'No one pulled the defendants by the hair and crashed their heads against the side of the van?'

'No, sir.'

'No one used terms of racial abuse against them?'

'No, sir.'

PC Bedford put up with the cross-examination without allowing it to upset him. It was just routine to him. His manner suggested that he was always being accused of punching defendants and using racial abuse, but he wasn't going to let slanders like that worry him or put him off telling the truth.

Again, he had a notebook in front of him to which he referred.

Donovan listened with growing despair. PC Bedford's story tallied exactly with what PC Logan had said. It wasn't what had happened. It was more lies. But would the magistrate see it that way? If he was likely to believe what one policeman said, wasn't he even more likely to believe it when there were two of them?

But Donovan didn't have more time to worry about that.

It was suddenly his turn. He was in the witness box, taking the oath, gazing round him petrified, feeling his mouth grow dry and his tongue swell up to block his throat. He licked his lips nervously and waited.

Mr Spence gave him a reassuring look and asked him to describe what had happened.

It wasn't so bad once he got started. It was still so vivid in his mind. It might have been only yesterday that it happened.

He told how he had called on Clive and how they had gone to Aunt Elsie's to borrow her organ. Then they had been stopped by a man.

'Was this man in police uniform?' Mr Spence asked.

'No, sir.'

'Did he say he was a police officer?'

'No, sir.'

'What was your reaction when he stopped you?'

'I were surprised. It weren't as if the organ were stolen or anyt'in' like that.'

'Did you swear at PC Logan or threaten him?'

'No.'

'What did you do?'

'I told 'im what were in the case.'

'Did PC Logan then caution you and tell you that you would be arrested?'

'I never 'eard 'im say not'in' like that.'

'What happened when PC Logan was joined by PC Bedford and PC Ward?'

'I got frightened. I couldn't understand what they all wants wit' us.'

'So you ran.'

'Yes, sir.'

'Into the block of flats.'

'Yes, sir.'

'But you must have known the police officers would follow you there and there was no way out.'

'Yes, sir. But I didn' think 'bout that. I just wants to get away from them. I were frightened what they was goin' to do.'

'What did you think they were going to do to you?'

Donovan swallowed and bowed his head. 'Beat me up.'

'What happened when PC Bedford arrested you?'

' 'E pull my arms behind my back an' shove me down the stairs. Then he push me against the wall an' punch me in the ribs.'

'Were you trying to resist arrest?'

'No, sir. I weren't doin' not'in'.'

'Did you have to go to the doctor's to have your ribs seen to?'

'Yes, sir.'

'Was there bruising there?'

'Yes, sir.'

'Then what happened?'

'I were taken outside an' made to lie on the pavement. Then the police grabs me by the arms an' legs an' throws me into the van.'

'Threw you?'

'Yes, sir. I lands on the floor.'

'Did anything happen on the way to the station?'

'Yes, sir. One o' the policemen pull me by the 'air an' bang my 'ead against the side o' the van. 'E call me a black bastard.'

As he uttered the words, the shame and humiliation of it all welled up inside him.

'Do you know which police officer did this?'

'No, sir.'

While giving evidence, Donovan glanced every now and then at the magistrate, apprehensive about what he might be thinking. But most of the time, the magistrate was staring down at his desk. He seemed to have lost interest in what was going on. Perhaps he had already made up his mind.

It was now Mr Watson's turn. He stood up to begin his cross-examination of Donovan. He had a way of glancing down at his papers and then suddenly raising his eyes at you over the top of his spectacles which Donovan found disconcerting. The eyes were bright and piercing.

'Were you angry when PC Logan stopped you?' Mr Watson asked.

'No, sir. I were surprised, that's all.'

'Didn't you swear at him and use offensive language?'

'No, sir.'

'I put it to you that when PC Logan stopped you, you became angry and began swearing at him and threatening him.'

'No, I never,' said Donovan. Why was Mr Watson going on at him like this? 'What right did 'e 'ave to stop me that way? I 'adn't done not'in wrong. I'd been loaned the organ. I 'adn't stolen it or anyt'in'.'

Too late, Donovan realised why Mr Watson had been going on. His voice was getting louder and more strident as he proclaimed his innocence. It sounded as if he was getting angry. A tiny flicker of a smile on Mr Watson's lips showed that was exactly what he wanted.

'So you think a police officer has no right to stop you?' Mr Watson went on.

'Not if I ain't done not'in' wrong.' Donovan tried to keep his voice cool, but he wasn't sure that he had given the right answer.

'Why did you try to escape when PC Logan said you were under arrest?'

'I were frightened,' Donovan replied. And then hurriedly added, 'But I didn' know I were under arrest. 'E never say so.'

'If what you say is correct, then why did you run? Doesn't that suggest you were guilty?'

'I were frightened I said.'

'I put it to you that you ran away in order to evade arrest. Isn't that so?'

'No.'

'PC Bedford was in uniform, was he not?'

'Yes, sir.'

'So you knew he was a police officer.'

'Yes, sir.'

'When PC Bedford caught up with you in the block of flats, you must have known that he intended to arrest you.'

Donovan was confused. 'Yes, sir. No, sir. I wasn't sure what 'e want. 'E didn' say.'

'I think you must have known, so why did you resist him and try to punch him?'

'I didn' resist. I didn' punch 'im. It were 'im what punch me.'

Mr Watson pursed his lips and gave Donovan a long look over the top of his spectacles that said more eloquently than words that he knew the defendant was lying.

But it was over. Donovan was free to leave the witness box. He stepped down and returned to his seat. His legs were shaking.

It was Clive's turn now. Donovan scarcely heard what he said to begin with. He sat numbly on the bench and brooded miserably on what he had just been through.

Had it been all right? Had he said the right things? Or had he simply helped to convince the magistrate that he was guilty? He just didn't know.

Clive was answering Mr Spence's questions in a mumble. Or was saying as little as possible, just 'Yes, sir' and 'No, sir'. He was keeping his head down and giving an impression of someone too timid to look you in the eye. Donovan wasn't sure it was a good idea.

The magistrate had to interrupt twice to ask Clive to speak up. Well, at least that proved he was listening, Donovan thought. That was something. Though the irritated way in which the magistrate had asked suggested that Clive's mumbling wasn't exactly helping their cause.

Mr Spence led Clive over the same ground that he had gone over with Donovan. What Clive said supported everything that Donovan had already told the court. The only new information was about what happened to Clive in the flats.

'So you were on the top floor of the flats,' Mr Spence said, 'when you were approached by PC Logan and PC Ward.'

'Yes, sir.'

'Did they caution you or say you were under arrest?'

'No, sir.'

'What did they do?'

'They push me against the wall an' thump me.'

'Then what happened?'

'They took me downstairs.'

'Who was holding you?'

'PC Logan.'

'What happened outside?'

'We sort o' trip up an' fall to the ground.'

'Did you do this deliberately?'

'No. I don' know 'ow it 'appen. It were a accident. I were feelin' dizzy. Our legs just sort o' mix up.'

'What did PC Logan do then?'

' 'E kick me an' drag me up.'

'Did anything happen in the police van on the way to the station?'

'Yeah. My 'ead were bashed against the side o' the van. I were called a black bastard.'

'Do you know who did this?'

'Yeah. It were PC Logan.'

Mr Watson indicated that he had no questions.

Donovan was alarmed. What did that mean, he wondered. Did Mr Watson think the case was so cut and dried? Was Donovan and Clive's guilt so obvious that there was no need for further questioning?

When Clive came and sat down next to him, his face was glum and miserable. He looks the way I feel, Donovan thought.

Aunt Elsie was called next. She took the stand and gazed defiantly round the courtroom. She read out the oath in a deep confident voice. Nobody was going to overawe her or prevent her from telling the truth loud and clear, and if they didn't want to hear it, then that was just too bad. Donovan felt his hope begin to revive.

Aunt Elsie explained how she had lent the boys the organ. Then she told how she had been going to catch a bus back to work when she saw a crowd on the pavement. She approached and discovered three men, one of them a policeman, talking to Donovan and Clive.

'What did you think was going on?' Mr Spence asked.

'It seem to be some row 'bout the suitcase,' said Aunt Elsie. 'They seem to think the boys 'ad stole it.'

'So what did you do?'

'I tells 'em the organ were mine an' I 'ad loan it to the boys. I 'ad a receipt fo' it, I says. I offer to show it to 'em.'

'Did the police officers take you up on this offer?'

Aunt Elsie snorted with contempt. 'No, they never. They wasn't interested in it.'

'Can you tell the court what you saw when the police officers brought the defendants out of the flats?'

'One o' them 'ad Donovan wit' 'is arms behind 'is back. 'E made 'im lie face down on the pavement. Then Clive were brought out. 'E sort o' trip up an' Clive an' the policeman tumble to the ground. Then the policeman got up an' kick Clive. I seen it.'

'That was PC Logan?'

'Yeah, that were 'im.'

'Then what happened?'

'The boys was thrown in the police van. An' I means thrown. It were like they was lumps o' wood or somet'in'.'

'Thank you, Miss Benson,' Mr Spence said.

When Mr Watson stood up to cross examine her, Aunt Elsie gave him a hostile scowl.

'There were other people about outside the flats,' Mr Watson asked, 'when the police officers were dealing with the defendants?'

'Yeah,' said Aunt Elsie. 'Quite a crowd.'

'So it would have been quite easy for the police officers not to notice you.'

'I don' see 'ow they could 'ave done that. I were makin' enough noise.'

'No more questions.'

Mr Watson might have finished, but Aunt Elsie hadn't.

'What I wants to know,' she cried indignantly, glaring at the magistrate, 'is why the police stops two boys goin' 'bout their lawful business. Why didn' they pay no attention to me when I tells 'em I loan the boys the organ? Why didn' they want to see the receipt?'

The magistrate waited impatiently until she had finished her outburst, and then waved his hand at her to show that she could step down. Aunt Elsie looked as though she was going to give him a bit more of her mind, but she thought better of it. She contented herself with glaring at him and sniffing. Then she went back to her seat.

Mr Abbott took her place.

'How long have you known the defendants?' Mr Spence asked.

'I have known the defendants for four and a half years,' Mr Abbott told him.

'Have either of them ever been in serious trouble in school?'

'No. Donovan has never been in any trouble. He has always been polite and friendly. Clive has sometimes been in trouble, but nothing that I would call serious.'

'You have heard the police officers say that the defendants swore at them and behaved in a threatening manner. From your knowledge of them, would you say that was in character?'

'No. I have never heard Donovan swear at anyone. I couldn't imagine him being violent. Clive can sometimes get a bit hot-tempered.'

Mr Abbott hesitated and then went on. He seemed to be picking his words carefully. 'He's sometimes been involved in fights with other boys, and he sometimes acts without thinking. But he has never attacked a teacher.'

'Thank you, Mr Abbott.'

It was time for the summing up. Both Mr Watson and Mr Spence were brief.

Mr Watson said there was no doubt. The evidence of the police officers showed quite clearly what had happened. The fact that the defendants had run away — something they admitted — proved that they had tried to resist arrest. Even if by some oversight the police officers had failed to give the defendants the proper caution, the fact that one of them was in uniform should have made it obvious that they were on official business, and the defendants ought to have done what they were told.

Mr Spence took up Mr Abbott's evidence and pointed out that it was out of character for the defendants to behave in the way the police officers had described. They had run away not because they were trying to resist arrest but because they had been frightened and had panicked. The police officers had failed to explain to the defendants what their position was.

He didn't mention the behaviour of the police after they had been arrested. Perhaps he thought it tactful not to.

The court stood up. The magistrate retired to consider his verdict.

Mr Spence and Mr Abbott went outside to have a cigarette. Donovan joined them. He needed some fresh air.

'I can see it all now,' Mr Spence said. 'That police officer who started it all. Logan? Young and inexperienced. He gets himself into a situation and then doesn't know how to get out of it. He overreacted. He charged into it, and then the only way he could get himself out of it was to put the boot in. Then, when the others arrived, of course they had to back him up. And then afterwards, in the canteen over a cup of coffee, they get together with their notebooks and work out their story.'

'Yes,' agreed Mr Abbott. 'I've known young teachers react in exactly the same way. And they've had three or four years' training. How long does a policeman get? Sixteen weeks?'

'That's what's wrong,' said Mr Spence. 'The training. They just don't get any idea of the kind of sensitivity you need when you're dealing with people.'

Donovan thought about his head being bashed against the side of the police van. And the name he had been called. That didn't show much sensitivity either.

'And what really maddens me,' Mr Spence went on, 'is the way they get away with it. They have no thought of the effect their actions have on people's lives.'

Clive pushed his head round the door.

' 'E's comin' back,' he said. His face was drawn and anxious.

Mr Spence and Mr Abbott ground their cigarette butts into the pavement. They hurried back to the courtroom.

Donovan should have known from the very beginning. Standing there with Clive, the magistrate staring sternly down at them, he knew what the verdict was going to be. Guilty. It was inevitable. Who would take his word against that of the police?

But it still hurt.

He only half heard what the magistrate was saying. Need to uphold law and order. Need to support the police going about their duties.

Then the magistrate came to the sentence. A one-year conditional discharge.

It was over. The court stood. The magistrate disappeared through the door behind his seat. They were free to go.

No one spoke until they got outside. Then Donovan's mum and Aunt Elsie let rip.

'It ain't right,' Mrs Bailey cried. 'It ain't fair. Those policemen just tells lies. They beats up my son, an' 'e the one what get punish fo' it.'

'That's 'em all over,' said Aunt Elsie. 'They can do what they likes, an' ain't nobody cares 'bout it.'

'Yes, I know,' said Mr Spence. 'But it could have been worse. So long as Donovan and Clive keep out of trouble for the next year, then nothing will happen.'

'That ain't so easy,' said Aunt Elsie. 'I knows 'em policemen. They'll be on the look-out fo' Donovan an' Clive all the time. They won't be able to leave their 'ouse. The police don' like people standin' up fo' their rights an' tellin' the truth an' lettin' the world know 'ow they treats black people.'

'Yes, you'll have to be careful,' Mr Spence agreed. 'You'll have to keep away from the kind of place where the police could catch you out.'

Donovan had only been half listening. His mind was still in the courtroom, hearing the magistrate say he was guilty. He couldn't bear it. He broke out suddenly, 'I ain't takin' it.'

The others turned to look at him.

'I'm gonna fight it,' he said defiantly.

'You mean you want to appeal?' Mr Spence asked.

'Yeah.'

Mr Spence became doubtful.

'I know how you feel,' he said, 'but I don't advise it. There's no point. The police have got their evidence off word perfect, and it's very difficult to win a case like this when it's your word against theirs. If we appealed against the sentence, we would have to take the case to the Crown court, and then if you were found guilty again, you might get a stiffer sentence.'

'What?' Donovan cried.

It didn't make sense. But then Mr Spence presumably knew about the law. It seemed, no matter how they tried, that there was no way Donovan and Clive could win. The spark of defiance was snuffed out almost as soon as it had spluttered into life. They would just have to accept defeat.

'Never mind,' said Mr Abbott, trying to console them. 'You know you are in the right, and we know you are in the right. That's what matters.'

Donovan gave him a brief unhappy smile. 'Yeah, I suppose so.'

They stood about on the pavement outside the court-house, not quite knowing what to do or say.

'Better get back to work,' Aunt Elsie said at last with a sigh.

'Me too,' said Mrs Bailey. She searched her son's face for a moment. 'You be all right?'

'Yeah, Mum,' said Donovan.

'I can give you a lift back to school,' Mr Abbott told the two boys.

Then he seemed to change his mind. 'After this morning, I don't suppose you feel much like it. Well, if you don't turn up, I shan't notice.'

'Thanks, sir,' said Donovan.

Mr Abbott and Mr Spence said their goodbyes and began to walk away. Then Mr Abbott turned back.

'By the way,' he said. 'I've been meaning to ask. It's been puzzling me. What happened to the organ?'

'Huh,' grunted Aunt Elsie. 'They just leave it dumped on the pavement. When they go, I picks it up an' takes it back to my flat. Like I says, they ain't interested in the organ. They just out to get the boys.'

That was certainly the way it seemed, Donovan thought bitterly. And they had succeeded.

Mum and Aunt Elsie lingered a while longer, worried about how the boys were taking the verdict. Then they too had to go. Donovan and Clive were left alone.

Clive began to kick despondently and half-heartedly at the brick wall of the courthouse. His face was cloudy with thought. He didn't seem to be aware what his foot was up to.

Neither of them wanted to talk about what they had been through.

'What you gonna do?' Clive asked eventually.

'I don' know,' said Donovan. 'Go 'ome I suppose.'

'Me too,' said Clive.

Donovan set off towards the High Street. But Clive didn't follow.

'Ain't you comin'?' Donovan called.

'Naw,' said Clive. 'I'm goin' to my own 'ome. Time I sorted t'ings out.'

He turned and walked in the opposite direction, his hands stuck in the pockets of his trousers and his shoulders hunched up.

Donovan watched for a moment and then breathed out deeply. He began to walk home. His whole body was empty as though every bone had been crushed. He had no feelings left.

Chapter 15

Guilty!

The word echoed through Clive's head as he strode along the pavement towards home.

How could it have happened? He was innocent. It was the police who were the criminals. Not acting properly. Beating him up. Keeping him in a cell.

Mr Spence had tried. So had Donovan's Aunt Elsie and Mr Abbott. His year head even seemed to believe that the chair leg from the window that just missed Mr Lewis was an accident.

But it had all been useless. It was only to be expected that the magistrate would listen to the police and believe them. Even when they were telling lies. You could see it in his face. The way he looked at you as though you were of no importance. As though you were hardly worth bothering with. As though nothing you said could be trusted.

Well then, what did it matter? Policemen, magistrates, they were all the same. They were all on the same side. There to make sure people like him were kept down. Kept in their place. Punished even when they hadn't done anything.

They called themselves the law and justice. That was a

laugh. They'd broken more laws and done more wrong in a few hours than he had in his whole life.

Guilty did they say he was? Right, he'd show them. He'd been punished for something he hadn't done. So why should he bother in future? Why should he have any respect for the law when it didn't have any respect for him?

He didn't know what he would do yet. What were those fancy words they used to describe crimes? Breaking and entering. Malicious damage. Handling stolen goods. Grievous bodily harm. There was a wide enough choice. He wasn't sure what his line would be. He'd have to think about it. He had contacts. He could make something of it.

After all, if they said he was guilty, why not be guilty of something? And get the benefit of it.

Of course, he'd have to be careful. What Donovan's Aunt Elsie had said was right. He was a known figure now. The police would be watching him. Just waiting to get their hands on him again on any old charge they could trump up.

Yes, he'd be on his guard. He wouldn't take any unnecessary risks. He'd make sure he covered his tracks and didn't make it easy for them.

But he was going to do something. He was quite determined. He was going to do something to get his own back on them.

In the meantime, he had to make his peace at home.

The idea had been growing in his mind for some weeks. Donovan's mum hadn't actually said anything, but he could tell from looks and silences that she was worrying about how much longer he was going to stay. How much longer she was going to be expected to look after him.

She'd been really good to him. Taking him in like that and accepting him. Giving him shelter, providing his food, helping him with the court case. Even buying him clothes when he needed them. Treating him just as she did her own son.

He knew his mum was giving her money. But it wasn't much. Not enough to cover the cost. No, Donovan's mum had done it out of the goodness of her heart. And that was something that touched him strangely. He couldn't imagine his own mum taking one of his friends in and feeding him for three months.

Of course, he'd thanked her. He was always telling her how grateful he was. And while a lot of it was just an act to keep her sweet, deep down he was surprised to realise that he really meant it.

But now it was time to move on. He couldn't go on imposing on her that way any longer. In any case, he could sense that he was outstaying his welcome. With the court case over, Donovan's mum was sure to raise the question of his future and what he was going to do.

He didn't want her to have to do that. He had decided to take the initiative himself. So that was why he was on his way now, getting closer and closer to home.

He didn't know what kind of reception he was going to get. At least there would only be Mum to deal with to begin with. That was why he'd chosen this time to go. If he could handle her all right, then he could face Dad when he got back from work. That shouldn't be too bad. For all his bark and bluster, Dad probably wouldn't kick up too much of a fuss once he found that Clive had his foot in the door, had re-established himself. A fait accompli, wasn't that what they called it?

It had worked those other times. There had been the rows. The storming out. The penitent return. And once in, after the first grumbles and verbal lashings, nothing more had been said. It was forgotten. As though nothing had happened.

Of course, he'd have to crawl. He'd have to give a real performance. Hang his head and say how sorry he was. Promise he wouldn't be bad again.

Well, he could manage that. He'd done it before. He'd had plenty of practice.

Funny how he'd been worried last time, coming home from the night in the police cell. That hadn't worked out.

He supposed he'd been too angry to play the part. Too bitter about how he'd been treated and too taken aback at how Mum and Dad had put all the blame on him.

This time he was prepared. He was in control of himself. He was confident he could bring it off. Somehow, he felt so much older, so much wiser. He felt he could achieve anything.

And if it didn't work out? If Mum and Dad wouldn't take him back? Well then, what did it matter? He would find something. He would make out all right. He would see that he did.

He pushed through the gate and rang the bell. There were snowdrops nodding beside the step. Soon there would be daffodils.

The door opened.

'I seen you from the window,' Mum said.

He couldn't tell from her face what she was thinking. She was just looking at him blankly.

'The prodigal return,' he said and laughed.

But Mum didn't seem to see the joke. She didn't laugh. She just went on staring at him as though he wasn't there.

'Suppose you better come in,' she said at last.

They went into the kitchen where she was in the middle of washing up.

'You eat yet?' she asked.

'Naw.'

She pulled a face and let out a weary sigh. She opened the fridge and took out some sausages.

Clive breathed a sigh too — inside. A sigh of relief. He knew Mum was just putting on a show. He had a feeling it was going to be all right.

'I'm sorry 'bout the trouble wit' the police,' he said contritely as Mum got out the frying pan. 'It's all over now. The case were this mornin'.'

'Oh,' said Mum turning to look at him enquiringly. Perhaps she was surprised that he was there instead of being in jail.

'Yeah, they give me a one-year conditional discharge.'

'What that mean?' Mum asked suspiciously.

'I gotta be'ave myself fo' one year,' he told her.

She gave him a scathing glance. ' 'Ow you gonna manage that?' she asked scornfully.

But Clive was even more confident now that it was going to be all right.

'Oh, I'm gonna be good,' he said humbly. 'I learns my lesson. Ain't the same livin' in someone else's 'ouse.'

He eyed her broad back hopefully, but she went on fussing the sausages and didn't turn round.

But something must have got through because she said, 'So you comin' back?'

'Yeah,' Clive said and then added hurriedly, 'that's if you'll 'ave me.'

Mum dished up the sausages and put the plate down in front of him. 'Reckons we ain't got much option,' she said.

She didn't sound exactly overjoyed, but then she didn't sound displeased either. She was accepting it as a tiresome fact of life.

So it was going to be all right. It hadn't been too painful. He hadn't had to crawl too much. He helped himself to a slice of bread and got stuck into his sausages. He suddenly found he was hungry.

' 'Ow 'bout Dad?' he asked. ' 'Ow 'e gonna take it?'

'I don' know what 'e think no more,' Mum said dismissing him. 'I gives up tryin' to work out what on 'is mind. 'E busy doin' out the spare room. Night after night 'e at it. I 'ardly sees 'im. 'E probably won't even notice you 'ere.'

That was all right then. Clive took another slice of bread and began to butter it. What had all the worry been about? It had been easy.

He had the odd idea that Mum might have missed him. She hardly ever went out except to the shops or to church. It didn't sound as if Dad was being much company. He was always working on some project or other. Mum might even be glad to see him back. Though it was like her not to show it.

When he had finished, he went upstairs to his bedroom. It was eerily unfamiliar at first. He had slept there all his life, yet three months away, and it was like the room of a stranger.

But gradually, as he lay on his bed and turned his eyes from one object to another, it all came back to him. The Bob Marley posters. The transistor. The pictures of Garth Crooks, Danny Thomas and Alex Williams. The wardrobe. The chest of drawers and the mirror. The desk with his books on it.

Yes, this was his room. This was his home.

Well, he would try to be the dutiful son. He would try to keep himself under control and merge with the scenery. He ought to be able to manage that. For a while.

Until the next time.

Chapter 16

All morning, Sandra worried about Donovan. In court. Having to face that ordeal. If only she could have been there to help him. To know what was going on.

She kept glancing at her watch and wondering if it was over yet. Had the magistrate given his verdict? Did Donovan know what his fate was? They must find him innocent, mustn't they? He was innocent. They couldn't find him guilty. That was unthinkable.

And yet the anxiety gnawed at her all morning. What if they found him guilty, and she wasn't there to comfort him? She could imagine what he would feel like. Let down and betrayed. Cheated and shamed. Angry and bitter.

She could see his face now in front of her, blurring the till. Looking like a little boy — hurt, bewildered, defenceless. She blinked her eyes and the image vanished. She couldn't bear to think of it.

It just wasn't possible. They couldn't be so unfair. It was obvious the police were in the wrong. They couldn't punish Donovan when he hadn't done anything.

But the worry went on all the same.

And there was another thing.

She knew she had behaved badly the night before. She felt

ashamed. She had been so cool and distant. She'd hardly said a word to Donovan. And what she had said hadn't been exactly encouraging.

She'd been upset at not seeing him for a week. She'd been annoyed that he was seeing so much of Clive. But most of all, she was still reproaching herself for going out with Errol. For the hundredth time since that evening, she asked herself how she could have done it.

Oh, she'd had her excuses. It was Donovan's fault for neglecting her. It was Clive's fault for taking up so much of Donovan's time. It was the fault of Clive's parents for throwing him out. It was the fault of the police for starting it all off in the first place.

But she knew now she had no one to blame but herself.

She hadn't spoken to Errol since that evening. Inevitably, they had seen each other and their paths had crossed, but Errol had just given her an angry scowl and said nothing.

Well, she could live with that.

What she wasn't sure whether she could live with was the way she had betrayed Donovan.

Perhaps she should have told him about Errol. But why burden him with more problems? He had enough to worry about without that. It was something she would have to work out for herself. She might tell him sometime. But not yet.

She tried to shake herself out of her depression. She was making too much of it. Yes, she had gone out with Errol, but nothing much had happened — fortunately. She had just got it wrong, that was all. She should just put it down to experience and learn from it.

And she had learned something. She realised now that the only person she wanted to touch and kiss her was Donovan. She loved him. She was sure of it.

Oh, she had been angry with him at the time, and she had nursed her anger and kept it going. But now she had snapped out of it. Now her mind was clear. She had no right to be angry with anyone but herself. She had been a fool.

She almost smiled. So Errol had had his use after all.

Then she remembered last night again. She had been angry and spiteful. She had turned her anger against Donovan, the anger she felt for herself. If only she had behaved differently. If only she had given Donovan the love and support he needed.

Now, she felt a surge of love and longing for him. She wanted to make it up to him. She wanted to hold him in her arms and show him how much she loved him.

She looked impatiently at her watch. Was it finished? Did Donovan know? She had to find out as soon as she could.

It was her half-day. She could phone the minute she was free. Donovan's mum might be at home, and she would be able to tell her. Sandra couldn't remember whether she was on early or late shift. Well, it was worth trying. Anything was worth trying to get some news.

But when Sandra dialled the number, there was no reply.

She put the receiver down and stood for a moment thinking. What should she do? Perhaps Donovan's mum had gone shopping or hadn't got back from work yet. She could try phoning again in half an hour. But what if there was still no reply?

She could go along to the school and wait for Donovan to come out. But what if she missed him? Or supposing he objected? Supposing he was embarrassed to find her there?

It had been all right when they had both been at school. But she had never waited for him at the front gate after she had left.

In any case, she didn't want to be told what had happened in the street where everyone could see.

She stepped out of the shop and stood hesitating on the pavement. What was she going to do? She felt so tense and so miserable. Donovan had said it was the waiting that was the worst thing. She was beginning to understand what he meant.

Then she suddenly knew what she would do. She would go round to Donovan's house. His mum might be in by then.

And if she wasn't, she would sit on the doorstep until she was. Or until Donovan got home from school. Mum wouldn't worry that she hadn't gone straight home from work. Not while it was daylight.

Yes, that was it. She would sit on that doorstep until someone came who could tell her what had happened. Then at least she would have her fears relieved. Or know the worst.

She set off briskly along the pavement.

Donovan still felt numb. He unlocked the door and went into the house. It was empty and silent. He switched on the radio, just to have some noise, just to have some company. Anything, to blot out the thoughts surging through his head.

But the thoughts went on.

The future seemed so bleak. Empty like the house. What was there to look forward to? A year of being branded a criminal. A year of watching every step and every shadow to make sure the police didn't trip him up again.

A year without Sandra.

Because he was sure he had lost her. He was sure it was over between them. Her attitude the previous evening had convinced him. Scarcely a word to him. No warmth. No sympathy.

But why? What had gone wrong? He knew he hadn't been seeing her so often lately, but there were reasons. There was Clive and the exams and the court case. Surely she realised that?

Then what? Perhaps she had just grown tired of him. Perhaps she had found someone else. Perhaps he would never know.

He remembered what Clive had said about girls. They were all the same. Chat them up a bit, flatter them, and they were yours for the taking.

But Sandra was different. Wasn't she? She wasn't like that. He couldn't bear to think of her like that.

Whatever it was, it seemed to be finished. He didn't want

it to end like this. He didn't want it to end. He loved her. But then, he might not have any say in the matter. It might not be up to him. Sandra might already have made up her mind.

He opened the fridge and looked inside. He grunted to himself. Even though the world was coming to an end, you had to eat.

He made himself a cheese sandwich and poured out a glass of milk.

Just as he put the last square into his mouth, the doorbell rang. Chewing and cheeks bulging, he went to answer it.

It was Sandra.

For a moment, he was so surprised that he just stared at her, his jaws frozen. What was she doing here?

Sandra looked taken aback too.

But Donovan's surprise suddenly gave way to a feeling of wild hope. She was worried. She had come to find out what had happened. Her eyes were filled with concern and anxiety.

He gulped and swallowed his mouthful of sandwich and said, 'Hi.'

' 'Ow did it go?' Sandra asked.

Her eyes were searching his face, dark and troubled. Her lower lip trembled slightly. Donovan found himself gazing at her face, lost in wonder that she should be so beautiful and that she should care. Her face was so delicate, her feelings so clear, it was like being able to see inside her head.

He dragged his eyes away and opened the door wide for her to come in.

But as he followed her into the living room, he was overcome by embarrassment. How could he tell her? What would she think of him? To have to confess his shame to her.

'I come round to see what 'ad 'appened,' Sandra explained. 'I thought you mum would tell me. I didn't expect to find you 'ere. I thought you'd be at school.'

'Mr Abbott said take the afternoon off.'

'I see.'

Donovan knew she was waiting for him to tell her, but he couldn't find the words. He couldn't bring himself to speak about what they had done to him.

'You still 'aven't said,' Sandra pointed out. There was a slight impatience in her voice.

There was nothing for it. He would have to confess.

He turned away and muttered miserably. 'They found me guilty.'

'Oh, no,' Sandra gasped.

He felt the touch of her hand on his arm, but he didn't respond. He still couldn't look at her.

'You don' think I'm guilty, do you?' he said.

He could hear the fear and appeal in his voice.

'Oh, Donovan,' Sandra cried. ' 'Ow could you?'

Now he looked at her. She had stepped back. Her eyes were bright with anger. 'Course I don' think you're guilty. Don' you know me? Don' you know I cares?'

Yes, he did. And then again, he wasn't sure.

Her eyes softened. She came near and put her arms round him.

'I knows what you been through,' she said.. 'I knows 'ow you suffered. An' I've suffered too. Thinkin' 'bout you an' what goin' on in you mind. But it over now. Finish wit'. Can' not'in' they says change my feelin's fo' you. I knows they gets it wrong. But I don' care what they thinks. I don' care what anyone think.'

She drew him to her and pressed herself against him. Her hands were round his waist. She rocked him gently backwards and forwards.

He clung to her. She was so strong. Like a rock a drowning man might cling to and know that the sea would never have him.

He held his head back so that he could see her face. Her eyes were shining. She was the same Sandra as before. Whatever gulf had grown between them had been bridged. It was as though nothing had changed. How could he ever have doubted her? He felt ashamed.

'I were just confused,' he said. 'But it all right now.'

And it was. Suddenly, a great weight had been lifted from his shoulders. The ordeal was over. It was in the past.

He was smiling. He was happy. What did it matter what the world thought? He had Sandra. She believed in him. She loved him.

Nothing else was of any importance.

Rhodri Jones
Different Friends
It was learning the truth about Azhar that shocked Chris into changing his attitude to love, making him think for the first time what the word really meant.   0 233 98096 2

Hillsden Riots and Getting It Wrong
Two of Rhodri Jones' most powerful novels reprinted in one volume. Both are concerned with the problems confronting black teenagers in urban Britain.   0 233 98708 8

Slaves and Captains
A version of Herman Melville's *Benito Cereno*, the true story of an 18th century slave ship and the strange events that occur on it.   0 233 98356 2

Them and Us
This is a collection of tough short stories about young lives, shaped by neglect, misunderstanding, prejudice and, sometimes, friendship.   0 233 98709 6

Pete Johnson
Catch You On the Flip Side
A sharp, lighthearted look at what happens to a boy, accustomed to girls falling for him, when he falls in love himself.   0 233 98074 1

Geraldine Kaye
A Piece of Cake
In this second Amy story, a sequel to *A Breath of Fresh Air*, Geraldine Kaye skilfully weaves the threads of the old slave life in Jamaica with modern Amy's Bristol life.
0 233 98712 6

Great Comfort
Comfort Kwatey Jones is half British and half Ghanaian. She loves being in Ghana, but when she goes to stay with her grandmother there, she discovers that she does not know the country and its traditions as well as she imagines.
0 233 98300 7

Someone Else's Baby
Partly because of her conventional family Terry tries to ignore the fact that she is pregnant, but the birth of her baby completely changes her life.   0 233 98575 1

John Kirkbride
In Reply to Your Advertisement
Kevin Daughtry may not have a job but he is a persistent and imaginative letter writer and through his application letters and the replies he receives we get to know him more and like him better.   0 233 98344 9

Thank You For Your Application
Kevin Daughtry, once an unemployment statistic, now has a job and ambitions to write. Efforts to be 'great' result in rejections, but a more popular style seems likely to win through.   0 233 98446 1

Sorry, Not Quite
Inspired by the acceptance of one story Kevin Daughtry soldiers on, in spite of withering rejection letters. Perseverance wins, and fortune once again smiles as Kevin refuses to take 'no' for an answer.   0 233 98717 7

Elisabeth Mace
Under Seige
The fantasy world of a sophisticated board game become an obession with Morris Nelson and the characters involved in the game more important than the people around him.
0 233 98345 7

Beware the Edge
The perils of dabbling in the supernatural.   0 233 97908 5

Sue Mayfield
I Carried You on Eagle's Wings
For Tony caring for an injured seagull was especially important because he felt so inadequate about helping his mother, who was dying of multiple sclerosis.   0 233 98576 X

Suzanne Newton
I Will Call It Georgie's Blues
Bitter family tension threatens the youngest son of a preacher in the American Deep South.   0 233 97720 1

Bette Paul
Ladlass
When Lyn collapsed with diabetes on a field study weekend, her life changed dramatically. She not only became the reluctant focal point of student and family politics, but fell in love.   0 233 98710 X

Eduardo Quiroga
On Foreign Ground
A young Argentinian soldier in the Falklands remembers his love affair with an English girl.   0 233 97909 3

Lorna Read
The Lies They Tell
Ann is an ordinary teenager until a blow to the head leaves her with thought-reading powers and the knowledge that a prospective candidate is lying to the electorate. Proving it turns her into a temporary celebrity.   0 233 98444 5

Caryl Rivers
Virgins
A bitter-sweet story of American high school girls growing up in the fifties.   0 233 97791 0

Malcolm Rose
The Highest Form of Killing
A chilling tale, starting with a tragedy on a Devon beach and ending in horrific tension, which highlights the dangers of manufacturing toxins for chemical warfare.   0 233 98589 1

Son of Pete Flude
Seb, son of pop-idol Pete Flude, is cheerful by nature and no fool. Both qualities help him survive an evil kidnap by drug dealers seeking to counter an undercover police operation.   0 233 98711 8

Michael Rosen
The Deadman Tapes
Paul Deadman's curiosity is aroused by eight remarkable tapes, apparently the confessions and life stories of a group of young people. Who are these people? Where are they now? Did they know each other? Who made the tapes?
0 233 98443 7

Andy Tricker
Accidents Will Happen
The author's own moving account of a motorbike accident which left him paralysed, and his struggle to regain a measure of independence.   0 233 98095 4

Rosemary Wells
The Man in the Woods
Is he an ordinary hooligan or a more sinister figure mysteriously connected with events of the American Civil War of a hundred years ago?   0 233 97785 6